ICE TRAP

A Novel of Suspense

KITTY SEWELL

A Touchstone Book
Published by Simon & Schuster
New York   London   Toronto   Sydney

Touchstone
A Division of Simon & Schuster, Inc.
1230 Avenue of the Americas
New York, NY 10020

First Touchstone hardcover edition February 2008

For information about special discounts for bulk purchases,
please contact Simon & Schuster Special Sales at
1-800-456-6798 or business@simonandschuster.com.

Designed by Carla Jayne Little

Manufactured in the United States of America

10 9 8 7 6 5 4 3 2 1

Library of Congress Cataloging-in-Publication Data
Sewell, Kitty.
    Ice trap : a novel of suspense / Kitty Sewell. —1st American ed.
        p. cm.
    1. Welsh—Canada—Fiction. 2. Surgeons—Fiction. 3. Father and child—
Fiction. 4. Canada, Northern—Fiction. I. Title.

PR6119.E96I28 2008
823'.92—dc22

                                                        2007031472

    ISBN-13: 978-1-4165-3997-1 (alk. paper)
    ISBN-10: 1-4165-3997-2 (alk. paper)

ICE TRAP

PROLOGUE

Shores of Coronation Gulf, Arctic Ocean, March 2006

He didn't take the snowmobile as the elders advised. Like most boys, he enjoyed the roar of a noisy engine, but lately he had started to appreciate the sound of his own thoughts. He liked the rumbling and cracking of the sea ice, the rare gust of wind, the crunch that his mukluks made in the snow as he walked—and making progress by his own exertion made him feel more able, more in control.

He packed a knapsack with a few supplies, just enough for the day, and clipped a rope to the collar of his dog. The husky had belonged to an elderly neighbor, but over time, and with some stealth, the boy had made her his own. She was a large furry devil, fierce when provoked, loyal but unaffectionate.

He hung his rifle over his shoulder and slipped a flare gun into his outside pocket. He would be unlikely to need them for self-defense; the dog would see off any unwanted company. He double-checked his gear as he'd been told so many times to do, and then they set off from the village toward the sea.

First he had to cross the shoreline. He stopped there for a moment to consider the way forward. Massive ice sheets were crushed against the coast by the sea. Giant slabs had slid on top of one another or been pleated like paper, incandescent peaks reaching toward the sky, pinnacles, some felled and shattered, as he imagined a forest of ancient trees would look. He was a strong boy, tall and broad for his age, but when clambering across the jagged ice and shouting words of encouragement to the dog—sometimes muttering impatiently in the language of his people—his voice betrayed his youth. He was anxious to be out there, wanting to be a man.

Panting from the exertion, they emerged onto the open ice. With snow goggles shielding his eyes from the glare, the boy scanned the horizon. The vast expanse hid little, but it still held surprises and a man had to be observant. With a few words to the dog, he started out. After an hour he turned westward, following the distant shoreline. Striding at a good pace to keep out the cold, he scrutinized the world around him, looking for tracks. He knew there was only a vague chance of finding any fox. One rarely saw them wandering in an aimless fashion. The sly little critters scuttled furtively behind polar bears to feast on the leftovers from seal hunts, quickly making themselves scarce if danger threatened. There were intermittent tracks of both bear and fox across the ice, one set large and heavy, depressing the thin snow, the other tiny and nimble. Most tracks were days, even weeks old. He didn't really mind. The graceful little fox was more appealing alive than dead, and the darkness of blood on its snow-white fur had always made him light-headed. He told himself that this expedition was more about the challenges of solitude and independence. Yet he knew he needed practice, to harden himself. Men must hunt to survive. Men must kill.

Walking in silent contemplation made time slip away. He stopped twice, sat on his haunches to drink the hot sweet tea from his flask and share a couple of strips of dried meat with the dog, but being motionless made him uneasy. It was very cold and best to keep walking. As the sun was making its low arc across the sky, he had turned northward, then eastward, and was returning from where he had come. The dog was patient, bored even, sometimes walking with her eyes closed. Despite his goggles, the boy's eyes were also beginning to feel the strain. There were no shadows but their own.

Yet now he did see something. His heartbeat quickened at the fresh tracks diagonally across his path: a bear, possibly only an hour away, maybe less. The prints in the snow were large, and the boy anxiously scanned the horizon. The tracks disappeared into the graying distance. A slight tremor rushed up his spine. *The people* had an inborn respect for polar bears. As the old men said: *Fox lead the hunter to Nanuk, whether or not the engagement is a happy one.* The boy smiled at this foolish saying, but he felt vulnerable, wishing he had listened to sound advice and not come out on the sea on foot. He looked toward the shore and tried to measure the distance. The village was just visible. Smoke from the chimneys rose straight up into the still air in sharply defined columns. Half an hour at a trot, perhaps more, he wasn't sure.

The dog had woken from her torpor and was walking briskly in the direction of the tracks, pulling the boy by the rope he had tied to his belt. The boy tugged sharply at the rope and shouted at her, but she did not much respond to commands; she never had. Annoyed, he booted her in the flank and she slowed reluctantly. A fearsome growl boiled in her throat, and the fur on her back had risen. Perhaps the source of her interest was just a seal hole, but the boy doubted it. He knew that the dog had caught the scent of the bear, and true to her wolf ancestry would welcome the chance to tackle it.

Though there was still plenty of light, he decided at once to return to the village, and after a brief tug-of-war with the dog they started back. But the wind was downward from the bear, and the dog, her snout twisting and snuffling, was reluctant to abandon the prospect of a good scrap. She kept turning and growling, stopping to take in the scent upwind, while the boy kept urging her with some force to go shoreward. Their battle of wills continued when suddenly the dog flung herself around and tore in the opposite direction, almost yanking the boy off his feet.

There, in the distance, was the bear. It must have heard or sensed their presence and turned from its route. Now it was following them. The triangle of black dots, the nose and eyes of the bear, soon came into focus in the gray light. They were fixed on the boy and the dog, no doubt a welcome sight of food. The boy stood immobile, all at once his strength draining away, making his knees tremble. He fought a sudden urge to urinate. The bear was becoming larger and clearer with each moment. It was approaching them with a peculiar lumbering gait. Its movements were deliberate but not obviously aggressive. Neither were they cautious nor mindful. Just purposeful. The bear was unusually large, but its winter thinness showed clearly through the pale yellow pelt. What finally jolted the boy into action was a sound traveling across the silence between them, the distant rasping, slavering breath of the starving animal. His thickly gloved fingers fumbled in his pocket for the flare gun. His hands were shaking as he loaded the flares, while shouting frantically at the dog to stop pulling and leaping. He could let her go, but he was still hoping that her snarling and yelping would see the bear off. The boy shot a flare with some skill. With a burst of light it hissed through the air and landed at the bear's feet. The bear stopped for a moment, sniffed at it suspiciously, then raised its nose, its head moving slowly back and forth. Finding the flare not a worthy deterrent, it started up again, this time moving faster, more aggressively.

The boy fired off another half dozen flares in quick succession, but the bear dodged them and kept coming. The boy got the rifle ready. Shooting the animal was his last recourse. A wounded bear would become crazed with rage and its movements would be even more unpredictable.

Handling the heavy rifle, the boy's hands were quivering and clumsy. He could not afford to remove his inner gloves with the danger of his fingers freezing, in which case they would be useless. Already, with his fear and his trembling, the cold was setting in. He could not stand there, motionless, much longer. The bear was now a mere thirty paces away and it was best to set the dog loose. With panic rising in his chest, he untied her and she charged toward the bear. The bear stopped, disconcerted. Its mouth was open as it watched the bundle of fury hurtle forward, then circle it and in one leap clamp her jaws around its hind leg. The bear twisted and turned to get at the dog, but she hung on as if all her strength were centered in those angry jaws.

The boy shook violently as he watched them battle. He had been told never to show fear of a bear, but the reality was different from the blustering stories of the elders, often told and much embellished. This colossal and furious animal was a terrifying thing; no man could deny it. Awestruck, he saw that his canine partner had no such fear. Small as she was in contrast to her opponent, she threw herself into the fight with a purpose born of ancestral rage.

Not knowing what else to do, the boy aimed the rifle at the bear. The dog would not let go, but some moments into their crazed dance the bear tore loose from her teeth and fled across the ice with its attacker in pursuit.

The boy shouted for his dog, but seeing her disappear into the distance he turned and started running toward the shore, rifle in hand, leaving his knapsack on the ice behind him. The village was farther away than it looked, but he ran heedlessly, his frozen fingers and toes coming back to life with the blood pumping vigorously through his body. He could see the houses clearly now, and he slowed a little, the sound of his heart pounding in his ears, breath deep and rasping, his lungs at bursting point with the icy air. The noises in his body prevented him from hearing the soft crunch of snow behind him. The bear was approaching him swiftly but silently from behind. The first he knew was the dog barking a warning signal. The boy turned and saw the bear bounding straight toward him. Then he saw the dog, injured and trailing blood, still in pursuit. As if time had no purpose, the boy just stood there, wondering how the bear had gotten around the dog and what sort of damage it had inflicted on her.

The bear charged, but at the last moment it stopped abruptly in front of the boy and raised itself to its full height on its hind legs. It was but five paces away and its shadow darkened the snow. The boy's reactions were quick, and he aimed the rifle at the shaggy chest, but at the instant of firing the bear had come down on all fours and the bullet vanished into the air.

A swipe of the gigantic paw sent the boy skidding across the ice. A crushing pain in his chest left him breathless. He knew that bar a miracle he was going to die. In one leap the bear was on him and, although the boy felt nothing of the pain, he heard his leg rip like rotten moose hide.

The dog, too, was mortally injured, but her loyalty to her master and hatred of bears gave her the strength to renew her attacks. Dazed by shock, the boy watched her frantic efforts to distract the bear and wondered why he had sometimes treated the faithful bitch with such casual disregard, taking her so much for granted.

The bear was anticipating a good meal and, compared with the agile and pesky dog, the boy was immobile and waiting for it. The bear swatted at its tormentor in irritation. Still the dog sprang away from its claws and kept nipping at its hind legs, making the bear spin around and around in frustration and fury. In a moment of clarity, the boy saw his rifle nearby and he tried to crawl, but in vain. He could not move; he could barely breathe.

As he struggled to draw air into his lungs, something began to change within him. A quiet composure settled in his chest. He knew that the end was near, yet found that he had no regrets. As he allowed himself no further thoughts and feelings, his fear also ebbed away. His body relaxed and with the courage of impending death he turned his head to face the inevitable.

With mild surprise he saw a man, stooped and ancient,

emerge from behind the frenzied churn of white and gray fur. The boy recognized him from sometime long, long ago. Wearily, the old man shuffled across the snow toward the boy.

"Come, son," he said. "Take my hand."

He held out his gnarled hand to the boy, but much as they strained to reach each other their fingers would not touch.

PART 1

CHAPTER 1

Cardiff, 2006

D r. Dafydd Woodruff looked down at his wife's face, a trifle detached. It was too early, in his mind, to be making love. Isabel was an insomniac and in the hours of dawn she made a habit of nudging him awake, poking him with her knees, grazing his back with her nipples, tossing and sighing.

Yet when she'd finally aroused his interest and gotten her way with him, as she had this morning, she often seemed far off somewhere, half pretending to be asleep. He knew better. Her eyes were shut too tight and her forehead had that tell-tale furrow of concentration. To Isabel, this was work. As their rhythm gathered momentum, she stretched her arms above her head and grabbed two posts of the headboard. The bed rocked, slapping rudely at the wall. Screws had come loose on the bed frame—they did so periodically—and Dafydd kept forgetting to tighten them. He tried to moderate his movements, but Isabel groaned in complaint.

When a rosy flush appeared on her chest and her thighs tightened around his hips, that unfortunate sense of duty engulfed him. As always, he tried to join her, closing his eyes and hoping the tide of her climax would pull him along. But, be damned, no.

"Keep going." She opened her eyes, alert and gazing at

him with feigned menace. "Don't think I'm through with you."

"Are you kidding?" he reassured her and continued, but no amount of gritting of teeth could save the occasion. That deep ambivalence he felt about the whole business had a direct link to his vital parts. He slowed to a stop.

"That's it?" she said with a strained lightheartedness. "My last fertile day."

"Oh, c'mon, sweetheart," Dafydd said and rolled away from her. "It's not as cut-and-dried as all that."

Though Isabel's face was pink with the heat of the exertion, she yanked the sheet up to her chin and stared at the ceiling. Dafydd heaved a sigh and turned to face her.

"Look, Isabel, I'm sorry. Your body might work by the calendar, but mine doesn't."

"All right," she said. "But do please explain what exactly *I'm* doing wrong?"

"Oh, God, Isabel, let's not. It's five o'clock in the morning." He plopped onto his back and looked through the skylight at the looming dawn. Wearily he reached for her hand.

"Let's sleep. Your last fertile day hasn't even started yet."

"If you say so." She turned her back to him but soon her breath changed, becoming deep and calm. Dafydd tried to switch his mind off, sweep away that exasperating sense of failure, but the cacophony of the birds in the garden seemed unusually shrill and startling. He shivered and hugged the covers around his cooling body.

He had finally dozed off when he heard the postman push the mail through the letterbox. The flap clicked open and the mail poured with a whoosh onto the hall tiles. He resisted being pulled back from a dusty sun-drenched place with a sharp blue sky, but the effort popped him to the surface of wakefulness like a cork through water.

He glanced across Isabel's sleeping form at the alarm clock. It was just after seven. Isabel was on her back, snoring softly, and had the sheet pulled over her head against the light. He ducked under the covers to join her. She was almost his own height, and her long legs disappeared down the murky extremity of the bed. In the darkness he looked down at their naked bodies, of the same species, yet so different, and according to medical science quite incompatible. That union, sperm to egg, did not want to take place though they had tried in a variety of ways, exhausting almost everything that was on offer. Rhys Jones, an ob/gyn specialist with an impressive track record, had reluctantly admitted defeat. He'd patted them on the back and reassured them that a pregnancy could still happen naturally, given time and patience, consulting thermometers and calendars, but Dafydd knew he was alluding to a bloody miracle. They were in their forties.

Besides, he'd just about had enough. It was destroying what little passion was left between them. The thread of desire on his part had become so fragile it frightened him. He'd tried to tell her—that something vital had been lost, that he now felt too old to be a father—but Isabel was unwavering in her determination to press on.

He got out of bed, put on his dressing gown and went downstairs. In the kitchen he put the kettle on and opened the blinds. It was bleak. A typical drizzly Cardiff morning. Dead leaves stuck to the wet windowpane, and there was green mold on the sill. He couldn't remember when he had last seen the sun, though it was supposedly still summer. Shoving a scoop of coffee beans into the grinder, he listened to the frenzied whir, tuning his ear to his wife, trusting the noise to wake the dead. Not a sound from above. He breathed in the pungent aroma, an incongruous mix of Mediterranean seaside bar and morning responsibilities.

While the coffee was brewing he went to pick up the mail. Spread out over the floor in the hall was the usual heart-sink pile. He scooped up the letters and sorted them into three stacks on the hall table: his, hers, and junk. Hers was by far the biggest, reflecting the surge of work that was coming her way. Yet the bills seemed to be all in his name. He took his handful of envelopes back to the kitchen. There was the agenda for the talk he'd promised to give in Bristol, a tedious affair that would need a lot of research. Flicking through the rest, he found the only vaguely interesting item was a baby blue envelope of flimsy airmail paper, addressed to him in curious childlike handwriting. He peered at the unfamiliar stamp. Canadian. The postmark quite clearly said Moose Creek, Northwest Territories.

"*Moose Creek?*" he blurted out loud, staring at the postmark.

Dafydd turned it over. There was a shiny sticker in the shape of a blue elephant sealing the flap. Perhaps someone had unearthed something he'd left behind, or someone getting in touch for old times' sake. After all this time? The thought brought a slight tightening in his abdomen, and he slit the edge of the delicate blue envelope with his forefinger.

Dear Dr. Woodruff
I hope you don't mind me writing to you. I think
I'm your daughter. My name is Miranda and I have
a twin brother, Mark. I've wanted to find you for so
long, I've nagged my mom to death about it. Then a
nice English doctor who came to look at our
hospital helped my mom to find you in a medical
directory.

In case you have forgotten my mom (Sheila
Hailey), she is the beautiful lady you were in love
with when you lived in Moose Creek (it's a dump so
I don't blame you for leaving, honest). Now that I'm
old enough (almost thirteen), she's told me all about
it. How you had to go back to England and how
the two of you couldn't get married or anything. It's
such a sad story. I wrote it all out for an essay for
school. I called it "A Love Story" and I got an A for
it. Miss Basiak loved it.

Please write or phone as soon as you get this letter.
Love, Miranda

Under this was a box number in Moose Creek, and a telephone number. For a time he stood motionless in front of the sink. Two, three times he read the letter, uncomprehending, until he became aware of his feet. The cold of the floor tiles had numbed them as if he were standing on bare ice. He looked down and saw frozen toes, swollen and blistered with frostbite, feet blackened by dying tissue. A girl, half naked and rigid in the snow . . . the beautiful endless snow. Flickering at the edge of this blinding whiteness were the sharp features of the little fox, a shadow creature of his conscience. He'd been told by an old man, an Inuit shaman, always to heed its presence. Dafydd's heart started racing. This belonged to a strange episode of his past, and he felt suddenly and unaccountably afraid.

"Hey!" Isabel's voice from above jolted him. "Coffee smells good."

"Coming," he shouted back. Shoving the letter into his dressing gown pocket, he resumed his morning routine.

Isabel smiled appeasingly as he handed her a mug of coffee, but he didn't notice her contrite expression. His thoughts were on the letter, racing, sifting through a myriad of half-remembered details. Sheila Hailey . . . that's crazy . . . impossible.

"Listen, sweetheart, I know I was being . . ." Isabel began, then stopped. "What?"

His resolve to keep the bizarre letter to himself was dashed. His past life was one thing, but he was hopeless at concealing things from her in the present. "I've had a letter. It seems someone has got me mixed up with someone else."

"Really?" She cocked her head, smiling at him. "How much and at what rate?"

Jesus. This wasn't particularly funny. He sank onto the bed beside her. "Brace yourself. It's quite weird." Reluctantly he took the envelope out of his pocket and gave it to her. "See what you make of it."

Isabel looked at him as she placed her mug on the bedside table. She pulled the flimsy paper out of the envelope and unfolded it. He watched her face as she quickly read the letter, her lips silently forming each word. For a moment she was quiet, just staring at the paper. Then she read it again, out loud. She read it easily, her voice girlish with a distinct American lilt. She'd always been an excellent mimic. Her performance unnerved him, and for a second he wondered if she had written the letter herself. Some sort of joke. Or a test. But she was pale, her lips white.

Abruptly she flicked the letter onto his lap. "What *is* this?"

"What did I tell you?"

They stared at each other for a moment.

"Who is this person?"

Dafydd shrugged his shoulders helplessly.

"You left a pregnant lover behind in Canada?"

Red blotches were appearing on his neck. He could feel them, little explosions of heat. Isabel saw them and her eyes bore into him. She always read guilt, whereas he knew they were merely the marks of stress, always had been. At once he felt irritated.

"Oh, for heaven's sake. Of course I didn't."

"Well, what, then?"

He didn't know what to say and was asking himself why the hell he'd shown her the letter. It was only natural that she would be bewildered and want to question him. He could have ripped it up, binned it, thrown the coffee grounds over the remnants and it would probably have been the end of the matter.

"I know the name. Sheila Hailey was the head nurse at the hospital where I worked. But I can assure you I was never involved with her." The burning sensation spread upward, toward his face. "I swear to you that I simply can't have any offspring in Moose Creek. It's totally impossible."

The whole thing was absurd. "And let's not forget," he added sharply, "that my sperm count, as you so often remind me, is like three peas in a pail."

"Yeah, I know," Isabel agreed. "But that's *now*." She sank back against the headboard, taking small edgy sips from her mug. His fierce denial had apparently not reassured her.

Neither of them spoke.

Dafydd closed his eyes, swiftly running through his year in Canada. Could he have made someone pregnant without ever having found out about it? He'd never been promiscuous as such; it wasn't his style. Yet it wasn't impossible—it hadn't exactly been a celibate time of his life, but with his mania for protection an accidental pregnancy was unlikely. Anyway, this was about a specific woman, Sheila Hailey, a woman he'd never gone anywhere near.

"Could you have got drunk, shagged this woman and then forgotten about it?" Isabel asked.

He could understand her consternation, but he didn't like the hard edge in her voice. "Isabel, you know me better than that. And if you pardon, I've never done *shagging*."

Isabel smiled. "Of course you have, darling. Why're you being so defensive? It's a perfectly reasonable possibility."

He burst out laughing. "I'm *not* being defensive. Hell, you know everything about me there is to know. I'm telling you, it's a mistake. Or someone over there has gone stark-raving mad. Cabin fever or something. What do I know?"

He didn't want to hide things from her—she deserved better—but in fact she *didn't* know everything about him there was to know, not *absolutely* everything. Over the years of laying bare their past and their conscience to each other, admitting to all peccadillos, the most outrageous and the most indecent, he'd managed to leave out most of his Arctic experience, a window in his life too brittle and in some ways too precious to open up to her sharp scrutiny.

The radio suddenly sprang to life, set for eight. Isabel reached over to turn it off, but Dafydd put his hand out to stop her. "Let's hear the news."

"Now? Are you serious?" She glared at him for a moment and then turned the sound up loud. They pretended to listen to the discharge of the day's horrors and disasters, car bombs in Iraq, floods in China, and the continuing humanitarian catastrophe in Sudan. After a few minutes she bluntly turned it off. "Dafydd. Shouldn't we be talking?"

It took him a couple of seconds to come back to the present, his eyes to focus. He looked at his wife. The light from the window fell on her thick blond hair, shifting and iridescent like sun on water. The disturbance of their morning had made sharper her aquiline features. Her nose seemed more pointed and her keen brown eyes were piercing. She was a striking woman, particularly in adversity. She'd always complained of the disadvantages of being tall and strong-looking. Men never credited you with being vulnerable. You had to fend for yourself, open your own doors. She was right—Dafydd couldn't help himself smiling—she looked forbidding in the way only she knew how. She noted his smile and with a show of exasperation started to rummage in the drawer of her bedside table. A noisy search located a package of tobacco and some rolling paper. Dafydd watched her long, slender fingers grapple with the fragile paper as she rolled a lumpy, uneven cigarette, her wet tongue sliding back and forth along the gummed edge.

"Are you sure you want to do that?" he asked, although there was something faintly alluring about the foul habit. "You've quit, remember. It's been three weeks."

"Who's counting?" she retorted and lit the fag, puffing at it with concentrated pleasure. "Dafydd, could this be some kind of prank? Maybe it's a nasty stunt by some friend of yours with a sick sense of humor."

Absently he stroked her thigh. "Who do we know who'd think of such a thing? I don't think so. I've neither friends nor enemies with that great an imagination."

Isabel coughed and stubbed out the fetid roach on the birthday card he'd given her the week before. "What about someone from back there, that redneck backwater? Did you piss someone off? What about this nurse? Has she got anything on you? Could this be some kind of blackmail?"

Dafydd shook his head. "Nah . . . Can't imagine what or why. We're talking fourteen years ago."

"Seriously. Why would any woman try to pin paternity on a man so far away, a doctor, of all people?" Isabel hugged her knees with conviction. "A simple blood test would prove her wrong; anyone with reasonable intelligence would know it. I mean, she is a *nurse*? And the poor kids—*twins*—what sort of mother would let a child write in vain . . . to a father who wasn't?"

"I suspect it's just some young girl with some elaborate fantasy." He looked at the clock. He couldn't afford to lie about any longer. Patting her reassuringly on the arm, he made to get up. "Whoever she is, I *am* sorry for her."

"Wake up, Dafydd." Isabel banged her fist on the bed, upsetting her birthday card and scattering ashes on the bedclothes. "Not some girl with a fantasy. The *mother* has obviously gone to some lengths to find you. You think you can just close your eyes and—ping—the whole thing will just go away? That's so *you*."

Annoyed by her outburst, he got up and went to shower. He let a single jet of hot water beat down on his head, creating the blurry cupola under which he allowed himself no unpleasant thoughts, but this morning the exercise didn't work. Sheila Hailey. He could see her clearly, too clearly. He turned his face up to the spiky assault of the shower to cleanse himself of her image.

Dafydd sat on a stool between operations waiting for Jim Wiseman, the anesthetist, to get the next patient ready. He fidgeted, glanced at the clock on the wall and felt his impatience mount. He knew he couldn't afford to be distracted from the job at hand. He took a few deep breaths and flexed his rubber-gloved fingers to loosen the tightness in his hands. The day never felt right if he and Isabel parted on less than loving terms, and in recent weeks that unspoken tension between them affected their mornings more than any other time.

Her biological pulse throbbed the loudest in the stark light of daybreak, and she was often edgy. And now that damned letter. But he was utterly certain; the suggestion of paternity was preposterous. So why was he disturbed by it? Why even react to a sad misguided letter, a foolish suggestion aimed wildly at the wrong person from a distance of thousands of miles?

"All set," Jim called to him, having finally gotten the patient anesthetized. The jolly new scrub nurse, a young Jamaican woman, swayed her enormous hips in tune with some music in her head. His other assistants stood waiting for him, inscrutable behind their masks.

"What's that music you're dancing to?" he said to the nurse as he made the incision in the abdomen in front of him.

"I can't hear nothing," she said, her colossal bust quivering with laughter. "Perhaps you don't like that sort of music, Mr. Woodrot."

"It's Woodruff . . . and yes, you moving about all the time is a bit distracting. Do you mind?"

She misunderstood him. "Why should I mind, man? Everyone to his own opinion. I don't take no offense." She chuckled and continued swaying her hips.

Her impertinent response cheered him momentarily. Hell, they could do with some un-English sensuality around the place; everybody was so damned glum. They worked on in silence, the dancing nurse doing her job with exceptional skill.

Bloody Sheila, Dafydd mouthed quietly as he lopped off the offending appendix and tossed it into the specimen pot.

The nurse looked up at him. "Sorry, did you say something?"

"No, nothing."

She handed him some instrument and he looked at it for a moment, not sure what it was for. He realized suddenly that his niggling apprehension wasn't so much about the girl's letter and her bizarre claim; it was Sheila Hailey herself. If that woman had put her daughter up to this (if indeed she had a daughter), trouble was sure to follow; Isabel was right about that. But why now, fourteen years on, and with him on the other side of the globe? Perhaps bitterness and hatred had no limits in time and space. A momentary shudder passed through his neck and shoulders.

"You okay?" the nurse asked, looking at him. Jim's face poked around the drapes. The masks made it impossible to know what they were thinking. Both Jim and the nurse—he didn't even know her name—seemed concerned. Dafydd bent over the job with a renewed effort of concentration. He had a thorough delve around the bowels for a possible Meckel's diverticulum before starting to close up the peritoneum. In the end it was a very neat job, likely to leave only the faintest scar. The patient was a girl in her early twenties with a delightfully smooth tummy. She'd be happy.

Dafydd took off his gloves and gown and headed for the coffee room. He was on his laptop, putting down his comments for the patient's records, when Jim came slouching through the door with his customary stoop.

"All right?" Jim asked casually, pouring himself a cup of tarry fluid from the coffee machine.

Dafydd looked up. "Yes . . . why?"

"Is everything okay?"

Had his lack of focus been that apparent? Jim was one of the few people at work who knew him well; he was aware of the difficulties he and Isabel had been having, of the fruitless fertility treatments and all the attendant distress.

"Yeah, fine," Dafydd lied, and turned back to the screen.

"And Isabel?"

"Oh, well, nothing doing yet. She can't lay it to rest. At least she's got a lot of commissions on. She's taking off in all directions. I should be pleased, really. Who knows"—he laughed impatiently—"early retirement, perhaps."

"Don't be daft. You're in your prime. Look at you," Jim said, looking down at his own expanding girth.

Dafydd closed his laptop and started to gather his things. Momentarily he felt tempted to tell Jim about the letter, but instead he poked him in the belly and said, "Get on yer bike, mate. Don't just talk about it."

He didn't really want to go home. The allegation wasn't something that could just be shelved. Isabel would want to talk about it all evening. They would scrutinize the letter for clues. There would be more questions and there was nothing more he could add.

He wandered down the corridor, diverged into the men's lavatory and shut himself in a cubicle. Putting his briefcase on the floor, he sat down on the toilet lid. Someone came in, had a pee, coughed noisily and spat, then ran a tap. He watched a pair of slippers shuffle past and out the door. This was stupid. What the hell was he doing? He could be sitting in the canteen or on a park bench, or better still in a pub with a pint of beer.

He leaned his head into his hands. Moose Creek, of all places . . . Squeezing his eyes shut, he tried to picture the town, but all that came to him was a vast expanse of ice. He had always tried to suppress the memory of why he'd gone there in the first place, the incident that had spurred him to leave his blossoming surgical career all those years ago and go to that godforsaken outpost to which no sane human being, least of all a doctor, would ever dream of going voluntarily. But the impact of the catastrophe had never really left him. It was always there, skulking around in the recesses of his mind. This was one of many reasons he never spoke of his year in the Canadian wilderness.

Naively he had hoped that Moose Creek would be a haven from his shame. He had been so desperate to get away, he had no clue what he was going to. His only aim was to get as far away as he could, to the most remote place on earth as was possible to find.

CHAPTER 2

Moose Creek, 1992

Dafydd's fingers were embedded in the armrests, his knuckles white. The tiny plane seemed to be dropping vertically toward the ground, then bounced along the tarmac like a flat stone skimming across a pond. Finally it swayed wildly before slowing to a stop near the end of the runway. Dafydd exhaled gradually, gave thanks to some higher entity and shook his hands to restore circulation.

He gathered up his belongings, smiled at the sturdy stewardess who emphatically herded him and three other passengers toward the ambulatory stairs. There was an urgency in the dispatch, as the plane was on its way to Resolute, the last outpost to the North Pole. As Dafydd stepped out of the plane, the heat felt like a wall. The air was dense, motionless. Within seconds he felt clammy. A steady low hum permeated the stillness, the apparent buzz of insects, although none was visible to the eye.

Two taxis were waiting outside the prefab terminal building. Dafydd's fellow travelers quickly nabbed the cleanest of the two. The one remaining was a battered old Chrysler Valiant—an automobile he'd admired as a boy—with a nasty dent on the front bumper. Dafydd raised his eyebrows, and the woman behind the wheel nodded. He grasped his two suitcases and lugged them toward the car.

"I'll be damned," drawled the woman in a thick, unrecognizable accent as she attempted to help Dafydd load the cases into the trunk. "You'll be staying with us for a coon's age, by the looks of ya."

"Yep, for ten months." Dafydd smiled back at her jowly grin and got into the passenger seat, which was furred up with dog hairs.

"Watcha . . . working for the forestry?" The woman jumped in and stared at him unself-consciously.

"No," he said firmly, as he sensed he was in for a grilling. "Could you take me to the Klondike Hotel?"

"Gotcha." She revved up the engine and tore out of the gravelly parking lot, leaving billowing dust mountains in the still air.

"Watcher business, mister?" she insisted, giving his immaculate navy suit a good inspection. "That there fancy gerrup is gonna look mighty sorry in a day or two." She chuckled.

"What do you suggest I wear?" Dafydd said testily, watching his trouser legs sucking up the dog hairs as if by osmosis.

"That 'pends on you job, mister," she tried again, "and you ain't neither trapper nor logger." She cackled heartily at this assertion and then, taking her eyes off the road entirely, she turned to him to wait for an answer.

"I'm a doctor," he quickly informed her.

"*Right on!*" She squealed in delight. "That's what I figgered." She swerved slightly to miss the ditch. "No one ain't so glad to meet you as me, I do declare." She detached a chubby hand from the steering wheel and grasped Dafydd's in a hearty grip. "I'm Martha Kusugaq. I've got a canker on my foot that's hurting real bad. It makes driving a real pain in the ass. Look." She reached down and popped off her shoe to show him a pus-filled growth on the side of her instep.

"Bad one," Dafydd agreed and fixed his eyes on the bumpy, curvy road ahead, hoping she would do the same.

"You'll be at the clinic tomorra?" she asked, turning to him expectantly.

"I expect so." His first patient . . . already!

"Okay, tomorra, then. Got yerself a date." She slipped the shoe back on her foot. "Them docs we got here are *shit,* I don' mind telling ya. You ask me anything an' I'll give you the low-down." She was obviously hoping for a barrage of questions, but when none was forthcoming she looked at him again from under her fringe and asked with a hint of suspicion, "What kinda cause brings a nice-looking guy like yerself to this neck o' the woods?"

There was absolutely no reason to get ruffled, he told himself. Nobody knew anything about his background, apart from a straightforward CV. The hospital director, Dr. Hogg, hadn't even checked his references. Anyway, he felt sure that if they knew why he was here, it wouldn't have mattered in the least. Young surgeons didn't come to Moose Creek for a lark.

Martha studied him with undisguised curiosity, waiting for his response. "Why do you ask that?" he inquired teasingly to mask his discomfort. "Are you saying this isn't a fit place for a nice bloke like me?"

"Bloke?" Martha cackled. She put her foot hard on the brake to avoid a small furry animal darting across the road. "Oh, it's an all right place, for the likes of me anyway. Around here we call this the assho . . . backside of the world." She turned to him in that direct way she had. "They all come here cos they got noplace else to go. Workwise, that is."

"Who?"

"You know . . . doctors."

Dafydd felt his jaws clench involuntarily. "Have we got far to go?"

"See, we've got our own kinda medicine. I picked up a few tricks from my granny." Again she gave him her sideways glance and chuckled low in her throat. "Bet I could teach *you* a thing or two."

He capitulated and burst out laughing. So did she. He felt sort of acknowledged, as a human being at least, seeing as all doctors were *shit* (if only she knew).

"Should I start to worry?" he asked. "You're taking me an awfully long way."

"Mind you watch yerself, good-looking kid like you. There are plenty wimmin who wouldn't mind getting their sticky paws on you, I can tell ya. Watcha . . . thirty, if a day?"

He smiled. "Close, but I'm not telling."

He looked her over surreptitiously. She was somewhere between forty and fifty. There was no doubting that she was an indigenous Indian. Her head and neck were stout, sitting comfortably on broad, padded shoulders. Coarse black hair was braided in a single plait down her back. Her bust was small in relation to her potbelly; thinnish muscular legs were encased in some type of leggings. But she had a smooth, fresh face and her eyes had a mischievous gleam to them.

The town was coming into view. It seemed entirely flat, not a building over two stories high. It looked dreary and dry. Surrounding the town was sparse coniferous woodland and in the far distance hills or mountains. The heat shimmered above the buildings. They passed a motel of some feeble clapboard construction. Its low, rickety cabins lined the road, followed by Colleen's Café, another tumbledown building. The car hurtled along a broad main street. Dafydd stared in dismayed fascination. This is it? he thought. He'd seen an aerial photo of the town on a faded postcard, enclosed by Dr. Hogg with the job description. The picture had looked quite exotic; a genuine subarctic outpost covered in snow and ice. A tourist leaflet described the place as *in the midst of spectacular scenery, with tall mountains, raging rivers and sparkling lakes, endless boreal timberlands thinning toward arctic tundra.* The reality was a collection of ugly, dusty, dilapidated buildings, set among thousands of square miles of desolate forest. He had to remind himself that this was late summer. That white, eerily mysterious landscape belonged to deepest winter when temperatures plummeted to fifty degrees below zero. He'd be exposed to it soon enough.

Martha screeched to a halt alongside a bizarre grandiose-looking edifice. It had a false front, like on a western movie set. The elaborately carved window frames and elegant balconies were fake, made of cheap molded plastic now cracked and discolored. A sign, KLONDIKE HOTEL, dangled from gilded chains.

"Here y'ar," Martha declared with a hint of proprietorial pride. "Can't get any better than that . . . not around these parts."

She turned around to look him directly in the eye.

"Now, you listen, Doc. You wanna taxi, anytime, night or day, you call me, right?"

"Thanks, Martha, but I tend to walk everywhere. It's a tiny town." He laughed, pointing up and down the road. "When am I ever going to need a taxi?"

"You just wait," Martha scoffed. "You'll soon be like the rest. Nobody walks around here. It's either too hot an' dusty, or too cold an' slippery, or you're too hammered. Most likely the last." Her voice softened a bit as she accepted a twenty-dollar bill, no change. "You look after yerself, young man. I mean it. This town's no kid stuff."

Several men were loitering outside the plastic portals of the Klondike Hotel. They seemed to be mainly indigenous Indians. In the bright sun they looked dried up and shrunken; short, squat men, poor-looking. Some of them appeared drunk, although it was only three in the afternoon.

As Dafydd heaved his suitcases toward the door, one of them darted forward and tried to grab one case out of his hand. Dafydd resisted, bewildered by the sudden assault. A brief struggle ensued, each of the two men clutching the handle and trying to wrench the case from the other. The rest of the men leaning on the wall of the hotel started sniggering. Nobody made a move to intervene.

"I'm not trying to rob you, mister," his assailant exclaimed, letting go abruptly. Dafydd lost his footing and stumbled backward, falling over his other case, which he'd dropped to the ground.

"I was only going to give you a hand," the man said, look-

ing down at him where he was sprawled on the dusty sidewalk. "What you get here is a good ole northern welcome."
He shrugged, an impertinent grin on his dark face. "Take it or
leave it."

Dafydd jumped up and dusted himself off. "You could have
said something." He was sure that the man had made him trip
over on purpose.

"Okay," said the man. "Can you spare some change?"

Dafydd looked at him coldly for a moment. He was unnerved
by the confrontation and wondered if these men had taken him
for a visiting businessman and fair game, or would this kind of
covert animosity be a daily nuisance.

"Are you serious?" he said angrily, determined to have the
last word.

The men laughed. Somehow they appeared to be on his side
now, and the incident suddenly seemed less menacing. Looking
back, he saw Martha Kusugaq standing by her taxi with her
arms folded. He thought she gave him an imperceptible nod,
some stern encouragement. With as much composure as he
could muster, he carried his heavy cases into the lobby.

He had a surprisingly good meal in the hotel restaurant. Moose
pie, their specialty, with lingonberry sauce and rice. The house
wine was well on the sweet side, but he drank it because it did
what it was supposed to do. He was alone but for an elderly
couple in a corner. They were working their way through a bottle of some dark amber spirit and two packets of cigarettes, his
and hers, smoking doggedly in silence.

By contrast, the "beer parlor" was bustling. Dafydd had a
good view of the bar through an archway, from which an abun-
dance of smoke and noise trespassed into the restaurant. Men in
rough clothing jostled for space around the small tables, while
miniskirted waitresses dashed to and fro balancing enormous
trays full of brimming beer glasses on one hand, an arm held
aloft to clear the heads of the customers.

A couple emerged through the arch. They saw Dafydd and approached.

"Dafydd Woodruff?" the man inquired.

"That's me."

In the dim reddish light the man looked handsome and erect, if perhaps a bit on the lean side. His hair was blond and wavy, extending a fair way over his shoulders. He wore a pair of snug jeans, worn thin, held up by a belt of tooled leather with a large intricate silver buckle. The woman was a striking-looking redhead, dressed in a short, tight leather skirt. Her bust strained from a fitted white shirt. Despite the provocative clothes, she looked austere. They were of a similar age to him, early thirties or thereabouts.

Dafydd, somewhat puzzled, tried to place them as he shook the extended hand, but the man's long hair and casual appearance gave no clues.

"Ian Brannagan," he offered at last.

"Of course," Dafydd exclaimed, trying to hide his surprise. There was something distinctly unmedical about his future colleague. "I didn't expect to find . . . I didn't think I'd meet anyone until tomorrow."

"You'll be in the thick of it tomorrow." Ian Brannagan slapped him lightly on the shoulder and sat down, pulling out another chair beside him for the woman. She looked inscrutable, but Ian Brannagan looked open and friendly despite the sharp angles of his face. He had a square jaw and a long nose. His lips were thin and pale, but his smile was generous, showing a large number of good teeth. Closer to, he looked careworn and tired, both of face and dress.

Dafydd turned to the woman, waiting to be introduced.

"I'm Sheila Hailey," she said, offering her hand in a firm clasp, but no further explanation.

"You're a godsend, my friend," Ian Brannagan said. "We've been desperate since our last one, Monsieur Dr. Odent, left us, two weeks ago now. There's fucking chaos up at the hospital."

"Really?" Dafydd leaned back in his chair, trying to look relaxed. Fucking chaos! And *I'm* what they need?

Ian Brannagan lit a cigarette and looked at the remains of the moose pie on the plate. "Mind if I smoke?" He sat back and studied Dafydd in a detached but sympathetic manner. The woman beside him was equally fixed on him, if less affably. She sat back from them somewhat, her slim legs crossed casually.

"How long have you been here, Ian?" Dafydd asked.

"Oh, just a year or so." Ian's brow furrowed slightly. "Two winters, to be sure. Jesus, time flies."

"But you like it here?"

"So-so," said Brannagan noncommittally and took a deep drag on his cigarette. A long tip of ash was forming on the end of it and he saw Dafydd looking at it. There was no ashtray. He allowed it to drop into the pastry shell that had contained the succulent moose. Dafydd flinched involuntarily. Lesson number one, he thought resolutely: no airs and graces.

An attractive dark-haired waitress emerged from the bar and came up to their table. She turned to Ian with evident familiarity. "Can I get you and your friend a drink?"

"Please." Ian's eyes locked with hers for a moment. "Get us a couple of bottles of Extra Old Stock. Iced tea for the lady."

"I know what 'the lady' drinks," the girl drawled impertinently, then hesitated. "You the new doctor?" She placed her hand on her hip and studied Dafydd with sharp expert eyes.

"This is Brenda," Brannagan cut in, putting his hand out to touch her somewhere midsection. "You be careful around her. She takes no shit from no one. Do you, sunshine?"

Sheila Hailey coughed up a withering chuckle while the two men watched Brenda turn and go. She owned a pair of well-filled legs that emerged assertively from under a tight red skirt and disappeared into fancy-looking two-toned cowboy boots. Her straight black hair swung pointedly from side to side with every sharp little step. Brannagan muttered something appreciative, then said, "Oh, Christ, you drink beer, don't you? Trust me not to ask."

Dafydd laughed, realizing there was no need to make a favorable impression. Not with Brannagan anyway. He seemed a pretty curious specimen for a doctor.

"Are you attached in any way?" asked Sheila Hailey suddenly.

"I beg your pardon?"

"Are you single?"

"Ah, well, yes."

Brenda's boots clicked their way back across the wooden floor, and she neatly popped the caps off the bottles with one hand. She turned coquettishly on her heel and clicked her way back to the bar, buttocks grinding proudly against each other under the slinky red fabric.

"Give the man a moment to settle in, will you?" Brannagan said to Sheila, nudging her affectionately with his elbow.

"Oh, God, I'm not interested in the least," she said, smiling for the first time. "I'm just trying to work out how long he'll stay."

Dafydd felt his neck prickle with the heat of indignity, but he didn't want to appear lacking in humor. "What's it to you?" he said lightheartedly.

Though the woman was stunning to look at, with a heart-shaped face, large piercing eyes, and a mass of red loopy curls, there was something deliberately obnoxious about her.

"Relax," she said, looking him in the eye with a faintly condescending smile. "You'll be very much wanted around here. If you're any good, that is."

Both Ian and Sheila laughed, while Dafydd broke into an unfortunate blush.

"Come on," Ian said, patting him on the arm. "She means as a surgeon, not as a man."

Trying to cover his annoyance, Dafydd turned to Sheila. "So are you connected with the hospital, or are you . . . a friend of Ian's?"

Sheila and Ian exchanged a quick glance. Dafydd noted in

that fleeting transaction not warmth or affection, not passion, but something else. Something connected them.

"I'm your head nurse," Sheila stated in a manner that clearly meant that she was his boss. Ian looked at her deferentially; it seemed he openly accepted her authority.

The chain-smoking couple in the corner had roused themselves from their torpor and were having an argument. The three of them listened to the drunken squabble for a few minutes. It seemed to be focused around the pair's respective rights to a certain pickup truck. Sheila lifted her glass and tossed back the last of her iced tea. Dafydd noticed her neck; it was slender and as white as porcelain but for a shower of pale freckles, barely visible in the muted light.

She stood up. "We start at seven forty-five sharp. Be on time." As if to either emphasize or to soften her command, as she passed his chair she put a willowy hand on Dafydd's shoulder, a touch that cooled the skin under his shirt and made him shiver slightly. "Please," she added as an afterthought, and without a word to Ian she was gone. Ian smiled resignedly and shrugged his shoulders. "That's Sheila," he sighed.

A group of large women burst in through the archway, clad variously in jeans, peaked caps, and checkered shirts, looking just like female versions of archetypal lumberjacks. They sat themselves noisily at a nearby table. Ian threw his head back and laughed at Dafydd's alarmed expression.

"Perfectly nice girls," he admonished in a whisper. "You can't be too fastidious around here."

"Well, *you* tell *me* what sort of social life you have here," Dafydd murmured.

"Womenwise do you mean, or generally?"

"I mean generally."

"You interested in anyone, you could always ask me about her first." Brannagan winked. "I'll tell you if she's worth it."

Dafydd felt his irritation mount afresh. Okay, he was green, but he wasn't stupid. At the same time he knew he should take it on the chin. He may well need an ally. Brannagan was an outsider like himself, but clearly the man with the know-how.

"Tell me about Moose Creek."

"Ah, you'll find out; it won't take you long. Just over four thousand souls, about half Déné and Métis Indians, some Inuit and every white misfit under the sun. An unholy mixture. Livers like Swiss cheeses. If you don't like people, there are plenty of bears—blacks, grizzlies . . ."

"How many people actually work in the gas plant?"

"About five hundred, perhaps."

"And the rest . . . what do they do?"

"There's quite a bit of logging. The stuff gets shifted only in the winter when the ice road is open. Tourism is getting to be the latest. People wanting to hunt and canoe the rapids." He hesitated a moment. "You can buy just about anything here. Illegal substances, anything you want." He paused to bite off a hangnail. "Some trapping . . . illegal dogfights . . . welfare, of course."

"It doesn't have the look of a very prosperous place."

"Could have been." Brannagan leaned forward in sudden animation. "They planned to build a mother of a pipeline some three, four years ago. It was a big deal. There's enough oil and gas up here to put the whole Middle East out of business. But did they?"

"I read about it. That must have been a blow."

"You gotta be kidding. Every kind of dropout came flocking north in anticipation. Virtual gold rush stuff. Some of them are still here. Everybody was hoping for a pot of gold without having to do much for it. Why do you think they built this ridiculous place?" Brannagan gestured around the mock-rococo room with a sneer. Directly he held up two fingers in the direction of the bar and nodded. The noise from the bar was deafening even at a distance. Hoarse manly laughter dominated the cacophony with periodic shouts and occasional shrill feminine shrieks. Shortly, another waitress brought two more bottles.

"This here is Tillie," Brannagan offered with a wink.

Tillie was a woman of indeterminable age, anywhere between twenty and forty. She was very short but of vast proportions. Even so, she was strangely attractive. Her sparkly blue eyes, a button nose and rosebud mouth looked like isolated islands in an undulating sea of facial flesh. She had a mass of curly yellow hair. Her whole persona brought to mind a very voluptuous, and adult, Shirley Temple.

"Howdy, Doctor," she said in a sweet voice. "Welcome to Moose Creek. I hope you like it here."

"That would be a warm, motherly bust to rest a weary head on," sighed Brannagan when Tillie had gone, "but she's not interested in that sort of thing."

Brannagan's uninhibited behavior and his total lack of manners suddenly infected Dafydd. Perhaps he was getting drunk. He imagined himself casting off his wretchedness in this place where nobody knew him, where he could be anything he bloody well wanted.

Brannagan was smiling at him, evidently reading him perfectly. "So, you're leaving something behind. No one back home pining for your return?"

"No," Dafydd said curtly. After a pause he said, "That's not true exactly. I had to put my mother in a nursing home before I came out here. Parkinson's, but she's completely on the ball. It wasn't a nice thing to have to do. My only sister is married to an Australian. We've not seen her for four years. I tried to get a job down under so I could catch up with her, but then this came up."

Brannagan studied him with hooded eyes, his head cocked to one side. "Yeah, that's what I was referring to. Why this?" Here it was again. If only he could be allowed to put the whole business behind him completely. He would never speak of it again if he had a choice. He had to forget if he was going to be safe and effective.

"I was bored, restless, needing a change," Dafydd said, trying to sound nonchalant. "I'd just finished my training and didn't want to walk into a surgical job that would incarcerate me for the next thirty years."

"That so? Funny choice of destination, though," Brannagan insisted, peering closely at him through the smoke of his cigarette. "I saw your CV. Pretty impressive. You could have had your pick."

Dafydd nodded wearily as his justifications dried up. "So what's your excuse?"

"Oh, Christ." Brannagan sighed, clearly trying to sound even more drunk than he was. "How long have you got?" He looked at a nonexistent watch on his arm. "I 'spect you're moving into your trailer tomorrow. I've a feeling it's not been cleaned since Odent left, and he had some funny habits; I'll tell you about them sometime. You better muck it out yourself, just to be sure." He swayed slightly in his seat, then tipped back the rest of his beer. "Tell you what. You don't *have to* move in there, just because Hogg calls it the 'locum trailer.' He pockets the rent cos he owns the bloody thing." Ian's laugh had a mocking undertone, and he slapped Dafydd on the shoulder. "If you don't like it, you tell 'im . . . right, buddy?"

"Got you." Dafydd stood up stiffly. He'd had enough.

"No, man, I'll get this," Ian put one hand on Dafydd's wallet while he fumbled around his pockets with the other. "You're the new kid on the block. This is on the clinic."

Every bone and muscle in Dafydd's body ached. His head spun and his chest felt raw. A combination of jet lag, change of atmosphere and general overload, plus too much sweet wine and Extra Old Stock. He suddenly yearned to be horizontal.

"Bright and early, my boy." Brannagan made a clatter of chairs as he got up. "Hogg's a hopeless manager, but he's a stickler for timekeeping. So is 'the boss,' as you no doubt gathered."

Saying goodbye to Ian Brannagan, Dafydd went to find the stairs that led to the safety of his room. After rummaging for his robe he slipped across the hall to the bathroom and ran a bath. Submerged up to his neck, he dozed, but eventually the cool-

ing water made him shiver and wake. The noises from below
had abated: perhaps the bar was closing. He had no idea what
time it was. He got out and dried himself off on a dingy yellow
towel, threw his bathrobe on and made for his room. In the narrow corridor he ran straight into the dark-haired waitress.

"Hi, Dafydd," she said, studying his loosely tied bathrobe.

"Well, good night," he exclaimed.

"Can I get you anything . . . a nightcap? I could bring it to
your room if you'd like." Dafydd looked at her, speechless. Was
this what he thought it was? *Plenty wimmin would try it on . . .*
wasn't that what his shrewd taxi driver had told him? And they
obviously wasted no time.

"Thanks, ah . . . Brenda. I'm fine, but thank you anyway."
He feared he must seem very naive. She was a seriously sexy
woman, but just like that . . . tonight?

Brenda smiled. "You sure about that, now?"

"Aha . . . yes," he said.

"Okay." She shrugged cheerfully, showing she was not
slighted by the rejection. "You have a good night, now." She
turned briskly and her arse swayed voluptuously as he, mesmerized, watched her walk away from him down the hall.

There was a steady pounding against the bed. He could feel the
vibrations of each thump traveling up the length of his spine to
his skull. At the same time it felt as if someone were knocking on
his head with a small hammer, sharp angry raps. He woke and
jerked himself upright, peering around in the darkness. There
seemed to be no one there, but the pounding continued, in fact
increasing in speed and urgency. Suddenly it stopped dead and a
long, low groan followed. Dafydd strained his ear to locate the
source of the unearthly noise. Then voices and laughter.

Damn. The wall separating him from the copulating couple
was like cardboard, and their bed was immediately next to his.
After a few minutes of husky conversation, his spent neighbors seemed to fall asleep. As he listened to the sound of their

breathing, he was sure he could feel the feathery draft of their exhalations across his face. He climbed out of bed and looked at the wall. He tapped it lightly in a few places and it undulated softly. Cardboard indeed. One of the two lovers banged on the flimsy material with a fist. It shook ominously.

"Fer chrissakes," came a gruff man's voice, "people are trying to get some rest here, you know."

"Exactly," Dafydd retorted quietly.

He tried to settle back on the knobbly mattress. There were bits of grit around his bare buttocks and he reached down to investigate. They felt like crumbs, perhaps even dirt from someone who'd not bothered to remove his boots. Hogg's filthy trailer could certainly not be any worse, no matter what Dafydd's predecessor, "Monsieur Dr. Odent," had perpetrated on it. One of his neighbors farted. Dafydd huffed and turned his back on them, drawing his knees up into a fetal position to protect himself from further insult. He slept fitfully for a short while but woke with a start.

It was seven months ago, to the day. Even now he could remember the uncountable numbers of tequila shooters he'd been forced to down, interspersed with triple Jack Daniel's and several pints of beer. Jerry and Philippa, two of his high-living colleagues in Bristol, had organized the bash in his honor. Partly to celebrate his thirty-second birthday but mainly because he was through with his training and was ready to apply for consultancy posts. He'd gotten to bed at five the following morning, grateful that he'd booked the day off work as part of his annual leave.

At seven the phone rang.

"Woodruff." It was Briggs, the senior consultant. "I can't see you down for any list."

"Ah? . . . No, I've got the day off."

"Never mind. I want a favor from you."

No sooner had Dafydd hung up than he had some dark forebodings, as if the damage done to his brain by the massive amounts of alcohol he'd consumed had opened up his sixth sense. If only he'd phoned the bastard back and refused to do his bidding, told him he was still drunk or whatever. Instead he staggered into the shower, followed by Tylenol, mouthwash, and instant coffee, dressed in the least dirty shirt he could find and some tracksuit bottoms and actually got into his car and drove to the hospital. What the hell, lots of people did it, getting loaded and going to work the next day. Junior doctors were known for their binges, a form of escape from the unrelenting work schedule, the crushing responsibility and the hours of studying for exams.

He'd gone straight to the ward to see the little boy, Derek Rose, and his mother, aware of his red-rimmed eyes and telltale breath, but he needn't have worried about making an impression. Sharon Rose was a poor single mother in her twenties, in frayed jeans, a cheap donkey jacket, and, by the look of her yellowed, anxious fingers, dying for a fag. She was the sort of unfortunate woman who thought doctors were omnipotent, men and women in white coats whose opinions should not be challenged since they could do no wrong. He wished he had put her right, there and then; told her he was not in a fit state to operate on her son. But Briggs had intimidated him and rubbished his objections; Dafydd was supposed to be a fully fledged pediatric surgeon, on the brink of consultancy, and Briggs's references were going to be extremely important.

As he was scrubbing up for the operation, that feeling of apprehension persisted. It was something other than just his nausea and slightly trembling vision; more a sense of impending misfortune. But he was a realist, not prone to superstition. Much as his instincts told him to back out, he carried on and pulled the latex gloves onto his hands. All seemed to go according to plan. The removal was easy; he thought he'd been worried for nothing. He held the boy's kidney in his hand for a moment. Then he looked at it more closely and was puzzled. But for some minor inflammation, it didn't look particularly diseased, although a small cancerous growth was clearly visible on the X-ray. No doubt the tumor was internal, but still . . . As he reached forward to place the kidney into the bowl the nurse was holding out to him, the registrar assisting him quite suddenly whispered something in his ear. There was a tense urgency to her voice, and she grabbed his arm hard, far too hard, and pointed to the X-ray. His hand stopped in midair and he peered at the plate. His heart lurched sickeningly and he felt the blood drain from his face.

It could happen and did happen—not often, but it did. With all his labored care and concentration, the disaster came down to a label. He'd not looked closely enough at the label on the X-ray, and now he saw that the small white sticker was at the back of the plate. The picture of the boy's internal organs was turned the wrong way around. It was so crazy—it was the stuff of cartoons, had it not been for the fact that a child's whole future life was put in appalling jeopardy. He'd been too focused on the actual operation, the boy's flesh and blood, to think of double-checking with the mother or reading the boy's notes properly.

The impact of his disastrous error made him feel faint; he had to let the registrar take over. The bile was rising in his throat and he rushed to the lavatory, leaving a shocked and panic-stricken team to deal with the aftermath, a frantic search for a transplant surgeon who could perform the reattachment.

His own aftermath had been to face Sharon Rose, to tell her what he'd done. At least he'd done that. Her disbelief had been shattering, his shame and remorse absolute. A severe depression followed, which numbed him to the core. It was easy to understand how some doctors took their own life.

His suspension from duties was immediate, pending an investigation. Briggs called him at home and told him to enjoy his "gardening leave" and that he would testify to Dafydd's competence. It was an "unusual circumstance" after all.

"Yes. A game of fucking golf," Dafydd said out loud into the dark, unfamiliar room, recollecting the "unusual circumstance" that had made Briggs ask him for this catastrophic favor.

At the time his career had seemed destroyed. He was uncer-

tain about his future as a doctor, regardless of the outcome of
the inquiry. Two months later he was acquitted. Briggs was held
responsible for the blunder since he was the senior consultant
in charge and Derek Rose was his patient. The whole business
was smoothed over as a "systems failure." It was no victory for
Dafydd. The little boy had now been relieved of his cancerous
kidney, but his once perfectly healthy kidney was now imper-
fect, vulnerable. *And it was his doing.* He would gladly have
given Derek one of his own kidneys had it been feasible.

A noisy rattle started up, hot water traveling and hissing
through pipes. It must mean that morning was approaching.
He hauled himself out of bed and went to the window. He drew
aside the blackout curtain and was astonished to see broad daylight. It was still only three forty-five. He tugged at the window. It was designed to open only a fraction, but he reveled in
the draft of cool air. An insect screen hung loose on its hinges.
Looking at the street below, he saw that everything was covered
with a layer of dust. Everything in sight looked sprayed with
fine gray powder. No wonder Martha Kusugaq had sniggered
at his good suit.

A lone dog sauntered down the middle of the road. It was
a thin, scabby thing, but it looked cocky enough. It stopped
and looked up at him with beady eyes, then set off at a trot toward its destination. Dafydd shaded his eyes against the bright
light and followed it until its skinny arse had faded into the
distance, along the road leading north. Up there somewhere, on
the shores of the Arctic Ocean, lay Inuvik and Tuktoyaktuk. Six
hundred miles southeast lay Yellowknife. Nothing but a couple
of tiny settlements in between. Gripped by a sudden despon-
dency, he pulled the dusty curtain across the sunlit night and
got back into bed, between the top sheet and the stained pink
satin eiderdown.

CHAPTER 3

Cardiff, 2006

> *Dear Dafydd,*
> *I'm glad you've responded to Miranda's letter, al-*
> *though I can't see why, at this stage, you'd want to*
> *completely disillusion her. Well, I suppose it must*
> *come as a bit of a shock, having had all these years*
> *to forget what happened, and then being reminded*
> *of what you left behind. You obviously have had no*
> *curiosity or sense of duty, since we've never heard a*
> *word from you. You've had almost thirteen years of*
> *freedom from commitment and worry, and now I'm*
> *afraid it needs to be addressed. Raising twins with-*
> *out a father has not been easy, financially or other-*
> *wise.*
>
> *I know you are married, but I'm sure that your*
> *wife, as a woman, will understand your obligations*
> *toward your natural children.*
>
> *You have my number. There is no point in putting*
> *it off.*
>
> *Yours sincerely Sheila Hailey*

A storm had been forecast and the wind whipped fiercely around the back of the house. Dafydd sat at the kitchen table, poured himself a glass of wine and waited for Isabel to read the letter. She stood by the window and held the letter up to the light, like she sometimes did with money, checking for counterfeits. Except he knew this little ritual was for his benefit. The way she squinted at the paper, her eyebrows practically meeting in the middle . . . What he *hadn't* shown her was a snapshot, enclosed with the letter: a plump dark-haired girl with her arm around a thin gangly-looking boy with long red hair. As twins went, they looked totally different from one another, and neither of them looked remotely like him.

"Read it, for God's sake." Under the table, his hands folded the envelope over and over, into a tight little cube. "What do you expect to find? Fingerprints?"

She glared at him. After reading it, she turned to him. "You *wrote* to them. Why on earth did you do that? I thought we agreed—"

A loud clatter saved him from her annoyance, temporarily at least. Both of them hurried to the dining room and peered through the window down the long, narrow garden. The tool-shed was rocking on its hard standing with each gust.

"That shed's about to go flying." Dafydd stared at the tiny structure, harboring a hidden delight in the forces of nature, even when potentially destructive.

"Why are you doing things behind my back? I thought we decided to deal with this together."

"If that shed hits the conservatory . . . Hell, look at the trees." The house was of sturdy Victorian construction, but the two enormous copper beeches in the garden were far too close to it. "Let's hope our insurance is in order."

Isabel grabbed him by the arm and sharply turned him toward her. "Fuck the trees. Fuck the insurance. Tell me about *this*." She raised her voice over the howling wind and jabbed at the letter, which was still in her hand.

It hadn't been a week since he wrote to the girl. He'd imagined that the post would be slow in the Northwest Territories.

It used to be. He looked at Isabel's agitated face. Her eyes, dark and intense, bore angrily into his.

"Listen, I thought about it and decided I didn't want it hanging over me, so I just wrote back and explained to the girl that her mother had made some sort of mistake, and that I couldn't possibly be her dad. And I wished her luck in finding her real father. That's all."

"I'd like to see what you said."

He hadn't kept a copy of his letter and now he realized that it would have been prudent to do so. "Hey . . . I'm sorry." He grabbed her and pulled her to him. "I know we're in this together, but let me deal with it. I did give Andy a ring and he advised me to write and tell them they'd got the wrong person. I'll sort this out. Trust me, okay?" He wanted to sound confident, but Sheila Hailey's letter was shockingly unequivocal. It was a real test of Isabel's trust, and her misgivings floated over him like a wet cloud. Her body felt rigid in his arms.

"No." Isabel untangled herself from his embrace. "Make it official. Ask Andy to write directly to this Sheila woman." She pulled out her old pouch of tobacco from her shirt pocket and rolled a cigarette. "I know what you've told me about Sheila and all this stuff between the two of you, so don't bother repeating it, but she sounds pretty confident. She's obviously after money and thinks you're going to give it to her."

Isabel was probably right about Sheila, but he couldn't understand that a bit of money could be worth the trouble and the damage this whole charade could cause her children. He toyed with the idea of contacting some Canadian child-protection outfit and asking them to investigate. After all, the woman was unbalanced, she had to be. Should she really be in charge of two vulnerable adolescents? He felt strongly about it. The girl had been drawn into a fantasy where he was the father she yearned for, the man who might bring deliverance from . . . God knows what strange and dysfunctional setup . . .

He left Isabel standing by the window and went to get the wine glasses from the kitchen. He took them into the conservatory, an original construction they'd often slept in throughout the six summers of their marriage. Now it seemed dank, drafty, and vulnerable. The structure would soon be unsafe. It occurred to him that there wouldn't be another summer.

"Come in here," he shouted to Isabel. "Let's be part of the elements."

Isabel followed him, peering anxiously at the glass roof. Wrapping an old quilt around her, she tucked herself into a corner of the sofa, well away from him. Her tall frame looked pared down; she had lost a bit of that slight spread around the hips that she was forever trying to eliminate. Her face was pale; her prominent cheekbones cast deep shadows on her cheeks, and her thick shoulder-length hair had recently been cut, rather clumsily chopped off on a whim, into a bob that didn't much suit her. She'd never been pretty, at no time sweet, but she was in possession of an extraordinary erotic appeal, a grace and composure that made heads turn. He remembered how awe-struck he'd been at first.

As he looked at her he felt the rise of his frustration. The timing of these missives from Canada was seriously unfortu-nate. He'd been waiting for the right moment to tell her . . . but how could he spring this on her now?

"You know what, Dafydd? You should ask them to submit to DNA testing. I have a feeling they won't let up until you take a stand. This business could drag on . . ."

He moved toward her, taking her hand. "You're right." Her hand was cold and looked bluish. He kissed it tenderly. "Let's deal with it. I'll ring Sheila Hailey and tell her to do a blood test immediately and not to contact me in any way until it's all done. I'm sure that'll be the last we hear from them."

"I feel sorry for those kids." Isabel sighed and put her head on his shoulder. "You'd be such a wonderful father." He could hear the grief in her voice. Raising her hand, she drew her fin-gers through his hair. "It may sound crazy coming from me, but in some ways it wouldn't have been an altogether bad thing. Part-time parenthood, having children over the summer holidays. I think I could have handled it. Perhaps it would have been the best thing that could have happened to us. At least they would have been yours."

Dafydd drew a deep breath, closing his eyes. "Oh, you don't mean that."

"Don't they say that childless couples who adopt children, when the pressure is off, suddenly find that they're pregna—"

"It's a myth," he interrupted brusquely. Perhaps *now* was the right time to tell her. Yes, why not now?

"Isabel, there is something we need to talk—"

A strong gust of wind rattled the panes of glass and they both got up simultaneously. The storm tugged at the structure, making the wooden joints squeak and wail like an infant in pain. At the end of the garden the shed was bouncing and rattling, when the wind quite suddenly embraced it and rolled it like a beach ball across the grass. It wedged itself against the fence.

"Jesus," Dafydd gasped. "Let's secure the hatches and bolt the doors."

"I'll tie you down," Isabel whispered into his ear and grabbed his hand, pulling him away from the window toward the stairs. "Nothing cures a falling birth rate like a hurricane."

The wind increased as he was trudging through deep snow, following a small fox. The snow was dry and powdery and crunched loudly underfoot. Tall trees towered over him, spruce and fir. With each step his feet sank deeper into the snow, and the wind whirled the icy flakes into his eyes. He couldn't see where he was going and realized that he had lost the tracks of the fox. It had scurried ahead. He called to it, knowing it was trying to lead him somewhere. Somewhere vital, somewhere he had to go.

He felt a sudden excruciating pain in one leg. He threw his head back and screamed. The echo of his scream reverberated among the trees. Wolves howled back at him from afar. He saw that his leg was gripped in the jaws of a leg-hold trap and wildly he twisted and turned to get free. The black-steel teeth had penetrated his ankle right through. Blood pulsated from the gashes, coloring the white snow a scarlet red. The wolves had approached and were in a circle around him amid the trees. The night was black and he could barely see them, but their yellow eyes shone as they observed him in silence. He brought his leg up to his mouth and started gnawing at his flesh to free himself . . .

Isabel stroked his forehead. "Wake up." She patted his cheeks lightly. "I think you're coming down with something. You're drenched. I'll go and make you a cup of tea."

"No, don't get up. I'm fine. It was just a dream."

It was four o'clock in the morning. The wind still whipped over the roof gable just above their heads. The dream had left the stench of terror in his nostrils. He'd had a clear insight into the feeling of being hunted, and of being trapped. He shivered and looked at the alarm clock. Then he remembered their plan. He calculated the time difference. Reluctantly he got out of bed.

"Do you want to hear this, or shall I go downstairs?"

Isabel looked puzzled, and he pointed to the phone. She resolutely shook her head.

He got into his tracksuit and a pair of thick socks.

"I'll be back." He smiled.

He took the phone into the living room and unfolded Miranda's letter. It still gave him a shock to see it. Not because of what it alleged, but because of the sudden turbulence it had caused in his life, dredging up things that he had worked hard to forget. He found the telephone number and dialed.

"Hello."

He recognized the voice instantly, even after all this time.

"It's Dafydd Woodruff here," he started formally. "We need to talk." Irritatingly, his voice shook slightly and his mouth had gone bone-dry.

"Not a moment too soon, Dafydd," Sheila Hailey said lightly with an amused edge to her voice. "You got my letter, then?"

"Why are you doing this?"

"I'm 'doing this,' as you put it, because Miranda has been at me for a couple of years asking who her dad was, and finally I thought it wasn't fair to keep her in the dark any longer. Mark doesn't care, but he should know too."

Long-buried emotions rose like the flame of a blowtorch inside him.

"What kind of idiotic stunt are you trying to pull?" He stopped himself; it wasn't good to start on that note.

"You can rant all you want, Dafydd," Sheila said coolly, "it won't make a bit of difference. You're the father of my twins, and you might as well get used to it. Take your time. In the meantime, you could start paying a bit of maintenance for them. After all, I've let you off for almost thirteen years."

"I've never laid a finger on you," Dafydd exclaimed, then cringed as he remembered what he'd done.

"Oh, Dafydd, come on. I know you were drunk and all, but surely you can't have forgotten." She sounded calm and reasonable. "First you drugged me to get me into bed, and then when I was pregnant and asked you at least to abort it for me, not only did you refuse but you assaulted me. You're lucky I didn't go to the police. You're really nothing but a thug under that slimy British snobbery."

"Just a minute. The abortion . . . of course I refused . . . it had nothing to do with me. What the hell are you talking about, drugging you, getting you into bed? None of that happened." Dafydd paused in disbelief. "You're accusing me of rape?"

"What did you think it was? A friendly poke? Difficult to prove, since it happened at your place, and I could do without the hassle. You know what the Moose Creek grapevine's like." She laughed. "They'd love it, wouldn't they? Just imagine."

A clear picture of Sheila came to him, her obnoxious red hair, the mocking blue eyes. He forced himself to swallow his outrage and try to sound composed.

"I want nothing to do with you or your children. If you're planning to harass me any further, I want to have a DNA test."

He paused, waiting for her reaction, but she said nothing. "I didn't think you'd be too keen about that."

"No sweat," she answered easily. "Do you want to organize it, or shall I?"

"Oh, I'll sort it out. Don't you worry. And let's get it over with as quickly as possible."

"That suits me just fine. Then you'll have to pay for it. I'll get the blood samples done tomorrow if you want."

She'd agreed. Thank God. That should be the end of it. "No, wait until you hear from my lawyer. Andrew McCloud. I'll talk to him today. He'll arrange the test with a certified laboratory."

"I'm not going anywhere for your sake," she said firmly. "I'll do whatever I have to, but the blood samples can be taken right here at the hospital."

"I'm sure that'll be fine. It makes no difference where or how you give blood. It's *my* DNA that's in question, not yours."

"Listen, Dafydd, I knew you'd want a DNA test. That's okay by me. I realize it's necessary, but you *are* the father of my children, and I know you know it. Come on, be realistic, why would I be bothering with this if you weren't? Why would I be wasting my time?"

"This conversation is pointless."

"Do you want to have a word with Miranda? She's dying to talk to you."

"No . . ." He hesitated. Then he heard Sheila call the girl's name. Might it be a good idea to speak to the girl and at least put her in the right? A couple of seconds passed and then he had no choice.

"Hiya, Dad." A bright confident voice. "How're you doing?"

"Hello, Miranda. Look, I'm afraid your mum has made a very big mistake. I'm very sorry that you're being put through all this . . . for no reason . . ."

"Don't worry, Dad." She said it with such warmth and enthusiasm, he felt pained.

"No, really, I *am* worried. You mustn't think your mother is right. I'm afraid I'm going to have to prove to you that I'm not your father. You mustn't take all this too seriously."

"Did you get the photo my mom sent? I think I look like you a little bit," Miranda chirped, unperturbed by his protestations. "We managed to get a photo of you from *Moose Creek News,* from when you first came to work here, and another one from a party at Mr. Bowlby's. I know it's a zillion years ago, but you're real good-looking. Mark's got red hair like my mom, but I'm like you . . ."

The receiver was grabbed from the girl.

"Okay, you've said hello," Sheila said matter-of-factly.

"'Bye, Dad," the girl shouted down the phone.

Dafydd hung up and sat still for a few minutes, giving himself time to recover and wondering what to tell Isabel. Sheila's accusation of rape was grotesque, absurd, almost funny. She must have lost the plot somewhere along the way. Or perhaps she'd had so many men she'd forgotten with whom she did what. Perhaps she was just plain crazy. But that was fine, as long as the test went ahead. When the results came through it would probably stop any further harassment. She'd move on to someone else, poor unlucky sod, someone closer to home.

Slowly he got up. He was grateful that Isabel hadn't wanted to listen. It would have really shaken her. Sheila sounded so remarkably confident and rational, Isabel would doubt his honesty, until the test came through anyway.

He climbed the stairs like an old man. He felt worn out. In the bedroom, Isabel was curled up on the bed. When he reached down to stroke her hair she raised her head and looked at him, her eyes cold. The telephone extension was in her hand and she pointed it toward him. "Don't touch me," she said.

"What? Isabel, now, listen—"

"No, *you* listen," she hissed. "I heard her and it's obvious, isn't it? She wouldn't be doing this. Why do you bother going on denying that you fucked her? Just admit that much, at least. Give me the benefit of—"

"I bloody didn't," he protested, his voice rising. "I absolutely *did not* have sexual fucking intercourse with the woman."

Isabel glared at him. "I'm impressed. You didn't have sexual fucking intercourse with the woman, but you got her pregnant *somehow.* Ha! Would I love to know how the two of you managed it."

"Isabel. For Christ's sake. Now you're being—"

"If you're so fucking clever, why can't you do it to *me*?"

"Oh, God. Enough now!"

"Not enough for me, *darling.* You should be trying harder, since you're obviously so good at it."

"Well, I'm through with trying," he blurted furiously. "I've *never* got anyone pregnant, and you know what, Isabel? I've had it with the whole damned business. I don't want any children, not hers, not yours, not anybody's. Do you hear me? I've been doing nothing but inseminating you and trying to flog a pregnancy into existence, and look at us. Where is the love in it? I've tried to tell you, but you just—"

He stopped. What was he doing? They stared at each other for a moment. Disgusted with himself and appalled by his tactless outburst, he saw with regret the shock begin to register on Isabel's face. She'd heard him, really heard him, finally. She got up from the bed and, raising her arm, she threw the telephone with some force toward him. It missed his shoulder and crashed into the wall, leaving a dull gash in the plaster.

CHAPTER 4

Moose Creek, 1992

Dafydd fumbled with the odd assortment of keys. They were tarnished and rusty, but there was no need, the lock was broken. The door had been pried open by some crude device, probably a garden-variety screwdriver. Hogg had warned him about the state of the trailer, even offered to pay for an extra night or two at the Klondike, so that it could be restored from the effects of a break-in.

"Just a couple of little things," Hogg had said vaguely. "The stove needs reconnecting, and one of the windows is cracked."

Dafydd had decided that there was no way he would spend another night being rocked by the motions of the copulating couple and chafing his arse on someone else's grit.

"Dr. Hogg . . . Andrew . . . I don't care what needs replacing"—his own assertiveness had surprised him—"but if you don't think it's fit for habitation, I'll look for something else. Ian tells me that there's quite a surplus of empty trailers around town. He told me I could get one within the hour."

As the senior partner of the hospital and clinic, Hogg, with Sheila Hailey as his sidekick, seemed to be a virtual one-man band. A short, corpulent man in his mid to late forties, he'd been one of the first doctors to come to Moose Creek. He owned the trailer park and a few other businesses, and he seemed quite naturally to expect newcomers like Dafydd to line his pockets. We'll see about that later, Dafydd had thought, and held out his hand for the rusty keys.

Hogg had quickly offered him a couple of twenty-dollar bills from his wallet. "Get a woman to clean it for you. There's a very amenable lady in the trailer next to the gate, Mrs. Breummer. She'll do it for you this evening. She's always in dire need of money."

The door swung open, hanging loosely on its hinges. Dafydd left his suitcases on the porch, brought by Martha, who'd appeared to be waiting for him outside the Klondike when he was checking out midafternoon. He stepped inside. Broken glass, cigarette butts, used condoms, and soiled clothing covered the floor. A window was shattered and an electric stove had been yanked from its filthy position and hauled over on to a sofa. There were sprays of reddish brown on one wall, dried blood by the look of it. Dafydd wondered if someone might have been killed, but a quick inspection of the bedroom and bathroom yielded no cadaver.

A "break-in" indeed; more like a pack of squatters on a binge. He felt suddenly furious. What a way to treat a newcomer who'd traveled halfway across the globe to do a job no other sane person would touch. But really, it was his own fault. He'd insisted on having the keys. How could he possibly approach the lady in need of money and ask her to tackle this abomination?

His first instinct was to leave, but Martha had departed in her sorry taxi and the evening was getting on. Oh, what the hell, he thought angrily, this is just fitting, it's absolutely bloody perfect. I have it coming. At least for one night. He brought his suitcases inside the door and hauled out his only pair of jeans. Rolling up his shirtsleeves, he set to work.

"Almighty mother of Jesus." Martha stepped through the door, raising her hands heavenward. "I just remembered my nephew telling me he'd been at a party around here. I thought I'd better come back and check that it wasn't in this precise trailer." She looked around and shook her head sadly. "Can you beat that?"

"What in heaven's name do they do?" Dafydd blurted out. "I've never seen anything like it."

"Just kids havin' fun." Martha crossed her short hefty arms over her belly. "Actually, I've seen worse. You don't rent no trailer to no native kid, any kid for that matter. Goes without saying." She shrugged expansively to show that cause and effect was a concept beyond question.

Dafydd looked at her, dismayed. "So this is pretty normal. Everyday sort of stuff. That's what you're saying?"

"Listen." Martha placed her hands squarely on her hips. "Tell you what. You give me a few bucks and I'll help ya. I got my barf kit in the back of the Valiant." She held out her plump palm, and Dafydd handed her the twenties, which were still in his shirt pocket. They set to it and between them hauled the stove back into its place, but not before Martha had removed the grime from the floor with her barf spatula. They swept up the debris and poured bleach over everything.

The woman with financial problems came, too, and so did a selection of other neighbors, pulled to the scene by curiosity and a certain sense of community. They, too, had had to put up with the mob that had partied in the trailer. Various contraptions for cleaning were brought, as was a thermos of coffee and some stale blueberry muffins. A young lad brought a cloudy old piece of Perspex, and it was deftly put over the broken window with industrial packing tape.

In spite of the generosity and the practical help, Dafydd sensed a wariness in his new neighbors. Even Martha abandoned her usual jocularity in the presence of the others and spoke to him in rather clipped tones. Perhaps doctors were as contemptible as she had intimated.

"If there's anything you need, now, ya hear, you just come right on over, Doctor," said a weedy middle-aged man with a shaggy mustache and long bushy sideburns. He wore a blackened cap, behind which trailed a stringy gray ponytail, and trousers held up by some Mexican-looking suspenders.

"Please call me Dafydd," he said to them all, "and I'm very

grateful for your help. If I can do anything at all in return, just let me know." The weedy man was the last to leave. He stopped on the porch and, taking Dafydd lightly by the arm, brought his face up close. His breath was overwhelmingly sour.

"I'm Ted O'Reilly . . . next door. What you just said . . . well, there's something. The Frog . . . the guy who was here before you, from Montreal way, he used to give me something for my leg. It's in a bad way. Pain alla time." The man winced to demonstrate how much he suffered.

"Do you want me to have a look at it?"

"Naa, nothing to tell. It's inside . . . er . . . in the bone, see?"

"What did he prescribe you?"

"Oh, no, it wasn't like that." The man hunched his shoulders uneasily. "He thought it was easier to bring the stuff . . . straight from the hospital . . . Seeing that I'm right next door."

"What was the medication called? Do you remember?"

"Valium, or something like that."

"But that's a tranquilizer." Dafydd sensed this was leading somewhere he didn't want to go.

"That's okay. It was mighty effective."

I bet it was, Dafydd thought, and wondered what Dr. Odent had gotten in return for his "treatment" of this unwholesome fellow.

"I don't think Valium's the best thing for your leg."

"I used to give him a bit of cash for his trouble."

"I think you'd better come to the surgery."

The man jumped back. "Surgery? No, really, it don' need operatin' on."

Dafydd suppressed a grin. "I meant come to the *clinic*."

"I don't get out much. Don't like walking. It's the pain, see?"

Dafydd sensed that it wasn't the last time he was going to hear this request. The man stank of alcohol and body odor, and his scrawny hands trembled slightly. He looked sixty but could be as young as forty.

"I'll give you a lift to the surge . . . to the clinic. Any morning you like, and you can come back by taxi."

"I'll get you home, O'Reilly," Martha interjected from behind the door.

The man jumped again, caught red-handed by somebody who knew better.

"Sure thing." He scuttled down the stairs from the porch. There was no limp to be seen. Martha emerged from her hiding place, brushing vigorously at her clothes with her stubby fingers as if to rid them of the grime they'd been exposed to.

"Now, there's a good example of the kind of individual you want to avoid," she admonished Dafydd. "Pity you have him next door."

"I thought you were going to bring your cankerous foot along this morning. I was waiting for you."

"Yeah, well," she drawled morosely, "some of us have to toil for a livin', believe it or not." She was holding two mismatched trainers in one hand, her barf box under the other arm. She looked satisfied, as if she had fulfilled a resolution and thoroughly indebted Dafydd to her for the foreseeable future.

"I'll take these sneakers, if you don't mind," she said, holding the defiled shoes up for his inspection.

"Oh, come on." He laughed. "Put them in the binbag. They're not even mates."

"Binbag? You mean throw them in the garbage?" she scoffed. "Poor kid. You evidently have no reckonin' where on God's earth you find yerself located." She got into her car and with a skid of tires she drove herself off toward the low red disk that was the sun.

There were no sheets or blankets, and Dafydd laid himself down on the soiled mattress fully dressed. The back of his head was perched on a fresh towel he'd brought from home, laid over a folded sweater, and he covered himself with his bathrobe, new

from Marks & Spencer in Swansea, his hometown. It seemed
light-years from this hellhole. With his eyes closed against the
perpetual light, he pictured M&S's immaculate food section.
Clean, decent people, in well-cut clothes and behaving in an
ordered and well-mannered fashion, buying dependable food in
good-quality packaging. Altogether a picture of health, happi-
ness, and good sense.

He half sobbed, half laughed out loud, then stopped dead.
The walls were thin here, too, and the trailers were only fifteen
feet apart. O'Reilly might have heard his maniacal eruption,
and would be convinced that here was another nutcase of a
doctor. One who'd eventually be an easy pushover, probably
ending up popping all sorts himself. Dafydd wondered if it was
the place that drove these people to apathy and addiction, or if
it was that the dregs of society were pulled here in the first place.
Either way, he'd better hang on to his last shreds of sanity.

Much as Dafydd constantly strived to end his penance and
overcome his loss of confidence, Derek Rose's little face reared
up in his mind. It seemed always to be there, not a flat round
childlike face but pointed foxlike features framed by straight
blond hair, trimmed as if a saucepan had been placed on the head
for guidance. Right this minute, his mother, Sharon Rose, was
probably in her flat on some dreary Bristol council estate caring
for her sick child. Dafydd wished she had sued him and Briggs
for compensation, and they might have been able to move somewhere nice, even buy a decent house, but she wasn't that sort of
woman. He'd been forbidden to do anything for her and Derek,
offer them anything. It wasn't done, an admission of guilt.

It made no difference that the tribunal had found him not
guilty of negligence or misconduct, that his suspension had
been overturned. He was incompetent, irresponsible. The question that was constantly on his mind . . . should he really go on
with medicine? How else was he going to earn a living? And
where? Back home in Wales . . . certainly not soon. Not for a
very long time. Perhaps never.

He fell into a fickle sleep, peopled by small somber children, a procession of men like O'Reilly, and himself flailing, drowning, in a sea of cigarette butts and soiled trainers.

"Bright and early." Hogg grinned patronizingly as he passed Dafydd in the hospital corridor. He stopped and grasped Dafydd by the sleeve with his fat, rather feminine fingers. Hogg had been there for a good many years, apparently, but the little man's accent and demeanor were still quintessentially British and Dafydd couldn't help himself smiling.

"I didn't introduce you to anyone yesterday morning . . . my apologies. I'll have more time tomorrow."

"There is no time like the present." Dafydd grinned at him, pleased for the opportunity to stuff the man's timekeeping clichés back down his throat.

"Right you are, right you are," Hogg said briskly, leading the way down the corridor.

"Here's the office . . . fax machine, photocopier, patients' records." Hogg pointed with a chubby forefinger around the dingy room containing two smoking secretaries, but didn't bother to introduce him, then frog-marched him farther down the hall as if Dafydd were a pesky schoolboy wanting to be shown around a new school.

"There's the dispensary." He waved casually toward a metal-plated door. "We keep it locked. We had a bit of bother with one of your predecessors, but really I shouldn't mention names. Drugs are popular in these parts, and not just for pain relief." He laughed, and for the first time looked Dafydd in the eye.

"Heavens. Don't worry. I *will* understand, we *all* will, if you find this place a bit like the Wild West at first. A young man like yourself from a rather sheltered environment. Believe me, I know what it's like. I've been there myself. When I first came here I felt quite out of my depth."

"I'm not exactly a spring chicken," Dafydd protested, laughing. "I've actually—"

Hogg raised his hand to hush him, "Ah, here we are." He had

stopped at another door, and his demeanor changed in a subtle way. His rounded shoulders hunched a little further, and the feminine aspects of his persona became more pronounced. He knocked at the door ever so lightly, an ingratiating smile playing on his lips. He put his ear closer to the door. Dafydd read the plastic plaque on the door: SHEILA HAILEY — HEAD NURSE.

"The lady we want to meet is not in her office, but you'll run into her soon enough. She's my very right-hand person here, you understand." He bent toward Dafydd and whispered, "It's well worth your while to cultivate her."

"I've met her already," Dafydd said. "She formed part of my welcome committee."

"She did?" Hogg looked momentarily uncertain. "Well, well, of course she would have. She's very thorough; nothing slips her by."

Again he grasped Dafydd's sleeve and led him on.

"Sheila knows the ropes, even better than I do. Anything you need, anything at all, anything from the dispensary, she's your woman."

"Hogg, is that me you're referring to?" Sheila Hailey came striding out of a ward behind them. "The young man is going to get the wrong impression."

She joined them and they all laughed awkwardly at her little innuendo. Hogg put a proprietorial arm around her shoulders.

"Sheila, you've met Woodright, our new recruit. He's a first-rate surgeon, according to his references, and is already proving himself an early bird. Just like you and me." He squeezed her shoulders tightly and her full breasts rose slightly under the pressure. "We might have to share our morning coffee with him. That'll be a first, won't it?"

Dafydd felt sick, a sensation he often had when he felt in dire need for a quick repartee but could find none. "I'm . . . it's Woodruff," he blustered ineffectually as the two looked him over like a prized side of beef, each in quite a different way and quite apparently for different reasons.

"Yes, very nice. He'll do," Sheila said, and their eyes met momentarily. There was an unmistakable authority in her presence, covered up by this playful come-on. Her eyes were of an unusually deep blue. She wore a lot of makeup around them for which there was no need. The rest of her face was clean, milky white, covered by pale pink freckles. In broad daylight her hair looked inflammable, a tumbling mass of red coils. Dazzling, but he was already wary of her, although he couldn't say exactly why.

Hogg had no such reservations. He gazed at her with undisguised admiration. Yet apparently he had a wife, Anita. According to a nice nurse named Janie Dafydd had met the morning before, "Anita suffers from post-viral fatigue, and Hogg doesn't believe in the disorder. Thinks it's *hogwash*." They'd had a good chuckle about that. Janie was the only really likable person he'd met in Moose Creek so far. Twenty-six years old, married to a hardworking trapper, with two children already and another on the way.

"Hogg's right," Sheila said, extricating herself from the possessive grasp. She stepped forward and put a slender, freckled hand on Dafydd's forearm. "I'll look after you."

After barely a week on the job, he had his first real challenge. The foreman at the mill called for a doctor to come to the scene with only a vague description as to the nature of the accident. Hogg suggested that Dafydd should go, as a way of familiarizing himself with the "industrial misadventures" of his new working environment. From the furtive look on Hogg's face, coupled with a few evasive words. Dafydd deduced it to be something gruesome and he was daunted by the thought of what he would find. With good reason. At a later count, the body of the man was in 142 pieces.

As he sat in the ambulance waiting to be admitted into the main yard, he wondered if the task of gathering human remains formed part of his job. The job description had been vague: *general practice, routine surgery, some obstetrics, psychiatric experience useful.* Mortician? He knew this call-out had to do with dead bodies, scraps of bodies. Perhaps Hogg was right about him being a bit out of his depth. He wasn't used to lots of dead bodies, let alone in bits.

The foreman received him at the door of his mobile hut. He apologized for bothering the doctor and pointed to Dafydd's superior knowledge of anatomy. "My men wouldn't know what's what," he said, averting his eyes from the yard behind him, "but some of them won't mind giving you a hand." He winced and quickly added, "That wasn't very nicely put, was it?"

Not meaning to, Dafydd found himself smiling at the pun. There was something so surreal about the whole situation that he couldn't quite take it seriously. He hadn't as yet seen anything and was unsure where to begin.

"Let me get you some sturdy plastic bags," the foreman offered helpfully and disappeared into his office. A few men in orange overalls were milling around quietly, waiting. "Oh . . . and here"—the foreman held out a tangle of yellow rubber—"you might want some gloves."

"What actually happened?" Dafydd asked the swarthy teenager who began following him around as he cleaned up the scene of the accident. The boy was holding out an orange plastic bag for Dafydd to drop the pieces into.

"He was pumping up a tire on the hauler over there," the boy explained, pointing to a massive vehicle with the wheels standing eight feet high, "and the tire just blew, literally exploded." The boy threw his arms out and imitated the sound of the explosion, accompanied by a spray of saliva.

"Nah," an older native man cut in, "you got that all wrong, kid. He was 'temptin' to heat the nut with a blowtorch, to loose it up, see. It was the heat that made it pop."

The man's body had been torn apart by the explosion. Bits of flesh, bone and tufts of hair had been flung up to fifty yards away. Shreds of black tire covered everything like a spew of molten lava. Larger body portions were lying about, red and glistening in the sun, vivid against the black of the yard, with its

bits of oily machinery. A part of the skull lay empty and smoth-
ered in dust like a shard of an ancient vessel. Dafydd picked it
up and examined it briefly. This bowl-shaped piece of bone had
contained the brain of a man his own age. Only an hour ago it
had been thinking and feeling, looking forward to the end of his
shift, getting home to his wife and children. Dafydd dropped the
piece into the plastic bag that the youngster was proffering him
quite eagerly. He felt faint in the heat, and the smell made him
nauseous. His gloves were smeared with blood and his armpits
were saturated with sweat. Drops of perspiration were slipping
from his forehead and found their way into his eyes.

The boy showed no hint of revulsion. He stared in fascination at the various organs and limbs that were gathering in the
sack. He put the bulging bag on the ground and scurried off to
fetch another one.

The men recruited to help hung back and poked in the dirt
with the toes of their steel-capped boots. It was too much even
for these hard-nosed individuals to touch the flesh of their dead
colleague. The driver who had brought Dafydd to the yard was
equally unwilling. He should have been doing his share of the
job, but he was tinkering with a collapsible stretcher beside the
ambulance, pretending it was out of order.

The foreman had called the dead man's wife, and now he
came out to inform Dafydd that the woman was at the hospital, waiting for her husband to be brought in so that she could
identify him. She was apparently wanting to do this, not now,
but yesterday. The foreman shrugged his shoulders and spread
his grubby fingers in a gesture of helplessness.

"I can't do this any faster than I'm already doing it," Dafydd
snapped. "Perhaps you'd care to help me?"

The foreman shook his head, a sudden look of dread on his
weather-beaten features. He glanced at his men, and obviously fear-
ing a loss of face he turned back to Dafydd and said, "I'll do my job
and you do yours. That way we don't step on anybody's toes."

He winked at the men and chuckled sheepishly, but the men
said nothing and continued poking in the dust with their boots.

Only the boy laughed. He reached into the bag and pulled out part of a foot with his bare hand.

"Here," he said, offering the bloody lump toward the foreman, "you won't be treading on *his* toes. Look. I've got them right here."

Horrified, the foreman paled and backed away, almost tripping over in the gravel. Without a word he turned and walked quickly toward his hut. Now some of the men were smirking and tittering. The humiliation of the chief honcho seemed a light relief after the trauma of the accident. The boy looked at Dafydd, pleased with himself. Dafydd returned his smile and nodded. He wondered if the kid was really old enough to work in a sawmill. Perhaps he would get fired over his impertinence.

They drove the grisly cargo back into town. The ambulance driver was a stocky man of Eastern European extraction. He rambled on endlessly about the horrors of his job, intermittently masticating and cracking a well-used wad of bubble gum. Dafydd switched off and looked out at the brooding woods on both sides of the road. These forests spread for hundreds of miles; how easily a man could get lost . . .

". . . she was in a culvert under the bridge—you know, the one by Mile Sixteen. Her body plugged it up and the water kept flooding the road, see, otherwise they might never have found her." The driver paused for effect and looked meaningfully at Dafydd. "The murderer is still on the loose, probably right here in town, under our very noses. They couldn't find anyone with a motive. I mean, the husband had another woman, but it was a friendly arrangement an' all, no one had any cause to murder the poor girl."

"Terrible," Dafydd commented absentmindedly, thinking of Bristol and how lucky it was that he'd not caused someone's death with his incompetence. He had yet to tell Hogg that he would absolutely not operate on children. He bit his lip hard and turned to the driver.

"How long have you been here?" he asked without interest.

"Ah, les see . . ." The man narrowed his beady eyes and

rubbed his unshaven chin in concentration. "Well, it was some-time around '84. My old lady . . ."

Dafydd nodded. He was piecing together the dead man's body parts in his mind. How would he do it? Lay them out on a table in the hospital basement, the so-called Pathology Department. Piece them together like a giant puzzle. He sat up with a jolt as he remembered the wife waiting to identify the body. Giving bad news to a relative was another thing he wasn't sure he could handle as yet. Plus, the foreman had omitted to describe the state her husband was in. He would have to talk her out of it somehow.

". . . and I had to put my arms around the guy's chest and pull so's Brannagan could cut the feet clean off. You shoulda seen the blood pumping from them, even with a tourniquet. There was no way we could have had that beam off him. The way the friggin' thing was wedged . . ."

Sheila Hailey stood on the steps at the staff entrance waiting for him when the ambulance pulled up.

"I've told the woman that she can't see the damned body, but she's not having it," she said to Dafydd while she watched impassively as the ambulance man carried the five bags around the back to the basement door.

"I'll talk to her," Dafydd said, somewhat surprised by Sheila's callous approach. In the few days he'd known Sheila, he was no closer to understanding what this woman was about. She was an excellent nurse with an enormous capacity for hard work, but there was a coldness about her that he'd felt from the very moment they met, disguised by flirtatiousness and an infinite willingness to be helpful. He supposed her pitiless attitude to some patients was the result of the rigors of the job, having hardened herself through having seen the worst. The biggest mystery about her was why a woman of her looks and obvious ability would hole herself away in a place like Moose Creek. Possibly, like himself, she'd done something . . . He'd try to ask someone about her, Ian or perhaps Janie when he'd gotten to know them better. Somehow he couldn't imagine getting close enough to ask her in person.

He wondered fleetingly why he was so interested as he pushed past her through the narrow door. She didn't move aside and his arm skimmed against her breasts. He jerked his shoulder to deny the contact and walked quickly down the corridor.

"I'm telling you," she called after him, "she won't listen. She's completely hysterical. I tried to shoot her up with something but she's—" Dafydd, mortified, swung around.

"Stop shouting," he hissed. "Anyone can hear you."

She looked startled, then smiled. "We're not big on privacy here."

Dafydd turned away and hurried toward the room where the bereaved woman was waiting for him.

"What's up?" Ian Brannagan said to him as they met in the corridor. "You look quite pale."

"If ever a man needed a drink . . ." Dafydd blurted.

"You're talking to the right guy," Ian said, taking Dafydd by the arm. "I was just on my way down for a quick one at the Klondike. Grab yer gear and we're out of here." They skipped down the stairs and walked quickly down the hill toward the main drag, kicking up dust with every footstep. It was just after six but the sun was beating down on them and the air shimmered. The heat made it worse: the stench of the dead man's flesh was still clinging to Dafydd's nostrils. He felt the imprints on his chest where the wife had thumped him in hysterical grief, and his hands were still tingling from the grasp that he'd had on her wrists. It felt as if he'd been through a major incident himself. It was a relief to enter the plastic "marbled" columns into the cool reviving darkness of the bar. They sat down at a small table under the air-conditioning unit. It was early enough and the place was still half empty. Brenda sailed up to them with her tray of filled glasses. "No, darling. Extra Old Stock," Ian told her.

Brenda looked at Dafydd. "What do *you* want, honey?"

"Scotch, please. A double, on the rocks."

Brenda's face was somber, and when she brought him his

drink it was brutally generous. "I heard," she said and patted his shoulder sympathetically.

"Already?"

"A few of the guys from the mill were just in," Brenda whispered.

"Wait," Ian frowned. "Don't tell me what sort of 'Welcome to Moose Creek' mission you were sent on until I've had a few."

No sooner had Ian downed half his bottle in a swallow than Brenda came back and tapped him on the shoulder.

"Call for you, buddy. You're to go straight to Emergency."

"Shit." Ian tipped the rest of the bottle down. "Can't the doctor on duty have a moment to fortify himself?"

As Ian sauntered off, Brenda remained by the table. With a sigh she put down her heavy load and proceeded to curl her shoulders around and around, groaning extravagantly. She sat down on the chair Ian had vacated, with her back to Dafydd.

"Do us a favor, Doc, pinch my shoulders, will you, give them a quick rub."

Dafydd looked about the bar but nobody seemed interested in the interaction. He put his hands on her shapely shoulders and proceeded to massage them firmly. She was wearing a skimpy red top held up by two thin straps. The warmth of her flesh felt healing on his hands after the grisly duties they'd been subjected to, and he entered into the spirit of the kneading and rubbing with his eyes closed. Her soft black hair caressed his forearms, and without thinking he gathered it together in his hands and let it slide through his fingers. Brenda moaned softly, and he opened his eyes.

"There you are," he said briskly and gave her a perfunctory pat on the back. "Occupational hazard, I guess, but you must be as strong as an ox."

She turned around and looked at him. Taking hold of her tray, she lifted it up onto her shoulder.

"I'm off at seven," she said. "Do you want to go for a drive? I could take you to Jackfish Lake." She laughed quietly. "It's the Riviera of the North. We could have a swim."

"Hell, why not?" After the various ordeals of the day, he could certainly afford himself any escapade he liked. A swim . . . he could sure use one.

At nine the sun was still high over the horizon, and he was floating on his back in a murky brown pond with floaty reeds snaking around his ankles. Every few moments, horseflies were dive-bombing him, and he had already ascertained that their bite was extremely unpleasant. There was nothing for it: when he heard the approaching buzz, a big gulp of air and head down into the water, water that in itself contained foreign animal life of many sorts. He just hoped that none of them would slither up one of his lower orifices or attach itself to his skin.

Brenda was on the stony beach in an orange bikini, lighting a barbecue in a rusty old drum, left there for the purpose. *Some Riviera.* He smiled to himself. Still, a pleasant end to a harrowing day.

"You can come out now," Brenda shouted to him. "The smoke keeps them away."

He swam toward the shore, then sprinted out of the water, self-conscious in his blue-and-white-striped boxer shorts. A family was just packing up their paraphernalia, leaving Dafydd and Brenda to enjoy the last of the evening on their own.

Brenda glanced at him as he struggled to put his shirt over his wet skin. "You don't have to get dressed. It'll stay warm for ages and I won't attack you." She laughed. "Although you're in a mighty nice shape."

She was right. It was still hot, and the smoke kept the dive-bombers away. He took off his shirt again and lay down on the blanket she'd brought.

"Well, I've got two burgers, two buns, and two potatoes, and nothing to put on them but ketchup," she said apologetically. "And the essentials: cold beer." She popped the cap off a bottle and handed it to him. He looked at the shoulders he had touched so intimately. Her upper body was indeed like a dockworker's, with a broad, muscular back and small, hard breasts. Her waist was slim and her thighs and buttocks overtly feminine, seemingly bursting with smooth brown flesh. She was so close to him he could smell her skin and feel the reflected warmth of it. He hastily rolled onto his stomach to disguise his incipient arousal, pressing the cold beer bottle against his forehead. Then he had a sip and laid his head down for a moment, letting the sun warm the cool skin of his back. For the first time since his arrival he started to loosen and relax.

Brenda was stroking him between the shoulder blades.

"Hey, it's getting late. And your burger is cold."

Dafydd came to with a start and saw that probably an hour had passed. The sun still seemed high, but it was cooler and the woods were totally silent. He sat up and rubbed his eyes. The barbecue was still smoking heavily, but the air was pleasant and suddenly the murky pond looked beautiful, with pink clouds reflecting on the still black water.

"How boring of me to fall asleep," he said.

"I enjoyed watching you," Brenda said. "You looked delectable, like a fallen angel."

He laughed awkwardly. A gust swept over them, and the smoke billowed over the water. Dafydd shivered and reached for his shirt, but she knelt in front of him and without a word gently pushed him back onto the blanket by his shoulders. He didn't protest when she laid herself on top of him, covering him with her whole length. It felt so snug and safe, it was hardly sexual. Her hot flesh felt like a heavy blanket. He put his arms around her and they lay quietly for a moment. He stroked her hair with one hand and with the other he fiddled absentmindedly with some strings at her hip. Abruptly her bikini bottom came loose and his hand found itself on her naked buttock. She lifted her head and they looked at each other.

"And the other side," she said.

There he was, pinned under an assertive, wanting woman, on a beach in the middle of the subarctic forest, with not a person for tens of miles around. And now his cock was straining to unfurl itself under the pressure of her belly. There seemed to be no turning back. He quickly untied the other string and pulled the orange panties off her with one sharp yank. She groaned huskily and put her mouth over his.

In the tension of the last months he'd ignored or forgotten his sexual needs, and this sudden reawakening made him painfully hard. He pulled her upward so he could reach down and feel her, while she tugged ineffectively at his shorts. As they grappled, panting and laughing, their hipbones ground painfully against each other. Grasping her thighs, he pulled her knees up so that she was kneeling over him.

"Go on," she urged him, her face flushed and her eyes large and brilliant. "It's okay . . . I'm on the pill."

Dafydd thought fleetingly about the need to protect himself, but before the idea was even formulated his hips had somehow been liberated from his shorts. He found his objective and pulled Brenda down onto him, meeting her in a single forceful thrust. She gasped, then grinned brazenly at him, as if this was what she'd had in mind all along. She put her feet flat on the ground and, squatting over him, she began to ride him vigorously. Something about her complete lack of subtlety excited him, but it excluded any other emotion. Her eyes were glazed and she no longer took notice of him, engaged as she was in her own pursuit. There was no need for him to move. This woman is fucking me, he thought, astonished at the sheer strength of her thighs. He looked down at their exposed genital interaction, feeling quite detached, like a piston in a shaft, like he was being pumped by a well-oiled machine. Beyond this he saw his pulled-down boxer shorts with their ridiculous stripes (they would *have* to go) and beyond still the slightly ruffled pond and the clouds going from pink to gray. Nevertheless, the intensity of her fucking soon brought him to the edge, and he grabbed her waist to still her, but she was in charge and seemed oblivious to his gesture.

"Wait, stop," he whispered, already knowing it was too late. He cried out; it was more painful than pleasurable, simply too intense. His whole insides recoiled. She slowed down, obviously disappointed.

"I'm sorry," he said. "It's been a while."

"Relax," she said and popped off him in rather a perfunctory way. "We'll try it again in a minute."

In a minute . . . Christ! He knew he could do something to make her come, at the very least, but an enormous lethargy overwhelmed him. He felt almost drugged. He put his arm around her and they lay cooling in the light evening breeze, with the eerie sound of an owl hooting nearby. In spite of his torpor, his senses were acute, as if his very skin were hearing the sounds of the forest and smelling the scent of sex and smoke and pine. There was a vigorous splash, as if some large fish flapped the water's surface.

They kissed, but now it seemed almost too intimate. They didn't know each other, after all. Her breath was quickening and he pulled back. He didn't really want to make love, or, rather, have sex with her, again. Slipping his hand between her legs, it was soon clear what would do. Within half a minute he'd brought her to a climax.

"Do that again," she commanded after a short recovery, and he did, with an equally quick result. She seemed moderately satisfied with this labor-saving reimbursement of her efforts.

"I guess we should think about going," she said and sat up. "This is bear country." Dafydd sat up, too, alarmed, and looked around him. She laughed. "Why do you think I lit the barbecue? For the horseflies?"

In silence they got dressed and packed up the stuff of their picnic. They drove back to Moose Creek in the deepening dusk, past the sawmill where only hours earlier he'd gathered up a man in plastic bags, and here beside him a woman, alive, throbbing, and whole in the flesh. He was in a very foreign place and he wondered what this encounter meant. Perhaps there would be some expectations, some assumptions, but almost certainly not. Brenda was an emancipated woman who seemed to follow her own impulses. Besides, she had probably found him too restrained and inadequate a lover. Either way, he wasn't able or willing to commit his bruised inner self to anybody.

CHAPTER 5

Cardiff, 2006

A thick gray cloud hung over Cardiff. Dafydd scanned the skies, bowed his head against the drizzle and headed for the doctors' car park, where his ancient Velocette Venom motorbike was plonked impolitely in the middle of a row of gleaming Jaguars and BMWs. Normally he took great pleasure in parking the old brute among the erection-substitutes, but for some reason today his mode of transport seemed a sorry statement, juvenile and embarrassing. He'd spent most of his life getting wet on motorbikes, but right now he could have done without it.

He slapped on his pudding-bowl helmet, zipped up his leather jacket, pulled on his waterproof trousers, strapped his briefcase to the pillion seat, and began the operation of starting her up. The kick start had a habit of kicking back, like a hammer blow, putting his knee at risk of early arthritis.

"Come *on*," he growled and looked up to see Ed Marshall smile condescendingly in his direction as he unlocked the door of his brand-new Saab and slid in onto its soft leather interior. Mercifully the Velocette exploded into being, and Dafydd roared off, leaving behind him a cloud of blue smoke.

It was late September and the days were getting shorter. Instead of going home to an empty house, he rode aimlessly toward the sea. The rain had almost stopped when he parked by the seafront in Penarth. The Esplanade was deserted, bar a woman trying to stuff a drenched and filthy retriever into the back of her hatchback. The dog wasn't having it, and the struggle continued until the woman gave in and allowed the dog onto the passenger seat. The jingle of a distant fruit machine in the pub merged with the gentle clatter of the sea rolling pebbles up the beach.

He sat astride the bike watching the grayness deepening. Two cars full of youths pulled up beside him. Loud rap music blasted from the windows, combined with hoarse shouting and girlish laughter. He looked over and wondered at their wanton exuberance. As a teenager he'd never drunk beer, smoked dope or snogged girls in cars. He hadn't had wheels until he was in medical school. He'd been his widowed mother's dream, disciplined, studious. He hadn't even lost his virginity until he was twenty-one. After that he'd done his best to make up for lost time.

A girl in one of the cars caught him looking and gave him a so-what-are-you-looking-at stare. She stuck her tongue out at him and wiggled it provocatively. For a moment he was fascinated by her boldness, but her eyes had something hard about them. She smiled then and rolled down her window, calling out, "Hey, man, you're lush . . . for an old guy." Her friends shrieked with laughter. He didn't understand teenagers; they were a different species. They intimidated him. He turned his eyes back to the sea.

He thought of Jim Wiseman. His wife had gone off with a Dutch pilot and left Jim with their three teenage children. Dafydd had gone over one evening to commiserate with him. There'd been all manner of youths draped over the furniture, TV blaring, plates of half-eaten food on every surface, the telephone forever engaged. The unlucky devil was facing a future of single parenthood, yet he lived for his kids; he loved those spotty, gawky, oafish things. A part of Dafydd had yearned to understand and experience this; another part of him found it incomprehensible and terrifying. Anyhow, it hadn't happened and it was too late now.

He got off the bike and rummaged around in his briefcase, extracting the remnants of a bottle of Glenfiddich that a grateful patient had given him. There was no point in going home, since Isabel had gone off on a job in Glasgow. Her new contact, one Paul Deveraux, contractor extraordinaire, was urging her to join him full-time as his interior designer. He'd dangled a carrot in her face for a few weeks now, a large new hotel in Glasgow, part of a major chain, and Dafydd had encouraged her to go. That way she'd get to know the guy and could make up her mind if she wanted to surrender her hard-won independence. By God, they needed space from each other, at least until the DNA confirmation came through. Her coldness toward him during the last few weeks had made them like strangers to each other. Whether she believed his denials about Sheila Hailey or not was less of an issue, but she'd been clearly distressed by the appearance of a packet of condoms on his bedside table. She'd understood that his resolution was born out of months of reflection and that he really meant what he so insensitively had sprung on her the night of the storm, but the technicalities of the decision were just too much for her.

"You won't be needing those."

He'd said nothing, hoping she didn't mean what it sounded like she meant. He, too, was annoyed. Not only did he have to shell out hundreds of pounds to disprove the allegations of some crazy woman from the distant past, but his own wife treated him like something that had crawled out of a sewer. Isabel wouldn't give him a chance to talk about how he felt, and less still share her own feelings. Much as he'd apologized for his callousness, she'd simply retreated into cool silence, speaking only when it was necessary.

Surreptitiously he took a swig. Superb stuff. He took another. Then he tucked the bottle inside his jacket. He looked out over the channel, but the mist lay heavy and the Devon coast was barely visible. Penarth Pier stretched far out into the water, a graceful structure and apparently very old. He had not been out on it since he first moved to Cardiff eight years earlier. It seemed a very long time. He'd taken the job partly because it was perfectly respectable and partly because of a need to return to his roots. His mother, Delyth, was Welsh born and bred, but she had married his father, a crusty northerner, and moved away to Newcastle. Not until Dafydd had gone to Moose Creek back in 1992, her husband having been long dead, had Delyth insisted on returning home, to a nursing home in Swansea, and there she had died not long after his return. Since his marriage to Isabel, *her* Welsh roots were another incentive to stay in Cardiff. Her parents were Italian and still ran their ice-cream bars around South Wales that had made them, a poor immigrant couple displaced to Wales by the war, a bloody fortune.

Dafydd passed the long-defunct turnstiles and wandered out along the wooden deck of the pier. A few fishermen in lumpy waterproof clothing sat immobile by the railings, eyes fixed on their rods, in total isolation from each other. Whatever they needed to get away from, this seemed as good a venue as any, since none of them appeared to be catching any fish. Dafydd walked past them, peering into their buckets, but not one of them looked up or seemed keen to make conversation.

There were covered benches on both sides of the structure, little booths that hung out over the water where lovers could shelter from the wind. Today there were no lovers; it was not a romantic kind of an evening. However, the seats were dry and he sat himself there, taking small swigs from his bottle as he observed the tankers easing themselves up and down the smooth waters. The tide was receding down the channel, sucking the water away with some speed and gradually uncovering the brown sludge beneath the pier.

He huddled his jacket around him and thought of his job. This whole business of the spurious paternity claim had done him one favor. It had brought to the fore his general inertia, a sluggishness that had steadily crept into his life. It seemed he'd be resigned to do what every other medical consultant did:

work conscientiously, salt away the money, pay off the mortgage, and wait for retirement. Then life was supposed to begin
in earnest, in the form of one long game of bloody golf. That's
when most of them had heart attacks and died. He knew all
this—it had happened to his own father—but his own pathetic
little rebellions against the surge of this trend, such as rejecting
car ownership and refusing to do private practice, were not, in
fact, making him feel heroic. Perhaps, when the DNA business
was out of the way, things could change. Some kind of new
start, in his life as well as his marriage.

It was dark now, but he didn't mind. The clouds had dis-
persed a little and the lights of Weston-super-Mare flickered
weakly. He had promised himself he would take the old paddle-
steamer across someday, but it had never happened. He tipped
the bottle back and drained the last of the whiskey. It seeped
into his bloodstream and left a glowing sensation in the extremities. Getting up, he tossed the bottle into a bin and walked
back along the deck. The fishermen had not moved.

The pub on the Esplanade was open and he needed a pee.
Just as well to have a pint and a bag of peanuts.

There was nothing in the house; the fridge was empty but
for Isabel's various vitamin bottles and Chinese herbal remedies that were supposed to stimulate fertility. Two hours
later he returned to the Velocette feeling really good. It was
great to have some time on one's own to think. He would
do things differently when this whole ridiculous business
was over. He would dust off his guitar, perhaps even take up
bloody fishing, he could use a bit of solitary meditation, get
back into running, get his butt as hard as nails. Bin the telly
and read all those books he kept buying and never made the
time for . . .

He swayed slightly as he pumped the kick start, and a fleeting thought about the wisdom of getting on his bike passed
through his head, but hell, it must be at least nine, maybe even
ten; the traffic would have eased off. He was such a goody-
goody he didn't even have a single point on his license.

Hooray. She started straight off. He patted the petrol tank affectionately. Lovely old girl, this one. He pulled out and rode up the hill along the cliffs as they rose from the beach and followed the one-way system that swept one back into the town. He didn't see the give way sign by Westbourne Road, and as he rode on, cautious but totally drunk, a green Volvo smashed diagonally into him at thirty miles an hour.

Dafydd became aware of a light somewhere far away. The light felt fragmented and was scattered across his retina like tiny droplets of mercury. They bounced and leaped, making his eyeballs hurt unbearably. He tried to shut his eyes but found that they were already closed. To escape the torture of the light, he turned his head away. His head was large and heavy like a ball of lead, and as he turned it, it pulsated with waves of pain.

Slowly he recognized extensions to his head. Heavy, numb appendages that were his arms and legs. He opened his eyes a fraction, and inches from his face he saw metal tubes on a green background. He knew this from somewhere and felt heartened by it. He allowed himself to go back into the darkness of deep sleep.

A pain shot through his wrist, and he looked at it. It had been bitten by a fox. The fox was still there, looking at him intently, its eyes green. Moving restlessly from side to side, it suddenly shrieked. It was a startling sound, a warning. It turned and darted off over barren, snow-covered ground. He wanted to run after it and called for it to wait. Struggling to move forward, his legs were heavy and rigid, like logs. The effort made him nauseous and this forced his eyes to open. He was in a room somewhere. He tried to sit up, but his body didn't want to cooperate. His head thumped relentlessly, and he gently lowered it back onto the soft surface where it had been. In the distance a piercing noise sounded, like an alarm. His hand moved upward and found that his mouth was covered with something. He fumbled over the surface of it. It was hard and cold and he pulled it off. His forehead felt puffy and remote, as though he were wearing a hat. Awareness trickled gradually into his mind, and he became fully awake. He was in a hospital room with his head bandaged. Presently he could feel the edges of the bandage with his fingers. It frightened him and he sat up. The sudden movement caused him to retch, and he looked around in desperation for some kind of receptacle . . . there was an aluminum pot on the stand beside him. As he vomited, his head felt like it was bursting like an overripe watermelon hitting concrete.

A nurse came up to him and gently eased his head back on to the pillow.

"Mr. Woodruff. You are in the Acute Medical Unit. Don't worry. You are all right. You've had an accident on your motorbike.

"When?"

"Just a few hours ago. It's just a concussion and a bit of a graze."

"What happened? Is anybody else injured?"

"The driver of the other vehicle is fine, but apparently *you're* lucky. Nothing worse than some cuts and bruises. Your bike, well . . . it's totally wrecked."

"Oh, shit, no," Dafydd groaned as his head started thumping anew.

"You've had a scan, and the inside of your head is okay. Just a little shake-up."

"I don't remember anything."

"That's okay. You've been . . . well, sleeping it off. You were perfectly conscious when the ambulance brought you in." She chuckled as she wiped his face with a wet cloth. "You caused a bit of a ruckus, apparently." She paused. "But you did give consent in the end . . . to having a blood test."

"What do you mean, consent?"

"To the police."

"Police? What did I . . . ?"

"Dr. Thakurdas will be with you shortly," she said quickly.

"Don't bother yourself about it now. Just think of yourself as lucky, Mr. Woodruff."

He let go of everything and fell back into another deep slumber. Someone took his pulse, and he could hear people talking about him, using his name, but he was too tired to listen. No doubt he'd been given something; the relentless pain in his head seemed to have vanished. He seemed to be sliding backward. He signed some book and then kissed Isabel. The strange woman presiding over their wedding was dressed in a flouncy smock with tiny flowers on it. It blew wildly in the draft as she retreated backward through a heavy oak door. Isabel turned to him. "Are you sure you want this?" she asked. Of course he did; he loved her. She was stable, good to hold on to in a storm. He looked down at the coat he was wearing. It was tatty, like a derelict's coat, and turning the pockets inside out he cursed himself. He'd left something behind in Canada. He missed someone; he was torn with angst that he had left her. She was soft and beautiful, and so, so far away he could never go to her again. He looked at the tall woman beside him. Her name was Isabel, not that other strange name. He gritted his teeth hard to keep from crying and turned on his side, pulling the flimsy sheet tight up over his face. There was a knocking at the door, knocking and knocking. Sheila came in and asked if he would perform an abortion on her . . . now, right away.

He shook his head, slowly, so it wouldn't hurt. An abortion? Here?

"I'm not feeling too good," he said, trying to sound convincing. "Why don't you fly to Yellowknife? You'd be back in a day or two. Nobody will know."

"Oh, come on . . . All that hassle for a trifle? Besides, my boyfriend doesn't know about the pregnancy. He'd be suspicious if I went away." She came up to him and sat down on the bed. She wasn't wearing her uniform but a very short green suede skirt, and though he tried not to look he could glimpse coils of red pubic hair between her thighs.

"How do you mean, he'd be suspicious?" he asked, knowing this somehow involved him.

She was quiet for a moment.

"Look, the baby—" Leaning forward, she put her hand over his. "The baby is not his."

"Really?" Dafydd snatched his hand away and stuck it under the covers.

She sat back, looking at him pensively. "You don't know him, do you? Let's put it this way, if he found out . . . he'd make mincemeat of every man I know. Including you. Definitely you. You know why, don't you? Remember what you did to me?"

Dafydd tried to think about this. He didn't understand what she was on about, but he absolutely did not want some hairy-arsed ax-wielding redneck coming after him.

"Ask Dr. Odent," he groaned, wishing she would go. "He does abortions in his trailer, and I've heard he likes very short skirts. Or Hogg. You know how much he fancies you . . . He'd do it."

"No. You know what a small place Moose Creek is." She laughed. "I wouldn't want things to get around. Besides, you and I have a shameful secret."

Moose Creek? Surely he was in Cardiff? Dafydd closed his eyes tight, hoping she'd evaporate into the ether. It wasn't fair. He was ill.

"C'mon, Dafydd, don't be such a bloody prude." She prodded his arm lightly. "Here in the wilderness things like that are done all the time. If your sensibilities are that easily offended, you shouldn't be here at all. You're not in some distinguished British hospital."

"But I am," he protested weakly. "This *is* a distinguished British hospital."

Sheila laughed. Her teeth were pointy, like a cat's.

Her mocking cackle made him angry. "You know damned well how dangerous it is. Really, you could bleed to death. It's illegal and it's unethical—"

"Oh, come off it," she hissed. "You and your fucking ethics . . ."

Someone patted him on the shoulder and Sheila lost her edges. There was a rush in his ears as he felt his bruised body roll over on the bed. He wanted to throw up. He might be absolved if only he could vomit and get rid of everything.

"Are you in pain, Mr. Woodruff?" Dr. Thakurdas asked, shaking him lightly by the shoulder. "You were crying and whimpering in your sleep. We were a bit worried about you."

CHAPTER 6

Moose Creek, 1992

He was about to knock, then looked at his watch: 8:38. Ian Brannagan was not a morning person, that had become abundantly clear. He looked around. The tiny one-story house had a porch running right around it, just like houses he'd seen in the southern U.S. It had a disused garden with remnants of a white picket fence. Very quaint, out here in the sticks all by himself with no one for company.

This notion was dispelled when a yellow dog sauntered up to him from nowhere, wagging its tail. Dafydd had always loved dogs but had never owned one. "Not much of a watchdog, you," he said, then realized that the dog was an overlarge puppy. He scratched the affectionate beast behind the ears and it licked his bare knees.

Beside the door were two wicker chairs. One had an animal skin draped over it. Dafydd touched it, then bent to sniff the pungent smell. A curious smell, animal and a concentration of smoke. Caribou hide. He knew the smell from a pair of embroidered boots, mukluks, he'd bought from a native woman.

He sat on the chair and waited. The dog sat beside him, leaning heavily against his thigh. The sun was already scorching, but in the cool of the porch mosquitoes buzzed nonchalantly. Already he was covered with insect bites. He'd always been a feast for blood-sucking creatures. A woman dermatologist once told him, quite unprofessionally he'd thought at the time, that it was his dark good looks and his fine skin that made him so appetizing. He rubbed at his chewed-up ankles, but it only served to intensify the agony.

A plane flew overhead. He watched it fly southward. Although he hated flying, he was seized by a yearning to be on that very plane, but it disappeared toward civilization without him, leaving a thin vapor trail. Leaves were already starting to curl at the edges. Autumn came early in the north.

"What the hell?"

Ian Brannagan's head had emerged from one of the windows. He looked years older first thing in the morning. "It's Sunday, man. What are you doing here?"

The puppy was in a frenzy of excitement, chasing its tail all over the porch.

"Thought you might want to go for a walk or something."

"A walk?"

"Yeah, like in getting exercise, fresh air, that sort of thing."

"You're out of your mind."

Ian's head retracted into the dark interior, but a few minutes later he emerged, fastening the impressive silver buckle on his belt. His upper body was bare. It was white and lean, but well defined, a ragged bulging scar running from his nipple diagonally across his torso and down beyond his belt.

"My God, that's a bad job," Dafydd blurted. "What was it? A heart-lung transplant?"

"Nah, a scrap."

"Looks like a visit to the taxidermist."

"Oh, no. Those guys do a real good job around here. If you catch anything I'll introduce you to a good one. A real master."

"I'm not into killing animals, but if I was, what would it be?"

"Take your pick. Dall's sheep, mountain caribou, and goat a bit higher up. Moose, wolverine, black bear, grizzly, and wolf a bit closer to hand. Mind you, some species are protected, and you need a license. Easy to get around all that, though. Just ask me." They sat in silence for a moment. Ian looked ill. He was deathly pale. His face, vaguely contorted, betrayed some kind of pain.

"Are you okay?"

"Yeah, I'm okay." Ian sighed and rubbed his face with both hands. "Just a mother of a hangover. Nothing that a walk can't cure."

Under the trees the air was cool and still. Everything looked brown, except in the clearings, where vegetation erupted vividly green against the dark interior of the forest. They had walked for an hour directly from Ian's house into woods. Dafydd swatted at the mosquitoes but Ian seemed impervious. He had taken his T-shirt off, and the insects alighted constantly on his body. In places they swarmed like black clouds into the eyes and nose, making Dafydd flail at his face in a panic. He'd read that during the bug season these clouds of mosquitoes and black flies could drive both man and caribou to the brink of insanity.

About to emerge into a clearing, they saw something large and brown. A massive bull moose was tearing at the grasses at its feet. Ian put his arm up as a sign to be silent. The dog, Thorn, instantly lay down at Ian's feet, nose tucked in between his front paws. They stood motionless and watched this colossus of nature as it went about its business. At the shoulder it was far taller than a man, and its immense antlers easily spanned some six feet. Dafydd saw Ian slowly raise his rifle.

"Damn you . . ." Dafydd cried out, knocking the rifle sideways, "don't do it."

Thorn flew to his feet and growled, and the moose's head swung up, elegantly balancing its heavy load. It stood stock-still for a second, its nose flaring, then it turned and galloped through the trees in what appeared to be slow motion, seemingly weightless.

"Jumpy, aren't we?" Ian said testily. "That's how accidents happen."

"All right, but I told you I didn't like it."

"I wasn't going to shoot it, buddy; I was just aiming for fun. There's no way we could have carted that thing back to the house."

"Yeah? And I was supposed to have guessed it?" Dafydd snatched up his bag and walked out into the sunshine, but Ian called after him.

"That's far enough. You can easily get lost. Let's head back."

On cue, Thorn raced forward to round Dafydd up and herd him back, barking and dancing around his feet.

The episode had bothered Dafydd, and Ian seemed grim. They walked for a time in silence. Dafydd hoped his outburst would not be held against him. He'd grown to like Ian, despite the man's occasional insolence and crude manners. It was vital to have some sort of friend. Ian was unusual, damned unusual for a doctor, slightly mad, in fact. He had problems. Probably booze, maybe something else. He chain-smoked and was often very tense. There seemed to be no woman in his life.

Dafydd turned to him and broke the silence. "Ian, do you have a girlfriend . . . or woman friend?"

"No, not really."

"No female company at all? You were quite friendly with the girls in the Klondike," he persisted. He couldn't help wondering if Brenda . . .

Ian smirked. "Do I get laid, you mean?"

"Okay, do you get laid?"

"Don't worry, this place is the Shangri-la of easy sex."

"I didn't mean . . ."

Ian went resolutely ahead and they walked on in single file. Ravens squawked loudly as they passed under their nests. The noise of their crowing reverberated eerily around the trees. They weren't following any particular path—in fact there was none—but Ian seemed to pick his way on even ground. He seemed to know the route.

"If you want to get laid, my friend," he said suddenly without turning around, "make sure you don't pick our friendly head nurse."

"Oh, not a chance . . ." Dafydd blurted out. "But why the warning?"

"Have you seen those sharp, pretty little teeth she's got? They can do a lot of damage to one's manhood."

Dafydd stopped, surprised. "Do you mean that literally or symbolically?"

"Both, I mean both."

"Jesus!"

"Count the days and she's going to be thrusting those pointy tits up against you."

Dafydd laughed. "It sounds like you've been there."

"And I'll be damned if I won't go there again."

Was Ian hinting to stay clear of Sheila because she was his territory? It didn't quite sound like it somehow. "She's all yours," Dafydd said to be sure he understood.

"Hell, no. Sheila doesn't work like that."

"Do you mind that?"

"C'mon, you've got it all wrong. She can do what the hell she likes. It's nothing to do with me. We have nothing going, no kind of commitment anyway. I only warned you because it's easy to get hooked, and there's always a price to pay."

"Do you mean that literally or symbolically?"

Ian threw his head back and laughed, showing his beautiful teeth and looking suddenly young and vital, his good humor restored. Then he seemed to reflect on the question.

"Both, man. Both. You'll see."

The trees were still dense, so they were probably nowhere near the cabin. Dafydd fixed his eyes on the movement of Ian's long, thin legs in front of him. He tried to step in Ian's footsteps, but they were not in sync with his. A cigarette dangled from Ian's fingers, and he flicked it away from him. Dafydd looked at the dry pine needles on the ground. Wasn't that how forest fires started? He heard a branch crack behind him, and he flinched, then a loud rustle of leaves and twigs. A bear? Wolverine?

"Ian, wait," he called and ran to catch up. Ian's rifle swung reassuringly from his shoulder. They walked side by side, amiably but out of step.

"That scar of yours? What was it? Not a fight, surely?"

"Oh, the scar. It's old. I was thirteen. I tried to rescue a dog . . . my dog, from a house fire, and I practically hung myself from a rod on a metal banister."

"Oh, God. Sounds ghastly."

"The dog survived, just," Ian said dully. "My parents didn't."

"Ian, I'm sorry."

Thorn suddenly raced off into the shrubbery, snarling at some real or imagined foe. They stopped, and even Ian looked disconcerted. A moment later the dog returned with a hare clamped proudly in his jaws. Thorn dropped it in front of his master.

"Good kid," Ian crooned, patting the yellow head. It was obvious why he had no particular use for people. He'd discovered early who man's best friend was. Ian bent forward attentively, examining Thorn's fur.

"Shit, you're covered with fleas," he exclaimed.

Dafydd looked down at the dead hare. He saw the fleas literally flying from it, in all directions but mainly onto Thorn. We all abandon a sinking ship, he thought. We all do it. Even fleas. Only Ian didn't . . .

He had yet to do any operating lists, for which he was grateful even though it was supposed to be part of the job. It turned out that, bar dire emergencies, most patients needing operations were flown off to Edmonton or Saskatoon. Not because the hospital wasn't suitable; it had an operating theater with reasonably up-to-date equipment. Hogg's policies had more to do with avoiding any major risks and responsibilities, to do as little as possible for maximum profit. Hogg had clearly hoped to widen the scope of available treatment, but in Dafydd he found a reluctant surgeon. But then, what go-getting surgeon would be enthusiastic about risking his hide in some hole of a town in the middle of nowhere for a ridiculous wage?

Instead, Dafydd launched himself into his role of GP and saw a procession of disgruntled patients in his consulting room, a hovel that felt and looked like a prison cell. Much to the amusement of the staff, he'd said he'd prefer seeing some people in their homes. They had tittered at his request and dismissed it as a British eccentricity. Why would he bother, they wondered, when most people had cars, and if they didn't, a taxi or an ambulance would bring them to the clinic where he could deal with them at his leisure?

"We don't want to start a trend here," Hogg had warned him. "People are spoiled enough as it is."

"Just a few," Dafydd insisted. "I'd like to see how people live, what they do."

Hogg patted him on the shoulder and said, "You do what you feel you have to do, young man. In a day or two you'll be only too grateful to do it our way. Mark my words."

A few weeks into his locum he set off toward his first "home visit" in the clinic's old Chrysler. It was mid-September and the sun, although bright, no longer warmed. The gravel road snaked lazily around copses of spruce and fir. Some eight miles out of town, reaching the crest of a hill, he recognized at once the shimmering landscape of the postcard that Hogg had sent him. He stopped and got out of the car. The views were breathtaking. Lakes of strange and irregular shapes glinted within the massive expanse of the Mackenzie Valley. The river itself flowed mightily toward the Arctic Ocean. In the distance to the north, barren tundra began, while westward the snowcapped peaks of the Mackenzies receded toward Alaska. It seemed impossible to see so far, but perhaps the distance was some kind of visual illusion caused by the clarity of the air. He thought he could see the curvature of the earth, but even that had to be impossible, as the horizon encircled him. He turned slowly around and suddenly felt as if he were in the center of *everything*. A feeling of euphoria came over him.

He looked up and saw a large bird circle overhead. It looked like a crane, with a long neck and a wide wingspan. It soared higher, its wings lit up into a vivid pink. Dafydd followed the bird upward toward the sun, but when it disappeared in the glare he came back down into himself with a jolt. He exhaled, disappointed. Still, there was something more to this complex and perverse existence. Perhaps a glimmer of hope. Life would go on, no matter what.

He got back into the car and sat for a moment, then looked at the piece of paper with the directions that Sheila Hailey had written for him: *Signposted Mile 12.5, turn left down track for three miles, right at fork, cabin situated two miles on.*

"You don't have to do this, you know," she'd told him. "We just send the ambulance to get him, that's what it's for. Anyway, the old man has a grandson who—"

"I want to," Dafydd insisted. "Sleeping Bear sounds interesting. I'd love to see his place."

"You *are* a blue-eyed boy wonder, aren't you?" She'd peered at him through half-closed eyes. "Get rid of the tie . . . you look plain ridiculous. You're off to see a moth-eaten half-dead old native, not some head of state."

The track was practically impassable. After almost half an hour's drive straight into virgin wilderness, he finally drew up in a small clearing dwarfed by firs. A cabin of rough-hewn logs, with a timber-shingled roof, stood in the middle. Several cars, in various states of dilapidation, were scattered around the yard, and a clothes line held some remnants of tattered cloth.

He got out of the car as an elderly Indian man appeared from somewhere carrying a bundle of sticks, kindling perhaps. His hair was waist-long and thin, tied by leather straps into two tails, one below each ear. His clothes, too, were leathery, although their origins were vague. They were stiff and black with the substances of rugged living.

"Mr. Sleeping Bear?"

"Call me Bear. Everyone does." The man offered Dafydd a filthy hand partly enveloped in strips of cloth that may once have been bandages.

"I'm Dr. Woodruff." Dafydd shook the ancient hand and motioned toward the cabin. "I thought I'd save you a trip into town. Shall we go inside and have a look at you?"

"That carrot-topped nurse sent word about you. There was no need for you to come alla way out here." The old man scrutinized Dafydd's freshly ironed shirt and silk tie with squinting eyes, obviously thinking that he was far too clean to deal with sickness. "There ain't no need for it no more. I'm feeling myself a whole lot better."

"But I've come all this way just to see you," Dafydd protested. "At least let me have a look at you. It won't harm."

"Come on inside," Bear invited with a sweep of his free arm. "I'll brew you up some coffee."

The cabin was very dark, and Dafydd drew a sharp breath as several pairs of eyes glowered at him. Several pairs of furry lips drew back and bared yellow fangs. All in absolute silence.

"Hush, boys," Bear admonished them soothingly.

The huskies, some six or seven of them, immediately obeyed and lowered themselves back onto the floor.

"Don't pay them no heed," Bear said, laughing, and Dafydd stepped warily over the threshold and entered the dwelling.

"How come they didn't bark when I drove up?"

"Ha," Bear exclaimed triumphantly, delighted to be asked. "I've got them trained like so. And it's a feat, don' mind telling ya. Most folks will say you can't stop a husky barking, bar taking a log to its head." Bear rubbed his hands together gleefully. "Someone tries to get in here while I'm out, get themselves one helluva surprise. They get no kinda warning, see?"

Bear pointed to a battered old armchair and Dafydd sat down. He wished he'd listened to the carrot-topped nurse and dressed more casually. His adherence to professional deportment was ridiculously out of place.

"What if the person is on a friendly mission?" he asked. "Like the postman or someone lost?"

"Postman?" Bear repeated, surprised. "We ain't got those out here." He set about spooning large quantities of instant coffee into two tin mugs. "If someone's stupid enough to try and get into my place uninvited, don' matter to me if they're lost or friendly, they'd be giving my dogs here a good feeding." He cackled maliciously and poured boiling water from an aluminum kettle into the battered mugs. "To tell the God-honest truth, nobody comes this way for no reason. And that reason could be all sortsa things bar cordial, see?"

He hobbled up and gave Dafydd a steaming cup of black coffee. It was laced with something sweet and unmistakably alcoholic. "I've got this growth on my ass."

"Let's have a look in a minute." The coffee was bitter but reviving. Dafydd's eyes had grown accustomed to the dark. The one-room cabin had a heavy wooden table with a chair on either side and a small gas cooker with its canister strapped to the wall. A cracked mirror hung over a ceramic bowl on wooden legs. There appeared to be no running water. In another corner stood a double bed with an ornately carved headboard. The homestead reminded him of an open-air museum he'd loved as a boy, depicting life in the Middle Ages.

The old man himself looked the archetypal Indian chief, just like he'd seen them in the westerns. The long, hooked nose and dignified bearing. The gaunt, bronzed face, thin lips and hooded eyes, the plaits. The only thing missing was the feathered headdress and the loincloth. Dafydd studied him with delight and admiration. Could he perhaps ask to take the man's picture, or was that tactless? Come to think of it, Sleeping Bear didn't look like most other Indians he'd seen around. The aboriginal population was stockier and shorter. They had tendencies to obesity, and their faces were round.

"So you live here on your own?" The man seemed well over eighty, but his rugged appearance didn't betray his frailty.

"Yep, sure do," Bear answered proudly, "and don' you go

sticking your nose in and try to change that. I'm going to no bloody institution, I'm telling ya."

"Well, let's sort out the growth on your arse, then. That way you can go on looking after yourself."

"I've got a grandson who visits me now and then. He makes sure I got everything I need." Bear couldn't get his trousers down and it took some convincing to get him to bend over the table.

"How have you managed . . . to use the toilet?" Dafydd asked as he used a stitch cutter to cut away the stale fabric of Bear's trousers where it stuck to the festering sore on his buttock.

"I don't," Bear replied sheepishly.

"What does he do?" Dafydd asked, trying to mask his horror at the old man's decrepit condition. "Your grandson."

"This and that," Bear answered evasively. "Hey, are you trashing up my best pants?"

"Good God, man," Dafydd exclaimed as he uncovered the infected growth, "how have you lived with this?"

Half an hour later, the wound cleaned up and dressed and a hefty dose of antibiotics having been administered intravenously, Bear looked pale and weak. Dafydd helped him onto the bed and tucked a stinking blanket around him.

"I ain't coming into no cotton-pickin' hospital, if that's what you gonna say. My grandson will see to me. He'll look in."

"You'll need more injections, and we should be doing some tests," Dafydd argued. "You'll have to come in, if only for a couple of days."

"Nope, you can't budge me from 'ere." He seemed to fall asleep, and Dafydd went out to inspect the sun-bleached rags on the clothesline. There was a two-legged garment that may once have been a pair of long johns, and he pried it away from the rope. As he stepped back into the cabin, the dogs immediately got to their feet and bared their teeth menacingly. Their master was asleep and vulnerable, and Dafydd had no doubt that they could kill him.

"Hush," the old man said from the bed, and the dogs laid themselves down again, keeping their pale and beady eyes on the intruder.

"Here's a pair of something." Dafydd handed him the article and plumped up some pillows behind his back. "I'll bring you something else to wear when I come and check on you."

They sat in silence while Bear slurped noisily from the remains in his mug.

"Why are you here?" he asked suddenly.

"To check you over, to make you better."

"No . . . I mean here, here in this place where nobody wants to come, 'cept those who have a reason, like myself."

"I've . . . run away from something," Dafydd said, at once stupefied by this confession.

"I thought so." Bear picked a black particle from his left nostril and flicked it to the floor. "What exactly?"

"A little boy . . . his name is Derek Rose. I messed up his operation, and I'll have to live with it for the rest of my life. That's why I'm here, to try to put it behind me." The dogs got up and crowded around, suddenly less distrustful.

"Everybody makes mistakes."

"Not where I come from."

"Masters of the friggin' universe, are they?"

"No, but you hope you're above mistakes like that. If you're not, you shouldn't be doing it."

"In cloud cuckoo land, sure. In real life it happens alla time." He reached out and patted Dafydd on the hand. "You'll pardon yourself. It's all about letting it run its course. And getting back up on the horse that threw you."

"You think so?"

"I know it." He thought about it for a few moments, then smiled. "What goes around, comes around, as they say. That's what you're doing now, isn't it? Your atonement, putting something back, even if it's out here in the boonies."

Dafydd nodded. There was plenty to do, to put things back. Every day of his working life could be dedicated to atonement.

Bear handed him his mug and motioned him to top it up out of a labelless bottle.

"Is Sleeping Bear your real name?"

"Hell, no." Bear chuckled. "My real name is . . . or used to be . . . Arwyn Jenkins."

"Jenkins?" After a second of confusion Dafydd said, "I suppose some ancestor of yours could have been Welsh or something."

Bear laughed so hard that the top half of his dentures came loose from his gums and flapped wildly. "My dear boy, you greatly underestimate my age." He kept chuckling and giggling while trying to press his teeth back into place. "When I was born, white man had never set foot in this part of the world. In fact, I was the first European to arrive in Moose Creek. There were only three shacks there at the time."

"European?" Dafydd repeated, dumbfounded.

"That's right. I'm Welsh, born and bred."

"You don't mean . . . But your face . . . and . . ."

"Most folks don't know this about me, 'cept the old-timers, and there ain't no need to go reminding them of my background, now, is there?" He gave Dafydd a sharp look.

"Certainly not. You can count on it. I'm half Welsh myself."

Sleeping Bear disclosed that he'd escaped some difficulties in Wales and come to the area in 1934, and after some years of hardship he eventually married an Indian woman who gave him two sons. Dafydd listened in fascination and more than once found it hard to suppress an urge to smile from ear to ear. This typical, storybook, wise old Indian turned out to be a Welshman from Pontypridd, probably a next-door neighbor of his own grandparents.

"And how did you come by your name?"

"Well, see, back then, when I first arrived, I couldn't hack the winters. You've got that bit to come, young man, you'll see what I mean. Mind, it's all very royal now, with heated houses and cars to take you places real quick, but back then you walked and you froze your ass off. I lost me a few toes. Wasn't used to it, see?"

Dafydd glanced at Bear's weathered boots and wondered how many toes a man could do without in this sort of terrain.

"So I holed up all winter in my cabin with the fire going. The Indians had laughs at my expense, but they were kind folks and brought me grub and firewood."

"So you hibernated?"

"You got it," Sleeping Bear exclaimed enthusiastically. "And the name kinda stuck."

He proceeded to pull on the tattered long johns over his rough boots and chortled quietly at some old recollections of his own.

"So did you adapt to the winters eventually?"

"Sure thing. Had to. You'll see what it's like when you face your first winter here, and that's real soon. By the third winter I was teamed up with a wife and a baby on the way. I had to bite the bullet and go out trapping. Later, when the town grew, I had a business cutting ice blocks from the river and a team of horses to pull them into town."

There was a faint sound of a car, which brought the dogs on the alert immediately. "Well, I'll be dipped in beaver spit and pelted with moose droppings," Bear burst out. "That'll be my grandson."

He jumped out of bed and darted out into the yard, all pain and disability forgotten. A short, sturdy, middle-aged man with long black hair got out of a gleaming pickup truck. He looked suspiciously at Dafydd but shook his hand when Bear introduced them. "This here is the new medicine man. He trashed my pants, but he cleaned me up real good." Bear leaped around like a frisky adolescent. "He come alla way out here to look me over."

The grandson said nothing but stood fast, looking at Dafydd with round, jet-black eyes.

"Well, I'll be off, then," Dafydd said. "I'll be back with more injections. I'll teach you to inject yourself. That way you can stay put." He got into the car and started off.

"Don't forget the pants," Bear shouted after him.

He drove back along the bumpy track and saw that his shirt-sleeves were already filthy. A mixture of blood and pus had smeared the front of a good shirt, probably ruined it. His tie hung limply like a lost erection. He took one hand off the steering wheel and combed his fingers through his hair. It was getting long. Dark curls were corkscrewing at his temples; he could see them clearly out of the corner of his eye. The fresh strands of gray reminded him of why he was driving down this dusty track in a dented old Chrysler, instead of astride his gleaming Velocette, weaving in and out of a traffic jam in Bristol. At least he was still working, trying to put something back. A wise old Indian, Dafydd smiled, was the first person to perceive the depth of his devastation.

He had one more visit, just on the outskirts of Moose Creek. One of the so-called suburbs. Soon enough the gray housing subdivision came into view on the left of the highway. He wet his hand from the bottle of water on the passenger seat and tried to smooth down his unruly mane.

"Aren't you gonna give him sump'n?" the young woman demanded, placing her hands on her ample haunches. Her skin was sallow and her hair had a lanky look, as if it had been combed through with cooking oil. Her man was glued to a game of baseball on the television and hadn't once turned or acknowledged Dafydd's presence. The intermittent cheering of the crowds within the confined space sounded strange and eerily discordant with the depressing existence of its occupants. The little boy coughed, a wet phlegmy cough, but he didn't have a fever.

"It's just a common cold," Dafydd reassured the woman.

"You can't jus' walk off and not give him sump'n," she said aggressively and literally blocked his exit with her broad hips.

"All this cigarette smoke"—Dafydd gestured bluntly around the room with a sweep of his hand—"could have something to do with his cough."

"Bullshit," the woman declared, unconvinced, and the man on the sofa half turned his head toward them. She pointed a forefinger toward Dafydd's chest. "He's coughed since he was a little tiny kid. Hogg's told me his lungs are fucked."

"I'm not surprised," Dafydd retorted, trying to keep the sarcasm out of his voice. "Give him some Vitamin C, junior aspirin, and some clean air, and his cold will get better in a couple of days." He knelt and ruffled the abrasive tufts of hair on the youngster's head. Taking courage from his conviction, he turned to the man. "Why don't you take him outside? It's a lovely day. A bit of sun would do him good."

The man again half turned his head, but his eyes never left the screen.

"What's that supposed to mean?" the woman protested. "D'ya hear that, Brent? The doctor here wants you to take the kid's fucked-up lungs out into the open air. Can you beat that?"

The Brent-person was still not responding. Dafydd wasn't sure whether there was something brewing, and the man might suddenly fly into a rage, or whether his apathy and indifference were absolute, beyond redemption. Either way, it was unsettling.

"That's all I can do for your son. I think the rest is up to you, really."

"You've done *nothing*," she spat after him as he quickly walked toward the car. "I'd say you're a plain danger to children," she called. "Negligence, that's what it is."

A couple of women came out on their porches to investigate the shouting. Dafydd felt his neck flush red with anxiety as he got into the car. A plain danger to children, how right she was. He felt ready to capitulate on home visits. As it was, his general practice skills were in fact very rusty and people seemed to have expectations of miracle pills and potions that would set them right. Apparently Dr. Odent had been a walking pharmacy, happy to do private deals.

Dafydd started the car, then hesitated and fished for the prescription pad in his case. A course of antibiotics wouldn't hurt the boy, even though it wouldn't do him any good. But the thought of knocking on the door and eating humble pie . . . The words "white trash" popped into his head and he said them out loud. A disgusting expression, but now he knew exactly what it meant.

"So did we do our thing, then?" asked Sheila.

He'd noticed that she made a habit of leaning against doorposts with her arms crossed in a way that pushed up her breasts. The smooth white mounds swelled right out of her uniform. She was smiling, her tongue flicking out to moisten her lower lip.

"What thing is that?" Dafydd was in no mood for her digs. He was sitting in the doctors' mess trying to make sense of the patients' records. Sleeping Bear had had nothing written in his notes for several years.

"Playing doctor."

Dafydd stopped to consider how to take these increasingly frequent jibes, disguised as they were by a pretense of being witty and good-humored. She seemed to want reactions out of him. It gave her some sort of kick. She obviously wanted to see how far she could push him.

He raised his eyes for a second and smiled at her. "Yes, I did," he said lightheartedly and continued shuffling the papers. His mother's voice came to him from the distant past: *Bullies want you to be scared. If you ignore them they have no fun and move on to the next kid.* She had drummed this into him daily, and it was good practical advice.

Sheila remained at the door. Dafydd glanced up at her quickly. "Anything else?"

He couldn't fault her boldness. She looked at him in a way that forbade dismissal. "You know something?" she said, then paused for effect, forcing him to keep eye contact. He shrugged his shoulders impatiently. "If you're not careful you'll get a reputation for having no sense of humor."

"Whose type of humor are we talking about?" he asked.

"Listen. It wouldn't hurt you to loosen up a bit, not be such a tight-ass. We work closely together, and here we have our own way of doing things. It would help you to try and fit in."

"*Tight-ass,*" he said evenly and returned his eyes to his notes. "Is that what you called me?"

Out of the corner of his eye he saw Sheila drop her boobs and put her hands to her hair, smoothing the wild red fringe away from her face. She had gone too far and she knew it.

"Don't take it personally," she said, laughing. "But this is exactly what I mean by no sense of humor. We're all in it together. No one in this hospital is better than anyone else."

"Is that so?" Dafydd looked up at her again. Her eyes bore into his and her mouth was just slightly open, waiting for a challenge. "It seems to me that you have plenty of power over others," he said. "I would never have guessed that *you* considered *yourself* an equal, the way you throw your weight around."

"Have it your way," she snapped and turned to leave. He chuckled wryly. Sense of humor . . . ? On whose terms?

"What is it you want from me?" he called after her, not really meaning to ask.

She slowed her stride but clearly could not give him a direct answer. Dafydd blew out a lungful of air. He shouldn't engage in her banter. Perhaps he was flattering himself, but he sensed that complicity would soon lead to a sexual approach. The truth was, she scared him.

Sheila turned suddenly and walked back into the room.

"Listen. You think the world is such a big place, don't you? You thought you could come and hide up here? I know why you're on the run. I found that out in no time, so don't be so bloody smug with me." Sheila shifted from one foot to the other, a slight flush on her face. Her eyes sparkled with barely concealed satisfaction.

Dafydd caught his breath. Damn it all.

"So what?" Though he was shocked, he tried to sound nonchalant. There really was no point in denying anything. "What are you going to do about it?"

"Nothing," she said, smiling. "Just lay off that conceit of yours, that slimy British self-righteousness. Considering where you come from, it's totally out of place."

She had approached him, and he felt disadvantaged by his sitting position. He stood up and faced her. "Conceit? Self-righteousness? Sheila, I'm stumped. Believe me, I'm humbled enough by what I did. My confidence is rock-bottom, which is the very thing you are hitting on all the time."

Sheila didn't answer. She seemed to realize that he was right, so he boldly went on. "I'm trying to figure out what your problem is. Is it men in general, or British people, or doctors, or losers, or anyone whose qualifications exceed yours? Or perhaps you just don't like my face. I'm trying my best here, just getting to grips with the job. I just don't understand why I rile you so."

Sheila stood her ground, but she was clearly thrown by his forthright appeal. "No," she said finally, "you don't rile me in the least. I'm too busy to get riled by temp doctors, people who use this place only as a stop-off. This is my patch. I just want to see it running right." She looked slightly flustered as she turned and left.

This is my patch. True, she was a big fish in a small pond. Where else could she wield such power? It certainly seemed *one* reason why she was stuck in Moose Creek. Dafydd sank down into his chair and exhaled. He was dog-tired.

CHAPTER 7

Cardiff, 2006

The bright morning sun that shone in through a window seemed at odds with the unstrung feeling in his gut. He felt out of control, not remembering the details of the accident of the night before. The crash, the police officers, the ambulance, his own belligerent refusal to have his blood alcohol level tested: he had no recollection of any of it.

Dafydd watched as a nurse who seemed no older than a schoolgirl drew the curtains around his bed. She stood by, looking eager and interested, while a tall, good-looking man with smooth chocolaty skin was prodding him gently and removing the bandage on his head. Zafar Thakurdas cackled and joked while he inspected the shallow cut on Dafydd's head.

"It was a rolling pin job, then, Dr. Woodruff?"

"Rolling pin?"

"You come home late in the night, very bad for wear, and the wife is waiting behind the door with a rolling pin. Then *crack*, she got you."

The young nurse tittered and Zafar winked at her.

Dafydd was in no mood for tomfoolery and just closed his eyes in protest. "Husband, take this: *crack*. You fool around with girls and I get you fine and dandy." Zafar Thakurdas swung the imaginary rolling pin. "In my country the wife sneak up on you in the night, and *slash*." He grabbed a stitch cutter off the tray and swiped at the air above Dafydd's groin. The nurse giggled shamelessly.

"You're showing off," Dafydd groaned at the young doctor.

A stern face appeared around the curtain. Zafar drew a sharp breath and straightened his back deferentially. "Dr. Payne-Lawson," he said, smiling broadly, "I'm just seeing to Dr. Woodruff's . . . er . . . scratch on the head here."

Dafydd raised his face and cursed silently at the sight of the medical director, an unpopular man with whom he'd never gotten on. The ever-growing string of aggravations in his life now included having his physical predicament, and his humiliation, witnessed by his own superior, at his very own place of employment.

Payne-Lawson came in and peered down at him.

"What have we here?" There was a hint of malevolent glee in the man's eyes. He sniffed the air, and his face hinted at a mild revulsion when he saw the vomit that had splashed the edge of Dafydd's pillow. Dafydd knew he looked awful. He had a black eye, his beard growth was exuberant, and there was crud under his fingernails. His mouth tasted, and probably smelled, as if a herd of Algerian camels had passed through it.

"I take it you're not fit for work this morning?" Payne-Lawson guffawed superciliously, but his eyes were small and mean.

"Not indeed," said Zafar Thakurdas. "He needs a few days' rest. His head is concussed."

Payne-Lawson rudely ignored the registrar. "I understand you were under the influence of alcohol at the time of the accident."

"Not particularly," Dafydd muttered.

"Rubbish, Woodruff. I'm sure you're still intoxicated. Your blood alcohol levels were through the roof. The police officers said you'll be banned from driving for at least a year. I sincerely hope that it won't interfere with your on-call duties. Well, we'll have to talk about this later."

"Yes, later," Dafydd agreed. "Although I don't think any of it concerns you."

"Wrong, my friend. In my role as medical director I have an obligation to query the . . . ah . . . unlawful behavior of the medics under my jurisdiction."

The stitches in Dafydd's head were stinging and he was close to being sick, although there was nothing but a cup of tea in his stomach.

"At this moment I'm a patient here, George. I've had an accident. I have a crack in my bloody head and a severe concussion." Dafydd drew a breath. "So listen, 'my friend,' quit harassing me before I vomit on your shoes." The words that left his mouth took him by surprise. Maybe it was the morphine injection that made him so careless. He cringed inwardly, knowing that he had just dug himself a big black hole . . . coffin-sized. Payne-Lawson could make life extremely unpleasant for him.

"I don't like what I'm seeing, I have to say," Payne-Lawson said frostily, but he'd stepped back in case his shoes might get splattered. "A couple of people have commented on your performance over the last few weeks. If there's some sort of personal problem, I recommend that you take some leave. I heard . . . about your wife going off."

Dafydd was shocked at this. Doctors rarely gossiped or shopped each other, even when they didn't get on. He wondered who might have talked to Payne-Lawson about him. Anyway, he was wrong, his wife had not "gone off," damn it.

"As far as I know—although you may know something I don't—my wife is on a business trip. Is it strictly necessary to discuss my private life here in front of everyone?"

"All I'm saying is that it seems to have a bearing on your performance."

Zafar, although slightly childish, was a man of impeccable ethics. With obvious distress he turned to Payne-Lawson. "Please, please, could you be waiting until later, perhaps? Dr. Woodruff is in my care. He is getting agitated. It's not good. His head is bad."

Payne-Lawson opened his mouth to argue, but his voice was drowned out by the sudden sharp wail of an infant in the next cubicle. The scream drowned out all the other myriad noises of the Acute Medical Unit.

Dafydd felt as if it were himself screaming. The vibration resonated and clanged like a million bells within his head. Sleep . . . if he could only be allowed to sleep. Just sleep and then wake up from this bad dream. Wake up to his real life, as it had been, steeped in normality and contentment.

In the afternoon, twenty hours after the accident, he was deemed fit to go home. Margaret, a kind and motherly nurse he'd met before, brought his clothes, and he started to put them on. He struggled with his trousers; his knee did not want to bend properly. His head felt large and as if his brain were swollen within it.

"Your wife just rang. She's near the M4 junction, so she shouldn't be more than an hour. Poor thing, she's been driving all day. All the way from Glasgow, dear, dear, dear."

Dafydd tried to button his shirt but his left wrist was bruised and Margaret bent to help him.

"You be sure to take it easy for a couple of days," she said gently. "Go on, Dr. Woodruff, why not tell your lovely wife to take you on a holiday in the sun? Tenerife, or one of them islands. Lovely there, it is. You can fly straight from Cardiff, it's a doddle."

Dafydd regarded her suspiciously. "Really . . . does *everybody* know?"

Margaret's gray eyes, crinkled at the corners from fifty years of smiling, looked stern. "They loves a good bit of tattle, Dr. Woodruff, but you pay them no notice. I could tell *you* some stories that would make the hair on the back of your neck stand up." She bent toward him and, putting her warm hand on Dafydd's, whispered, "I'm sorry about the driving ban. I just wanted to mention . . . my son Llewellyn has a lovely Ford

Fiesta. He's twenty-six and unemployed since two years. He's a good driver. Solid. If you need . . . he wouldn't want a lot . . ."

Dafydd flinched. He'd not actually given any thought to the consequences of this disaster. What was this going to mean? A year, possibly more, without his own transport. How could he have done that? Perhaps that's what you get for all the self-righteous moralistic carping about drunk drivers. Thank God he'd not hurt anyone, or worse.

"I may well do. Thanks, Margaret. I'll get back to you."

He lay back on the bed and waited. A holiday in the sun was not such a bad idea. He'd put it to Isabel right away. He certainly could take a couple of weeks' sick leave, and hopefully she'd finish her Glasgow thing soon. Ideally, they'd have the lab results from Sheila's paternity claim first.

He came sharply awake when Isabel strode into the room. She looked radiant, dressed in a skin-tight black trouser suit and high-heeled boots. It was obvious now how much weight she'd lost in the last few weeks—stress, no doubt, but it suited her well. Her hair had been cut once more, shorn almost, but very stylishly. Though past forty, she looked boyish, tall and confident like right out of a fashion magazine. Dafydd felt a stirring that reminded him of being in love, and lust, with her.

"My God," he said, "Glasgow suits you."

"Oh, Dafydd." She came quickly to the bed and sat down, looking at his face. "What on earth happened? God, I was frantic when Jim rang. I got in the car and haven't stopped."

"You look as fresh as a daisy," he said and hugged her back, thinking it was the first time she'd hugged him for weeks.

"Oh, darling, look at you, your face . . . your gorgeous, handsome, lovely face." She cupped his face and kissed him on both cheeks. "Are you hurting anywhere?"

"Not really. I'm just stiff and bruised, like having been in a boxing match."

"How could somebody *do* this to you?" She shook her head, looking earnestly into his eyes. "I knew this would happen. You're far too vulnerable on that stupid bike."

Dafydd got a glimpse of something that didn't feel right. Maybe she'd been feeling guilty about the way she'd treated him, perhaps about doubting his honesty, and was going over the top to put it right. It didn't suit her to exaggerate; it wasn't her style. If nothing else, she was forthright and plainly spoken, verging on blunt.

"Isabel, let me put you in the picture straightaway. It was me. I was drunk and I'll lose my license for at least a year."

Isabel's hands dropped from his shoulders. "You're kidding?"

"No."

She was mute for a moment, then her voice was brusque. "What the hell were you thinking?"

"Shit happens," he said and looked at her searchingly.

She turned away and laughed a dry incredulous little laugh.

"Aren't you going to ask me if someone else was hurt?" he asked.

"Why, you'd tell me, I'm sure." Her voice had taken on a sharp edge, and it was easy to read what she was thinking.

"You shouldn't have bothered to come, right?"

Her true feelings flashed across her face. "If you must know, it's one hell of an inconvenience."

"I'm sorry Jim took it on himself to ring you. He should have asked me first. I wouldn't have inconvenienced you."

"Well, Paul was adamant that I should come down. He said he'd hold the fort for a day or two."

"How good of Paul." Dafydd snorted.

"Oh, come on." Isabel touched his arm. "I wanted to come to take you home, get you some food and stuff, but I've got to go back tomorrow. This job is just too important."

"Of course it is."

They looked away from each other, and Dafydd suddenly saw his briefcase, sitting under the bedside table. It looked as if it had been savaged by a pack of large dogs, by the looks of it the worst casualty of the accident, not counting his beloved bike. He stared at it in consternation for a moment, but then thanked the Almighty that it was merely the receptacle for his work papers, not his brain. He was supposed to be lucky, but he felt gutted. He needed *her*. It was bad enough; what had happened to him was of his own doing and some punishment was to be expected, but he wished it wasn't coming from her. He wished she would excuse him, exonerate him, the person he really was: responsible, capable, trustworthy, the man she knew and supposedly loved. But he knew it was not just the accident, it was Sheila Hailey and her allegation, it was the fact that he failed, time and time again, to be a real man, with real live sperm that would finally make her into a real woman, a whole woman, a mother. And now he refused to even try. He'd failed her . . . in every way.

CHAPTER 8

Moose Creek, 1992

The month of November was exceptionally harsh. During some nights the temperature plummeted to minus fifty degrees. Thick snow already submerged the landscape. A white immovable blanket had settled on the forests. The air was very still and clear.

By contrast, the streets of Moose Creek were dirty. The mountains of snow and ice that were shoveled high on every street corner were mixed and remixed with the grime of human habitation. Dafydd had slipped and twisted his ankle on the filthy ice that covered the sidewalks. He was not alone. Many a broken limb and cracked skull resulted from this perilous situation. Nobody seemed to complain about it. When the odd Monday coincided with goodwill, materials, and manpower, a truckload of sand would sometimes be strewn haphazardly across roads and walkways, but on the whole the inhabitants were expected to watch out for themselves.

Dafydd saw his patients in the clinic, but outside of work hours he was stuck in his freezing trailer. The place was depressing and stank unbearably, especially since a tomcat had sneaked in and spent a whole day at his leisure spraying clothes, furniture, and bedding. Mrs. Breummer, still in dire need of money, had helped Dafydd scrub it out, but no amount of bleach could quite restore it to its previous smell. As the full winter approached, he tended to spend more time in Ian's cabin. Occasionally Ian offered him a meal, extracted from tins, or Dafydd brought take-out pizzas that were all but frozen when he got there. If Ian had his way they would have lived at the Klondike, in the bar specifically. The sweet and demure Tillie had been promoted to assistant manager, despite her incapacitating obesity, and Dafydd had become her foremost priority among the customers, the one most deserving of good measures. Ian was not such a choice patron in Tillie's eyes, but he benefited by association.

Brenda was always her businesslike self, affable and with a stinging sense of humor. She never once alluded to their encounter at Jackfish Lake. While he was grateful for this, Dafydd couldn't help wondering about her coolness. Had he so disgraced himself, or perhaps she was tied up with someone else? Maybe she preferred to keep herself free from entanglements. After all, Moose Creek was a place where your actions were everybody's franchise. There were moments when sheer sexual frustration and the memory of her voluptuous thighs riding him in that magical wilderness made him want to grab her, ask her to repeat the experience (somewhere indoors), but he held back because it seemed too forward and too complicated. And when he realized that Ian sometimes slept with her, he knew his resolve was justified. There was no doubt that sex, in all its human complexities and manifestations, was an important part of the arctic winter. What else could people do, incarcerated indoors?

A few times he'd ended up in the motel room of a very spirited traveling saleswoman. Anette Belanger was a tall bottle-blond woman in her mid-thirties. She was well suited to the rigors of her job, which was selling frozen foodstuffs to hotels and restaurants in the most out-of-the-way places. Her booming laugh and her wild stories of travels in the catering business to all corners of Canada always amused him. She brought a small measure of delight into his onerous existence, and her solid white body seemed an honest place to lay himself down on, particularly as she kept insisting he should do so.

After her fifth visit to Moose Creek, she called him and said she wouldn't be coming anymore. Her husband hadn't liked her being away all the time, so she'd gotten another job in her hometown of Calgary. That was the first he'd heard of any husband; she must have sensed that Dafydd stayed clear of married women. So much for honesty.

The swollen ankle put paid to another thrill. Ian had given him an old pair of cross-country skis, and he'd sent for some ski boots from a catalogue. Gliding through the forests, using the sunken tracks conveniently left by snowmobiles, he'd experienced a silence and a blinding whiteness that was beyond anything he'd ever known. It was beautiful to more than just the senses. It brought him closer to something eternal, a hint of immortality, a long, white sleep.

The days were short and getting shorter. He had only an hour, squeezed into his midday break, to get out there for a fix of light and air. As the month wore on, it made no difference whether he could or not put weight on his foot. At under minus thirty degrees, skis would no longer glide and the anesthetic effect of the cold turned dangerous. A numb foot, cheek or ear could turn into a frostbite within minutes, and stopping for a pee was a hazard a man should not risk. Dafydd had no choice but to stay put. He felt he was going half mad from inactivity and claustrophobia. He strapped his ankle and limped around town, wearing his moose-hide mukluks that gripped the ice. The main street was always bustling but the rest of the town seemed deserted. Nobody walked anywhere, except en route to shopping, drinking, and hell-raising.

Dafydd's first casualty of the cold was a young Inuit girl who'd been either raped or was a drunken but willing participant in a gang bang. The deed took place in a van in a disused parking lot, and when they had finished with her the girl was kicked out of the vehicle and left to fend for herself. She never even got her parka back on and was frozen solid by the morning when she was found. The three youths were sitting in a cell meant for one, adjoining the police station, awaiting transfer to the Yellowknife prison.

The event had unsettled Dafydd. He'd seen plenty of gruesome deaths in the four months since his arrival, but this one was particularly disturbing. When she was brought in, he'd not known the exact circumstances of her death. However, there was no doubt that sexual activity had formed part of her last few hours. If felt like another violation, parting her legs stiffened with cold and rigor mortis, to take the necessary swabs. It would not do to leave it until Dr. Gupta, the visiting pathologist, made his rounds, in case there was a possibility of foul play. The girl was so young, sixteen or seventeen. Her skin was the translucent white of death, but apart from a large black bruise on her hip she looked healthy, as though she were asleep. Remnants of red nail varnish dotted her toenails, scuffed and forgotten since the last days of sunshine and sandals. The smile frozen on her lips unnerved him. He would rather have seen signs of torment, just to know that she had struggled to live. But hadn't Ian said that death by freezing is a painless, even somewhat pleasant experience, a bit like drowning? Part of his discomfort was a vague feeling of desire. The girl was beautiful, not in the way he normally perceived beauty, but she was the most exotic creature he'd ever examined. Her jet-black hair was coarse to the touch. Cheekbones so high that they pushed at the lower eyelids, like eyes convulsed with laughter. Looking at her taut, compact young body, he felt an urge to stroke it. At the same time it made him feel queasy and disgusted. What the hell was he up to, having semi-erotic feelings for a corpse? A sign of madness, cabin fever, or just loneliness? He realized that he really missed Anette's warm, breathing body, short-lived as the affair had been, and there was no one else. He pulled a sheet over the dead girl and called for the porter to wheel her down into the basement morgue.

The same night, Sheila phoned him to come and deal with a man who had been brought in unconscious. It was four o'clock in the morning by the time he got to the hospital, and the night was at its coldest. The man had been discovered lying in a snow-filled ditch by a waitress departing from an all-night extramarital rendezvous (how Sheila was privy to the intimate particulars of the poor woman, Dafydd did not bother to question).

The casualty, a native man by the name of David Chaquit, was warming up and coming back to life, although still in an alcoholic stupor. He'd been lucky. He was wearing thick enough clothing and couldn't have been out there for very long. Dafydd and Sheila manhandled him onto a trolley, where he lolled and giggled, winking at her and drooling. He had a broken wrist that was easy enough to deal with, but his left ear had been in prolonged contact with the ground. It was swollen and white, practically transparent, like ice itself.

Dafydd set the wrist, then pulled off his rubber gloves to get ready to return to his trailer. The night was so cold he feared the Chrysler would have died while the sump heater was unplugged in the hospital parking lot.

"What about the ear?" Sheila said rather sharply. "Why not deal with it now?"

"I'm leaving it until tomorrow."

"It *is* tomorrow," Sheila said.

"In that case I'll come back later."

"Your delicacy for the grubbier parts of the job is rather cute." She was smiling but her eyes were flat; the sharp blue of the irises seemed dimmed by lack of sleep. "Someone's got to do it, though . . . have you thought of that?"

Dafydd felt the prickles of heat rising on his neck.

"I have every intention of dealing with it. I'd rather Mr. Chaquit sobered up first. I'd like to talk to him about it. That's reasonable, isn't it? How would you like to wake up one morning minus an ear? Anyway, I want to see how much of it can be saved. It's far too early to tell."

Immediately he felt irritated by his rationalization. There was no reason to explain himself. He wasn't accountable to *her*.

She was looking at his neck with her head cocked to one side, and he remembered. She knew of the black stain on his heart, she knew of his fears and insecurities. She read him like a book. Though she didn't exactly refer to it directly, she held her *knowing* constantly over his head.

He turned away abruptly and limped out of the theater.

"No danger of gangrene, then?" she called after him.

"Certainly not," he said without looking back. Bloody woman, they might as well hire *her* as the doctor. It seemed she would have the last word no matter what. He knew he would have to take her to task sometime soon, challenge her in some way. But he loathed the idea, because there was no doubting that she would bring up his shame. He would re-act defensively. Anger tended to make him inarticulate and blundering, sometimes downright stupid, and she would be delighted to have further cause with which to ridicule and de-skill him. In fact, her understanding of human frailty was admirable. Though most people respected her, and some even seemed to like her, they all did her bidding—even Hogg bowed to her will.

"Oh, come on," she called to his back. "Let's whip it off. The sooner we can send him on his way. Believe me, people like him have no use for the aesthetic part of the hearing apparatus. It's just a piece of expendable flesh." She'd followed him into the mess. "You're here now. I promise I won't let anyone call you in the morning. I'll tell them you had a god-awful night. Emergency after emergency . . ."

Dafydd stopped and looked her in the eye. "What a good-hearted offer, but no." He pulled his parka on. "You look like you could use a few hours' beauty sleep yourself. I'll see you in the morning."

"No, you won't," she snapped. "I'm off in a couple of hours."

"Oh, well then."

But Sheila was not predictable. The hardness of her expression melted and she cocked her head a little. "I could use some stimulation," she said, her voice husky. Dafydd felt himself reddening again and she smiled seductively, folding her arms under her breasts. "I'll do it myself . . . and you can watch me," she whispered. He stared at her in confusion.

"The amputation, you twit." She laughed now. "I've done them before. Hogg often lets me."

She got him, and it *was* quite funny. He could have laughed, but he didn't want to give her the satisfaction. "I think not," he said and left her standing there propping up her boobs.

Dafydd stopped in the parking lot to breathe in the cold air. The woman had no scruples at all. *Piece of expendable flesh . . .* He just hoped he'd never find himself under her nursing care. God knows what she'd chop off. Better stay well and sober at all times.

He looked into the night sky, pinpricked by the sharp white of stars. The arctic winter was slow to dawn. He could see the morning approaching by the lights being switched on inside houses and trailers. People waking and preparing for the day. Children to be bundled into layers and layers of clothing; husbands defrosting pickups inside garages; wives donning snow boots and parkas to drive the short distance to the school and the supermarket.

The idea of meeting someone in Moose Creek had never occurred to him, but what if he *did* fall in love with someone? He'd never actually been in love, not properly, he was pretty sure of it. Lust, many times, even passion . . . There had been Katrina, his first. He'd certainly been totally infatuated for a good many months, but the feeling fizzled out as they found they had nothing in common. The only other woman he'd felt strongly about was Lesley. She was a colleague who had rented him a room in her house after her husband cleared off. They became lovers for a year, then stayed firm friends. She was twelve years older than him, but she was attractive and stimulating. She was also a practical woman, extremely supportive, and had been invaluable in helping him pass his exams. The affair was long over when the catastrophe with Derek Rose happened, but she turned out to be his only real ally. Yes, he had loved her very much, still did.

Two weeks before Christmas there was a party at Charles and Shirley Bowlby's. They owned an insurance/travel agency and had a large, comfortable house in a new subdivision on the outskirts of town. Martha drove him out there. On the way she gave him his instructions.

"I'll be waiting for you at two, sharp. That's when they start to wind down, mostly. Now, you be careful to come home with me, right? Don' get talked into going home with any wimmin. Once you stay the night, you'll never be rid of them, ya hear? You stay clear of that Hailey woman. Her boyfriend's outta town, but you don' want mess with a great big hulk of a logger's woman, now, do you?"

"Right you are, Martha." He was distracted by her reckless driving and the way she turned to look at him for confirmation . . . Two in the morning, and he was already tired. "I'd rather you came at midnight. I'm sure you need your sleep, too."

She laughed sarcastically. "Do you think you're my only fare, boy? I plan to earn me a good few dollars tonight. Them guys won't be doing much drivin'." She nodded in the direction of the pitch-black road ahead. "I reckon a couple of dozen people will be beggin' me to deliver them home. Can I afford to be nappin' the night away, huh? And I'm not dubblin' yer up." She snorted loudly at the concept. "One at a time . . . you gotta be kiddin'."

"You're some businesswoman."

"I'm as smart as I'm plain," she said and dropped him at the bottom of a long drive. "This is where I'll be waiting."

Dafydd was let in by one of the host's teenage sons. The boy took his coat away and left him at the entrance to a large living room already full of people. Hogg stumbled toward Dafydd with outstretched arms. He wasn't really a drinker, but he'd apparently had quite a few.

"Our golden boy," he bellowed. "Who haven't you met?"

"Oh, I think I know almost everyone. Don't worry, I'll introduce myself."

"This kid'll be staying with us," Hogg continued in his high-pitched voice to no one in particular. "He's my right-hand man." He patted Dafydd on the back and then pinched his cheek before heading toward a table of snacks. Anita, his post-virally afflicted wife, was nowhere to be seen.

The living room was hung with gaudy oil paintings, and the overhead light was too harsh. Some sixty or seventy people were gathered there in their finery, the entire collection of Moose Creek's Chamber of Commerce, RCMP and government administrators, senior hospital staff, the two school principals and their most presentable teachers, plus wives and husbands. All dressed in the best that Edmonton or Yellowknife could offer on a hasty pre-Christmas shopping trip. Still, it was an unexpected bit of glamour, and after a couple of very strong gin and tonics, poured by the hearty host, Dafydd felt himself enter a Christmas spirit of sorts. He didn't look too bad himself. His dark-chocolate-brown suit contrasted sharply with a crisp white shirt, and he wore the tie he'd picked up in Florence a year earlier while attending a conference. Just before Derek Rose. He fiddled with the soft, silky fabric and straightened the knot, reflecting on how he would have felt then, had he been able to observe himself here at the edge of civilization just a year hence.

He looked about for someone interesting to approach. Ian was standing by the ornately decorated Christmas tree, with his back to him, talking to a young woman he recognized as working for the town administration. The girl was looking up at Ian in a coquettish manner, laughing at his every pronouncement. Ian looked good. His blondish hair was quite long and curled over his shirt collar. Both the hair and collar looked clean. He'd swapped his jeans for tight black leather trousers, and even Dafydd could see what a girl would find attractive in the man.

The girl saw Dafydd looking at them and she said something

to Ian. He turned around and without so much as a word he left her standing.

"You're looking swish," he said, poking at the unusual tie.

"Hey, so do you, man," Dafydd said, imitating his accent. "Should you really leave that delectable girl to be snapped up by someone else?"

"I can always pick up where I left off." Ian lit a cigarette, took a deep drag and studied Dafydd with a comic squint. "Hey, c'mon. You need to lighten up. It's Christmas, for Christ's sake, and you're walking around like you have a stethoscope up your ass. Why don't you just enjoy the scene?"

Was that really what he looked like? An uptight, humorless twit, fulfilling the long-held Canadian opinion of British people. Perhaps Sheila wasn't harassing him just for the hell of it. Ian was right: He had a lifetime ahead of him, fretting about patients and their opinion of him. It was about time that he let go of his bloody neurosis, his fear of mistakes.

"I take your point. I'll try harder."

Ian laughed his rare face-splitting laugh and people turned their heads in his direction. "It's not about trying, you dope, just the opposite. You need to let rip."

Dafydd felt a surge of appreciation for the man, even though he was a fine one to speak of attitude. Letting rip and not caring about the consequences wasn't doing *him* much good, not his health, at any rate.

The girl had recovered from Ian's unmannerly snub and joined them. She was a well-filled, dark-haired beauty with hazel eyes and a broad expressive mouth, quite a bit younger than she appeared under the layers of makeup. She grabbed Ian's arm and pulled him toward her.

"Hey . . . introduce me to your friend."

"This is Allegra . . ."

She turned to Dafydd and started talking. She had a lot to say. Just a year out of high school but affecting the sexy, sophisticated femme fatale, helped on the way by glass after glass of cheap champagne. Her prattle was fatuous but endearing: the unavailability of *real* hairdressers, the lack of clothes stores, her last boyfriend and his innumerable shortcomings. Ian moved away. Latecomers piled in. Someone started playing "Silent Night" on an ill-tuned piano. Drink after drink appeared in Dafydd's hand. He wondered if there was a conspiracy to see him lose his composure, his stethoscope-up-the-arse manner, see him spill himself all over the place. It seemed to be a perfectly acceptable way in which to behave in this town. People came here because they'd done too much of that in some other place, or because this was the place where they could indulge it. Where else in the world could you live and let live in this way? He relaxed and tossed back whatever was handed to him. Looking around frequently, he tried to get away from Allegra, who had glued herself to him as if they were already lovers. She would be more than easy to invite back to the trailer, but he had Martha to contend with and he didn't want to use her transport for the transaction. Anyway, much as he ached for a warm female embrace, he was never totally comfortable with one-night stands, and the girl was not someone he would want to spend a lot of time with. Besides, she was too young and he had no condoms. In his befuddled mind he made a note of it. He should be practicing what he preached to his younger patients: if you're footloose and fancy-free, keep condoms on you at all times.

He disengaged himself from Allegra as tactfully as he could and headed for Elaine, a young teacher whose husband had recently perished in a light aircraft accident. Dafydd had examined the remains of this tall good-looking fellow and had been shocked at the state of him. He'd attempted an emergency landing on a cut line in thick fog. Although wide enough, the cut line was a mass of tree stumps and the plane literally broke up into pieces, fracturing the man's body in several places, including his neck and back.

Elaine was sitting by herself on a chair near the window looking out into the black night. She'd gained a large amount of weight since her bereavement. Her youth and beauty seemed to have vanished abruptly. He said hello and stood awkwardly beside her since there was nowhere to sit. The noise around them was deafening.

"Are you enjoying yourself?" she asked indifferently, her voice barely audible.

He bent down on one knee to be at her level. "How are the girls?"

"Still wondering when he's coming back. They ask me every day. It's driving me mad. I don't know what to tell them."

Dafydd tried to smile, to lighten her dark mood. "You're the teacher. You talk to children all the time. I'm rather a believer in telling it as it is. Even to children."

"When am I going to stop hurting?" she pleaded, looking him directly in the eye. Her face was contorted with pain. "If it wasn't for the girls, I'd join him this minute." She grabbed him by the sleeve and repeated, *"This minute."*

Suddenly he felt giddy. He was balancing on his haunches and his knees were groaning. He was too drunk to be dealing with this woman's grief. The party had given his spirits a kick and revitalized his enthusiasm for living, yet he couldn't have ignored Elaine, sitting there alone.

"I want you to come and see me," he said without much conviction. "Talking will help."

"We're talking now." She glared at him icily.

"A refill?" A carafe was held out toward his glass, and he turned to see Sheila standing beside them. He nodded. "Yes, please, Sheila." He was feeling generous toward everyone, and his newfound Christmas spirit almost included her, especially since she was smart enough to see he wanted to be rescued from the grieving Elaine.

"Dafydd, there's someone you must meet." He stood up and Sheila took him by the elbow.

"Excuse me," he said to Elaine as he was led away. They went into the family room at the other end of the house where a different party was taking place. The music was loud, the lights dim, and there was a conspicuous haze of cannabis. The younger contingent was obviously having an even better time of it. Sheila drew him into a little vestibule where coats were flung everywhere.

"Have a seat here for a moment," she said and pushed him back on to a chair covered in coats. She took a tiny vial out of her handbag. Dafydd watched in astonishment as she carefully poured a tiny amount of powder onto the back of her hand and snorted it up her nose through a slim silver tube. She held the vial out to Dafydd. He shook his head.

"You prude. Don't look so shocked," she said, laughing. "Just between us. No one's gonna see you. Hey, it's Christmas, and we're not at work."

He shook his head again but couldn't help smiling. Who would have thought it? Our rigorous hospital matron snorting cocaine in a cupboard. Well, if anybody needs to let rip and relax, she does.

"Where's this person you want me to meet?" he asked.

"She's standing right in front of you."

"I know you already."

"Oh, no, you don't."

"Oh, all right, then." He laughed. "I can see that there's much more to you than I could possibly understand."

She repeated the deed with her other nostril, blinked and rubbed her nose. It was true: he didn't know her at all and he was seeing a different side of her. There was nothing of the tough, businesslike head nurse who inspired respect and awe in colleagues and patients alike. And looking at her now, it was hard to imagine how she constantly tried to intimidate him. She seemed as meek as a lamb. In her state of blissful intoxication she looked young and almost touching, like a teenager. Her large blue eyes were positively angelic, and her mass of red curls stood like a halo of fire around her face. She was wearing an emerald-green minidress and her smooth, muscular legs were encased in the flimsiest tights. Looking down, he glimpsed the profusion of freckles on her thighs under the pale nylon. He felt suddenly uncomfortable and stood up.

When she saw that he was about to leave she moved forward,

cornering him against a coat rack. "Can't we be friends?" she said, reaching out and smoothing a curl of his hair away from his forehead. The touch was overly intimate and he wanted to be out of the airless cupboard at once, but that would make him look anxious and feckless. To her advantage.

"Sure," he said. "Does that mean you're going to stop mocking me at every opportunity?"

She traced his mouth with the tips of her fingers. "Oh, come on, don't take yourself so bloody seriously. Can't you see I'm trying to help you? You are so damned fastidious"—her hand dropped to grip his tie as she searched for a suitable description—"and *delicate*. You're far too scrupulous and prudent for this kind of place. Although, of course, I know why that is."

She laughed softly and pulled him toward her by the tie. "Honey, I've got your little game figured right out."

In spite of his Christmas good cheer and the drink, he felt himself go rigid as if he'd been punched in the stomach. He looked at her and saw the other Sheila, the one he dreaded and disliked. As his jaws clenched, a powerful urge came over him; he wanted to throw her across all the coats, yank up her delicate little dress and rip her tights, penetrate her and pound that inimical arrogance out of her, have her crying for mercy. Feeling hot and flustered by this sudden inexplicable impulse, he hovered between doing to her what he wanted (suspecting she might just let him) and running out of there. He took a deep breath, wrenched her hand off his tie and moved toward the door, but she stepped around him and blocked his exit. The gorgeous seductress in front of him seemed determined to get what she wanted, God only knows what, and for what reason. She must have known that he didn't want her (or . . . did he?), so why try, why expose herself to rejection when there were so many other men to hit on? Men who would do anything . . . Dafydd turned and looked intently into her eyes, trying to decipher what lay beyond that beautiful mysterious blue. She said she wanted to be friends, though he knew there was more, so *why* did she think she'd achieve it by cutting him to shreds?

She stared back at him, challenged by his wordless confrontation but completely misinterpreting it. "All right, show me," she said, her breath sharpening, her lips parting. "Show me you can be forceful. Take charge of *me*. My boyfriend's away. Come home with me tonight. Just this once."

Perversely, and almost regretting it, he saw his advantage. "It wouldn't work." He smiled, shrugging in mock apology. "You don't turn me on sexually."

Sheila stared at him in disbelief for a moment. "You're a fucking faggot, that's why," she hissed and walked out, leaving him standing, breathing the mixture of her perfume and damp wool. Oh, fuck! Why had he said that? Revenge was far from sweet. He was as bad as she was. A moment later, as he pulled himself up to leave, there was a soft knock on the door. Hogg stood there anxiously trying to peer past him into the vestibule.

"Sorry, I was looking for Sheila," Hogg said self-consciously, not at all the smug little autocrat of the hospital. "I thought maybe she was with you."

"She was. But don't worry, she's all yours," Dafydd said, not giving a damn. "Mind, she'll be in a foul mood, Andrew. Do yourself a favor and don't bother." He left Hogg standing, staring at his shoes in mortification.

Two hours later Dafydd was very drunk. He hadn't meant to get drunk, not *that* drunk. He found his coat and staggered out to look for Martha. It wasn't his time yet; she was busy ferrying other shipwrecked souls back to safety. He waited by the road, hoping to catch her or anyone else going into town. Just a few minutes passed and the cold was entering his body and numbing it. It wasn't so bad, like a seduction. He felt quite willing to accept the frigid slumber, a trance full of bliss and light . . . This was the very danger that he had never quite understood. He felt drowsy and about to sit himself down in the snow, but abruptly he came to his senses when he began to shiver violently. He started hopping on the spot and rubbing his gloved hands together, wishing desperately that he'd brought a hat.

A car came down the long drive and stopped.

"Get in," Sheila's voice commanded through a crack in the window. "You can't just stand there. You're drunk and it's dangerous. I won't be responsible for leaving you to freeze to death." When he hesitated, she added with a sneer, "I wouldn't touch you with a ten-foot pole. I'm taking you straight home."

They drove in silence. She seemed icily sober. He'd noticed that she didn't drink alcohol, but the coke must have affected her. She certainly was a woman in charge of herself no matter what connivance she was in the midst of.

She turned into the trailer park and stopped the car outside his porch.

"Look!" She pointed to the sky and turned off the ignition. Thin veils of white were undulating across the heavens. In turn they would flash like a whip. He had seen the aurora borealis on a couple of occasions but had been a bit disappointed. It wasn't as described in the books, a light show of different colors flashing wildly around the sky. Sheila turned and looked at him, and he held her gaze for a moment, then he lay his head back against the headrest and looked out into the night. The dancing shrouds were quite mesmerizing after all. His head was spinning, but he felt quite snug. The car was wonderfully hot, and Dire Straits was playing on the tape deck, making him feel at home.

He wanted to apologize for his spiteful comment. Why not? He'd been unnecessarily rude, wanting to hurt her in return for her unrelenting efforts to put him down. Though she was a difficult customer, she was not exactly an evil one; she was a damned skillful nurse, in fact, and very dedicated to hard work. They were just so utterly different, complete opposites. It was no wonder there was no understanding, no empathy. But they had to work together for several more months . . .

Just as he was thinking about how to offer her the olive branch, he felt her hand reach out for him. He made no move. He was too relaxed to react, too weary to resist. He longed for some physical contact . . . if only it wasn't hers. In a moment she had worked her way through the layers of clothing and expertly unzipped him. Her palm was nice and warm around his cold cock, and immediately he felt himself start to harden in her hand. She had not moved closer and he didn't look at her. With his eyes closed, he tried to lose himself to the motions of her hand. There was a perfunctory experience at work, almost nurselike. He reached over and touched her thigh. The thin nylon of her tights felt cool and slippery, and she moved against his hand, as if urging him to explore further. The image of Kerstin came to him, a girl with whom he'd once had a fiery affair. It was Kerstin who was masturbating him and it worked beautifully. His hand closed over Sheila's, guiding her to quicken the pace.

"Why don't we go inside?" Sheila suggested, her voice low and raspy.

Dafydd was trying to consider the possibility, but his thoughts were still focused on Kerstin. Now Sheila was trying to withdraw her hand but he held on to it firmly and a few seconds later he came, the waves of pleasure sharp and acute despite his drunken condition.

With a contemptuous groan, Sheila whipped her hand away from his crotch and wiped it on his coat. She started up the car and put it into gear.

Dafydd sighed and closed his eyes. He'd really done it now; he knew he was beyond redemption. "Sheila, I'm sorry, I didn't—"

"Get the fuck out," she ordered.

Dafydd tumbled out of the car and she drove off with a roar, skidding crazily on the icy drive. He searched through his pockets at length, trying to find his keys, aware that his fly was still undone. A hunch made him look up, and there at the darkened window of the next trailer stood Ted O'Reilly. Dafydd could clearly see the leering smile on his unshaven face. The man made a thumbs-up sign, accompanied by a few obscene movements of the hips. Dafydd groaned and turned away, trying to get the damned key into the lock.

CHAPTER 9

Cardiff, 2006

Dear Dad, I hope you don't mind me calling you dad. My mom has told me all about you being careful and not wanting to rush things until the blood tests have been all finished and stuff. That's OK. I understand all that, but I hope you will be a teensy bit happy about having a daughter and a son. I can tell you for sure that I am real happy about having a dad. All my friends have dads except Melissa and Cass, their parents have divorced and they don't hear from their dads no more because their dads left Moose Creek. That's real sad, don't you think?

We did the test two weeks ago now, that is to say, my mom had to give blood and Mark gave blood. I don't like needles so my mom thought it would be enough if Mark went. Well, we are twins, everyone knows that.

I wonder if you might want to come and visit when you find out that we are your kids. I sure hope so. I've got lots to show you, like photos from when we were babies and all that.

Lots of love
Miranda xxx

Dafydd read the letter twice, then let it drop onto his lap. There it fluttered in the draft that seeped belligerently in through every gap between the glass panes. Damnation. That poor kid is totally and utterly convinced, he thought. Bloody Sheila. The memories of her incongruous behavior and her pathological arrogance had gradually come to the fore; every day he recalled some interaction or other that they'd had, and how she'd ended up hating him with such intensity. But what was the point of all this? It just didn't make sense. Where on earth did she hope it would get her? No matter how much he guessed, speculated, and hypothesized, he just could not understand. The only explanation was some sort of delusion, madness even, or else a complete memory loss as to whom she'd slept with. Possibly due to drugs or alcohol. He supposed he would never actually find out. Sometimes, on waking in the night, he conjured up all kinds of ridiculous scenarios, ways in which she could have gotten hold of his sperm. She had once . . . masturbated him; he cringed just thinking about it. *But that was all.* It took place in a car, in subzero temperatures; he supposed the sperm could have been immediately frozen somehow. Could she later have transported some of it to her own womb? No—as laughable as getting pregnant off a loo seat, a towel or in a swimming pool. Perhaps something more sinister? Maybe she put something into his drink. A date-rape drug with total postcoital amnesia. He dismissed it all as ludicrous and physically impossible. And given that she had once desperately pressed him for an after-hours abortion, why on earth would she want to go to those lengths to get pregnant, by him, *a man she loathed . . . ?*

He left the letter on the sofa and trailed through the house, noting the sheer squalor it had fallen into. He and Isabel shared the housework equally, but in the two weeks she'd been away he had not had the impetus to do even his own share. What was the point of it when it all had to be done again? And what was wrong with paper plates once in a while? He'd not had a normal meal for days, living off various indistinguishable cling-wrapped lumps from the freezer and the pizzas and ready-washed salads that Isabel had dashed next door to buy at Ved Choudhury & Sons, but where in fact Mrs. Choudhury and daughters tended shop. Mrs. Choudhury had been horrified by Isabel's account of the accident and had offered to send one of her daughters over with cooked meals while Isabel was away. Isabel had declined the kindness, much to Dafydd's disappointment.

He went up to take a shower. He wasn't sure he'd had one since the day before yesterday. Throwing off his dressing gown, he got in, but much as he tried to switch off and let the flow of water cleanse his thoughts he could find no serenity in it. It was as if his life were crumbling at the edges, yet he had to concede that nothing truly threatening had taken place. Perhaps his existence had been so uneventful for so many years that these minor calamities seemed distorted and magnified out of proportion. The loss of his Velocette Venom was a blow—a beautiful relic of rusting metal on two wheels that had served him for so many years. She was pretty well irreplaceable, but also there was an unequivocal finality to her demise, the end of an age. Isabel would be restored to him properly once the DNA tests were done, and his driving ban, well, a year went by at a hell of a rate these days. The drunken driver image might take longer to lose.

He got out of the shower and started to tackle his stubble. His life had to go on; he'd overcome the snags. Be proactive. He'd get dressed and go back to work. Four days was enough of a convalescence. His black eye was now a bilious yellow, but so what? His knee should be able to take the pace and his wrist was almost all right. His pride would have to endure.

The week was coming to an end. He'd managed to keep his head down and get on with his work, ignoring the odd wink and smirk and sympathetic pats on the back. The weekend was ahead, and Isabel was supposed to be back midafternoon.

All morning he'd been in a state of fidgety anticipation. They had talked on the phone most days, and she seemed somewhat apologetic, maybe even embarrassed. Allusions were made to some sort of atonement, whether sexual, affectionate or simply domestic—he wasn't sure what she meant or why she felt he deserved it.

His pager bleeped shrilly while he was chatting with a woman about to have her gall bladder removed.

"I'm home," Isabel sighed when he finally got to a phone. "Thank God. What a drive."

"I bet. Listen, I was on call last night and I've been here since the crack of dawn. There's no food in the house. Why don't we have a meal out? I want to hear all about your venture. Let's go down to the bay. How about Eduardo's? Would you like that?"

"Great," she said, sounding pleased. "Are you coming home or shall we meet there?"

"Well," he said, hesitating, realizing that she'd forgotten that he no longer had wheels. "Let's meet there. In the bar. How about seven-thirty? I'll book a table."

They met in the parking lot. Isabel arrived in a taxi and seemed puzzled at the sight of him clambering out of Jim Wiseman's people carrier in which he'd thumbed a lift. She looked stunning in the soft black dress that adhered to her anatomy as if it had been applied with a spray can, over which a new cashmere shawl wrapped her shoulders. The shadows of hard work or late nights under her eyes, and the scarlet lipstick, made her look her age, but still she was impressive. He felt a sudden surge of desire such as he hadn't felt for her in a very long time, but there was nothing tender about it. He wanted her like he used to want her, years ago, before sex became an enterprise.

The restaurant was crowded. It always was these days. The current place to be seen. They had discovered it first, eight months ago when it was struggling to get off the ground. Eduardo, his loyalty undiminished, rushed forward with both arms outstretched. "Darlings, I gotto favorite table . . . Isabella!" He puckered his plump lips and gave her a noisy kiss on each cheek, then pumped Dafydd's hand with both of his.

They sat by the window overlooking the water taxi docking bay. There was just a shimmer of the sun's light over the water and Penarth's cliffs looked black. Lights twinkled along the marina, and the boardwalk below the restaurant was full of couples strolling, laughing, and drinking. Dafydd sank contentedly down into his chair and sighed with pleasure. This felt so normal, so right. He scanned the menu and raised an eyebrow. Eduardo was doing well, too well by the look of the new prices. The little man rushed up with a good bottle. He had an excellent memory.

"It's onna house, my friends." His warm, liquid eyes looked sad. "You donna come so often. I always make room for you. Anytime, you know."

The couple at the next table, wondering who they were, leaned toward each other in whispered speculations. Isabel looked like a movie star in the glow of the candle. Then she took out her fetid little pouch of tobacco and her Rizlas and proceeded to roll a jointlike cigarette, strands of tobacco sprouting from each end. Dafydd sighed and glanced at the couple next to them. The lady's face had changed dramatically from curiosity to unconcealed disgust. The husband snapped his fingers at Eduardo, who came running.

"Waiter. This is supposed to be the nonsmoking section." He jerked his thumb in Isabel's direction. "My wife is asthmatic."

"It's okay," Dafydd mumbled to them and cast a pleading look at Isabel. "Just don't light it . . . please."

Their precarious homecoming celebration suffered a slight setback. Isabel petulantly threw her cigarette onto her side plate. She was back on the fags good and proper, and when she was she liked to have a smoke with her drink. There were no other tables available. Eduardo looked distressed and kept making signals of solidarity and helplessness from where he was stationed near the door. It was distracting, and Dafydd wished he could turn his back on his solicitous host, but he was right in his line of vision. A tiny insect kept circling the three daisies in a vase that graced the center of the table. Isabel swatted at it and knocked over the vase. Water covered the starched white table-cloth. Dafydd dabbed at it with his napkin and tittered, "Dress her up—can't take her *anywhere*." She hid her smile behind her wine glass; it was a genuine smile.

"I've missed you." He took her hand in his and noticed that she wasn't wearing her wedding ring. A little circle of white skin stood out from where it had been for the last six years. He caressed the absent ring with his thumb and looked at her questioningly. "I took it off . . . I turned the hotel room upside down this morning looking for it. It must have slipped down somewhere."

"A Freudian slip, huh?" He smiled. "Good for business . . . not wearing it in Glasgow?"

She frowned and he wished he hadn't said that. She'd been so disagreeable during the last few weeks he felt he had to tiptoe around her moods, never quite knowing where they would fall. He'd almost forgotten what had so attracted him to her, her curious mixture of sophistication and mischievousness. A hell of a temper and she sure could hold a grudge, but he used to think it was part of her Italian allure.

He topped up her glass. The wine was fiendishly strong. She tapped her side plate with her long nails. It made a loud rhythmic clicking. Their neighbors glared at her. She showed them her unlit cigarette and they looked away.

Although the place was filled with people, everyone spoke softly, causing a mere hum of sound. The tables were too close together. Every word they said could be overheard. Dafydd waved at Eduardo, who was at the ready and rushed to their side.

"Eduardo, why no music? Can't we have that 1980s compilation, you know, the one you put together yourself?"

"I am so sorry," he said, mortified. "The system break down

today. It's terrible." He dashed off and fetched them another bottle. They were drinking too fast.

"Let's order. I'm getting pissed," said Isabel rather loudly.

Eduardo took their order and they leaned back in their chairs and contemplated each other. Isabel looked vaguely uncomfortable.

"What's the matter?"

"Dafydd. I think the letter arrived this morning. 'Cell-Link Diagnostics,' right?"

"Oh, really?" He paused, realizing suddenly that at least one of his troubles could finally be laid to rest. "You should have opened it. Then we could really have celebrated." He felt annoyed that she'd not told him on the phone.

She looked at him quietly for a moment, then said, "I've got it in my handbag."

It shocked him somehow. There it was, finally, within reach. "Well, what the fuck. Open the bloody thing," he said, sounding more rankled than he meant to.

She hesitated. "Are you sure you want to open it now?"

"Well, you brought it. Why wait? Open it."

She promptly took the envelope from her bag and opened it with her bread knife. He watched her intently as she read it. He would remember this moment for a long time to come, for the rest of his days. Looking at her face, he felt a rush of cold, as if a bucket of freezing water had been thrown over him. He grabbed the piece of paper from her hands. They stared at each other.

"You liar," she whispered, "you fucking liar."

He was speechless. It could not be right. He looked at the paper. The words jumped about wildly, but he made out his name and that of Mark Hailey. Minimum 99.99 percent certainty. He knew what it meant: paternity was an absolute certainty.

"Why did you do it like this?" Isabel asked him with icy calm. "I always thought of you as an intelligent and sensitive man. I gave you every opportunity to tell me the truth. I told you I would accept it. So you fucked somebody years ago. I wouldn't have cared about that. An accidental pregnancy could happen to anyone. If you admitted you could have forgotten, been drunk, been seduced, raped, *anything*." Her voice had risen and there was a hush around their table. "Even if you said you'd been crazy about the woman and still ached for her, I would have accepted anything as long as it was honest. But no, you've been harping on about not even going near her. You wouldn't let up. Why insult me like that? *Why?*"

He saw Eduardo coming toward their table with their fish soup. Dafydd waved frantically at him to stop him from approaching. The man became confused and came anyway. The couple beside them were staring blatantly, as were a few other people. Isabel lit her cigarette and took a deep drag, turned her head and blew the smoke over their table. The woman coughed hysterically, squinting and waving her hand across her face. Eduardo was in a fluster and put the bowls of steaming soup down in front of them, retreating backward with his head bowed, ignoring the summons from the furious asthmatic.

"And what about the other things she claimed?" Isabel hissed.

"Please," Dafydd implored her, "you can't possibly—"

"Well, you've been lying to me about everything else. It's a good thing for you that she won't be able to prove rape." She puffed at the roach but it had gone out. "It's too late for that, I suppose."

"There is no way I—"

"Oh, shut up. Why do I bother? I've been listening to your bullshit for weeks now. Don't give me any more, I can't bear it."

There was nothing to say. His thoughts were so jumbled that he could make sense of nothing. Dafydd looked into his soup and saw a crab claw floating among the other bits. He loved crab claws. Now he swore to himself that he would never eat another one for the rest of his life. Some sort of oath had to be given. Perhaps it ought to be celibacy.

"What are you going to do about this?" she said, jolting him.

He shook his head. "I don't know. Have you any ideas?"

She relit the fag and they sat in silence for a few moments. Dafydd looked up at her. Her face was turned hard, almost ugly, by her anger. Still, he desperately wanted to touch her, to bring her back. She seemed to be receding from him and it frightened him. He reached over the table to cover her hand with his, but she snatched it away.

"We'll challenge this," he said with sudden confidence, slapping his hand down on the letter in front of him. "We'll talk to Andy about it tomorrow."

"*We?*" she huffed, incredulous. "With this one you're on your own, mate." She got up and dropped the smoldering fag into her soup. Then she gathered her smoking paraphernalia, stuffed them into her handbag and snatched her shawl off the back of her chair.

He tried to stop her by grabbing her wrist. "What do you mean by that?" he demanded. "Where are you going?"

She shook him off and brushed past the fascinated couple, upsetting their table, almost knocking the woman's glass over with her bag. Drops of red wine splashed onto the woman's buttered bread and she grabbed an inhaler, wheezing from it in a phony panic. The man ignored her and stared at Dafydd, almost in commiseration.

"Hey . . . ! Come back here . . . Isabel," Dafydd called after her. "Don't be ridiculous. This is wrong. I swear it."

"Oh, just . . . fuck off," she shouted back at him half across the restaurant.

Dafydd was fossilized on his chair. He should have gone after her, but he found he couldn't muster the physical and emotional stamina it would require. Fuck it . . . let her go, he thought angrily. It seemed *everybody* was out to get him. Either he was suffering from dementia, amnesia or whatever other derangement or somebody had found a way to steal his sperm. Who the hell could do this? Falsify a DNA test? It was absolutely fucking outrageous.

He leaned his face in his hands to shut out the people who

gawked at him. After a few minutes Eduardo came up to the table and put a compassionate hand on his shoulder.

"You wanna come and sit in my office. I've got some Amaro from my hometown. The best in the world." He allowed himself to be led away, into a deep armchair in a warm womb of a room and a large glass of black liquid placed in his hand.

"Don't worry. I got taxi for Isabella. She's okay. I fight with my wife alla time. You make it up tomorrow."

CHAPTER *10*

Moose Creek, 1993

Dafydd's left hand was pressing down on her smooth white abdomen, his right hand deep inside her vagina. The situation felt utterly surreal. Sheila had hardly looked at or spoken to him in the three months since the fatal Christmas party, and here he was touching her in the most intimate way.

His first instinct had been to refuse, especially when she requested the appointment out of hours, *with no nurse present,* but Sheila had almost pleaded with him when she approached him in the corridor that morning. Her alarming pallor and red-rimmed eyes had a surprising effect on him: his loathing of her softened instantly. Of course, he was also curious to know what on earth would bring her to *him* for a medical appointment. On some other level he must have really wished to see some vulnerability in Sheila, see the real person within, but he argued this notion with himself. He merely wanted a cordial working relationship with the woman.

Here she was, for the first time truly exposed. She was, literally, in his hands, and he could see that this was perhaps the opportunity to forge a measured peace between them.

"Sheila, how could you not have noticed?" he asked carefully.

"As I told you, I've had two perfectly normal periods, and

no symptoms whatsoever," she said. "I mean, I've never been pregnant, so I don't suppose I'd be that aware anyway."

"So what made you think you were?"

Sheila looked at him, then rolled her eyes up in her characteristically scathing way. "Well, eventually one can't fail but to notice. There is this great big lump growing inside my abdomen."

"It's not a great big lump—far from it—but there's no doubt about what it is," Dafydd agreed, having been put firmly in his place. "You're at least three months gone, probably more."

"Shit." Sheila covered her face with one hand, while Dafydd put a wad of tissues in her other hand. He moved away from her, pulled his gloves off and drew the curtain around the examination couch. He waited in his chair, his thoughts churning. Three months . . . she must have conceived around Christmastime. She was fertile, obviously not using birth control . . . He shuddered, thinking about if she'd gotten her way with him.

He looked out of the window. It was dark outside. Somehow he felt he shouldn't be there alone with her at this time of the night, yet it was only just after seven. By the weather, if not by the calendar, it was still winter. He had imagined that it wouldn't snow anymore as it was late March, but there it was again, great big snowflakes dancing their way down from the heavens, landing softly on the windowsill.

Sheila took a long time getting dressed behind the curtain, and when she eventually emerged she looked shaken.

"Sit down and tell me how I can help you," he said gently.

She sat down opposite him. She was out of her uniform and wore a green suede miniskirt that seemed utterly unsuitable for the occasion and the weather.

"You *can* help me, Dafydd. We can do it now."

Dafydd was confused. "Do *what* now?"

"A termination."

Sheila looked him steadily in the eye. "You can do that for me, can't you?"

Dafydd braced himself. So this was why she had come to

him. But she knew that he didn't do terminations, so why? He was definitely pro-choice, but it was just one procedure he refused to do. He'd done only two in his career, when he was a registrar. He couldn't explain it, even to himself, but both times he'd been disturbed by them and suffered nightmares. Sheila had many times tried to take him to task on this "weakness" of his, seeing that in Moose Creek terminations were more common than actual births.

"I don't do them, as you know. But Hogg does, and Ian. Why don't you talk to one of them?"

"No way," she shot back. "I absolutely don't want either of them involved. You're the transient one, and you keep your trap shut, that much I've noticed."

"Sheila, there is no problem about arranging for it to be carried out elsewhere. You can fly to Yellowknife and be back in a day. I'll ring them tomorrow morning if you want."

"No, that's too close. They know everything about us up here."

"Okay, Edmonton, then. Better still."

Sheila seemed not to be paying much attention. Her eyes were glazed over and she was lost in thought. She still had the tissues in her hand, and she was shredding off little pieces and rolling them between her thumb and forefinger.

As if she hadn't heard a word he'd said, she looked up at him. "Really, I mean it. We *could* do it now. Hogg's on call, but there's nothing doing. There's no one in theater. Janie is on the ward with Phil. I don't mind doing it under sedation. It's only an hour of your time."

"For God's sake, Sheila, it's out of the question. You need a proper anesthetic and it's . . ." There were so many objections, but he couldn't think of any single one that she wouldn't immediately quash. He changed direction. "What's your boyfriend's stance on all this?"

"I've not told him. The thing is, he's a stickler for prevention. You wouldn't catch him without his condoms."

Was she telling him that the baby probably wasn't his?

"Condoms break," he offered ineffectually, knowing that this was rare.

Sheila thought about this for a few moments. "Yes, they do, don't they?" she said finally.

"Have you thought about the option of having the baby? I mean, you're, what, thirty-two?"

"No, I hadn't thought about it." She leaned back in the chair and looked at him, but she wasn't really seeing him. Dafydd felt nothing he could say or suggest would really make an impact, and unless she confided in him he couldn't really offer anything. Some idea seemed to be churning away in her mind; perhaps she was testing the notion of actually becoming a mother. Suddenly she focused her piercing blue eyes on him and, leaning forward, said, "No, I really *do* want a termination. Please do it for me." She moved restlessly and shook her head as if to rid herself of the idea of motherhood. "I just want to deal with it tonight. Can you understand that? Now that I know what it is, I don't want it hanging over me. I feel really uncomfortable with this. In fact, I can't bear it. Go on, Dafydd, *please*," she implored him. "A shot of Valium, a little suction, a quick scrape, and I'm out of your hair."

Dafydd gathered his thoughts. He had to say no, but he didn't want to upset her. She was still leaning toward him, her full milky-white breasts noticeably bigger, spilling over the neckline of her black sweater. Before he'd had a chance to say anything, she laughed, reaching out and tapping his desk with her forefinger.

"In a place like this you've got to do each other the odd favor. You owe me one, don't you? I did you a favor, remember? And I would do it again . . . or if you prefer, I'll pay you."

Dafydd cringed. "Sheila, don't do this to yourself. Don't offer me anything. You should know me better than that. I want to help you, believe me. What's the big deal about waiting a couple of days?"

Suddenly she started crying. Dafydd was floored. These were real tears. Genuine distress always moved him, and she was obviously more troubled than he'd realized. He jumped up and went to her, putting his hand on her shoulder. "I'm so sorry," he said.

She looked up at him. "Well, fucking do it, then."

"I'm sorry," he reiterated.

"You're sorry? Is that it? You pathetic fucking Limey," she snarled through her tears. "You're a useless idiot, you know that?"

Dafydd's hand was still on her shoulder. "Take it easy, Sheila," he said sternly. "You're upset, understandably. It's been a shock, but it's not a disaster. *You* should know that. Your hormones are probably all over the place. Just calm down and we'll sort something out."

She pushed his hand away and flew up from the chair. "Don't you think I can do that for myself? I asked you for a simple favor. But no, you're too fucking selfish and precious to help someone out. What the fuck are you doing here anyway? Just hiding away 'cause you can't face up to your own incompetence. I shouldn't let you come near me. If you can take out the wrong kidney on a child, you probably wouldn't recognize a fetus if one smacked you in the face." She let out a withering laugh and gave him a shove in the chest. He grabbed her wrist, too hard.

Later, he couldn't recall exactly how it happened. She lunged at him like a wildcat, and without knowing how he could have done such a thing he'd slapped her across the cheek.

They both stopped dead and stared at each other, their arms still entangled in a grotesque embrace. If nothing else, the slap had calmed her. She seemed to go quite limp. "You'll live to regret this," she said coolly, pushing him away but not too vigorously.

"Sheila, I'm already regretting it," he said, his voice shaky with a mixture of dismay and spent anger. "I definitely should not have done that, and I apologize."

"You'll pay for it."

"I'm sure I will. But I beg you to remember that you attacked me first. Even so, it was inexcusable."

"Well, do it, then. I'll accept the abortion as an apology."

"*No.*" Dafydd ushered her firmly toward the door. "But I'll gladly do anything to facilitate it for you. You just give me the word." He opened the door for her.

Sheila slammed it hard behind her. It knocked a print off the wall in the hallway. Dafydd heard the thud and a splintering of glass and Sheila's footsteps hurrying away. He opened the door and surveyed the damage, then began to gather the shards with trembling hands.

Had she attacked him on purpose, was she that cunning? It was hard to imagine, it had all happened so fast.

The cold hadn't yet abated. Everyone complained and said it was the harshest winter on record. They also admitted that this was said every winter, since almost every winter was as hellishly cold. The town was ugly, inundated by the filthy mountains of ice and snow, hard as concrete. All manner of waste was frozen within and on top; even the sidewalks were a kaleidoscope of refuse, immortalized under the glacial surface. It was bleak. The darkness didn't seem to lift; no one really noticed that the days were getting longer. Depression, domestic violence, and alcoholism intensified at this time of the year. Those who were not indigenous to this land of extremes were the worst affected.

Dafydd, knowing his own shortcomings, was resourceful. His ankle had healed quickly and he was back on his skis. As the light allowed, he spent more and more time out in the wild. He'd sent for appropriate gear and the hood of his new parka extended like a tube away from his face, reducing the sphere of his vision but saving the delicate protuberances like nose and earlobes. The magic and the silence of the white trees alleviated his own seasonal angst. There was little sign of life, which was both comforting and uncanny. The only visible creature was the raven. It's jet-black wings flapping in the treetops caused soundless avalanches of powdery snow and its startling shriek occasionally shattered the stillness.

Dafydd had been warned about grizzlies. They didn't always hibernate. A grizzly will stalk its prey in total silence. Unlike other bears, it has little fear of man but avoids the proximity of human communities. Out here, Dafydd was drawn to confronting his fear of death. He believed in dramatic endings, as long as they were quick. His fear of death had always fluctuated in tune with his state of mind. In happy times he hated the idea of life ending so irrevocably, but in the last year death seemed like no big thing. Either way, when his time came to go, he wanted it to be in style. Mauled by a bear or frozen to death in the subpolar regions would do, rather than by prostate cancer or, worse, fading slowly in a nursing home in Swansea like his mother.

Most Saturdays he skied out to Ian's cabin, taking a shortcut through the woods and approaching it from an angle where the road was out of sight. The smoke from the chimney could be seen from afar. Since there was rarely a gust of wind, the smoke rose straight up in a rigid column, high into the stratosphere. Then, as he came closer, the sight of the little shack buried up to its shingles in snow, surrounded by tall trees dressed all in white. It reminded him of childhood elves and trolls and adolescent daydreams of wilderness and survival.

The puppy, Thorn, now grown to the size of a slim St. Bernard, would charge along the snowmobile tracks to meet him. He sensed Dafydd coming a mile off. Ian, too, was always happy to see him. He wasn't exactly a loner, since he was prone to waste hours in bars talking to people he didn't really like, but the remoteness of the cabin spoke of some need for distance and solitude. Dafydd envied him the space and had even looked around for something similar himself. But now, as the time was drawing nearer to the end of his contract, it didn't seem so pressing to get away from the gruesome trailer.

One Saturday morning Thorn didn't come to greet him as usual, and when he arrived at the cabin he found the dog sitting beside a car. Sheila's car. Judging by the time of the morning it appeared that she might have spent the night. Brave man, Dafydd thought, risking those sharp pretty little teeth. Hadn't he said he would succumb to them again? He wondered how often those two got it on. And why. The animosity between them was palpable at times. At other times they seemed to have some sort of restrained dependence on each other. Favors seemed to be traded, excuses made. Still, would Sheila be sleeping with Ian, when the pregnancy was such a big issue for her? And would Ian be sleeping with Sheila if he knew of the pregnancy? Could Ian be the father, perhaps?

Just a week had passed since Sheila's request for a termination. He winced, half from cold and half from distaste. The unpleasant incident had put a nail in the coffin of his enchantment with Moose Creek. Anyway, since it had happened, Hogg had not once patted him on the back, nor repeated his hale hopes for an extended contract, despite the fact that Dr. Odent had decided not to return from his sabbatical, and no efforts had been made to replace him.

Dafydd stopped at the side of the house and hesitated. It was a long way back and he'd looked forward to the generous glass (or glasses) of hot toddy that normally awaited him. Thorn was cowering beside the vehicle, and Dafydd snapped his fingers, attempting to lure him away from it. He wondered if the dog had been just let out or if he'd spent the night outside. Perhaps Thorn was wary of Sheila. Dogs were quite perceptive, after all.

Dafydd stiffened when he heard the door creak, then Sheila's husky voice.

"You'll need me."

"No." Ian's tense voice. "Aren't you hearing me? I'm broke."

Sheila's voice rose in annoyance. "That's what you said last time. All right, you're cut off. I don't need this. It's too complicated."

"That's a risk I'll have to take, Sheila. I'm really trying this time."

Dafydd stood motionless and Sheila didn't see him as she got into the car. As usual, she was dressed in clothing utterly unsuitable for the weather. Sexy skin-tight black trousers with a waist-length sheepskin jacket, dainty leather boots. No hat, scarf or gloves. The car started up effortlessly and she revved the engine angrily, but then she sat still, looking down into her lap. Suddenly she covered her face with her hands, and her shoulders hunched. She seemed to be crying.

There was something pathetic about her huddled form. It appeared she was capable of ordinary human feelings, after all. She was obviously in the throes of some personal crisis, something more, or other, than a mere pregnancy. Perhaps she was just unstable; although her mask never cracked in any work situation, no matter how stressful. Dafydd shrank within himself, knowing how Sheila would feel if she knew he was a witness to her misery, but he couldn't move away without risking being seen. A minute passed, then she wiped her eyes with the back of her hand. Slowly and carefully she backed down the tracks and disappeared toward the road.

What business were they discussing? Ian was cut off . . . from what? Surely not her sexual favors? He wouldn't care about that. Perhaps he did. Things certainly were quite different from what they appeared.

He waited a couple of minutes, then skied up to the front door. Thorn's joy of life was totally restored. Ecstatically he threw himself at Dafydd, who fell backward into the snow laughing. His face, still buried in the hood, got a thorough going-over by a long wet tongue.

"What was that all about?" he asked Ian after he'd discarded his many outer garments and flopped in front of the woodstove, glass in hand. The big yellow dog was steaming at his feet. "I was just coming up. I couldn't help hearing what you and Sheila said on the porch."

Ian looked annoyed at having been overheard. His eyes narrowed and he looked sharply at Dafydd. "I live out here in the nowheres specifically to avoid being eavesdropped on."

"Do you want me to fuck off?" Dafydd prompted, trying to hide a smile.

Ian's face broke into a wry grin. "No, don't fuck off. I have no one else to drink with." He patted Thorn on the rump. "The dog can't hold his liquor. He's no bloody good."

Ian was quiet and pensive for a long time, smoking cigarette after cigarette. Suddenly a thunderous rushing sound enveloped them. Dafydd looked up in alarm. "It's the rising heat," Ian said, keeping his eyes fixed on the open door of the stove. "That's the last of the winter snow sliding off the roof." He lit yet another cigarette and looked at Dafydd from under the unkempt hair falling across his forehead. "I don't suppose she's asked *you*?"

"Sheila?" Dafydd said, having been taken unawares. "I understand it's common practice . . . after hours."

"Is that what she said?"

There was an awkward pause and both men bent down simultaneously to stroke Thorn. Thorn opened a lazy eye and blissfully plopped it shut again. Dafydd was hesitant. Perhaps Sheila had asked Ian to do the termination, but it really wasn't his place to discuss a patient's procedure, even less if she was a colleague. Still, the drink made him careless, and he was curious. "I can't understand why she was so resistant to going away to have it done."

"So she *has* asked you."

"I just refused to do it. It's not my sort of thing, as you know. I hate terminations at the best of times."

Ian shrugged. "Well, she changed her mind." He sucked faithfully on his cigarette, his fingers stained a deep ocher. "She's keeping the baby."

"You're kidding?"

"She's had more than one termination, and I think she's counting on the current boyfriend. He's quite an investment. Good-looking, lots of money, never married, no baggage. Personally I think she'd be better off with Hogg. He's been in love with her since he first clamped eyes on her marble breasts, and that's at least six years ago. He's got money and he'd drop Anita like a hot coal if Sheila just said the word."

"I wondered about that. So perhaps . . . so Hogg and she . . . ?"

"What do I know about it?" Ian laughed. "He wouldn't be getting it very often. She'd meter it out, that's for sure. He's good for advantages, but he's not exactly a sex kitten, is he?"

Dafydd held his glass out for a refill. "You know, sometimes I can't work this place out. Are there no standards or morals? Sheila seems to think nothing of juggling all these blokes. My God, she's a really, *really* bad girl. Wicked. They don't make them like that very often. I can't help but admire her gall. In fact, I could use a bit of it myself. In moderation."

"Well, take it from me, she's *not* bad. She's good, diabolically good."

"No, she *is* bad," Dafydd insisted, feeling all loose and glowing from the hot whiskey.

"That's right," Ian cackled maliciously, "you'd love to get your chops around her wicked flesh. And she knows it, too. Don't worry. We've all been through it."

"Not a chance." Dafydd hesitated a moment, wondering if there was a grain of truth in Ian's comment. "I'm not proud of this, but when she came to ask me we had one hell of a ding-dong and I slapped her. I can't believe I did it, but she attacked me and I just sort of lost it. I've been waiting to get arrested, but I think I can plead self-defense."

"No kidding?" Ian tried to look concerned but there was a glitter of delight in his eye. "I can't imagine you beating up a woman, a pregnant one at that. You're such a pussycat."

"Oh, for God's sake . . . I didn't mean to, but she was trying to rip my eyes out."

"Whooo." Ian blew on his fingertips and then shook his hands as if burned. "You'll wish you'd never done that." He leaned back in his chair and lit another cigarette. He looked unwell, as he often did. His youthful features were lined, creating an odd impression of paradox. In his spectacular laugh there was an impish boy, full of life and up to no good, whereas the brooding man was inclined toward self-destruction, deeply lonely and alienated. Dafydd had observed him closely and realized that he still had no idea who this man really was. He knew nothing about his background, beyond his parents' ghastly demise in a fire, where he came from and why. He never talked about himself and tended to dismiss questions. The only thing Dafydd knew for sure was that Ian was the only person in Moose Creek who had showed himself to be something akin to a friend. For that reason Dafydd was willing to excuse him his bad moods and occasional impertinence.

Not long had they sat there, enjoying the roaring fire and the steady drip-drip from the eaves, when dusk was on them and it was time for Dafydd to ski back, or get caught in the dark of the forest.

"C'mon, shtay," Ian suggested, slurring slightly. "I'll drive you home later." He lifted his bottle of whiskey, which was still a third full, and shook it cheerfully.

"Oh, yeah, really," said Dafydd, laughing. "That'll be some ride."

The quantity and the potency of the hot toddies didn't keep Dafydd from panicking when, on his way back, he skied straight into a bison. The enormous animal was lurking just around a bend in the tracks, hidden by trees. Beyond it were a dozen others, stomping and scraping at the ground to get down to the frozen vegetation. The blue light of approaching nightfall tinted the snow yet made every particle of the world around him stand out with frightening clarity. The bison looked sinister and menacing, its dark looming body moving slowly toward Dafydd on the indigo snow. Dafydd had heard stories of a wayward herd of exceptionally large bison living along the valley, having escaped decades ago from the park of an eccentric breeder in Alberta. It was a bit like the Loch Ness monster: stories abounded of the mysterious herd but nobody knew anybody who had seen the animals.

A loud snort from wet nostrils burst through the silence, a rasping inhalation of breath, and the lowered head seemed to come before a charge. Dafydd's instinctive reaction was to throw off his skis and run, but the exercise proved futile. No sooner was he off the track than he dropped chest-high into the snow. Thrashing and scrambling, he could make no forward progress. A few seconds passed and the panic subsided. He turned and looked at his bloodthirsty adversary, which stood calmly observing his antics, chewing on a twig. The gentle brown eyes were filled with pity for him. Dafydd slunk back to within six feet of the massive head and retrieved his skis and poles. He skied home through the deepening darkness, carried on a charge of pure adrenaline, feeling very humble and realizing that he wasn't quite ready for a sudden dramatic death.

Derek Rose was dead. Lesley, his colleague and former lover in Bristol, phoned him at work late one afternoon.

"Can you talk?" she asked anxiously.

"Yes, I'm just about finished for the day. How are you? Everything okay?"

She told him straightaway. She had just heard it herself from another colleague.

"But you listen to me, now," she told him firmly. "It had nothing to do with you, you hear me? The cancer had spread to his lungs. He didn't have a chance. Probably never did."

Dafydd was startled by the news. He couldn't respond.

"Listen," Lesley pleaded. "His mum will be okay. She's got a nice bloke and they're expecting a baby. She's going to have it right here in the hospital." She paused, waiting for him to react. "Dafydd, come on. She's known for a while that Derek was very ill. She knew it was coming."

Dafydd saw Sheila approach him and he tried to wave her away, but she stayed, arms crossed, looking cool and fierce, tapping her sleeve and glancing at her watch.

"Perhaps I shouldn't have told you," Lesley was saying now. "I thought I was doing the right thing . . ."

"Yes . . . no, absolutely. Naturally you had to tell me, Lesley. It's good of you to let me know. I'm . . . I'm going to need a bit of time to let this sink in. Can I call you later?"

He put the phone down and looked out of the window. The sun was radiant, with the promise of spring touching everything, yet the land didn't know it yet. It still thought itself frozen, submerged as it was under the blanket of winter. Yet he could see that the ice was rotting, breaking up, leaving a gray slush to take its place, soon to drain away. This spring belonged to the living; nowhere else in the world could this be more true, and he was here, safe and alive. Where was the justice in that?

"What's up?" Sheila asked. "You look like shit. Someone back home given you the 'Dear John'?"

"You could call it that, I guess." Dafydd turned to her, wondering if there was so much as a particle of compassion hidden somewhere behind those glacial blue eyes. "Someone's died."

Sheila paused, the hostility of their unpleasant confrontation in his consulting room still hovering between them, but to her credit she looked suitably somber. "I'm sorry," she said briskly, "but try to put it away for the moment. We've got three potential corpses on our hands. Three boys, half drowned and with severe hypothermia. They stole Bowlby's car and drove it out on the ice at Jackfish Lake. You can imagine the rest."

That night, after hours of erratic, fitful sleep, he slid into a dream. A small animal was nudging him. The wet, cool nose poked him in the side, again and again. But he was afraid of it, so afraid he couldn't move. In the darkness the animal looked down at him. It was a fox, small and sharp-nosed. He knew that it was Derek, come to ask him why he was dead: why Dafydd had killed him. He screamed and Sheila appeared. She, too, wanted answers: what was wrong with him, why he was such a coward, why he called for her, screaming her name. He didn't want her but he was angry, seething with rage, so he took her. He wanted to hurt her and she let him. She seemed to like it. Her white body glowed in the dark, the place between her legs the color of fire. He tried to force himself into every dark cavity of her flesh. When finally she resisted, he bit her on the breast, on the stomach, on the mound where the hairs swirled like the serpents on Medusa's head.

CHAPTER 11

Cardiff, 2006

"Read it," Dafydd said, and Lesley read the report out loud:

> Dafydd Eric Woodruff is not excluded from pater-
> nity. The results obtained are twelve thousand times
> more likely that Dafydd E. Woodruff is the father of
> Mark Jeremy Hailey than that they are unrelated.
> The probability of paternity given the DNA evidence
> is a minimum of 99.99 percent.

"Pretty irrefutable," she said, shaking her head.

They were sitting in the conservatory, having first swept the bits of glass off the sofa. A pane had finally pushed itself out of its rotten frame and exploded on the tiles, leaving a gaping hole, but the temperature was mild; an Indian summer of sorts. A midday sun shone in on a fresh breeze. It was surely the last good weekend before a long dreary winter.

Dafydd got up to fetch more olives and cans of beer from the fridge.

"Pass this by me again," Lesley encouraged him as she popped the tab off another Stella.

"I reiterate. *It is not true.*" Dafydd turned to her and took a deep breath. "I hurt her once, I admit that, but I did not have sex with her. I didn't, I know I didn't. It's impossible. I couldn't have . . ." He looked at his best friend and erstwhile lover and saw the doubt that crept into her expression.

"What do you mean, *you hurt her*?"

"I didn't . . . Well, she drove me to it. I didn't mean to."

"She drove you to what?" Lesley moved toward him, her face intent. "How did you hurt her?"

"Oh, no," Dafydd groaned. "Not *you*, too. I slapped her once in self-defense."

"Look, Dafydd." Lesley looked unhappy. "I should tell you this. A couple of days ago Isabel rang me from London."

"Isabel? Really? What about?" She and Isabel had never gotten on; they were like different species. Lesley was as cool and pragmatic as Isabel was fiery and impulsive.

"She told me that this woman is accusing you of having drugged and raped her."

Dafydd was shocked. "Isabel rang you to tell you that?"

"Well, yes. It was very awkward. She asked me . . . if you'd ever been violent toward me, when we were together . . . in our sexual relations." Lesley seemed embarrassed. She was, after all, very straight. Years of singlehood, hard work, and an obsession with obscure research projects had not made her more at ease with the vagaries of human relationships, and now, at fifty-eight, she was too unworldly to give a damn about sexual politics.

Dafydd stared at her. "Are you serious?"

"I was quite stunned, to be honest." Lesley sounded *too* serious for his liking. "Now, why would she ask me that?" she said.

He thought about it for a moment and said, "Perhaps because she's thinking of leaving me and wants some really juicy justification."

Was that really the reason? He felt he no longer knew his wife or what was going on in her mind. She'd changed. He knew he'd failed her, broken their pact. Their aim, their wedding gift to each other, was to have a family. He'd wanted it then; it seemed the right thing to do. She'd yearned for a child more than anything, but now that they'd failed and he no longer wanted to keep flogging that seemingly dead horse, she had cooled, emotionally moved on from him and physically made herself absent, using his supposed lies about his past as an excuse.

Then he thought about wealthy, handsome, sharp, thirty-eight-year old Paul Deveraux, her new partner. *Partner?* Dafydd had not been totally blind. The way she looked: transformed, slender, confident, *glowing* . . . Her new perfume, skintight clothes, faraway expression, her wedding ring *lost* . . . He drew a sharp involuntary breath. *She was having an affair,* that was it, *she was sleeping with that slimeball.* The realization, suddenly clear as ice, was shattering, not least because Isabel was conniving to discredit Dafydd in her own eyes and justify her actions. Why otherwise would she revile him so brutally about some long-ago mistake, one that he couldn't even remember (and, in his mind, had never taken place)? And that phone call to Lesley, inferring a propensity for sexual violence. It was a horrible, underhanded move, and not worthy of her. She couldn't possibly believe in the crazy notion of him as a *rapist.* He was an enthusiastic lover, or had been, and his fantasies could occasionally veer toward overpowering, subjugating, and possessing a woman he wanted, *but that was all it was.* Didn't everyone have those kinds of fantasies? Isabel and he used to share them; in their first couple of years she'd often wanted him to be Neanderthalish in his approach, she'd ask for it and he was only too happy to comply. What turned her on, turned him on, too. Was she twisting these little private scenarios of theirs to her own ends, or was she really wondering . . . ?

Lesley clapped her hands together in front of his face. "Hey, I'm still here."

"I'm sorry, Lesley." He turned to her and wondered if he should share this awful suspicion, but he had no actual proof of an affair and he still owed Isabel his loyalty. Instead he asked, "What was your answer? What did you say to her?"

"I should have told her to mind her own damned business, but I thought it wouldn't really help you. I told her you were a gentleman through and through."

Dafydd laughed. "A *gentleman*? How sexy! I'd say you just don't remember."

Lesley chuckled and looked becomingly pink in the face. "Well, it is fifteen years ago, at least. What do you expect?"

Dafydd took her hand and looked into her eyes. "Lesley. You *know* me. There is no reason I should lie to you, is there? Will you believe me if I say I never slept with this woman in Canada? I would like for just one person to give credence to my word of honor."

"Oh, for God's sake. Don't be so melodramatic," Lesley dismissed him with a cheerless laugh. "How can I, Dafydd? I'm a scientist. I know DNA testing is foolproof. It's miraculous; in fact it's changed everything. Look at all we achieve, the crimes we can solve—"

"All the fathers we can nail for child support," he interrupted. "Sure, Lesley, I agree with you." Dafydd looked through the gaping hole in the glass and saw the toolshed, still on its side in the garden, the scattered branches that the storm blew down, the wheelbarrow full of turf, abandoned weeks ago in mid-job. It would all have to wait. He'd had enough. There was only one thing to do.

"Listen, Les. I've just made up my mind. I'm going there. I've got holiday coming, and I can take some unpaid leave. I'm going to Canada to sort this out, if it's the last fucking thing I do."

Lesley clinked her can against his, but her face was neutral. "How do you suppose you'll do that?"

"I have absolutely no idea. If those kids look like me, I guess I'll have to accept it." He took the snapshot of Miranda and Mark from his wallet and gave it to her. "I don't see any resemblance there at all, do you?"

She looked at it briefly over the rim of her specs. "I'm sorry, Dafydd, but I think it's immaterial."

"We'll see."

"Well, bon voyage, then," seemed all she could think to say.

The weather had changed from one day to another. An unusually cold snap had Dafydd digging in the attic for his father's old sheepskin coat. There was a threat of snow, but the skies were holding back, waiting to shake loose and whiten the muddy fields of the vale. In the meantime it rained freezing needles that whipped in all directions.

Dafydd stopped on the road below the castle, got off his bicycle and fought off his cumbersome waterproofs. He wheeled the bike quickly up the hill toward the Roman wall, and when he raised his face against the icy rain he was dismayed to see that Isabel had gotten there before him. He'd not seen her car parked on the road or in the parking lot, and there were no other signs of human presence. This was her choice of meeting place, a strange one, although they knew it well, implying that even a pub would be too intimate.

She was standing up against the stone face to avoid the worst of the rain, looking as though at her post, leaning on the ancient wall, even dressed in a light-colored cloak, belted tight at the waist and flowing full to her ankles, and sturdy leather boots. Her demeanor was stern, her profile positively Romanesque, her short hair damp and clinging to her temples. She stood motionless, for a moment a wholly archaic apparition. He stopped and stared at her, but she looked far off, as if she were part of a distant past. The habit of tenderness for her came in a rush, overwhelming him, threatening to bring tears and stinging his eyes, yet when she turned, the coolness and self-possession of her gaze chilled him. He put the bike down, scrambled over the rocks and joined her in a crouch behind the wall.

"This is my new pad, as a single woman." She smiled and

flicked a drop of snot from the end of his nose with her fore-finger.

"It will be a lonely life. Cold and inhospitable," he said.

"Not as cold and inhospitable as yours might be."

"Mine is just a reconnaissance trip. I'll be back," he said with emphasis. "You *know* that." He waited a moment, looking at her. "What about you? Are you coming back?"

"I don't know, Dafydd." She picked at some lichen on the wall, then examined her nails. They were smooth and even. It appeared that she'd stopped biting them. "I don't know if we can repair things, but I admit I'll be interested to know what sort of conclusions you find for yourself over there." She searched her pockets for her gloves and pulled them on. "If ever I can understand what you're up to, what's going on inside your head. If I could only . . ." She stopped and stared at her boots.

Dafydd looked down, too, into the wet grass, and wondered if she was thinking of the picnic they'd had there, three summers earlier. There'd been an incredible sunset and the light had lingered. They'd eaten some dried-up petrol station sandwiches and drunk a whole flagon of cheap cider, strong as wine, making them giggly and rude. He'd pushed her down on the grubby blanket, whipped off her shorts and knickers and yanked down his fly. Lying spoon-fashion, he pulled a corner of the blanket over her naked hips. As she cried out, quite noisily for her, an American woman tourist prattled, oblivious, on the other side of the wall. "Gee, don't you just love it. He forced his troops to build it just to keep them from getting lazy. It says right here . . . Don't climb on it, honey. It might crumble and you'll break a leg."

"Why did you want to meet *here*?" he asked.

"I was curious to see if going backward could undo something." She turned her wet, pale face toward him. "I was longing to have something back. It's been devastating to lose everything."

"Everything?" Dafydd frowned. "There's still me, your husband, and our home together."

"Trust is a considerable thing. Don't belittle it." After a moment she added, "And finding that someone you thought you knew so well was in fact not that person at all, well, it's pretty bloody devastating."

"Yes, you're right, it *is* devastating," Dafydd said pointedly. She didn't seem to hear what he meant, but she let a sudden sob escape.

He felt suddenly detached. It was almost comical. Only months ago they believed their love was forever . . . Irreconcilable differences—or whatever it was called in the courts—could sneak up on one like a mugger in a dark alley.

Isabel was crying. Dafydd wasn't sure what her grief meant, for whom or for what she was weeping: him, their marriage, the child they would never have . . . or her own duplicity. He put his arms around her and she didn't push him away.

"I'm hoping to come back and explain it to you." He kissed her hair, rocking her gently. "But first I must explain it to myself."

There was no point in saying anything more. After a long moment in his arms she looked up at his face, then traced the red scar inside his hairline with her thumb. "Don't go having accidents like that."

"You should have stayed with me. I needed you desperately." His voice bore a touch of resentment, and he hoped she would express a little bit of regret. "You've made yourself absent and we never had a chance to talk."

Isabel had no regret or apology. She was blotting her mascara on a tissue and her face was no longer soft. She disentangled herself from his arms.

"There was nothing to say and I was angry."

"You can also be unnaturally callous."

Isabel laughed. "Are you calling me a bitch?" Looking blue with cold, she put her hands deep into her pockets and hunched her shoulders. "Anyway, Paul wanted me in London. There's this new project . . . life must go on. He's got lots of plans for us."

I bet! *Bastard* . . . Dafydd felt a surge of bitterness, and he knew he should confront her, but he didn't have the strength for it. It would just drive a greater wedge between them and he was leaving tomorrow. She would do what she liked anyway. Why give her a hard time? Why try to stop her? She'd have to decide what she wanted, without him there competing for her.

"I want to go now. I'm freezing," she said.

They started down the hill, Dafydd pushing his bike, and after a while Isabel pulled away from his side, heading in a westerly direction. Dafydd, lost in thought, didn't notice at first. He ran to catch up with her.

"I'll see you to your car."

"No . . . let's part here. I've been to the house and picked up some clothes and I'm driving straight back to London." She stopped and kissed his cheek, hesitated, then kissed the other. "Good luck, Dafydd."

"Do you love me?" he called pathetically to her back, but perhaps she didn't hear him. He stood and watched her go while small white dots danced around him. It had finally started snowing.

CHAPTER 12

Moose Creek, 1993

Dafydd had taken to weekly visits to the homestead of Sleeping Bear. The old man had survived the winter, miraculously, without any real help. His health had been excellent and the visits were mainly to restock Bear's supply of drink, tobacco, and newspapers. His food came from some unnamed source and consisted of repulsive lumps of meat, plus other grotesque substances of a bestial nature. He seemed to function just fine on them, but knew better than to invite Dafydd to share his meals. His stamina was in fact remarkable.

However, just as spring was actually thawing things out, on one of these visits Sleeping Bear was wrapped up in his bed with a high fever. Dafydd was certain he'd contracted pneumonia. At home, the old-timers of the profession used to call pneumonia "the old man's friend" since it saved the elderly from further decrepitude by a peaceful, painless death. Dafydd didn't believe in prolonging life unnecessarily and unkindly, but Sleeping Bear did not seem ready to go. He was like an old piece of hide. Soak it in hot water, grease it up and it would be as good as new. He was useful to no one bar his dogs, but there was still kindling to be gathered for the stove, pipes to be stuffed, and strong coffee with firewater to be drunk. Although Bear was hell-bent on staying put in his own bed, using his own tried-and-tested remedies coupled with some antibiotics by mouth, Dafydd finally put his foot down.

"You're bloody coming in, even if I've got to fasten your feet to the Chrysler and drag you there."

"I'll get you for this, you little shit. I knew you'd want to clean me up in your cotton-pickin' hospital. I have no call to go there. You juss wanna give me a bath, ass-all." As he got upset he started to shiver and shake. Dafydd picked him up in his arms, and the man, although fairly tall, was as light as a cardboard cutout.

"Put me down, or else," Bear threatened, although his resistance was crumbling. "I won't talk to you ever again . . . not for years, anyway."

"Look, old man. One more day here on your own, two at the most, and your dogs will be feeding on your flesh . . . what's left of it."

He carefully placed Bear on the back seat of the car, tucking him in with his filthy quilt and several blankets that were stowed in the back of the car for emergencies.

Four days later Bear was back on his feet, walking around the hospital corridors, his scrawny legs sticking out from under his green gown. In fact he seemed to be enjoying the comforts of the hospital. The dogs were fed by his grandson, and Dafydd was secretly supplying him with the drink that had pickled him for God knows how many decades, and without which he would surely give up the fight.

"Now, my young fella, listen 'ere. Make sure that carrot-topped nurse don' catch you bringing the stuff. She's one testy son of a gun. She'll boot us both out the door."

"Believe it or not, she has no say over me. I'm actually her senior."

"Gee whiz," Bear exclaimed, impressed. "Dip me in vixen's musk and roll me in goose feathers."

"Make that two of us," Dafydd agreed.

As the days went by, Bear made no move to get up and pack his things for a return to the cabin. Dafydd decided to let him stay until he was good and ready. Perhaps, having slept in a comfortable bed with clean sheets, eaten palatable food, and enjoyed the company of other old folks on the ward, he was taking to the creature comforts. For sure his cheeks had filled out. He was shaven clean and his waist-length hair had been washed and braided by Janie.

On the tenth day, Dafydd decided to challenge him.

"You getting soft, or what? I can't believe you're still lolling here as if you were infirm. I never thought I'd see the day."

Bear seemed unfazed by the bait. He motioned to Dafydd to lean closer.

"I tell you what I'm doing," he whispered. "I'm building up my strength for a great, long journey. I reckon it be my last one."

"What sort of journey?"

"I'm takin' meself up farther north. To the other side of Great Bear Lake. West of Coppermine." Bear was glancing this way and that, fearful that his plans might be overheard and thwarted by some busybody.

"That's mighty far. How are you planning to travel?" Dafydd asked, intrigued.

"Ah, well, there're a whole load of different possibilities." He stopped to sip furtively from the mug that Dafydd had provided him. "Years ago I'd have hitched up the dogs. But now, of course, one can fly." He looked slyly at Dafydd.

"I don't believe they fly to the Coppermine region from Moose Creek. I guess you've got to get yourself to Yellowknife or Inuvik and go from there."

Bear stifled a laugh. "There won't be no commercial flights where I'm going."

"Perhaps your grandson could arrange a pilot to take you there direct. Mind, that would cost a packet."

"Nah, my grandson doesn't approve of the friend I want to visit."

"Friend?"

"Yeah. I was kinda wondering. I thought you could use a bit of counsel. My friend is an *angatkuq,* an Inuit shaman. Not one of these newfangled self-appointed flag-bearers. No, no"—Bear tut-tutted and wagged his finger—"the *old* kind. The real thing."

"You think I need some counsel, do you?" Dafydd laughed. "How do you know this man?"

"Many years ago, much before you were born, he spent some time in Moose Creek. He came here after having been banished by his own people."

"What'd he done?"

Sleeping Bear's cheeky grin vanished and at once he looked impossibly old and grave. "He was asked to heal a child. The child was mortally injured and would have died regardless, but he blamed himself for the death. Then the missionary and the government people stuck their noses in and decreed to prohibit shamanism. The people listened to this and the elders decided to cast the shaman out. After many years the people forgot, and he was allowed to return to his land."

Dafydd stared at him and felt a sudden bitter ache inside his chest. He had hidden his grief for weeks, fearful of letting it erupt. He'd never even known little Derek, but the boy's fate seemed to be intrinsically linked with his own. His pointed little face and searching eyes came to Dafydd in his dreams, more often than ever since the boy's death. Dafydd fought the tears that seemed to well from the depths of his throat; he swallowed repeatedly but could not contain his sadness. Hiding his face in his hands, he took several deep breaths.

"I reckon it would be damned good for you to meet him." Sleeping Bear patted Dafydd's knee with his leathery hand. "And anyway, I could use the company."

The thaw had started in earnest. Water ran, dripped, slushed, and gurgled everywhere. The region had so little rainfall that not much farther north it was termed a desert, but still the ac-cumulation of snow over the winter released the torrents that flooded basements and made grubby rivers down streets, over-filling ditches and making the ground sodden. Some nights were cold enough to refreeze the whole lot to the core, leaving a glassy surface that created mayhem with cars and pedestrians. Nevertheless there was optimism in the air. Teenagers could finally revert to wearing skimpy garb and footwear, snowmobiles went in and trail bikes came out of storage and women planned their vegetable gardens, short-lived as they were going to be.

Dafydd's contract with the hospital was finally reaching its end and Hogg had come to think that Dafydd's departure would be a great loss to the community, or so he said to try to convince Dafydd to stay.

"I know you and Sheila don't always see eye to eye on things, but I'm sure the wrinkles can be ironed out, given time," he argued. "I'd like to make you a permanent member of staff at an excellent rate. A young man like you could have a great future in Moose Creek. The town will grow. Civilization will reach out to embrace us. Come on, David—I mean, Dafydd—do think about it."

For a brief moment Dafydd had vacillated. He didn't know what he was going home to, but there was his mother, quite ill and increasingly distressed about his absence. He felt he had to justify his surgical training, which he could hardly advance in Moose Creek despite the hair-raising emergencies that sometimes required his skills. The embrace of civilization would not happen for a long time, if ever. But more than anything he had to face the situation he'd left behind. He could not escape it forever. Perhaps in these extraordinary and demanding ten months he'd grown a little as a person, as a man, but as a doctor he still felt afraid of himself. He knew that the sooner he came face-to-face with his nightmares, the better. And much as he hated to admit it, Sheila was a factor in leaving the job. He could not foresee a harmonious working relationship with her, and with Hogg there was no contest between them: Hogg would never see *her* go.

* * *

Dafydd postponed his ticket back to Britain in order to accompany Sleeping Bear on his last quest. It took two weeks to make the necessary arrangement. The Chrysler was no longer available to him and in the end Bear's grandson offered them the use of a Ford station wagon for the long drive southeast to Yellowknife. From there they would fly straight north to the land beyond the Arctic Circle. Thinking that Bear's suggestion that Dafydd come along might have been due to a shortage of funds, Dafydd offered to pay, but there was no such motive. It appeared that there was a sizable sum of money earning interest in the bank. Bear's trapping and ice-hauling days had been profitable and he rarely touched his stash. Now he set about spending. Many gifts, tools, clothes, and gadgets for his host and his daughter.

In the meantime Dafydd roamed around on foot, enjoying the cataclysmic effect that spring was having on the snowy landscape he had so delighted in. He saw the town from a new perspective, not having to be under the constant threat of harrowing medical emergencies, or bored to distraction by one case of cough, flu or sniffle after another. He was free to *be,* without even having to worry about his behavior or if people trusted him. Just another ordinary unemployed citizen or a tourist, whichever suited his mood.

After all these months he felt safe about asking Brenda out.

"Just to thank you for the benefit of your bright face and good humor," he said to be clear. "A few drinks and a nice meal somewhere. How about it?"

The question of why he'd waited until his last week to ask her out remained unspoken, although he could see that she was puzzled. Anyhow, he would not have been able to come up with an adequate answer, not even for himself, except that she was not the sort of woman he'd fall in love with and there were too many others vying for her company. Yet there was absolutely nothing wrong with the lady. She was funny and sexy and talked a lot, running a witty commentary on everybody who was anybody in the town. He listened and laughed, feeling merry, coveted, definitely seen but absolutely not heard. What did it matter? He wondered why he'd deprived himself of her good company all this time. She could have been a much-needed friend, if that was possible after their tryst at Jackfish Lake.

Halfway through their meal in a smart new restaurant, Sheila walked in on the arm of a rugged beefy man with a massive jaw and bushy eyebrows. The proverbial lumberjack was in fact a clever businessman, Dafydd had been told, but he certainly looked the part. Sheila no doubt was a good match for him, making up with a surplus of feminine guile what she lacked in size. She looked stunning in a short, flowing orange dress, her legs strapped into knee-high lace-up boots. Dafydd glanced involuntarily at her abdomen and saw the unmistakable swelling.

From the door Sheila looked first at Brenda, checking her from top to toe, the expert eye quickly sizing up the competition. It appeared she found it not a threat because she smoothed back her red hair and dragged the boyfriend up for introductions.

"This is Dafydd, the young Welsh doctor you haven't met," she said without a glance toward Brenda, "the one who couldn't cope with the rigors of the north and is leaving town."

Although Dafydd had never seen her take a drink, her eyes had an unfocused look about them and her cutting comment seemed unnecessarily offensive. The boyfriend looked baffled and embarrassed but nodded briefly at Dafydd, then turned to Brenda, leaning forward and kissing her on the cheek. "Hi, honey. You're looking mighty fine. Enjoying your dinner?"

"Sure, Randy." Brenda looked at him with sparkling eyes. "Hey, why don't you guys join us?"

There was an awkward silence. Dafydd looked at his plate of spaghetti, aware that his mouth was plastered in tomato sauce, and a forkful of it had splattered his shirtfront. The indignity of the situation and the idea of sharing a table with Sheila made him forthright.

"No, Brenda. Not tonight." He looked earnestly at Randy. "It's nice to see you both but we're on a date. You two have a really nice evening."

Sheila pulled him lightly by the tie, putting her face close to his. "Aw . . . ain't that cute? You be sure to come and say good-bye to us all before you rush home to that shitty little country of yours." Brenda and Randy fell silent and looked at them. Sheila's rudeness seemed absurdly out of order. She straightened up and with a cool smile she grabbed her boyfriend by the arm and pulled him away.

Brenda looked from Dafydd to the back of Sheila. "Hey, what was that all about? Don't tell me you got on the wrong side of *her*."

"Not a bit," Dafydd grinned. "We're great pals."

"She looked stoned," Brenda mused. "She better watch it. Randy is quite a catch, and he's not into drugs. I sure know that about him, plus another thing or two."

After paying the bill, Dafydd excused himself and went to the men's room. When he came out Sheila was standing outside the door, seemingly waiting for him.

"What are you doing with *her*?" she asked, leaning against the wall with her arms crossed.

"Why do you ask?" he asked, taken aback. Sheila had never shown any sign of being jealous or in any way interested in his private life.

"You know, I'd hoped I'd seen the last of you." She looked unstable on her feet and there were tiny beads of sweat on her upper lip. "Be that as it may, I want you to know I'm going to do something."

"What?" he asked with foreboding.

"I'm gonna take matters into my own hands. Just so you know."

"What are you talking about?"

"I want your professional advice. What do you recommend, Dr. Woodruff? What would they use in little Britain? A hypertonic saline solution, applied with a catheter and a great big fifty-mil syringe? I could do it myself, easy, couldn't I? That would do away with the problem, don't you think?"

"Oh, for heaven's sake, Sheila, that's crazy," he exclaimed.

"Anyway, I don't believe you. You wouldn't. You're too far gone, anyway." Dafydd was troubled by her behavior. He wasn't sure if she was drunk or stoned or ill. "Listen, Sheila, you don't look well. Let me get Randy—"

"Don't bother. Thanks to you, that relationship is about to have the kiss of death. He's already asking about my thick waist."

"Not thanks to me, Sheila. It's not *my* doing. Why are you projecting all this shit on me? I did offer to refer you somewhere else. You could have had it done in any bona fide hospital."

"Projecting shit on *you*? You're *kidding*," she said. "After what you did—"

"What do you mean?"

"Never mind." She tottered slightly.

Randy came toward the lavatory, and when he saw them standing there together his expression changed. He stopped, warily scrutinized their faces and was about to say something but then thought better of it and brushed past them into the men's room.

"Listen, I want nothing to do with this business, I've told you," Dafydd hissed. "Besides, my contract with the hospital is terminated, over, finished! This is *goodbye,* Sheila."

"It was your fucking suggestion to have the baby. You put the thought in my head. All that bullshit about breaking condoms and stuff. Well, guess what I just found out? Randy's had the chop, years ago."

Dafydd reflected on this uncharacteristic confession. Sexually transmitted diseases were rife in the town, and Randy must have used protection because he'd never trusted his beloved, never knew where she'd been, never foresaw a future in the relationship. Sheila was a temporary diversion. He'd just used her, like she'd used him. Sheila was pointing her finger toward his face.

"Ever since you landed here with your sharp suit and your nose in the air, you've pissed me off." She leaned her head back against the wall, exposing her smooth white neck. Dafydd suddenly felt very sorry for her. Sheila's little plan to start a family

and become respectable was obviously on the brink of disinte-
gration. Despite her strong, capable exterior, she was actually
a rather messed-up lady whose glassy casing was cracking up,
whose plan had failed disastrously.

"Why is all this venom directed at *me,* Sheila?

She glared at him without answering.

"Do I perhaps remind you of someone? Is that it?" he asked
reasonably. "I've tried to keep my head down and just do the
job to the best of my abilities. Why does that make me such an
unmitigated arsehole?"

"Yeah, now that you mention it, you *do* remind me of someone." Sheila peered at him with dim eyes. "He was one pompous,
stuck-up, condescending twat. Exactly like you. Soooo aloof.
Soooo detached. I was never bloody well good enough for him,
no matter what I did. Just like you, he thought he could . . ."

Dafydd stopped listening. This shower of insults had an interesting element to it, but he was suddenly very weary. Sheila
was still haranguing him, but he knew that nothing he could say
would make any difference. He switched off and waited impatiently for Randy to reappear so at least he could leave Sheila
in safe hands.

At the end of the evening Dafydd and Brenda went for a
stroll around town. A mild spring wind blew and there was
a scent of pine in the air. The ground seemed dry for the first
time in weeks. He showed her the new running track behind
the recreation center. It was a soft path covered in wood chips,
on which he had recently been taking some morning runs. A
perfect half-moon shone down and showed it littered with beer
cans and other items of teenage consumption.

"If it wasn't so early in the year, I'd take you for a swim
at the lake," Brenda chuckled drunkenly. "You do remember,
don't you?"

"I do," Dafydd said, taking her hand and kissing it lightly.

"Making love out-of-doors . . . you can't beat it." She turned
and looked at him. He saw where this was leading and that he'd
better turn her right around and get her out of there, but already his

resolve was weakening. Christ . . . it had been months. One of his father's quirky educational gems came back to him: *Remember, my lad, a stiff prick has no conscience.* The concept of a stiff prick with a tiny brain, sly and godless, had puzzled him in childhood, and in the early days when he'd slept with a woman for the first time his father's admonition had popped up before him. Invariably he'd felt a brief divorce from his brazen self-gratifying member.

But Brenda was a fully grown woman, he argued with himself; what about *her* conscience? Why was it up to him to be restrained? In answer to it, Brenda had slipped her hand around his back and was stroking his bottom in a casual manner. He put his arm around her shoulder, and they walked farther down the path into the willow grove, away from the litter and the bright light of the half-moon.

The time of the journey had finally come. The preparations were all made. Dafydd had moved out of his trailer and put his belongings in storage with Ian, where he would spend the last week of his stay before flying home to Britain.

The ice road was melting and Bear's grandson had decided that he wouldn't get his car back in time, so they caught the last bus of the season. The thaw had accelerated and it was merely days before the road would become impassable and Moose Creek would be isolated from the civilized world, an island of self-contained endurance.

From Yellowknife they chartered a small plane to take them to Black River on the shores of the Arctic Ocean. The tiny hamlet itself was ugly, built mostly as it was from soulless prefabricated government-issue dwellings. From the plane it looked as if God Himself had thrown a handful of dice haphazardly across the ice. The only building of some beauty was a clapboard church, painted white and seemingly ancient. The place itself was spectacular. The ice blocks along the shore and the jagged icebergs in the distance shimmered in the clear air. Inland, the tundra seemed to extend forever, flat and bleak. It was black in patches, having lost some of its snow. In the far distance, white mountains lined the horizon.

They watched a tiny figure scurrying toward the airfield, and when the plane landed he stood waiting for them. The two old men greeted each other with many backslaps and handshakes. Angutitaq was as ancient as Bear, if not even older. He was shrunken in stature and bowlegged, and his face was crisscrossed with so many wrinkles that his features were buried deep within them. When he laughed the folds and ridges split apart and a mammoth grin offered two remaining teeth stained yellow with age and tobacco.

His house lay on the outskirts of the settlement. They walked the short distance from the airfield. The daughter was waiting for them at the house, and Dafydd was surprised at how young she seemed, considering the age of her father.

"What about his wife? Where is she?" Dafydd quietly asked Bear.

"She died in the influenza when she was pregnant with her second child. Don't mention her. We'll never hear the end of it. The influenza took most of his friends, too; it's a mighty sore point."

The father and daughter spoke to each other in their native tongue. Dafydd was astonished when Bear suddenly joined in, sounding fluent in the mysterious language. He had no idea that Bear spoke Inuktitut. Bear corrected him: the language of the Copper Inuit was Inuinnaqtun. "I've been around," said Bear, puffing his meager chest out. "I wasn't always holed up in Moose Creek."

The first evening was spent smoking, drinking tea, and eating in the tiny living room. There were many chairs in various states of dilapidation, a sofa and a small table in the middle. That table seemed to be the central point of much village hobnobbing. A steady stream of villagers came to look at the visitors and take part in the talk. Some of the elders stayed long into the night, conversing animatedly, alternating between Inuinnaqtun and, for Dafydd's benefit, a curious archaic English.

The food, bowls of plain salty noodles with bits of seal meat, and the tea were served by the daughter.

Angutitaq seemed delighted with his guests and the fascination they engendered in his neighbors. He held forth while smoking continuously on a cracked old pipe. In spite of the fact that he looked like something that had lain drying in a cellar for centuries, his mind was sharp and his humor peculiar. He talked rapidly, using his pipe as a pointer, waving it to emphasize his remarks. Each statement was punctuated by comical laughter. Dafydd sensed that he already knew why Bear had invited him, apart from the role of companion and general minder.

Uyarasuq, the daughter, moved like a shadow around the old men and women, filling up their tin mugs with tea and stoking the woodstove, occasionally letting rip a bell-like laugh, usually at something her father had said. Dafydd took Bear aside and asked him the approximate age of the woman, but Bear's grasp of time was unreliable.

"Where is her family? Doesn't she have a husband?"

"Sshh," Bear whispered, "don't mention her husband. Angutitaq holds very bad feelings about him. We'd never hear the end of it. He had a child with another woman. Now he's in jail for chopping off a man's fingers in a brawl." Bear chuckled quietly. "The scoundrel did do them all a favor. He was the main reason the elders voted to ban alcohol in Black River."

"Are they separated . . . or divorced?"

Bear looked at him uncomprehendingly. "He's in jail. I told you. Now, *sshh*."

Angutitaq tried to teach Dafydd the names of his guests, and Dafydd's attempt at pronouncing them caused tremendous hilarity among the old folks. They literally doubled up with laughter, tears rolling down their cheeks, and asked him to say the names again and again. Dafydd wasn't sure if they were laughing at him or at his ineptitude. An old lady named Kenojuaq, who sat next to him, patted Dafydd's thigh and drew his attention to some sort of tag on a leather string around her neck.

"My Eskimo number," she said in her singsong accent. "When

I was a young girl, the government told us that we had to wear them always, not to get them dirty or lose them. We were told to give up our names, because they were too hard to say. But most of us have found them again and taken them back."

"Do you still have to wear those?" Dafydd asked, appalled, looking around at other people's necks. This was cause for yet more merriment. Only the daughter didn't laugh; she looked pained. She leaned forward to whisper in Dafydd's ear.

"She won't admit it, but she's proud of her tag. It's lasted a long, long time."

Dafydd turned and looked at his host's daughter. Her face up close looked younger still, her skin fine and smooth like a baby's.

"Do you live in this house?" he asked her.

"No, not always." She smiled. "I have my own house."

But did she have a life of her own, he wondered, in this tiny settlement without roads, shops, restaurants, nothing at all apart from vast expanses of beautiful but frigid vistas? Everybody seemed to be so old. He would have liked to talk to her more, but she was busy, or didn't give him the opportunity. Her eyes seemed always to be elsewhere, although a few times he caught her looking at him. Finally, quite late in the evening, she sat down beside him.

"Do you like country food?"

"I like most foods. What exactly is country food?"

She bent toward him and listed them on her fingers, her brow narrowed in concentration.

"Well, caribou, that's the most country, either as *quaq* or *mipku,* or in a stew. Fish, smoked or *piffi.* Seal is good, particularly the flippers. *Hik-hik.* I've seen the odd goose and duck. They seem to have come early this year. If I see one tomorrow, I could shoot it." She looked up at him. "What would you like to try?"

"I'll have any of those," he said, smiling, "as long as it's country."

"Tomorrow," she said and went back into the kitchen.

Dafydd had a fitful night sleeping on the lumpy old sofa in his sleeping bag. The second day dawned and passed much as the first. People coming and going in the living room, eating, smoking, and drinking endless glasses of tea. He was longing to go out and experience the surroundings, but there was nowhere to go apart from straight across the flatness. He walked down to the shore at midday surrounded by five children, the only ones in the hamlet, all eager to talk to him about motorbikes and films. The sea ice rumbled and crackled ominously, in the throes of rotting and breaking up, and the children fell about laughing at his feigned terror.

Back in the little dwelling and forced into inactivity, he gradually relaxed and was content just to sit and listen to the endless ebb and flow of the old men's strange conversation. He wasn't used to this much leisure time and it was a novelty to lie back in an old armchair and be thoroughly lazy. He was lulled into a cozy stupor and found himself becoming mesmerized by the movements of Uyarasuq. She looked eerily similar to the girl whose frozen body he'd examined. The broad face and coarse black hair, the high cheekbones and wide-set, oriental eyes.

Finally all the guests had come and gone. The voices of the two old men blended into a hum of agreeable rhythms, while smoke from the woodstove added a beguiling haze to the small living room, as if he were watching an old grainy film. Outside, the silence was so complete that it was almost like a sound in itself, a white, empty tone that went on and on.

He felt so relaxed that he even wondered if the old boys were slipping him something in his tea. Or maybe *she* was. It was a luxury to let the hours just float away, reading the odd passage from a novel he'd brought, intermittently studying the Inuit woman, trying to understand what was underneath that exotic but rather reserved demeanor. It also took some stealth to do it in such a way that she, and the others, wouldn't notice his scrutiny. He started to fantasize about her. He thought of pulling her to him behind the door in the kitchen and of her responding passionately, pressing her breasts against him, her inky eyes boring into his. He imagined taking off her caribou-hide skirt and pulling her thick-knit sweater over her head to investigate the shape of her body. Everything under those bulky clothes was so hidden, so secret. Yet he was disappointed when on the third day of his visit she appeared, looking slim and Western in tight jeans and a sweatshirt with DISNEYLAND stamped across the chest.

"Have you been to Disneyland?" he asked, surprised.

She chuckled and shook her head.

"What do you do . . . apart from looking after your father?" He got up and followed her into the little kitchen, wanting to hear her speak English.

"I'm a carver," she said, turning away from him to hide a slight blush.

"Carver?" Dafydd moved around her to force her to look at him. "What kind of carver?"

"Stone carver. Soapstone, mainly. It's the easiest. Sometimes bone. The people do this. Half of us in the village make a living from selling carvings."

"Might I see some of your work?"

She walked around him to the sink. He followed, leaning over the sink and making a silly face at her. "Hi . . . talk to me."

She laughed, and her blush deepened. In the light of the window she looked almost childlike. Their eyes met for a second, and in the intensity of that look it occurred to him that he'd fallen in love with her. It was a childish, irrational sort of thing, but as soon as he acknowledged it he felt himself shiver with the pleasure of it. He must have lost his head, he felt drugged, the air, the silence, the sudden freedom and distance from people like Hogg and Sheila. He looked at Uyarasuq's innocent face and wanted to cup it in his hands and kiss her, but he didn't quite dare. It felt like being fourteen, when he was besotted with his Pakistani neighbor's daughter. She was a twelve-year-old girl with an otherworldly beauty, waist-length hair, and eyes black like caves. Back then, he never even got close enough to talk to the object of his young love, but in his mind he made love to her, day and night. The intensity of his passion was so pleasurable, so *miraculous,* he never tired of indulging it.

"I know this is cheeky to ask, but . . . how old are you?" He felt momentarily guilty about his erotic interest in her. Then he remembered that she'd been married. She couldn't be *that* young. A child bride, maybe, but not a virgin.

"I'll tell you," she said, "but I don't think it's polite to ask. I'm twenty-six next week . . . on Wednesday." She looked at him now, bolder. "But you'll be gone by then."

That was it. Of course. He would be gone. For her, what was the point of a little flirtation, even though it was harmless and would pass the time? There was always a danger of becoming familiar, of liking too much. She couldn't afford the luxury of engaging her feelings. In a place like this you were either stuck with people or else they would be gone. There was nothing in between.

"I'm not really a fly-by-night sort of person," he began. He wanted her to trust him, but what else was there to say? It was better to hide his sudden starry-eyed awareness of her, knowing it was folly.

Suddenly she reached up and touched his hair. "It's like baby hare's fur," she said, and smiled, "so fine and soft . . ." She twirled his dark curls between her fingers. Dafydd grasped her hand and put it to his lips, kissing her palm and wrist while studying her face for her reaction. He knew he shouldn't be doing this, that it wasn't fair. Her eyes were lowered and after a moment she pulled away.

"Yours is like a horse's tail," he said.

"What a compliment." She swiped at him with a kitchen towel. "Actually, I've never seen a horse, except in pictures and movies. I know they used to make mattresses out of horses' tails . . . in the old days."

"Yours would make an amazing mattress," he said.

She snorted in mock disgust, but there was a definite glint in her eye. She went into the living room, chucking large lumps of twisted wood into the woodstove. Her backside looked round and bold as she bent to the job, her legs quite short but well shaped. The jeans seemed incongruous, but maybe it was *him*, his romantic notions and ridiculous misconceptions. In spite of the extraordinary setting and her foreign features, she was probably a thoroughly modern woman.

The following morning he stood at the window watching a neighbor cut up a seal. The bright red blood looked angry on the white snow.

"Come," said Angutitaq and patted the seat beside him on the old sofa. "You are wearied and frustrated?"

"Not a bit. I'm enjoying your hospitality very much."

Bear got up and went into the kitchen, where Uyarasuq was washing the breakfast dishes. A lively conversation issued forth, mixed with riotous laughter. Dafydd listened, surprised, feeling jealous. She wasn't that shy after all. Perhaps, after the faithless husband, she didn't trust younger men. Maybe it was his foreignness that got in the way, or she didn't care for the way he looked at her.

Angutitaq was studying him intently. "You're a man who must resolve your pain before you can come back."

"Me? How do you mean?"

"You'll come back to Canada one day when the mist over your head has cleared. This silence will be calling you. You'll come back and settle down."

"Oh?" Dafydd didn't want to disillusion the old man unnecessarily, but he didn't believe that he'd be pulled back to this northern land. In spite of its spectacular beauty, the rigors of it that he'd come to respect and even enjoy, ultimately he belonged to the year-round misery, and the safety, of the rain and fog of his homeland.

Angutitaq coughed, breaking his train of thought, then pointed the stem of his old pipe toward him. "I know about the *quattiaq,* the child spirit that plagues you. Our old friend told me how you acquired the *quattiaq.*"

"I think it's *me*," Dafydd said quietly. "I'm the one who's doing the plaguing, and with perfectly good reason."

"That, too," Angutitaq agreed, nodding at length. "And the people . . . the people must find someone to blame, and it becomes necessary to carry their pain and take it away with one, far away."

"It wasn't like that," Dafydd protested. He didn't want his blame messed about with. "I did make a very grave mistake and I'll have to live with it. I ran away because I couldn't face what I'd done. That was the reason, plain and simple."

The door to the kitchen closed and the jolly interaction within was reduced to a rumble. The lump of wood in the stove crackled angrily.

"Of course. I know it myself. Still, you are like a clump of moss, soaking up the pain and holding it, taking it with you to all corners of the world. You are here"—Angutitaq threw his arms out to indicate the whole of the Arctic—"and you are still heavy, dragging the burden with you like an overloaded *kamotik*."

It was true: the weight of his remorse dragged at his very bones. They sat quietly for a long time looking into the fire. Angutitaq hummed quietly to himself. Suddenly he tapped Dafydd's knee with the stem of his pipe.

"I am seeing the *quattiaq* and he looks to me like a good spirit. He looks like a little fox with a long nose. But he is not angry." Angutitaq looked intently at Dafydd. "He is an innocent spirit, but in his eyes there is a lot of wisdom. If you let him, he could help you."

"*No*," Dafydd blurted out. "Don't you understand? I'm responsible for—"

The old man abruptly raised his hand and closed his eyes. "He is here. I shall ask him to show himself. Then you will not be so afraid."

Dafydd shook his head. "I don't know . . ." He swallowed hard. The child whose face haunted his dreams . . . how did the old man know of his foxy little features? He didn't like where this was going. It frightened him.

"*Unnirniaqqutit*," Angutitaq shouted out.

The room seemed to darken, as if some shift in time had taken place. It's in my mind, Dafydd thought. I'm agitated, unstrung . . .

Then the old man started to sing. "*Alianait, alianait, alianait . . .*" It was an austere-sounding song with few notes; perhaps it was a chant. He kept his eyes closed and folded his gnarled old hands over his chest. Dafydd felt self-conscious, wondering if anything was expected of him, but as the song continued for some time he felt more comfortable and grew to like it. The sounds from the kitchen had ceased, and a slight wind whistled around the corners of the house. Suddenly the room darkened again, as if night had fallen at once. Dafydd thought it eerie, but the song had calmed him and he didn't want anything to distract him. He leaned backward and closed his eyes against the dark. The peculiar melody went on, like an archaic hymn. Angutitaq's voice was so deep that he could feel the resonance of it right through the soles of his feet, rising through his legs and filling him up. He wanted to hum along but felt drowsy. Derek's little face came to him, but not the pale, sunken countenance of illness and death. A rosy face, eyes bright and alive. Dafydd smiled. Then he saw the fox within the face, its fearless grin, its long, pointy nose. It was the sharpness and wisdom of the eyes that really touched him, filled him with courage and drew darkness away from him.

Quieter now, Angutitaq's voice trembled slightly, as if the effort of singing the song was sapping his strength. Derek's features shimmered, softened, and went. The song drifted off, becoming hollow . . . like an echo from beyond the silent sky of the Arctic.

When Dafydd opened his eyes he was alone in the room. He was puzzled by the light outside and felt disorientated. The embers in the stove still glowed, but the house was quiet. No one seemed to be around. His body was stiff and he felt heavy-headed. He stood up and stretched. He yawned until his jaws creaked. Suddenly he was hellishly thirsty, as if he'd hauled himself across a desert. His tongue felt thick. He made his way to the little bathroom and as it had no window struck a match to light the *qulliq,* a soapstone lamp, filled with seal fat, carved beautifully into the shape of a half-moon. He drank mugs of water. He brushed his teeth. The mirror above the basin showed a three-day beard growth. His hair was too long, curly and un-ruly. Looking closely at his face for the first time in ages, he laughed. It was a face more like a drug-crazed hippie's, or just a ruin of a man—that was what he was, after all. Even so, he couldn't muster up the conflict he'd had with his own reflection. He remembered what it was like to respect himself . . . looking at his own face in the mirror and finding it rather handsome, dashing even, full of promise. Over a year had gone by since his life fell apart. Maybe a year was enough.

Standing there in the squalid little bathroom, he had an abrupt elevation of spirit, the burden loosening, floating away. The clump of moss being squeezed like a sponge and the fetid water draining out, making him feel light, fresh, springy.

He had a pee in the "honey bucket," then he took his clothes off and stood in the little tray that passed for a shower. The tiny jet of cool copper-stained water felt as extravagant as stand-ing under a mountain waterfall. He dried himself off and got dressed, then scraped ineffectually at his face with someone's razor, making his throat bleed.

In the kitchen he found Uyarasuq sitting at the table, per-fectly silent and still.

"The fathers have gone for a visit," she said. "They won't be back until late."

"What are you doing?" he asked, surprised.

"I'm resting my old bones," she said, looking fresh-faced, like a teenager.

"I must have been sleeping for hours."

"You said you wanted to see my carvings." He saw her white skin turning pinkish, and she turned her head away from him to hide it.

"I would love that. Where are they?"

"In my house." She stood up and directly put on her parka. He looked around for his own gear. It was rolled into his sleeping bag, which he'd stored behind the sofa. The air was mild, and the sky was a weak blue. He had no idea what time it was. Uyarasuq took him by the hand and led him purposefully around the dwellings to a tiny house near the shore. She lived in a one-room box, no bigger than the trailer his parents had owned when he was a boy. The air within was moist with the vapors of a gas heater. Long, thin shelves covered the walls from floor to ceiling, on which she stored all her belongings. Small soapstone carvings were everywhere: hunters with spears, whales, polar bears, seals, and birds. They were exquisite.

"These are remarkable," he exclaimed. "Where do you sell them?"

"In galleries of the *kablunait*," she said and winked. "You know . . . *white man.*"

If she was making fun of him, he didn't really mind. "So you *do* go south sometimes?"

"No. There is a research station a few miles from here. They take them for us . . . for a cut, of course." She had put a kettle on the tiny stove and hung up their parkas on hooks on the back of the door. "You're not *that* white, actually. Why did I think that all European people were fair? Still, you're made of a different material from me." She came over to where he'd sat down on a small stool, handling one of her carvings, feeling the cool, smooth stone. She put her hand into his hair and ruffled it like a child's. "Different material, soft, maybe a bit fragile." She laughed.

He looked up at her. How much did she know about him? Perhaps she had overheard his strange interaction with her father the shaman, or Bear may have told her why he'd brought him here. But there was nothing like pity or charity in the way she looked at him. He put the carving on his lap and placed his hands around her waist, feeling the slim narrowing from her hips, getting a measure of her. She didn't seem to mind. After a moment he let his hands drop.

"It's okay," she said.

"I'm sorry . . . I mustn't act on my impulses. *Kablu* . . . whatever you called us, we're terribly forward. It's that white imperialistic pighood . . ."

She laughed and, taking his hands, she returned them around her middle. He leaned his forehead against her belly; it rumbled hungrily. He pressed his ear to it to hear it better. There was something earthy and powerful about the sounds, like distant thunder and lightning, like eruptions of hot lava and calls of wild forests, like a tiny universe within. A different place, exotic, fascinating, and forbidden. He wanted to be there, inside her, enter her secret cosmos with his own flesh.

The kettle was hissing and she pulled away from him. He looked around and noticed the furnishings. She seemed to live on the bed. Spread on it were books, papers, clothes, sewing, and a plate with crusts of bread.

While she made tea, he got up to finger other sculptures; he couldn't help touching them. Each told a tale of the Inuit's relationship to the world and its creatures. He picked up one of a couple of lovers. The woman was sitting astride the man, also sitting, their faces broad with smiles, their limbs chunky, wrapped around each other.

She handed him a mug and they stood together, between the bed and a table.

"When is your husband coming back?"

"Never."

He couldn't think what else to say and perhaps she didn't like him prying.

"You want me, don't you?" she said.

"Yes." He reached out to touch her cheek. "I do. But don't think—"

"It's all right," she interrupted, "but it's been three years since I've been with a man. I wouldn't know what to do."

"You don't have to do anything. I didn't come here with any expectations," he said, feeling unsteady. "Can we sit?" They sat on the edge of the bed, sipping the hot tea. After a moment she

got up and started gathering the stuff on the bed, with some difficulty finding places to put them. There was no wardrobe, and
she placed the folded clothes on a shelf. The books and papers
were stacked up on the table. Dafydd felt weak inside, almost
panic-stricken. It was ridiculous; it wasn't as if he were a virgin
himself. He wanted it so much and yet he felt like an absolute
novice, hopelessly unsuave. At the same time he could feel a
strong stirring in his groin. That part of him didn't give a damn
about his battle with confidence and etiquette.

When she'd finished putting the things away, she took the
mug from his hand and went to turn off the light. A gray dusk
shone weakly through the window. Dafydd got up and followed
her. She was shorter than she appeared, and to kiss her he lifted
her off the floor. She laughed, but her shyness was gone. Her eyes
glittered in the dim room. "Take your clothes off," she said.

"Are you sure you want this?"

"I very much want it." She smiled and began to unzip his
body-warmer.

When he'd managed to get out of his clothes he realized he'd
not been naked for months, except to jump in and out of his
filth-infested shower. The muggy heat on his bare skin made
him more aroused. His erection swung like a lead weight before
him as he helped her undress. Her nipples were dark, sitting
high on her small breasts. He bent to kiss them and they hardened on his tongue like tiny pebbles. He didn't stop until his
neck was aching and he drew her onto the bed.

He couldn't help himself grinning at the sight of her bright red
satin knickers, and asked her where on earth she'd found them.

"In a catalogue, of course." She chuckled, tapping him on
the nose. "What did you expect, panties made out of birch bark
or seal hide?"

"Yes." He laughed. "I *am* disappointed."

"And clumps of moss for sanitary pads?"

"Absolutely." How well she had read him.

He peeled them off, careful not to tear the delicate stitching.
"Did you wear them in anticipation? Did you plan this?"

"Yes . . . but I always wear beautiful underwear just to remind myself that I'm a woman." If they hadn't been so glaringly *present* he might have stolen them from her, but she would know and think he wanted a trophy. She wouldn't be altogether wrong. Being here, in this bed with this beautiful and exotic woman, was the highlight of his year. A moment never to be forgotten. He looked over her pale body, the details of it smudged by the slowly darkening night. Her small black triangle was just as he'd seen it in his erotic ruminations. He kissed it, rubbing his nose in the coarse texture of her pubic hair, smelling her. He was already perilously close to coming, but he forced himself to hold back, trying to think cold things, difficult things. They kissed, for a long time lying side by side, pressed together. She laughed suddenly, a sound of pure joy, and it made him laugh, too.

He wanted to talk a little, hear her voice and look at her more closely, but she slid down along his body. The sensation of her mouth enveloping him was overwhelming and within seconds he shrank back. Much as he desired this woman, he couldn't trust his self-control, and he didn't want to invade her in that way, losing himself carelessly. He drew away from her and laid her on her back so that he could pleasure her. The tender folds beneath the black triangle were virginal, childlike. Momentarily he felt troubled and had to remind himself that she wanted him, too, she was a woman, far beyond the age of consent. Nevertheless, his attentions made her cry.

"Is this not okay?" he whispered, alarmed.

"Yes, it's wonderful. Don't stop." She had reasons to cry, sadness, loneliness, frustration. Here was love, even if it was only for some short hours, to be cruelly snatched away. Tomorrow he'd be gone. He couldn't think of it himself. Suddenly it was devastating. Then his need took over and he stopped thinking. He pulled himself up and hovered over her, licking at the tears that had run down her face.

"Can I? Are you protected?"

She nodded. "It's a safe time," she said. He knew there was no such thing as a totally safe time, and why would she be protected? From what, out here, with no man? So he drew away from her, jumped up and searched frantically through his clothing for his wallet with the dog-eared condom packets that had followed him around for so many months.

"I don't mean that I don't . . ." he began as he pulled on the unsightly rubber.

"It's fine. Everything is fine," she reassured him.

Her tightness hurt them both. She winced. He whispered apologies and started to withdraw, but she grabbed his buttocks with both hands to keep him where he was, soon asking him to move, to thrust. When her pleasure came, he let go, releasing himself with a force that made him see the stars behind his eyes.

He made his way toward his host's house. The sky was finally black but the night was lit. The sight of the billions of dazzling stars made him stop in wonder. The sheer enormity and brilliance of the universe was something that he'd never properly experienced. Day by day the light would grow now, the fading dark quickly giving way to the arctic summer when there were no stars.

He walked along the path, smiling and humming. The vapor from his exhalations into the cool air was like Thor's mighty breath, blowing life into storms and clouds and thunder. He felt powerful, brimming with strength and vigor, like a boy on the brink of manhood. Proud, fulfilled, expectant, his blood hot. He laughed out loud at himself. Damn it all, he was madly in love, crazed with desire and totally stupid. But he also felt at peace, a radiance that was soft, gently spreading inside him. He didn't allow himself to think any further. Certainly not of the future. Nothing must interrupt what was happening to him.

Suddenly a distant noise like shattering crystal made him stop and look up. The aurora borealis flashed across the night sky in an eruption of colors. Long tails of red, yellow, and green whipped from one end of the horizon to the other. Multicolored sheets climbed and descended in an intricate dance. It was the most extraordinary sight, and Dafydd stood motionless, awed by the beauty. He'd been told about the phenomenon of the unearthly sound. The music of the northern lights was a rare experience; many people spent their entire life in the Arctic without ever hearing it.

He wanted to run back, drag the sleeping Uyarasuq out of her cozy bed and make her share it with him. It would link them, in this enormous temple under the sky, like no other ceremony ever could. But he knew it couldn't be, so he walked on, his eyes and ears alive. At least he would take this with him, this day, this night, wherever he went. Because of it he was rebuilt, made whole again.

Sleeping Bear was quiet, not his usual impish self.

"Guess what, young man?" he said without enthusiasm. "We're getting a ride in a helicopter."

"Really? How's that?" Dafydd said, tucking into a slice of *nattiaviniit,* the meat of the seal born last spring. His appetite was obscenely huge, and he looked over at Uyarasuq and winked covertly. She smiled and cut up yet another slice.

"That young priest . . . not the Anglican, the bloody Jesuit"—Bear made as if to spit on the floor beside him—"has arranged for us to be picked up by that pack of weather people on the research station."

"That's nice of him . . . and them," Dafydd said through a mouthful. "Have you canceled our pilot?"

"Yep. It'll save us a few bucks," Bear concluded grimly, struggling with his own meal, which was hard on wizened teeth, although Uyarasuq had cut it up for him into tiny pieces. "They're flying to Yellowknife for a concert. Imagine it. The money they have to spend on frivolities like that." Bear flicked his thumb in Uyarasuq's direction. "Thanks to her carvings, no doubt. Fucking wolverines."

Uyarasuq put her hand on Bear's shoulder. "We do okay, Grandpa," she said soothingly. "Are we going without?"

Bear looked at her with a tenderness that Dafydd had never seen in the old man. He patted her hand but said nothing. Angutitaq emerged from the bathroom looking frailer than ever. It seemed that his back had bent even farther, and his legs bowed out unsteadily. Perhaps he'd partaken in a furtive drink of Bear's bottled medicine.

In spite of Dafydd's exceptionally good spirits, the mood of the party as a whole was somber. There was a finality about this breakfast. The two old men must have known that this was surely their final meeting. Uyarasuq was downcast for her own reasons, and Dafydd was living on some unprecedented high that he knew would suffer a hideous collapse as soon as he was returned to the stark reality of going home. *Home?*

Bear had been right about his need for counsel, but never had Dafydd imagined the form that it was going to take, and the profound effect it was going to have. Losing his heart, inexplicably, to a woman he hardly knew was another matter. It had never happened quite like this, and he hoped that leaving this extraordinary place would put everything into perspective. He'd been bewitched: how else to explain the whole experience?

Half an hour later there was the thunderous roar of the approaching helicopter. A chorus of huskies barking wildly blended with the intrusive noise. Angutitaq patted Dafydd on the shoulder. "If you learn to be quiet, the little fox will come to you. He will tell you things no one else will. Talk to him when you are troubled."

While the two old men spoke quietly together outside the door, Dafydd pulled Uyarasuq to him in the kitchen.

"I don't regret it," she said firmly, but her eyes looked large and too shiny.

He held her coarse hair, pulled her head back and kissed her deeply. Much as he searched through his mind for some adequate declaration of his feelings, he could not find a single one that would make it all right.

PART 2

CHAPTER *13*

Moose Creek, 2006

More snow was expected, according to the lady who checked him into the Happy Prospector B&B.

"Winter is setting in well and truly. What choice do we have, huh?" she said, head cocked to one side, waiting for him to add his own reason for wanting to endure this forthcoming ordeal. Dafydd just nodded sagely in agreement. She asked for ID and proceeded to carefully copy down the details from his passport. She looked at his picture for a long moment, then looked up at him.

"I *remember* you," she exclaimed, delighted. "Dafydd Woodruff."

"I'm sorry," Dafydd said, looking closely at her pixie face. "I probably should remember you, but I'm afraid I don't."

"Don't you worry. I can rightly take that as the best possible compliment." She laughed merrily, looking genuinely very pleased.

"I've put my foot in it somehow," Dafydd conceded, embarrassed.

"Not on your life . . . I used to work in the Klondike. I'm Tillie. Does that ring a bell?" Dafydd stared at her. Of course he remembered Tillie. She was the obese Shirley Temple lookalike who always had a nice word for him and a smile, a true smile. He'd enjoyed her attentive ministrations at the Klondike, offered in a caring, motherly fashion, vigilant of his every need in the way of food and drink.

"Tillie . . . I can't believe it," he exclaimed. "You look wonderful."

Behind the Formica counter stood a woman in her early forties, slender and fit-looking, with a lovely youthful face and blond ringlets gathered in a girlish ponytail. "Whatever it is you've done, you should patent it. You'd be the richest woman in the Western world."

Tillie blushed becomingly. She really was very pretty. Smooth, lovely skin, tiny ski-jump nose and small red rosebud mouth, just like a doll.

"Tell me to mind my own business, but how did you do it?"

"A very nice doctor who worked here for a while fixed me up. I was feeling tired all the time and he discovered that I had a *very* underactive thyroid. I got some pills and the weight just dropped off."

"Dang, I wish I could have taken credit for the discovery," Dafydd said with feeling. "I missed my chance to be a real hero. Perhaps I wasn't very . . . imaginative in those days?"

"You were just fine," Tillie said. "Anyway, I never saw you about it, did I, so you never had a chance." After a moment she added, "Lots of people really appreciated you. Some were real disappointed that you left after such a short time. They were getting used to you . . . and your ways."

"Ah, yes, my ways." Dafydd smiled. "Fastidious to the point of absurdity."

Tillie smiled back, seemingly unsure of what he meant. "Let me show you your room." She led the way up a narrow staircase to the first floor. A dark corridor contained a row of plastic doors. It looked unspeakably depressing. However, when she threw open the door to number 6, the room itself proved bright and spacious, with an overlarge bed over which hung a purple canopy. Tillie saw him looking at it.

"This is my best room." She went up and stroked the purple

velvet lovingly. "I get the occasional honeymooners. They're usually very pleased with . . . the bed."

"This is great, Tillie. I'm really glad I found you. I would have gone straight to the Klondike, but the taxi driver had never even heard of it."

"It burned down some years back. Right down to the ground. Mr. George was arrested." Tillie smoothed some nonexistent wrinkles from the purple bedspread. "He was thrown in jail for arson. He couldn't pay the mortgage. We all felt real sorry for him. Such bad luck."

Dafydd scrutinized the face of this innocent-looking woman. This was Moose Creek. He'd forgotten the code by which seemingly ordinary people lived their lives and exonerated themselves in the face of adversity. Arson was totally justified if you couldn't pay the mortgage. A man had to do what a man had to do. He had an overwhelming urge to tell Tillie why he was there. Ask her opinion about why a woman in this place would get herself pregnant and then keep quiet about it for years and years. Maybe she even knew something about it, about Sheila and the children. He sensed that she would understand his predicament, sympathize with him. But then again, why should she? She was a woman and would see life from a woman's perspective. Especially a wronged woman, a single mother left alone to struggle with twins. He thought better of it; he might need the purple bed for some time to come.

"When do you serve breakfast?" he asked.

The town had changed, grown. Since the highway had been joined up, people were coming up in droves. Most didn't stay long, but between the oil and gas exploration, and the talk about diamond mining, a tremendous increase in ecotourism, plus the antithesis—hunting, fishing, trapping and prospecting, and other more shady pursuits—there was a steady stream of enthusiastic pioneers crowding the new bars. They held forth in booming voices about returning south with pockets full of cash, diamonds or gold, beer glasses raised in premature self-congratulation.

New negotiations about a pipeline were under way, but now the aboriginal new rights to the land asserted themselves. The process was painfully slow, since the different native tribes had to agree among themselves as well as with the government and the oil giants. These details were of no real import to the new-comers, who lived hand to mouth until the elusive rain of gold would descend on those who had the stamina to remain.

Dafydd allowed himself to be updated by Tillie's colorful account before he left the Happy Prospector, luggage yet to be unpacked, and wandered around the town taking in the chang-es. New dreary buildings replaced the old shabby ones. There were no concessions to aesthetics. Everything was purely utili-tarian. He missed the idiotic grandiosity of the Klondike that gave the main street its wacky Wild West flavor. Another large and expensive hotel had been erected, the inside of which was supposed to be magnificent, but it still looked like a giant shoe box.

The first snow had come and almost gone, but it was al-ready very cold. It was just about dark at four forty-five. The shops were starting to close, and Dafydd quickly crossed over the road to the Hudson Bay Company department store, now renamed simply the Bay, to buy himself some long johns and a parka. He was astonished at the sophistication of the store, which previously had held only some dusty frills for frustrated housewives but nothing of real use. He walked down the main street to the "liquor store" and bought a bottle of Southern Comfort.

After returning to his room, he turned on the television, opened the bottle and poured himself a good measure in a mug. Taking off his shoes, he stretched out on a pink lounger. The Southern Comfort had an instant effect, a warm liquid rush to the extremities and a glow inside the skull. He caught the tail end of the news. It told sketchily of some catastrophic air disas-ter in Europe, as if Europe were some small country somewhere, as remote and inaccessible as Tibet. A never-ending string of commercials followed. Dafydd fiddled unsuccessfully with the remote control when there was a knock on the door.

"You have a phone call, Dr. Woodruff. I'm afraid you'll have to take it in reception," Tillie called through the door.

Dafydd put his shoes back on and made his way down, perplexed, wondering who could possibly know he was there. Tillie handed him the receiver and discreetly slipped out through a door marked PRIVATE.

"Dafydd Woodruff here."

"Dafydd Woodruff." The unmistakable voice of Sheila Hailey. "You could have had the courtesy to let me know you were coming here."

"I thought that would be the least you'd expect, an immediate visit to assume my responsibilities as a father. How did you know I—"

"There are responsibilities, all right." She laughed wryly. "But it wasn't necessary for you to come here. I told you that in my letter."

"Well, I don't take instructions." Dafydd felt his antagonism toward her rising like sewage in a blocked drain. "Here I am, and I'd like to meet the children as soon as possible."

"Hey, slow down. I think we need to get together first and talk."

"Where and when do you want to meet?"

"Nowhere public. Why don't I come over to you? At least we can speak in privacy."

"Are you sure you want to take such a risk? After what you went through," he said sarcastically. "You *do* remember, don't you . . . the rape, and the drugging, of course. Let's not forget." He clenched his jaws hard, knowing it was sheer stupidity to let himself go down this road. Nothing, absolutely nothing would be gained by it.

"Oh, cut the crap," she said angrily. "I'm not afraid of you. Only cowards behave like you do." She paused. "Listen"— her voice softened—"let's talk . . . sensibly."

"Okay. My place, then. When?"

"How about right now?"

She was still quite beautiful. Thinner than he remembered her. Her unusually high breasts sat slightly lower on her chest, but quite magnificently. Her hair had dulled somewhat in color and was more orange than red. The piercing blue eyes had sunk back, the lids curved high and deep. They reminded him of Greta Garbo. A conspicuous absence of lines on her face and neck made him guess she'd had some nips and tucks. Perhaps the faithful Hogg had had a go, or Ian, if either was still alive and kicking, and still here. She still looked late thirties, although she was near enough his own age.

"You're looking . . . in good health," he said, holding out his hand to her. In the hour since their phone conversation, he'd downed another couple of measures of Southern Comfort and decided to keep things as cordial as was humanly possible.

"Actually, you're not so bad yourself." She shook his hand, smiling. "Maturity becomes you. Gray temples always look so sexy on a man, and all that hair . . ." She boldly looked him over. "Very trim, and not a trace of a beer gut. You don't see that around here in a man your age."

He pulled up the pink chair for her and he sat on the bed.

"Whoa," she exclaimed, looking at the bed. "In a tacky sort of way it's quite sexy. Just keep in mind that you've already got two to support."

"Your good humor remains unchanged." He smiled courteously and showed her the bottle but she shook her head. He poured himself another one.

"Let's get right down to it," he said. "I'd like to meet the children as soon as possible. In fact, I'd like to meet them before we talk about anything else."

"My lawyer says that I should have a minimum of two thousand dollars a month."

He studied her tight expression and wondered if this was all about money. "You know, I'm baffled about this odd timing of yours. All that money. All those years. What stopped you from nailing me earlier?"

Sheila sat back in the lounger and crossed her slim legs. She didn't answer him straightaway but studied him with undisguised interest, taking in his shirt, his jeans, his boots. "I didn't need the complication," she said finally. "It was Miranda who set this farce in motion, wanting to know who her dad was. You can't blame her, I guess."

He tipped the mug to his lips. "Good stuff, this," he said, looking at the label of the bottle, buying time, almost squirming with discomfort under her scrutiny. He had to talk about it. It had to be done. He drew breath, knowing it would be difficult. "I want you to know that I still don't accept it. I don't know what you've done to swing this, but there's got to be an explanation. You and I *never* had sexual intercourse."

"I don't believe it." Sheila laughed. "Talk about denial." Her delight was genuine and it made her quite pretty. The sharpness of her look mellowed, and she gazed at him almost sympathetically. "You're a doctor, for heaven's sake. If you hadn't voluntarily passed on your sperm, how on earth did you think I might have laid my hands on it? I'm quite flattered that you think I'm such a magician."

She was exasperatingly right; much as he had twisted and turned the possibilities, his paternity had been proven after all.

"I might accept that I have passed on my sperm, as you call it. But *how,* that's what begs the question. It's quite possible that you could have slipped some drug into my drink at that party." As soon as he said it, he felt stupid. Spoken out loud, it sounded quite a pathetic theory.

Sheila smiled and shook her head. "That's a cute little turnaround. Me drugging and raping *you.* Little old me carrying an unconscious man into his place and performing—"

"Just leave that for the moment," Dafydd interrupted, but she pressed on.

"And why the hell would I want to do that? Why on earth would I want *your* baby . . . of all people?"

Yes, it was a question he'd pondered endlessly and couldn't possibly find an answer to. She recrossed her legs and her denim skirt rode up a bit on her slim thigh. He glanced down involuntarily and saw the freckles on her legs that were dark enough to show through her tights. He remembered being both fascinated and repelled by her mass of freckles. Her whole body was covered in them. As soon as he'd thought it, he wondered with dread how he could possibly know such a thing. Probably, he'd just visualized her naked body, her thighs, her buttocks, her back, imagined it all freckled, but again, why would he, in his mind, want to strip her naked?

"I'll tell you my side of the tale if you like, just to refresh your memory." She paused to let him protest, but he was too curious to hear what sort of story she'd cooked up.

"We got back to your trailer and I was feeling very woozy. First you had me masturbating you in the car, and I admit I *sort of* consented to it. Then you invited me in for a cup of coffee, saying I shouldn't drive any farther in my 'condition.' I even remember you saying 'doctor's orders' about three times. You were quite smashed yourself. The next thing I know, I'm naked, laying face down on a bed, with a pillow under my hips and you giving it to me from behind. You were really going for it and you're quite big, aren't you . . ." she said, looking pensively at his crotch.

"I asked you to stop several times, but you wouldn't have it. At one stage you even tried to penetrate my backside, but I'm not sure how far you got. My every orifice was sore as hell the next day. Even my throat was chafed raw. And I had a migraine like nothing I've ever known. What the hell was that stuff? I thought I knew my pharmacology, the various date-rape drugs, but *that* stuff . . . I was aware of most of what was happening, and I remembered it afterwards, but I had no strength to resist you."

Dafydd stared at her. At first he almost marveled at her nonchalant exposition, telling of the alleged rape as if she were describing a tea party, then he shuddered involuntarily and felt queasy. The picture she had painted was so vivid, her matter-of-fact account of it was so chillingly artless, anyone hearing it would believe her.

"My God, woman," he groaned, "you have one hell of a talent there. That *tale,* as you called it, was quite realistic."

"It seemed to me, looking back on it, that you must have been *on* something yourself. That's probably why you can't seem to remember it. Your stamina was astonishing. You just went on and on. I don't think I've ever been . . . done over quite like it."

"And it was me you think you remember, in that drugged-up state?"

"The crazy thing is," she continued unperturbed, "though I didn't really like you much, I probably would have gone to bed with you if you'd just asked nicely. You really were quite a tasty little morsel in a meaningless sort of way. But, boy, you really blew it. It was quite unbelievable that you then refused me the abortion." She shook her head. "How you must be regretting that now."

Yes, she was right. He should have set aside his principles on that one occasion, and possibly he wouldn't be in this bizarre situation now.

"That's one thing I've never been able to figure out," he said, changing tack. "If you really didn't want children, why didn't you go ahead and have the abortion elsewhere? Surely it was possible."

This made her angry. "You have a lot of nerve to ask that. You have no idea of what I went through." She got up out of the lounger, with some difficulty. The prone position disempowered her. She stood there for a moment with her fists tight, then went to the window. The bright lights of the frothing town center and the noises of cars and humanity spilled through the triple-glazed windows, clear and crude. She looked down onto the street and spoke with her back turned to him.

"Why the hell are we talking about this? It's no concern of yours."

"All right, but I think you were hoping to marry that big fellow, Randy whatshisname. And you found out too late that he'd had a vasectomy."

She laughed, as if the notion was utterly absurd. She came back from the window and sat down on the edge of the lounger, pulling it up toward him, far too close for comfort. "You've no idea what you're talking about."

Dafydd pressed on. "So what about adoption? I mean, as you were so totally disgusted with the idea of a child, was that not an option?"

Some emotion flickered across her face. He could almost have guessed that she felt hurt. Perhaps she really loved her children, although she was the least *motherly* woman he'd ever met. It wouldn't really be so strange. Most mothers did love their children, after all.

"I will not deign to answer that," she said coldly. "Let's get back to the business of child support."

"Fine."

"You want them to have all the things that their parents can offer, don't you?" she said, trying to sound more agreeable. She fastened her big eyes on him. "After all, they are your *only* children . . . our only children."

"What makes you think they're *my* only children?"

"Oh, trust me. I know a lot about you. I've talked to your wife on more than one occasion. She's been kind enough to fill me in on a few things . . . as I have with her. In fact, we got on real well."

Dafydd froze. This piece of news was something he'd never even considered. Isabel and Sheila exchanging information. Perhaps this was behind Isabel's phone call to Lesley. Although Isabel had every right to talk to anyone she liked, he felt betrayed. She was so bloody sure he'd lied to her all the way, but she hadn't been honest with him. She'd allowed Sheila to poison her mind.

"How dare you involve my wife in this." Dafydd's voice was cold. He sat back, wanting maximum distance from this woman. He wanted to get up and pour himself another drink, but she had him pinned by her mere proximity. He could smell her breath. It was warm and fragrant. Her small, even teeth were glinting white, her throat was milky. He could imagine putting his hands around her soft, slender neck and squeezing hard. It occurred to him that if he'd ever had sex with Sheila, he would have wanted to hurt her, to wipe that smirk off her face and put bruises on that freckled body. The very thought startled him. Perhaps she brought out this violence in people . . .

"Listen." She must have read his face because she flicked the air with her hand as if to sweep away his hostility. "Let's not argue. What good does it do? All this is pretty clear-cut, isn't it? I'm not planning to be totally unreasonable. I think it would be nice if you could get to know the twins a little bit, and as soon as arrangements have been made for regular payments you can go back to Wales and get on with your life. All I'll ask of you in the future is a monthly check for a reasonable sum . . . taking into consideration that there is quite a bit owing for previous years." She smiled now, trying to be conciliatory.

"Don't count on anything, Sheila," Dafydd said. "When I see the children I'll decide if I accept the DNA test. Judging by the photo you sent me, they don't look anything like me."

"Don't be ridiculous," she said. She got up and started to put on her rust-colored coat. It looked expensive, not from the Bay. "I've got a new lawyer . . . in Inuvik. His name is Michael McCready. You can have a talk with him. He's real good, and he's a nice guy." She handed him the lawyer's card.

Dafydd stood up to see her out. "When do I meet them?"

"How about Saturday? That'll give me time to prepare them. Come for lunch." She turned to him again at the door. "Do me a favor and don't speak to people about this or tell anyone why you're here. You can tell Tillie we're discussing a possible locum sometime in the future. Not that I care that much, but it's just

easier for all of us if we avoid all that gossip. Think of the kids
. . . spare them that."

We'll see, Dafydd thought as he closed the door on her. She's
not going to stop me from making a few inquiries.

There was daylight when Tillie knocked at the door. Dafydd
had crashed out in the chair, fully dressed. When he woke to
the persistent knocking he had no idea where he was, or indeed
who he was. Jet lag and general exhaustion had finally claimed
him, eased on their way by half a bottle of Southern Comfort.

The sheer unreality of being where he was, and the expectations heaped on him, the loss of his unruffled life, the loss of his
marriage—as it had been—all seeped back into his conscious-
ness like the slow trickle of sand in an hourglass, filling up the
numbed and empty space with dread. He staggered toward the
knocking.

"Dr. Woodruff," Tillie called through the door, "I'm finish-
ing up in the kitchen. I'll make you something quick, if you
want."

"No, thanks, Tillie. I'll grab something later," he called back.

For a moment there was silence. "But you didn't go out for
anything last night . . . Why don't I fix you a couple of eggs and
some nice hot buttered toast? I'll bring it up to you."

Dafydd opened the door and Tillie peered at him, her eyebrows furrowed with concern. "And a good strong cup of coffee?" she added anxiously.

"Yes, all right. But just coffee." Dafydd rubbed his chin. It
had the consistency of an industrial sander, and his eyes felt
swollen as if he'd spent the night crying.

"You okay?" Tillie took a step forward and put a tiny hand
on his arm.

"You're very kind, Tillie. I don't want any special treatment.
Tomorrow morning I'll be on time." He paused and patted the
small hand. "However, that coffee is going to be a lifesaver. And
please call me Dafydd."

CHAPTER *14*

Dafydd spent a couple of days on his own, trying to adjust to his situation. He tried to remain calm and rational, reminding himself that no actual catastrophe had occurred. He was alive and well, Isabel was alive and well and so far there had been no mention of divorce. He still had a job to return to, even though, such as he left it, the prospect was unappealing. If he absolutely had to, he was young and fit enough to support these kids, financially at least, for many years to come. These things happen to men all the time. His problems were insignificant compared with some.

He walked a lot, straying out of town on the many gravel roads that had been constructed with housing subdivisions in mind. Trees had been felled in large square patches to make plots for future homes. He could not quite understand who would want to live in such an isolated situation, but then imagined it all developed into a nice neighborhood with streetlights and the sounds of lawn mowers or snowmobiles and children laughing. Here was virgin land for the taking. Seen from this different perspective, anything was possible if you just had the right attitude, the right stamina, and a good set of tools. Some people would give anything for this freedom from the throngs of humanity and this wealth of nature at their doorstep.

He tried out the various new bars. As a stranger, sitting in a corner he could reflect on things and at the same time watch and listen. The aboriginal people were generally bunched together as "natives" but they hailed from different territories, with different genes and different languages. The old-timers spoke Inuktitut and Slavey, but there were a few foreigners, Germans, Italians, and Americans, plus French-Canadians and folks from down south speaking their twangy English. This was a unique place, a melting pot of humanity on the fringes. He smiled when an image of the extraterrestrial bar in *Star Wars* came to him. He'd been shoved to the outer rings of his normal safe little universe, exiled to an alien outpost, accused of a crime he had not committed. He had no idea how long he would have to remain, what form his investigations would take, how he would fit in. Everything seemed unfamiliar, and yet he had been here, worked here and known the feeling of exile before.

Late on Thursday afternoon he was sitting in the Golden Nugget, drinking an ice-cold Labatt Blue, when a man approached him. He was a middle-aged to elderly native, quite considerably overweight, with a dour expression.

"Howdy," he said, doffing his peaked cap. "You won't remember me."

"No," Dafydd admitted, "I don't, to be honest."

"You were quite pally with my granddad, way back. You stuck him in the hospital once, and I rightly think you saved his life."

Dafydd lit up. "You're Sleeping Bear's grandson." He reached out his hand and the man reluctantly shook it.

"Dare I ask . . . ?"

"He died some five years back. Just turned ninety-nine."

"Good Lord, ninety-nine . . . Won't you have a seat? I'll get you a beer."

"Nah, no beer." The man sat down nevertheless. "Grandpa was keen on the liquor, but it's not doing the nation no good . . . the Déné Nation."

"Any nation," Dafydd agreed. "It's the world's favorite poison."

"For us it's poison in more ways than one. We can't handle it . . . it's not in our genes. How do you think we were robbed blind of our lands and rights by the white man?"

The blatant hostility toward his forebears was somewhat jarring, although Dafydd basically agreed with the man's sentiment. White men had robbed and plundered everywhere.

"Tell me about Bear," he said. "I knew he couldn't still be alive . . . but ninety-nine, that's a hell of an age."

"True," the man reluctantly agreed, "he was a tough old nut. He just slipped away one night. The dogs wouldn't let anyone come near him. I had to shoot the darned things, otherwise we'd never been able to put him in the ground."

"So did he continue living out at the cabin until the end, like he always said he would?"

"Yep."

"Amazing."

They fell silent. Bear's grandson looked uncomfortable. Dafydd wondered why he'd bothered to approach him at all. The man had never been friendly or shown any signs of appreciating the care that he'd given to his grandfather.

"I just wanted to say . . ." the fat man began. He looked around, getting ready to heave himself out of the seat. "The old man got your letters. He did treasure them. He asked me to write to you about something, he kept on about it, but I never took him up on it. His eyesight was no good no more, and he never was that keen on writing. I don't think he'd rightly ever learned how."

He paused, and Dafydd wondered what he was trying to tell him. "Do you know what it was about?"

"I dunno. I felt a bit bad about the fact that I never troubled with it. *But I'm telling you now.*"

With this he seemed to feel his deficiency made good, and the burden of it discharged. He got up and left with a gruff goodbye.

"What's your name?" Dafydd called after him. "I've forgotten."

"Joseph," he called back without turning his head.

Dafydd watched him waddle out of the pub, looking at no one. His stance said it all. There were quite a number of militant Indians, he'd read about them that morning in the *Moose Creek News*, campaigning for a prohibition of sorts. The other ninety percent of the town's population thought it was a tremendous joke. Fat chance indeed. He suddenly felt a strong sympathy with the sullen man. A man having watched the whole of his culture gradually destroyed by the steady encroachment of the white peril. And the self-destruct impulse, plus the genetic inclination, that had his fellow men and women drink themselves into apathy and stupor. Now drugs, too. If it wasn't dope and cocaine, glue and gasoline sniffing was always on hand for the youngsters who had one foot in the fast lane, an empty, shallow place of computer games and television, and the other foot on a vast and beautiful land of untold riches, which they had lost the knowledge to reap and respect.

As he walked home through the cold streets lit up by merry yellow street lamps, his thoughts wandered to Sleeping Bear. Arwyn . . . Jones or Jenkins. So the old bugger had tried to write to him after all. Dafydd was grateful for the well-overdue message. His letters had reached the old man and had given him some pleasure. He thought about their trip. The trip that Bear had called his last pilgrimage, and which had turned into such a pilgrimage for Dafydd himself. Much as that experience had done for him, he felt a profound sadness after it. A few letters had been written and rewritten to the woman with coal-black eyes and hair like a horse's tail, and never been answered. He understood why. Life had to go on, and living on a memory or an illusion did nothing for someone surviving that harsh milieu. It would have dragged her down. It was her land and her life, it was where she chose to be. Still, the terrible sadness after leaving her had unsettled him. He had imagined that his infatuation had been just that, superficial and short-lived, but his longing for her went on for months and months. Then, gradually, the ache dulled and she transmuted into a fantasy, someone he'd conjured up in his mind, and their passionate encounter . . . the stuff of impossible dreams.

When he got back to his lodgings, he stopped and looked at the sign above the door: THE HAPPY PROSPECTOR. He laughed out loud, shaking his head.

"It's not me at all, you know," he said to Tillie, who opened the door apparently waiting for him. Tillie looked bewildered. "But your place is splendid, a real haven for a lost soul," he added quickly.

"I've turned your bedcovers down for you, Dafydd," the tiny woman said with her usual solicitousness. "Anything else I can get you? Have you had any dinner?"

"I'm absolutely fine. Thank you, Tillie. See you tomorrow," he said. A thought made him stop and turn to her as she stood watching him climb the stairs.

"I just wondered . . . What became of your old colleague, Brenda? You two were good friends . . . Is she still here?"

Tillie's sweet face clouded over. "Yeah, she liked you, too," she said with a tinge of bitterness in her voice. "No, she got pregnant about the time you left, and decided to go somewhere more civilized. She went to live with her sister in New Mexico and then married an oilman. He's quite well off, and from what she tells me they're real happy. Three kids, including the one she had . . . She always wanted a family, *really,* although you wouldn't know it sometimes, the way she carried on, but she is real respectable now. Sorry, Dafydd."

"Hell, no," Dafydd exclaimed, embarrassed. "I was just asking. I'm a happily married man."

"Oh," Tillie said, also mortified and very obviously disappointed.

The hospital looked the same. Nothing had been done to it. Not even a lick of paint on the dull gray cement blocks. Quite

early the following morning Dafydd wandered in, mainly because he was curious but also with an impulsive purpose. He'd
ascertained that both Hogg and Ian were still in situ, plus three
other doctors to serve the increase in the population. One was a
retired army surgeon, Dr. Lezzard, who could perform the most
complicated operations while under the influence of a whole
liter of whiskey. All this according to Tillie, who was a mine of
information.

He had hoped to run into Ian in one of the bars, but untrue
to style he'd not been on the loose. There was, at the same time,
a certain trepidation about meeting him. A man his own age,
fourteen years on, what would he look like? What would he see
reflected in Ian that might say something about himself?

A young nurse stopped him in a corridor and asked if she
could help him. It wasn't visiting time and he was clearly tres-
passing. "I'm looking for Dr. Hogg or Dr. Brannagan."

"Are you a patient?"

"Ah, no. A former colleague."

"Dr. Brannagan is on sick leave at the moment. Dr. Hogg
is in a meeting, but he should be out soon. Would you like to
sit in the waiting room by reception and I'll tell him you're
here . . . Mr. . . . ?"

"Dr. Woodruff. Dafydd Woodruff." The girl turned to go,
and he called after her: "Excuse me. Does Janie Kopka still
work here?" She turned and looked at him curiously.

"Sure thing. She's my mum." She eyed him up and down in
a rather cheeky fashion.

"Please say hello from me. I'll try to catch up with her later."

He sat himself down in the waiting room, which had been
painted a sunny yellow but otherwise had the same plastic stack-
ing chairs for the patients to sit on. As he was flicking through
some hunting and fishing magazines, Sheila marched in.

"What are you doing here?"

"What's this, Sheila?" he chided her. "I'm a free man. I can
go wherever I want."

He wasn't sure, but there was clearly something more than

just irritation in her expression. She looked anxious, trying to hide it behind her nurselike authority. She was certainly most unhappy to see him there.

"Are you worried I'm going to tell Hogg about my new-found paternity?"

"Don't you dare," she shot at him. "Look, it's nobody's bloody business. Hogg and I are good friends. We go back a long way, but I don't want him to know about this." She shifted uneasily from foot to foot, her arms characteristically folded tight under her breasts. She looked older in her nurse's uniform, and even more commanding. Her hair was scraped back into a tight braid. Still, she was sexy, in an imperious, dominatrixy way. Dafydd smiled a little, realizing she probably didn't appreciate him seeing her like this.

"So how are you going to explain why you're in Moose Creek?" she insisted.

"Perhaps I'll ask him for a job." He felt a smug satisfaction with this opportunity to ruffle her. "I hear Ian is on sick leave. Perhaps I can fill in for a while, until he gets better. What's the matter with him, anyway?"

"I wouldn't bother with him if I were you," Sheila said sharply. "Anyway, he's away and not coming back for weeks." She closed her eyes momentarily, and he could see her jaws moving angrily against each other. "Don't even think of asking for a job. I'll oppose it all the way. Anyway, it would be illegal. I wouldn't hesitate to contact immigration if . . ."

He raised his eyebrows to indicate that Hogg was approaching them.

"Well, well, well, a blast from the past." Hogg chuckled and shook Dafydd's hand. "Just what we need, eh, Sheila? You wouldn't believe how much we could use you at this very minute . . . Holiday?"

Dafydd glanced at Sheila. "Yes, just a tour, for the hell of it."

"Jolly good, jolly good." He looked just the same as before, although he must be pushing sixty. He had a good crop of hair that wasn't even graying . . . or perhaps he had it colored. The way he looked at Sheila made it immediately obvious that he was still as besotted with his head nurse. They all chatted about the town for a few moments, then Hogg was hopping to be off. His restless energy was unabated.

"Look, old chap. Come to the staff cafeteria and have a bite with us at one-ish. We all want to hear how our young recruits have expanded their horizons and come up in the world." He stopped and glanced at Dafydd. "You're still in medicine, I take it?"

"I'm a consultant surgeon in Cardiff."

"Well done, well done," he said with some respect. "Good place, good place. Cardiff. I did a locum at the Heath once. Who'd have thought it?"

Before Hogg had a chance to scurry off, Dafydd grabbed the opportunity to ask what he'd come for.

"Hogg . . . Andrew, I'm just curious, do you remember a tenant that you had in the trailer park, Ted O'Reilly? I wonder if you'd know where he might be. I know it's a long—"

"O'Reilly? Of course I know where he is. He's here."

"Ah . . . where?"

"Here in the hospital. I'm treating him myself. He's had a foot amputated due to his diabetes . . . I told him it would happen if he didn't look after himself."

"Why do you want to see him?" Sheila asked warily. "Is he a friend of yours?"

"Yes. Which ward is he on?"

"If he owes you money or something, you might as well write it off." She sniggered, glancing at Hogg.

"I'd like to just say hello," Dafydd insisted.

"You can't see him now. It's not visiting hours," Sheila said.

Hogg looked admiringly at her. "You can see who keeps the order in this hospital, can't you?" he said to Dafydd, shrugging his shoulders up to his ears and offering his chubby palms up to the heavens. "What would I have done all these years without her?" He excused himself and marched off in his jaunty, purposeful way.

"*He's* not changed," Dafydd commented to Sheila, who still stood, arms crossed, guarding his next move. "He always looked as if he were in control of everything, but it's all show, isn't it? Are you managing . . . between the two of you?"

"Look," Sheila said, moving closer to him. "Stay away from my workplace. You have no business here at all. Don't bother coming to the cafeteria. I'm telling you . . ." The threat in her voice was unmistakable. Dafydd was curious. She had no reason to care about where he went and why; she had never given a toss about what people thought of her before. Surely she must have expected him to come to Moose Creek after being told, categorically, that he was the father of her two children? But it was obvious that his presence in the town had made her profoundly uncomfortable.

"See you on Saturday," she said, "not before then." She turned away and left him. Half an hour later Dafydd phoned the hospital from Tillie's and asked for Janie. She was delighted to hear from him.

"Patricia said there was this choice hunk of a doctor asking after me. She'd forgotten his name, or she pretended to anyway. I couldn't think who it could be."

Dafydd laughed. "Can this choice hunk take you out for a drink sometime, or will he be in mortal danger from some other he-man?"

"No way. Eddie would be delighted to be rid of me for an evening so he can practice his golf swings in front of the TV. How about Friday night? The Chipped Rock Café at eight? We'll be the oldest ones there by about twenty years, but who cares, huh?"

"Great." He wrote it down on a piece of paper. "Janie, you wouldn't happen to have a phone number for Ian? Sheila says he's not in town right now. Is that right?"

Janie was quiet for several seconds. "He's at the cabin. I was there last week to check on him. He's in quite a bad way, Dafydd. You'll be shocked when you see him." She gave him Ian's phone number.

"Just one more thing . . ." Dafydd said.

"Shoot."

"When can I next visit a patient of yours?"

"Hi, there. I don't suppose you remember me," Dafydd said to the shriveled man lying on top of the bed in striped pajamas. The only thing recognizable about him was the bushy mustache and sideburns and long greasy hair, now practically white.

"I'll be darned," O'Reilly said after he opened his eyes. "I tole you my leg was bad, but you never believed me." His mouth was like a round hole, with neither lips nor teeth to obstruct the view of the black crater within.

Dafydd glanced down at the bony blue leg that ended in a freshly scarred stump. "Well, all right, my mistake . . . but there seems to be nothing wrong with your memory."

"Oh, Miss Hailey was here earlier and reminded me of you. Mind you, doctors come and go in this town like politicians to a bordello. I can't keep track of 'em all, but you did stand out in my mind." He winked lecherously, his ravaged face split apart by a broad grin.

So bloody Sheila had gotten to O'Reilly before him, but did she know why Dafydd wanted to see him? She *couldn't* know. Dafydd glanced around and saw the only two other men in the ward looking curiously at O'Reilly's visitor.

"Listen." Dafydd bent forward. "I'll leave you to rest in a minute. I just wanted to ask you a question. I'm counting on your good memory," he said, hoping flattery would spur the man's recall. "I know it's a hell of a long time ago, but do you remember the night I came home very late to the trailer with Miss Hailey? We'd been to a Christmas do . . . You were standing in the window and saw us . . . *fooling around.*"

"What *is* this trip down memory lane?" O'Reilly cackled loudly. "Miss Hailey was asking me the same thing. She says she'd rather forget it happened and gave me strict instructions not to blabber. Sorry, buddy."

Dafydd sank back against the chair, seething with frustration, knowing how pointless this endeavor was. Fourteen years on, he was sure O'Reilly wouldn't remember anything, booze-addled as his brain was, but at the moment it was his only point of reference. "I wouldn't have thought you were the type to take orders from a woman."

O'Reilly shrugged.

Dafydd leaned forward again and looked hard at him. "What did she offer you as a compensation for not blabbering? I'll better it."

It was the wrong move. O'Reilly suddenly looked hostile and he glanced toward his ward mates. "What the fuck are you talking about? Look . . . she asked me if I'd seen her go to your trailer. Well, hell, yes, I did. So what's the big deal? All the doctors who lived there did the same."

Dafydd stared at him. "With Shei . . . with Miss Hailey?"

"Did I *say* that?" He gave Dafydd a cold stare. "That's the very reason I remember the occasion. I was mighty surprised to see her there. I figgered she was far too fancy for that fucked-out flee-ridden mattress in your rat's nest of a trailer. Take a look at her, for fuck's sake."

Dafydd grabbed his arm. "What you saw that night was no big deal, you're right about that, but it took place in the car, didn't it? Cast your mind back and be honest, man. *She didn't come into my trailer, did she?*"

O'Reilly tore his arm out of Dafydd's grasp. "Sure she did. I saw the two of you go in together as plain as day, wrapped around each other like you couldn't wait to tear yer clothes off." O'Reilly snarled, bad-humored. "What *is* this shit? Why the hell don't the two of you get together and retrace yer steps? Think of the fun you'd have." He laughed unpleasantly. "Leave me out of it. I've got my own troubles, case you haven't noticed."

Dafydd considered how much money it would take, but he sensed it wouldn't get him anywhere. Between Sheila's keen persuasive power and her money (and/or pills?), O'Reilly obviously thought her a better bet for the future.

"A lot is riding on this, O'Reilly. You might be called to be a witness in court," he tried, but the threat of the law didn't ruffle the old wreck in the least. And even if it came to that, O'Reilly was a remarkably good liar, disconcertingly so.

"Don't come hassling me again, ya hear?" he called after Dafydd as he hurried out of the ward.

Instead of phoning him, Dafydd decided to go straight out to Ian's place. He had a feeling that Ian might dissuade him from coming, and Dafydd was now determined to see how his old friend was faring. There seemed to be a cloud of mystery around his health; no one wanted to talk about it. Dafydd took a taxi out to the cabin and asked the driver to come back for him in an hour.

The place was very dilapidated. The porch had all but disappeared and shingles were missing off the roof. A low growl met him as he climbed the rotten steps. The growl intensified when he knocked. After a moment Ian came to the door. "Bloody hell . . . *you*!"

The first thing that struck Dafydd about him was his eyes. What were once the whites were a deep shade of dirty yellow, rimmed with a pinky-red. The skin around the eyes was loose and wrinkled, with the fatty, lumpy deposits of someone whose cholesterol had been sky-high for far too long. The rest of his face was gaunt and sallow, his hair still longish but the color of hay had turned to dead straw. He looked like a man who'd lived in a dark cave. There was even something musty about the smell of him. They stared at each other.

"Yes, me," Dafydd said and held out his hand. Ian took it limply but hung on to it for a moment. "Come in, fer chrissakes." The growling stopped abruptly and an ancient dog got up, struggling with arthritic back legs.

"Thorn, or one of his descendants?"

"I'm surprised you have to ask . . . he hates strangers."

The old hound's mangy tail wagged furiously as the dog

licked Dafydd's hand. He felt a lump in his throat when he patted the bony head. "I'll be damned. He recognizes me."

"So do I, man." Ian laughed and slapped him on the shoulder. "Come in and have a drink."

The place was filthy. Here lived a man who'd given up on everything. Ian poured scotch into two glasses and handed one to Dafydd. They sat down at the kitchen table, which was covered with half-eaten meals on greasy paper plates and empty tins of dog food. Ian caught Dafydd studying the remnants and fetched a trash bag. He swept the whole lot into the bag and tossed it into a corner. Thorn lumbered up to it and scratched at it insistently with a paw.

"Is he hungry?" Dafydd couldn't help himself asking.

Ian lit a cigarette and looked at him through the wisps of smoke that trailed up over his face.

"What the hell are you doing back here?" he asked, putting heavy emphasis on each word. He was reed-thin, apart from his abdomen, which was incongruously distended, like a balloon bursting out of the cavity of his shrunken torso.

"You have no idea, then?"

Ian was quiet for a moment, looking at him, his expression betraying nothing. His eyes strayed to one side in a flicker of distraction or perplexity. Then he smiled. "You've come to snitch my job . . . finally. Just waiting for the moment to pounce."

Dafydd laughed. "In fact, Hogg was suggesting something like it."

"No, honestly. What *are* you doing back here?"

Dafydd hadn't really decided what to tell him, but someone had to be privy to his reasons for being there and the best person was no doubt Ian. He was one person who knew Sheila; he knew her more than well.

"I'll tell you, if you tell me what the hell is going on with you. You look sick as a dog, and you're off work."

"Nothing out of the ordinary. I drink too much . . . and sometimes my liver protests. I'm on holiday at the moment whatever anybody says. I have three weeks coming to me."

"Should you really be doing that?" Dafydd said, pointing to his glass, then regretting it instantly. It was none of his business, and Ian quite rightly ignored the question. Thorn had managed to rip open the plastic bag and was spreading the contents over the floor, nibbling at the scraps.

"Don't you have a tin of dog food somewhere?" Dafydd asked, making this his business.

Ian got up and rummaged in cupboards. "Actually no," he said, clearly irritated. "I'm very short on supplies."

"Tell you what. Seeing that you're not altogether well, I'll do some shopping for you tomorrow if you tell me what you need. I've got time on my hands."

"Thanks, pal. I'd be much obliged." Ian plonked himself heavily down on the chair, looking exhausted from the effort. "I stay clear of the town these days. Can't stand the way it's going."

"How *is* it going, do you think?"

"All these assholes all over the place. I came here cos I wanted to get away. Now it's become *away* for a never-ending stream of jerks." He threw out his arm. "Have you not seen them in the bars? Have you *seen* the bars?"

"Yeah." Dafydd swirled the sour whiskey in his glass. Thorn came up to him and rested his head in his lap, looking up at him with eyes full of sad wisdom.

"C'mon," Ian prodded. "Why the hell have you come to Moose Creek? This ain't no holiday destination."

"Why not? Seen plenty of tourists around the place."

"Not *your* type."

"Well, here goes: Sheila claims I'm the father of her twins." He paused to let Ian take this in. "At first I thought it was a joke, or she'd gone mad, but when she wouldn't let up we had a DNA test. It confirmed she was right, and you can't argue with DNA, can you?"

"Bloody hell." Ian whistled and shook his head, staring at Dafydd in frank stupefaction. Then he threw back his head and laughed, reclaiming a shadow of his former charisma. "I *knew* it. I knew you were hot on her, no matter how much you tried to deny it . . . So you had your rocks off with Sheila." He laughed again, but abruptly he became serious. "What does she want?"

"Just the usual. Money . . ."

"Christ." Ian drew his fingers through his lank hair. "What will you do about the kids?"

"I don't know." What was the point of trying to tell Ian he was convinced that the pregnancy had happened by some insidious trick, some sly theft of his sperm? It would just cause an outbreak of yet more hilarity, although that in itself was almost worth it. It heartened him to see a glimpse of Ian's old sensuous appeal. The ugliness that had overtaken him was too depressing, the haggard derangement of his body and soul made Dafydd feel profoundly melancholy. Looking at Ian, life seemed such a short affair.

Ian got up and excused himself, disappearing into the bathroom. A good ten minutes passed in dead silence, bar Thorn's intermittent wheezing. Dafydd was just about to call out for him when he heard the toilet flush noisily and Ian staggered out, his face white.

He sat down and poured himself a small top-up. "It's funny," he mused, "I used to half believe they were *my* kids. There was a lot of speculation around town. Her then-boyfriend threw her out on her ear. He knew he wasn't the one, and she's always refused to say. Latterly I thought Hogg might have been the culprit. Ever since Anita left him, he's been trailing around after her like a dog in heat . . . He'd do anything for them. He didn't seem to give a shit about the fact that it started people talking. But then he's always been in love with her."

"Well, I'm just going to take one step at a time. I'm meeting them tomorrow."

"Nice girl, well . . . you know, a normal impertinent adolescent. The boy is a bit of a dark horse. You can't get much out of him. I've a feeling he is extremely sharp. Looks strange, too, face like a spook." Ian looked at him in earnest commiseration. "Better you than me, man."

"I wrote to you a few times, you know. How come you never answered?" Dafydd asked. He'd felt hurt that Ian hadn't thought him good enough a friend to keep in touch with. But seeing him now, it was plain that he was not a man with initiative. Besides, Ian had always lived day to day, and where people were concerned it was probably a case of out of sight, out of mind. The hoot of a car horn saved Ian from answering the redundant question. Thorn howled on pure principle, looking bored.

"That's my taxi."

"Hey . . . take my car. I don't need it for a couple of weeks. That way you can keep bringing me supplies."

"Do you mean it?" A car would, in fact, be quite handy. He could take the kids on some outing. Perhaps get away on his own for a day or two . . . see the wilderness.

He paid the taxi for the fare, and drove Ian's car back into town, having promised to return the following day with food, drink, and cigarettes.

CHAPTER 15

"This is Miranda . . . and this is Mark." Sheila shoved the boy in the back while the girl reached up to place a modest kiss on Dafydd's cheek.

In the last few weeks Dafydd had gradually come to accept that, in theory, impossible as it appeared, much as he doubted he'd ever unravel the means, *these children were probably his.* He'd not really felt anything for them, apart from pity and concern, so he hadn't anticipated the effect that this meeting was going to have on him. The reality of seeing them for the first time shocked and moved him. His heart raced, and he felt himself flush very hot. His eyes felt moist. It made him furious, this uncalled-for exposure of himself in front of Sheila.

Miranda was a radiant young girl, a little on the plump side, already showing signs of physical maturity, unless her bra was stuffed with rolled-up socks the way his sister used to do when she was that age. He scanned her face for some recognition of his own genes, and indeed she had dark, curly hair. She had a full mouth like him, curled up at the corners. Her eyes were wide-set and dark brown under a broad forehead. If anything, that mouth reminded him a little bit of his sister, a slightly lopsided smile showing lots of teeth. At the same time, he wasn't sure . . .

The boy looked so unlike Miranda it was hard to believe the

two were related, and he had nothing that Dafydd could identify as belonging to his clan, yet there was no doubt that he was
Sheila's through and through. There was the mass of unruly red
hair, which he'd allowed to grow long and was wearing in an
impressive ponytail. His face was thin and very pale, he was
gangly and quite tall for his age, looking more like fifteen than
thirteen. Like his mother, he had an excess of freckles, his eyes
were almond-shaped and gray, pale like dishwater, much different from Sheila's dazzling deep-sea blue. They would not focus
on anything, certainly not on Dafydd, and he stood awkwardly,
refusing a simple greeting.

"Don't be a jerk, Mark," Sheila said to him. "Can't you just
pretend you have some manners? Dr. Woodruff here is your
father, and he's come a long way to meet you."

"Now, wait, Sheila," Dafydd said. "Why should Mark be
impressed by that? He never asked me to come, and I don't
blame him for thinking it's a pain in the . . . backside."

Miranda burst into a giggle and pressed her hands to her
mouth. Dafydd smiled, too, and reached out his hand to her.
They shook hands formally, with Miranda taking a while to
pump his hand in an exaggerated fashion. She was trying to
make up for her brother's deficiency, and with a refreshing dose
of humor. He then offered his hand to Mark, who, taken off
guard, touched his clammy adolescent palm to Dafydd's for a
fleeting second.

The house was large for the town, comfortable and tastefully
furnished. Sheila looked striking in tight, pale yellow jeans and
a yellow sweater. For a second he had a vision of impeccable
domesticity. Himself with this attractive woman and their two
comely children, in this stylish contemporary home. A perfect
setting for a breakfast-cereal advertisement requiring a stereo-
typical healthy, happy family.

They went into the living room, but Miranda grabbed his
hand. "Come and look at my room. I want to show you my
stuff." He allowed himself to be dragged away, grateful for the
sheer normality that this girl exuded. They spent a good twenty

minutes looking at her posters, childhood toys, music collection, and photo albums of the kids in their infancy. She asked him if he wanted some of the photos and he accepted a couple of snapshots. He stuck them into his wallet. Sheila called them down to have lunch.

She'd cooked a roast. "Isn't this what you folks in England eat?" she said with a smirk as they sat down around a large table.

"Some do. I don't eat a lot of meat, between the foot-and-mouth outbreak and mad cow—"

Miranda put her face in her hands and giggled helplessly. "Foot and mouth, mad cow . . . ?"

"Well, yes. It's a few years ago now . . . they're diseases that affect—"

The boy suddenly spoke. "I'm vegan. I can't stand the idea of eating the putrid flesh of dead animals. Nor do I drink the secretions from cow udders, or eat their by-products."

"Oh, for Christ's sake," Sheila groaned, "not now."

"So how do you get your proteins?" Dafydd asked, trying not to grin.

"Beans, tofu, nuts, and seeds," the boy said, loading up his plate with potatoes and vegetables before anyone else, "mainly peanut-butter sandwiches. Bread and nuts make a whole protein."

"I thought peanuts were legumes, not nuts," Dafydd said.

The boy looked up at him for the first time. "True. But they still work together."

Dafydd looked at the surly youngster. Not only was he disconcertingly sharp, but his looks were strange, both sinister and fragile at the same time, with his thin face, deathly pallor and his cold eyes. On the other hand, most likely there was a very vulnerable young lad under all that, in this house of strong, assertive females. Dafydd hadn't seen any interaction between brother and sister and wondered what their relationship consisted of. In terms of both appearance and personality, they couldn't be more different.

In the end it was quite an easy lunch. Miranda made every-thing go smoothly with her attentive questions and her infec-tious laugh. Even Sheila seemed remarkably jovial, trying to make the best of an undesirable situation. He looked at her closely a couple of times. *The mother of my children.* He rolled the concept around his mind for a moment and tried to put aside his experience of her as a dangerous, vindictive, and cun-ning man-eater. A reasonable mother, a good provider, a good homemaker, a presentable woman, strong, a worthy role model, as long as you didn't look too closely, do too much sniffing in the corners . . . in closets.

"What next?" he said to her when the kids were out of the room for a moment.

"Next . . . let's sort out the money and then you can be on your way back home. Meet me here on Friday. The kids are in school and I've got the day off."

"All right. But I meant what next in terms of me spending time with *them*." His eyes flashed toward the kitchen, where they were clattering around with dishes, talking in quiet voices. "I'd like to see them on my own. Perhaps separately."

"Why is that necessary?" she asked. "It's not a good thing for them to get too close to you and then you're out of their lives. I can't see how that would help you, either."

"I'm not buying that, Sheila. Either I'm their father or I'm not. You've forgotten what you told me, haven't you? You're only do-ing this because Miranda wanted to get to know her father."

"All right, then," she hissed between clenched teeth, glancing toward the kitchen, "but I expect you to be discreet. I've given them strict instructions not to tell anybody, although Miranda can't keep a secret if her life depended on it. Just try to arrange something that doesn't involve crowds of people."

Dafydd lowered his voice. "What's your problem? Why is it so important? I'm as acceptable a father as anyone. I think it would be better for them just to be able to be open about this. Having a father is far better than not having one, in everybody's eyes."

"This is *my* business," she shot back. "Your opinion is not required."

They glared at each other briefly before the twins came back, carrying a fruit salad and a bowl of ice cream. Mark looked suspiciously from his mother to Dafydd and back. His pale, watery eyes seemed to penetrate beyond the skin.

"Do you have to go already?" Miranda asked as they finished the meal and Sheila appeared with Dafydd's parka in her hand.

"It looks like it," Dafydd said. Miranda was a girl who would have no problem confronting her mother. She had no doubt inherited her quick thinking, and she was assertive and outspoken. Dafydd found himself hoping that if she was his daughter, she also had some of him, his basic simple nature and modest needs, his benign disposition. He said goodbye. The boy, in his rasping voice, huffed a quick "See ya," whereas Miranda gave him a hug. Here was a kid who thought she'd struck gold: finding the father she'd longed for. In her eyes he had to be perfect. It was quite a role to live up to.

Dafydd settled into a pattern of visiting Ian every morning, taking him papers, food and very reluctantly the whiskey that had become Ian's curse of choice. There were signs of a small effort being made at detoxing, which in Ian's case meant drinking a bottle per day instead of two. Dafydd wanted to tackle him about his addiction but decided to wait until they'd recovered some of the old ease and intimacy they'd had. Ian had shut the door firmly on his own emotions and apparently had no close relationships at all.

Dafydd did not see the children for the entire week. He phoned Sheila almost daily to remonstrate with her for unreasonably keeping him away from them, but she rejected his requests, telling him to stay put until Friday and "talk to my lawyer and make arrangements for child maintenance with my bank." Dafydd did neither. She seemed to be hoping that keeping him away from the children would somehow pressure him into sorting out their financial arrangements, but her logic didn't work on him. He felt in no particular hurry. The more she told him to speed up the process, the more he felt he should stay put, to see what would give.

Almost two weeks had passed since he'd arrived, and he'd telephoned the personnel department in Cardiff telling them he was applying for a sabbatical. Though they weren't too happy about it, there were plenty of precedents. Other doctors had done it, some on a regular basis. He pleaded a personal crisis. Well, hell, wasn't it? All sorts of rumors had circulated the hospital before he left, his drunken accident, his run-in with Payne-Lawson, his errant wife . . . it had all added up to some inspired stories. He was glad to leave all that behind for a time and let the dust settle. Leave Isabel to make some decision, make or break.

When Friday came around, he left Ian's earlier than usual in order to keep his appointment with Sheila at her house. The snow had started to fall in earnest, and flakes as large as quails' eggs descended relentlessly from a white velvet sky. They fell in slow motion, but thickly, and getting out of the car and up to Sheila's front door had Dafydd covered in white fluff. When she let him in, he removed his parka and shook it vigorously out of the door.

"Why did you tell me that Ian was out of town?" he asked her straight off.

"I didn't want you to gang up with him. He's bad news. But that didn't stop you, did it? I hear you're out at his place most days. As long as you never take the kids there."

"I have no intention of doing that. Anyway, why the hell should you care what I do in my spare time?"

"I'm sure it hasn't passed you by that Ian is a raging alcoholic. He is a lost cause . . . and a sad fucker," she added with a cold disdain that shocked Dafydd.

"Alcoholism is a disease, Sheila. As a nurse, I would have thought you knew that."

"Like hell it is," she sneered.

They were standing in the hall. Sheila folded her arms and leaned against the doorpost in her customary manner. "Did you ring McCready?"

"No, but my lawyer is in touch with him."

She studied him for a few minutes, saying nothing. She looked different. Her normally immaculately brushed locks were in wild disarray and she wore no makeup but for some lip gloss that made her mouth look wet and slippery. She was dressed in threadbare jeans with two rips on the left thigh, and a tight T-shirt, a white lacy bra showing through the worn-out cotton. It was an odd outfit for her, very casual, sloppy almost, but nevertheless devastatingly sexy. He wondered what she'd been thinking when she dressed, what psychological maneuver she had in mind for the occasion. He could see there was some conflict turning in her head. Despite her seductive appearance, he knew she was angry and frustrated, but obviously reluctant to let him have it, although she never used to have such restraints. Finally she spoke.

"Don't you want to get back home?" she asked reasonably. "I can't see why you'd want to drag this out. I think we should settle on the figure McCready suggested." She looked him up and down, quite boldly, her eyes lingering somewhere around his belt buckle.

He felt a strong urge to leave. He felt in danger on her territory, alone with her. He hadn't forgotten what she was capable of. She was a she-devil incarnate, lovely to look at, intriguing, alluring, until she was spewing malice and contempt all over you, or worse. But these meetings with Sheila had to be gotten over with.

"Here, I'll hang up your coat by the vent," she said pleasantly, reaching her hand for his parka but without moving. Then, shattering the illusion of the good hostess, her eyes wandered down to his crotch. Dafydd felt his neck burst into a bloom of crimson and cursed himself for allowing this idiotic little interaction.

"Let me get you a cup of coffee . . . or something stronger?" she said and smiled.

"Coffee," he said, his voice as cool as his neck was hot.

"Just make yourself comfortable," she said, shoving him toward the living room and handing him a copy of the *Moose Creek News*.

The living room was curiously sterile, devoid of personal things, not even the kids' stuff. He sat back and tried to concentrate on an article about the drug problem in the town and wondered if the children, *his* children, might already be exposed to drugs. After a moment he heard the front door clicking open. He got up from the sofa and wandered to the window. Instinctively he took a step back when he saw Sheila, covering her head against the falling snow with a jacket, opening the trunk of Ian's car. He couldn't see what she was doing but he quickly backed off and sat down, his heart beating quite fast. A bomb came to mind, but then he dismissed it with a smile. Why kill him when there were all these riches to be had? She couldn't flog a dead horse. Was she just snooping? It seemed odd.

A minute later she returned with two mugs and sat down. She looked searchingly at him. In the reflected light of the whiteness outside the window, he saw that there was a tiredness about her. Darkish rings depressed the chalky skin under her eyes. Perhaps his presence in the town was more stressful for her than he imagined. She sipped quietly at her coffee for a moment, then, taking a deep breath, she pulled herself up.

"Now," she said, "I want to talk to you about Mark. There are a couple of options. A special school in Winnipeg. It costs twenty-two thousand dollars a year, but it's supposed to be excellent. If you don't want to pay for that, there are other, less attractive options."

"Special school? What are you talking about?" Dafydd asked, perplexed. "There seems to be nothing wrong with his intellect."

"On the contrary, but it's the behavioral side that I no longer want to put up with."

"You never said he had a problem."

"Well, I'm telling you now."

"Teenagers tend to be moody and difficult. That's normal," Dafydd protested. "Does Miranda know about this . . . sending him away?"

Sheila looked down into her lap, momentarily flustered. "Absolutely not. And you're not mentioning it, do you hear?"

"So she wouldn't want to see him banished to some—"

"*No*. But I don't care for his insolence. He has a dark side. I think it's not doing her much good. She worries too much about him. She should be having fun with her friends. Normal kids."

"Hmm . . . his dark side. I wonder where that hails from."

"Listen here," she said, her voice rising. "I spent most of my childhood in all kinds of boarding schools, and not half as nice as the one Mark can go to. What the hell is wrong with that? You people over there send your kids away to be educated, you probably went to boarding school yourself." She tossed her head angrily. "So don't give me that bullshit morality of yours."

"And what is it you'd like him to learn in such a place?" Dafydd asked.

"To fend for himself, for one," she countered, her voice harsh. "*I* had to, and it did me a power of good. You learn to look after number one."

"I believe you there *entirely*," Dafydd agreed. "You do know about that."

Sheila looked as if she wanted to wring him out with a heap of insults, and Dafydd almost smiled. This was the real Sheila, the one he knew. He much preferred her flashing anger to her bedroom eyes.

"Look. You've got to make some decisions pretty quick, or you're going to end up with a whole pile of lawyer's fees. I don't want you staying around here for very much longer. There should be no need. Surely your wife wants you home?"

"Oh, no, she doesn't." Dafydd laughed. "You've seen to that."

"Actually, I don't give a shit about your domestic situation. I just want things settled. I want some money in the bank by the end of next week. Like I said, two thousand a month is the going rate for someone with your earnings. So let's get a move on, shall we, or I'll have to take some further action."

"What do you think you can do to me?"

"Slap you with a court order, that's what."

He stood up, not having touched his coffee, and went into the hall to fetch his parka. But Sheila had this way of knowing when to step back, just in time. She followed him out into the hall and stopped him, putting her hand on his chest.

"C'mon, Dafydd, it doesn't have to come to that," she said placatingly. "Think about it. Let's keep things easy . . . for their sake. You want the best for them, don't you? Just be reasonable."

"The best for *them*? Like being sent away to some ghastly 'special school'?" The very idea that she planned to use *him* and his money to get rid of her son outraged him. "I'll pick them up tomorrow morning at ten. If that's not okay with you, I'm taking the next plane out of here and you'll have to pay your fucking Mr. McCready to chase me and my checkbook around the world."

He drove the car down a road leading to a playing field. The thick layer of snow covered up a series of nasty potholes and he bumped his way to a stop. He got out, stepping through ice up to his ankle in a freezing puddle, swore loudly and went to the back of the car. There was no lock on the trunk. Did Sheila know this? He opened it but could see nothing at all, bar a pair of mold-covered boots, the deflated spare tire and some greasy rags. He lifted these articles one at a time but discovered nothing untoward.

Lifting the corner of the soggy mat that lined the trunk, he spotted the item. Not a ticking bomb, but a package the size of a paperback, wrapped in bubblewrap and secured with transparent tape. He felt it. It contained many small elongated articles, hard, making a sound of grinding glass as he handled them. He wondered why it was there, who it was for, and toyed with the idea of unwrapping it, but his natural respect for other people's property made him replace the mysterious package where he found it. He backed the car out of the treacherous lane and headed for Tillie's place for dry socks and the lunch she'd insisted he'd have in lieu of a missed breakfast.

The three of them were sitting in Beanie's Wholefoods & Cafeteria, an establishment that evidently was not doing too well in this mainly redneck community, eating Beanie's beanburgers. With a view of the street, they looked at the people, now dressed in proper winter garments, gingerly shuffling along the icy sidewalks. Pickups with enormous tires crawled along, while a couple of dead cars littered the road in front of Beanie's, each topped with a tall hat of snow.

They were the only customers, served by a young man—Beanie himself, presumably—with long hair and a caftan that swished around his long legs and constantly threatened to trip him up. Miranda averted her face from the sight, as there was a danger of bursting into fits of giggles. She bent her head to the job of wolfing her burger when she remembered something and dug in her little red leather handbag. She handed him an envelope.

"My mom asked me to give you this. It came to our box number, but it's for you. Who's it from?"

"Doesn't your family back home know where you're staying?" Mark asked sharply, ending an hour-long silence during which he'd been engrossed in a magazine about computer software.

"Actually, no," Dafydd admitted, mortified. He'd thought about Isabel almost every night in a state of languid sleep, conjured up her pre-letter face and caressed her long slender body. It hadn't occurred to him to let her know where he was, mainly because she'd been adamant that he should go away and not bother her until he was back. She knew she could e-mail him whenever she wanted, or try his mobile, so why hadn't she? Still, it was imprudent not to let her have a contact address and phone number just in case. Suddenly he was eager to have something of her, if only words on paper.

"Would I be rude if I read this now?" he asked the twins.

"No," they said in unison. He tore open the envelope, and Miranda inched closer to him in an attempt to read over his arm.

> *Dafydd.*
> *You've been gone over two weeks and I haven't heard a thing from you. I thought you might have had the decency to contact me and give me some clue about what's going on. I sent you an e-mail, but it came back, so I'm sending this letter to Sheila Hailey's box number since you've not given me your address.*
>
>   *I'm having a hell of a time here, you should know, since the house was burgled last week and the place totally ransacked and vandalized. They got in easily through the conservatory. The damage is in the thousands. The police say it's the work of young-sters. As you know, there isn't a lot to steal that's worth anything but they went around with cans of red and orange car paint and sprayed the furniture, the paintings, the clothes in our wardrobes, even the inside of the fridge, curtains, towels, and—I'm afraid—your Russian icon. Just for the hell of it. I've taken the icon to a specialist restorer—can't tell as yet. I can't find your guitar, so unless you took it with you I presume it was nicked. The police say someone's got to live in the house, or this will hap-pen again. Squatters might move in, all sorts of other horrors. To be honest, I find it terribly depressing to*

*be there and Paul needs me in London until this job
is finished.*

*I phoned the hospital and they told me that you'd
requested a month's sabbatical to follow on from
your three weeks' leave (it would have been nice if
you'd told me, so I didn't have to ask your secretary
about your plans).*

*To avoid any further disasters I suggest we might
try to get someone to stay in the house for a few
weeks. Paul has a niece who is at the university here
and lives in some hovel; she'd be delighted. If you
could be kind enough to let me know how you feel
about this, so that I can set things in motion. The
place has to be cleaned and redecorated, and she and
her friends have offered to do the painting.*

Please e-mail me as soon as possible.

Isabel

"Oh, my God," Miranda yelled, having read most of it, although Dafydd tried to shield the contents with his hand. "That is just horrible. I'm not coming to visit you in England with creeps like that around. Poor lady. Imagine that."

She turned to her brother. "These guys broke into Dad's wife's house and sprayed all her clothes with paint."

Turning back to Dafydd, she asked, "Did she have lots of clothes?"

"No, she never was that interested in lots of clothes," he said, his voice strained, "but she always looked great, even in simple things."

"Jeezus, I'd flip out totally," Miranda said with feeling.

Mark sighed loudly and rolled his eyes, but a flicker of interest in the concept of a break-in with massive damage was clearly there. He looked as if he would have liked to ask some questions but had a stance of indifference to maintain. He patted his sister patronizingly on the head and then got up and went over to speak to Beanie. He was obviously a regular customer, the one place where a committed vegan latchkey kid could have his snacks while waiting for his mother to come home. It sounded as if the two had a great deal to say to each other. Miranda chatted on, telling Dafydd of the various designer sneakers that she had her beady eye on, and the various means by which she was going to obtain the money to buy them. Dafydd felt numb as he tried to listen, while stretching his other ear in Mark's direction, wanting to hear what this mute child had to say to the caftan man. Another part of him was struggling to suppress a strong feeling of doom, of irreversible calamity and a sudden sharp decline in optimism and hope. Much as he was actually enjoying this little outing with these mismatched children, he couldn't wait to get rid of them so he could phone home . . . home? Such as he had known it, there was no longer a home.

CHAPTER 16

The roads had frozen over and a thick layer of powdery snow had settled on the ice. The effect was like banana skins on a newly waxed floor. Dafydd hauled the chains out of the back seat of the old Ford and with difficulty fastened them around the tires. With a fearsome clatter he set out for Ian's place.

As he drove down the highway, approaching the turnoff to the cabin, the package in the trunk came back to his mind. It could only be for Ian. What did Sheila have that Ian wanted or needed? Perhaps it was something he'd sent for, using the hospital's address or Sheila's. But why this furtive way of delivering it? Why hadn't she just given it to him to give to Ian? Glass, shot glasses, glass sticks, glass tubes . . . glass vials. *Glass vials!*

Dafydd's foot hit the brakes without meaning to, and despite the chains he skidded sideways to a stop near the ditch. That's when he saw a herd of musk oxen lumbering along the narrow road leading to the cabin. He sat up, surprised, knowing the animals rarely ventured south of the tundra, some seventy miles away.

He'd heard that packs of wolves sometimes drove them southward. Spellbound, he approached them slowly, but at the sound of his clattering chains the giant oxen fled, curiously joining themselves to each other, shoulder to shoulder, flank to flank, and moving as one animal. The wild sweep of their long hairy skirts was like a dark wave, undulating gracefully as they galloped in this formation in among the trees. He remembered that Sleeping Bear had once told him that one pound of the fine underwool could be spun into a strand ten miles long.

"Have you seen those amazing beasts?" he asked Ian after bringing in his daily supplies.

Ian handed him the usual twenty-dollar bill, which never covered his necessaries, but was well made up for by the use of the car. "The musks? God knows what they're doing here. Thorn's going mad."

Ian poured out drinks from a newly acquired bottle and handed one to Dafydd. "You didn't come yesterday. I didn't have your phone number so I couldn't call you."

"Why didn't you look it up in the phone book or ring directory inquiries? The Happy Prospector, remember?"

"I kept waiting for you to come, and then I got smashed and couldn't care less."

"Was there anything particular you wanted?"

"Nah, not really. I was just getting used to you coming every day."

Dafydd waited for the moment when some excuse would be made and Ian would go rummaging in the trunk of the car.

"How's fatherhood, then?"

"All right, thanks. Miranda is really sweet, and feisty, too. Mark, I don't know . . . Sheila says he's got behavioral problems. Do you know anything about this?"

"He's a teenager, for fuck's sake; they're all *behavioral*. She thinks she knows everything, that woman. She's real good at manipulating and using people, but she knows fuck-all about humanity. She's like a scavenger, a wolverine. Did you know their nickname, 'the glutton'? That's her, all right."

Dafydd was taken aback by the bitterness in Ian's voice. Perhaps he, too, had reasons to detest the woman, other reasons. There certainly were some sort of shady dealings between them. He couldn't hold off anymore and said, "I believe there's a package in the boot of the car that's meant for you."

Ian looked startled.

"What did she tell you?" he asked sharply.

"Nothing. I just saw her put it in the car."

Ian hopped up surprisingly fast and scuttled out, returning at once with the plastic package. He hesitated, standing there in the middle of the room, looking to the bathroom, then to Dafydd, then at the package.

"Oh, for God's sake," Dafydd burst out angrily. "What sort of substance am I being made to carry? Just spit it out."

"Demerol."

Dafydd stared at him. "Demerol?"

"I thought you might have guessed. Before. When it started. I've been hooked on it for . . . years."

"How much do you use?"

"Oh, around a thousand mg. a day."

"A thousand . . . my God. How on earth do you get the stuff?" Dafydd had known of a few doctors getting hooked, even two or three in Cardiff, but over a decade . . . that's a long time without getting caught.

"Oh, come off it. Where do you keep that gray matter of yours?" Ian was about to add insult to his irritation but abruptly sank into himself and went for the nearest chair.

"What do you *think*?" he said, sighing deeply, putting his head in his hands.

"Not Sheila, surely?"

Ian looked up. "Have you seen that house she lives in . . . on her nurse's salary? Her clothes, her car, her furniture? Not to mention her bank account." He sat back in his chair and started to tear the package open with some difficulty. "Now look at how *I'm* living . . . on a doctor's salary. See if you can put two and two together."

"But how does she get away with it? Does nobody keep count . . . ?"

"Of course. *She* does. She's completely in charge of all the ordering, dispensing, and accounts. Haven't you seen that little bunch of keys on her belt? Nobody but Sheila sets foot in the dispensary. Even Hogg has to ask her for whatever he needs." He tore at the plastic with his teeth. "I live in terror of her holidays."

He finally liberated the many vials from the package. They popped onto the table, rolling in every direction, and he just managed to grab one before it crashed to the floor. "Mind, she's pretty good about stuff like that. As long as I pay her extra, she'll provide a good advance supply. Difficult to meter out, though," he said and smiled. "I actually prefer it when she's in charge. I tend to go overboard on things."

His hand closed on a vial and, in reflex, he was already rolling up his sleeve. "I'll just be a moment," he said, getting up.

"Just one thing before you go," Dafydd said, trying hard not to let sarcasm infect his voice. "Is this why I have your car? To save you the journey, or to save Sheila the journey?"

"Oh, no, that never entered my head. Truly. Normally delivery is not a problem, but since I've been home it's become a bit tricky. She hates the ride, and people notice. Seeing that you were coming . . . well, it was her idea. A stupid one, as it turned out. It's not like Sheila to be careless." He shrugged his shoulders and headed off toward the bathroom.

On impulse, Dafydd got up and left, driving off with a thunderous clanging of chains against the hard ice. In the rearview mirror he saw Thorn bounding after him, barking forlornly. Abruptly his anger and disgust dissipated and he stopped to say goodbye to the distressed dog. Thorn looked pleadingly at him, begging him not to abandon his master. *Don't go. He's got no friends. Don't desert him.*

Dafydd hugged the old mutt, burying his face in the warm, fluffy neck. He had no right to judge Ian. The man was an addict, not a fiend. He had never found out why Ian had come to Moose Creek in the first place, what need or misdeed had brought him here. Sure, the younger Ian had seemed reckless at the time, irresponsible even, but he'd been a good and caring doctor, always doing his share of work, often more. But his addictions had now taken him beyond this point. Nevertheless, Dafydd decided that it was not his business to police Ian's affairs; it was up to the hospital to know how he handled himself. He knew that much worse people had worked in Moose Creek; he'd been told some shocking stories by Janie. A genuine CV wasn't an absolutely rigorous requirement, and in a pinch a cast-out alcoholic or pethidine-addicted doctor, or one with a criminal record, or simply incompetent, dangerous or with dubious qualifications, could have his misdemeanors overlooked and be welcomed in this place where posts were often near-impossible to fill.

Dafydd backed up the drive and went in to join Ian, who by now was in a state of blissful inebriation.

I'm sorry I've missed your calls. I'm very busy. I've been offered a new commission. Paul has suggested I go in with him on a chain of hotels in Dubai. I'll be working from London, but I'll have to be on site quite frequently. I hope you're happy for me. This may be years of work. A free hand on everything, including restaurants, foyers, the lot. This brings me to another question. The Thompsons have friends who are interested in our house. Not as a rental, but to buy. They rang me out of the blue and offered £290,000. Marjorie must have filled them in on all that has happened to the place (and us personally) and figured we'd want to get out. Out of interest I rang an agent who came to look. He confirmed the price. It'd be more if it wasn't in such a state. I was astonished. Quite frankly, I think it might be the best thing. Let me know what you think. All the best for now. Isabel.

All the best, indeed. Dafydd stared at the screen. Whatever happened to love, kisses, hugs, and exes. What happened to longing, yearning, and missing? Paul Bloody Deveraux . . . who the fuck was he to lay claim to his wife? A powerful wave of grief rolled over him. A pain in his chest set itself like a stone, making him almost breathless. But he was sitting in Tillie's office and Tillie was hovering nearby, pretending to put papers into files.

He desperately needed to talk to Isabel in person but she was avoiding him very effectively. Perhaps he'd receded in importance so much that he wasn't worth talking to. Or was her thrust forward part of his punishment, to show him how redundant he was? He pressed *reply*.

> Isabel. The tone of your e-mail was painful. It makes it sound as if we are business associates, not partners in a marriage (we *are* still married).
>
> Congrats on your commission in Dubai. Obviously good for you, but perhaps you could let me know how you foresee *our* future together, if you think there might be such a thing.
>
> As for the house, that was quick on your part. I've been gone only three weeks, and you're dismantling our life. That house is my home, your home, our home. But by all means get rid of the damned thing. It's too big for us, anyway. A new start in a new house would perhaps be good for us. I'll leave it for you to handle, and I fully accept whatever decision you make.
>
> However, please have the courtesy to talk to me in person sometime soon. Ring me. Love, Dafydd.

He clicked *send* without reading it through. He had said what he felt and she should know about it. Ten seconds later he panicked and wished he hadn't been so stern, so *terminal*. And the house . . . they'd been there only six years, but he thought it was for keeps. He'd practically told her to get rid of it. If ever he wanted to have Mark and Miranda to stay, or to live, where would they come? The whole situation seemed utterly surreal. Tillie was moving around behind him, attentive to his mood. He felt her hand momentarily on his shoulder.

"You okay?"

"Yes, Tillie, thanks." He sighed and got up. Climbing the stairs, he felt depressed. He was thousands of miles away from his wife and any chance of a shred of intimacy, of understanding. But what was there for her to understand? He had to concede that it was a bit of an event to be a father, but he couldn't say that he was full of exhilaration and enthusiasm. In fact, the idea of getting close to these two vulnerable children and then merrily leaving them to fend for themselves now filled him with alarm. With all those thousands of miles separating them, how could he be there for them when they might need him?

In his room he looked around at the mess. The gaudy décor bounced off his eyeballs like a disco light show every time he opened the door. He'd forbidden Tillie to come in and tidy for the last two days—he knew instinctively that she shouldn't be folding his clothes, removing them for washing, smoothing his sheets and his pillow—with the excuse that she did far too much for him already.

He plopped into his chair and put his face in his hands, trying to blot out the contradictory options of his complex future. He was pretty well damned whichever way he chose to go. He couldn't stay here, not a chance, but what would he find on his return home? How would he feel if Isabel left him for that Deveraux slimeball? Where would he live?

There was a loud decisive rapping on the door. He flew out of the pink lounger and tucked his shirt into his jeans. It was a Sheila-type knock. He felt instantly angry at his own reaction. She had no business coming to his room unannounced. He sat down again, deciding not to respond. The knock was repeated, this time harder. Dafydd swore and went to the door. It was Hogg.

"Hogg!" he exclaimed. Hogg's brows narrowed. "Andrew . . . please come in." Hogg marched in and surveyed the room briskly, taking in the clutter and the unmade purple bed. "Sorry to burst in on you like this. I couldn't get through on the phone just now and I thought I'd just walk down to see you. It's a nice day, but the sidewalks are treacherous. That's all I need now, to slip and break a leg."

"You need mukluks," Dafydd said, pointing at Hogg's feet, which were clad in expensive Italian shoes. "They stick to anything. In fact, I'm planning a trip to the Friendship Center this afternoon to see if I can pick some up."

"You'll have a faint when you see the prices. Native crafts are well beyond the reach of us ordinary resident folks. Tourism has seen to that."

They were standing in the middle of the room and Dafydd cursed himself for forgetting to ask Tillie for some proper chairs. He pointed at the lounger, but Hogg, being hopelessly rotund, eyed up the prospect of getting in, as well as getting out of the hammocklike contraption, and said, "Why don't we pop across the road to the greasy spoon? They do a good old-fashioned apple pie."

Dafydd quickly laced up his boots and grabbed his parka, wondering what this visit was all about. Hogg was not a person who made social calls; neither had they ever become anything like friends. Hogg seemed quite a shallow person, but he did love Sheila, everybody knew that, and Dafydd wondered if this unexpected visit had something to do with her. Perhaps he had found something out. Maybe she'd told him. They marched across and sat themselves in a booth with a view of the street. Hogg greeted the waitress with exaggerated courtesy. "The usual, times two," he said, winking. "We missed you in the cafeteria the other week," he said with affected petulance. "I was jolly disappointed. I've been told that you seem to be staying on here . . . Is that correct?" He tapped the middle of the table with a short fat forefinger to encourage an explanation for this frivolous carry-on.

Dafydd was unprepared. Sheila didn't want the facts known. On the other hand, why was she able to dictate to whom he spoke? Granted, the children should be protected whenever possible, but Hogg was their GP. Surely he must know, anyway. He would have taken the blood samples for the DNA tests.

"Well, it's complicated . . . Can you keep this to yourself, Andrew?"

"Of course, of course. Fire away, fire away."

"It appears that I'm the father of Sheila's children. Actually, it is more than that. I *am* the father of Sheila's children. That's why I'm here."

The shock that hit Hogg drained the blood from his face, and for a moment he appeared about to pass out. He stared at Dafydd, but his confusion made his eyes seem out of focus and he looked as if he were seeing Dafydd through a haze.

"Are you all right?" Dafydd asked. Suddenly he remembered what Ian had said. Hogg acting as if he were the father. Perhaps he thought he was.

"Of course I am," Hogg huffed. "It just seemed such an un-likely . . . situation."

"I'm sorry to spring it on you, but you did ask."

"Of course, of course."

The shapely waitress with the Texan accent descended on them with two plates. All around her wafted a cloud of per-fume and the aroma of steaming apple pie. She swiftly fetched the caffè lattes, which were large like buckets and almost white with creamy milk. Hogg poured a generous stream of sugar from the dispenser and stirred his latte for a long time, looking into the swirling center in concentration. His appetite seemed to have vanished.

"Perhaps you should consider a DNA test," he said at last, "before you're totally committed to the idea."

"It's been done. I wouldn't be here otherwise. This has been one hell of an upheaval for me and my wife. I had no idea . . . until three months ago."

Small pearls of sweat covered Hogg's brow, and his deathly pallor had been replaced with a deep flush. Dafydd got con-cerned that the man might have a cardiac arrest or a stroke. He looked most unwell.

"I thought *you* might have done the blood tests on Sheila and Mark," Dafydd said. "I'm sorry. It was an assumption."

"Don't worry. I won't speak a word of it." Hogg's breathing was labored. He pulled out a large handkerchief and mopped his face. Grabbing the sugar dispenser, he poured yet another stream into his well-sweetened latte, seemingly in a daze. Again he stirred thoroughly, then he clinked his spoon a couple of times on the rim of the mug and placed it neatly on the saucer. He looked up at Dafydd. "I had no idea," he said.

"Well, Sheila is adamant that no one should know. Don't ask me why." Dafydd took a sip from the gigantic mug and tried a bite of the stodgy pie. "I thought it might have been the reason you wanted to talk to me."

"Oh, no. Certainly not." Hogg's tone was sharp and he waved his hand dismissively. "I actually wanted to ask you if you could do a locum. Ian doesn't seem to be in a hurry to come back. He's been off a lot in the last couple of years." Hogg leaned forward across the table and lowered his voice. "He's not too well. I have absolutely no cause for complaint, but . . ." He closed his eyes and shook his head, no doubt in a battle with himself about how much to confide.

"I could do a couple of weeks, I suppose, but what about work permits, et cetera?"

"Oh, don't worry about that. I'll handle it. Up here we have such things as emergency situations, and I consider this to be one. I can offer you five thousand dollars for three weeks. It's not an enormous amount, but it's the best I can do."

"Three weeks . . . ?" Dafydd did a quick calculation and realized that this would take him just past the end of his sabbatical. Well, another week or two wouldn't make much of a difference, although it was a bit disloyal. He wouldn't get fired, but he could clearly visualize Payne-Lawson's haughty, disapproving expression, the speculations around the hospital, and found that suddenly he didn't care.

"All right. When do you want me to start?"

"First thing tomorrow morning, eight-thirty sharp."

Dafydd smiled. Some things never changed. He looked at the little man, now brisk and businesslike as usual, completely recovered from his strange turn. Not enough recovered, however, to tackle the man-sized snack that he had ordered. He just looked at it with regret. He saw Dafydd looking, too.

"Really, I shouldn't be eating the stuff," he said, slightly embarrassed. "Here am I telling all these obese patients to cut down and be sensible. I should be putting my money where my mouth is." He laughed a big hollow laugh, trying to sound amused with himself.

After leaving the greasy spoon, Dafydd turned to Hogg on the sidewalk.

"I think Sheila is going to object to me working in the hospital. You'll have to do a job on her, Andrew."

"I would have thought she'd be happy," Hogg said with unexpected bitterness. "What could be better than having her family united, and her future . . . her former . . . eh, the father of her children working locally?"

"It's not quite that simple."

"I see. Well . . . what's the problem?"

"It's not exactly a harmonious situation. But perhaps you shouldn't let on that you know . . . for now," Dafydd said. "Personally, I don't see why it should matter. You're quite close to Sheila and the children. You seem to be her only real friend, and she trusts you, she said so herself."

Hogg's mood seemed to improve slightly by these revelations. "She's a headstrong woman, but I'll do my best to convince her that you're an asset to the hospital . . . for the moment."

They shook hands and parted.

"I'm employed," Dafydd said aloud and laughed. Then he winced. Déjà vu. There he was, back in Moose Creek, joining the losers, after yet another transgression back home.

CHAPTER 17

After twenty laps his back and neck ached. He'd swallowed what felt like two liters of water with a strong dilution of infants' pee and a serious dose of chlorine. His eyes stung and he felt vaguely sick. He stopped and attempted a few stretches in the water, realizing that not only had he gotten thoroughly unfit in just a few weeks but he was stiff as a board as well. He resolved to get his lazy butt to the pool at least three mornings a week.

He became aware of being observed by a figure sitting on the edge of the pool. It was the only other bather, since the recreation center had opened at seven and it was not even a quarter past. The lanky figure was recognizable mainly from its top, a reddish orange halo of hair, uncharacteristically out of its ponytail.

Dafydd swam over. "Good morning, Mark. You got an early start? You and me both." His voice was unnaturally merry and loud in the echoing emptiness of the pool building. He treaded water while being scrutinized by the cold, watchful eyes.

"My mom said you've got a job in the hospital."

"What the heck? I might as well make myself useful whilst Dr. Brannagan is si . . . is on holiday."

"She's mad."

"How do you mean?" Dafydd asked guardedly.

For the first time the lips of the lad drew apart in a semblance of a smile. "Not mad as in crazy," he said condescendingly, "mad as in fucking furious."

"Well, well," Dafydd said, trying to think of a suitable reaction to this. "She'll probably get used to it, don't you think? I'll try to stay out from under her feet."

"Why don't you just give her the money and skedaddle?"

"I'm here to get to know you and your sister." Dafydd felt his exasperation rising. He grabbed the edge of the pool and hauled himself up to sit beside the boy who was his son. "Wouldn't you like to get to know *me* just a bit? All this is hard to get used to, I admit, but I'm supposed to be your father, even if you think I'm a bloody nuisance."

The boy said nothing and Dafydd looked at their feet, which were dangling and splashing the foul water. Mark's were long and narrow, the shape of them so utterly different from Dafydd's own wedge-shaped paddlers. There was, in fact, not a single recognizable similarity between them. Mark's body was a sickly white, strangely elongated and scrawny and lacking in muscle tone. Freckles speckled every inch of him. Dafydd, too, was lean, but dense. There was nothing of his solidity and compactness of limb in the lad, but then again he was still very young.

Mark watched him study their differences. "You're *not* my father. I know that for a fact," he said and jumped into the water. He swam off in a surprisingly graceful crawl. Dafydd sat dumbfounded, looking at him swimming quickly back and forth. When he finally hauled himself out of the pool, Dafydd followed him into the changing room. It, too, was empty of early birds.

"Exactly what did you mean, I'm not your father?" Dafydd asked him. Mark was swiftly drying himself off, then disappeared into a booth to put his clothes on.

"I'm late for school," he shouted over the partition.

"Come off it," Dafydd called back, "it's just gone half past seven. I'll buy you breakfast if you get a move on."

They were seated in the cafeteria of the Northern Holiday Hotel, a mere five-minute walk from the rec center. Despite the sprint, both looked blue around the ears and nose from their still-damp hair in the minus-twenty temperature.

"There's probably nothing here I can eat," Mark said, scanning the menu.

"How about a big bowl of porridge with cinnamon and honey, followed by hash browns with baked beans and fried tomatoes and mushrooms, together with toast with margarine and jam, plus a fruit salad?" Dafydd said casually, fingering the battered corners of the plastic bill of fare.

There was obviously a crack through which a person could approach the boy, as long as it involved food. With the apparent lack of interest and understanding from his mother, and food purveyors in general about town, the poor kid had a hard time foraging for his vegan foodstuffs. His pale eyes took on a genuine glitter, but then his shoulders slumped and he said, dejected, "I doubt they'll have all that."

They did, and Dafydd, being naturally inclined toward the vegetable kingdom, joined him in the feast. When they'd finished scoffing it all down, mainly in concentrated silence, he tried again.

"I know all this has been sprung on you against your will, but we could try to just be friends."

Mark glanced at his massive watch. "Well, just *look* at us," he said. "We don't even look alike. You're absolutely not my father. To my sister, maybe, but not me."

"But that's just impossible," Dafydd objected. "I'm sure you know that."

"Well, I'm not your son. I just know it. Go bug someone else." He seemed to regret his last words and he said, "Well, I'm *real* full."

Dafydd was in a rush to get to the hospital. He thought now, a week on, that he'd been wise in agreeing to do the locum. Five thousand dollars would come in handy. Nothing was for free in this town, probably one of the world's most expensive outposts, and he would have to start paying Sheila something. He was no further forward in his search for the truth; on the contrary, it appeared as if he would have to accept his part in the making of the twins. Whenever he tried to think of the time of their supposed conception, his mind went blank, probably because he'd been over it so many times. And no one he'd spoken to could offer him any lead. Miranda had shown him their birth certificates, with no prompting on his part (but possibly Sheila's), and the dates tallied perfectly. Anyway, until he felt ready to leave, work was giving him another sense of purpose and stopped him from sitting around and ruminating.

Mark was right, Sheila had been fucking furious. She didn't want him around the hospital, and that was that. However, Hogg having personally recruited him meant she wasn't in any position to stop him. Her threats about the immigration authorities were hot air. Hogg knew his way around the obstacles. It was all in the paperwork.

"You told Hogg," she hissed when they were preparing to repair a baby's hernia.

"Yes, I told him. He promised to keep it under wraps." He had scrubbed down and was putting on rubber gloves. "*So what?*" he added irritably. "He's their GP. I'm astonished you haven't told him yourself. Anyway, who *did* take the blood from you and Mark for the test?"

Sheila looked away and the set of her jaw betrayed her tension. "What difference does it make?" she snapped. "It was one of the doctors here and he asked no questions."

"A *he*, then," Dafydd said, ruling out Dr. Atilan, the woman obstetrician, and Nadja Kristoff, a young GP fresh out of training. It didn't make any difference, but he was fed up with all the secrecy and underhandedness, and he liked to see her squirm a bit.

"God, you're a pain in the ass," Sheila said. "If it means *that* much to you, it was Ian. But leave the poor guy alone, will you? He's a dying man; he doesn't need your brand of third degree."

Dafydd was on the verge of saying, *Nor your brand of help to get there,* but held his tongue. He didn't want to compromise Ian. Instead he said, "Dying? What makes you think he's that ill?"

"His liver is fucked, in case you hadn't noticed."

He thought, his death will be a fucking great loss of revenue for you, bitch, but he swallowed the outrage he felt. He tried to fight his growing antagonism toward her; it didn't help the situation, but since finding out about the main reason for Ian's decline, physical, spiritual, and financial . . . he was disturbed by some of the fantasies he was having about Sheila, particularly after what she had accused him of. He *wanted* to hurt her. The thoughts unsettled him; he couldn't remember ever wanting to hurt anybody. He wondered sometimes if there was some unsound sexual motive behind his fantasies, but no, it was all anger, disgust, and outrage. She was evil, and he hated what she was, what she'd become.

The atmosphere during the operation wasn't good. Dafydd had asked Hogg to arrange his rotation never to coincide with Sheila's if possible, but was told that it was *her* job to write out the rotation. Much as they now loathed the sight of each other, she obviously felt she had to keep an eye on him. Other than his time with her, he was thoroughly enjoying the work, real patients with real problems. There were constant challenges, and he was mindful of his hard-earned maturity and experience. He could see that fourteen years ago he'd not been up to the job, not really. This was so different from his work in Cardiff. He found that he was now looking at the person, his color, his breathing, the feel of his pulse, instead of having his eyes fixed on monitors and video screens that dehumanized the process of medicine and turned his patients into organs and systems, to be removed or repaired. As the days went by he rediscovered his enjoyment of hands-on, grassroots medicine. It was often hazardous, sometimes frightening but occasionally very rewarding.

His last patient of the day was Joseph, Bear's grandson. He was thoroughly surprised to find Dafydd in the consulting room.

"What! I thought you were here on holiday," he said as he saw him sitting behind the desk. "Normally I see the army man. Lezzard. He knows about my condition."

"I'm just doing a short stint, filling in . . ." Dafydd said and studied the man's notes. He saw that Joseph suffered from adult-onset diabetes.

"Has Dr. Lezzard discussed with you the benefit of losing some of that weight?" Dafydd asked and a picture of Bruce Lezzard's tall and bulky form came before him, a man-mountain himself.

"No, he just prescribes me my injections."

"That's the point. You might be able to do away with the injections if you lost some weight . . . quite a lot of weight." He saw that realistically this would never happen and said no more. He examined the man and was surprised to discover that he was only fifty-eight years old. The climate was hard and life expectancy short. After a quick examination, he wrote out the prescription and handed it over. With a curt "Thanks," Joseph headed for the door.

"Do you have a family, Joseph?" Dafydd said to his back.

"Why do you ask that?" Joseph's tone was guarded but he stopped and turned around.

Dafydd shrugged. "It's just that I don't know anything about you."

"No, you wouldn't, would you?" Joseph replied with sarcasm. "Let me tell you something. Even my own granddad didn't. He never even met my children. I've got four of them. He didn't want to know."

"Well, yes," Dafydd said, trying to motion him to come back and sit down. He was curious about what made this man so bitter with the world, so obviously having nothing of Bear's good spirits. "I remember him telling me that your wife didn't much like him. Sleeping Bear apparently wasn't welcome in your home."

"*Sleeping Bear,*" Joseph sneered. Abruptly he came and sat down in the chair he had just vacated. "You thought you'd made friends with a real old indian, didn't you? But he wasn't native, he wasn't even born Canadian." He looked triumphantly at Dafydd. "Bet you had no idea."

"Actually, I knew," Dafydd said.

A fleeting look of surprise passed over Joseph's jowly countenance. "Well, I don't know what sort of picture you had of the old man, but he was far from the perfect family man."

"I gathered that," Dafydd admitted. "Things weren't always easy between the two of you, were they?"

"Now, hang on a minute." Joseph placed his fat palm on the table. "I cared about him plenty. I looked after him the very best I could. And he never thanked me for it. He was a selfish old so-and-so."

"He cared about you," Dafydd insisted. "I know he did."

"Hell, no. He hadn't a care for his own family. But he wasn't beyond spreading his seeds around the place . . ."

It was Dafydd's turn to be surprised. He remembered clearly the old man's stories about the hardships of his first years in the wilderness and how he fell in love with a beautiful Indian woman, how devoted he had seemed to the memory of his long and happy marriage. He talked about his wife often, a stoical, humorous and affectionate woman who did nothing but work and care for her family.

"What do you mean exactly?" he asked Joseph, who seemed to be angry with himself. He was staring at his boots with an irritated frown.

"Well, hell. I'd have thought *you* would know," he said in a sullen voice.

Dafydd laughed, trying to lighten the atmosphere. "I don't, but by all means tell me about it. The old man used to talk a lot about his wife and children, but he never mentioned any others . . ."

Joseph looked up, directly into Dafydd's face, his eyes puffed by edema. "Well, for example, I reckon you must have met his boy in Black River. Surely you remember that wild-goose chase you two went on."

Dafydd was baffled. "I don't remember any boy."

"Sure you do." Joseph clearly disbelieved him. "He had a kid with someone."

"I'm sorry. I don't know anything about it."

"Oh, come on. That's why you went. He had a woman up there."

"No, we went to visit an old friend of his," Dafydd said truthfully. It was almost laughable. Bear would have been ninety by then, and his days of "spreading his seeds around the place" would have been well and truly over. He even remembered the old man lamenting his lacking sex life, saying he'd not "had my jollies" since his wife died. Mind, Bear hadn't necessarily been a paragon of fidelity, and he'd been young once. Dafydd winced with unease. No one would have guessed that about *him* either . . . *spreading his seeds around the place.*

Joseph's hoarse voice pulled him back. "Have you any idea how this felt for me and my wife? I looked after him for years . . . and he left half of his money to that kid. Half to *one kid*. The other half split between the rest of us, and my sister, and her two kids." Joseph's right hand had clenched and the fist emphasized his points with small rhythmic whacks on the table between them. "I always told him I wanted Max to go to university. He's the smartest of the lot and wanted to become a lawyer. He's the one who would take over the fight for our rights and our lands. He was the one worth investing in. I told him many times. But no, there was precious little money to go around. I got the cabin but it wasn't worth a goat's pellet . . ."

"I'm sorry," Dafydd said helplessly. "I'm surprised he didn't tell me about this, about the—"

"Come, now. If you did know, I don't expect you'd tell me," Joseph said and stood up abruptly. "Anyhow, what's the point of talking about it? I just thought I'd set you straight. All these romantic notions about the old man, you weren't the only one who thought he was a true son of the native soil. It was just so much bullshit."

"I'm sorry you feel that way about him."

"I think he owed me, he owed Max. He knew the hopes we had for the boy. Smart as they come. That business soured my feelings for the old man, I can tell you straight."

"In that case I think it was very good of you to come up to me in the bar the other day and pass on his message. I sure appreciated that."

"Well, I always did his bidding, didn't I? And see where it got me."

When Joseph had left the room, shutting the door a little bit too firmly, Dafydd waited a few seconds and then burst into chuckles. The old devil. Who would have thought that Bear was running around having his "jollies" with women around the place, leaving offspring in his wake? If it was true, it wasn't perhaps the most commendable of traits. Dafydd tried to imagine the decrepit, none-too-clean old man in the process of seduction and it made him laugh afresh. Well, he thought as he gathered his notes, there's hope for us all.

Dafydd drove out to Ian, having changed his visits from mornings to after work, stopping off at the Co-op to get him his supplies. Twice he'd seen Sheila meddle with the trunk of the car in the doctors' parking lot but had done nothing about it. He knew he had to take a stand, but how? It was sheer madness to expose himself to arrest and deportation.

The sky was jet-black, not a star in sight, and the headlights of the car were weak. The previous week he'd stunned a moose cow in the middle of the road, but apart from this incident and the rare sighting of the musk oxen the forests were quiet, dark despite their snowy whiteness, devoid of apparent life. As the snow was building up, darkness was lengthening. The drive seemed longer than usual, Ian's dilapidated abode more remote than ever.

"You should consider moving into town," Dafydd said after unloading the Co-op bags. "And you could use a bit of help." His hand swept around the room.

"I like it here."

"Listen." Dafydd sat himself down opposite Ian at the table and drew a deep breath. "You've got less than two weeks before you've got to be back at work . . . You've got to get your act together. For a start, I don't think you can go on living here. If you want to, I'll help you. Why don't you consider renting an apartment in Woodpark Manor? They've got vacancies. The apartments are bright, clean and there's a gym in the basement. I'd go there myself if I wanted to live in Moose Creek. I'll help you rent a van to move your stuff. You'll be near the hospital and—"

"Hold it," Ian snapped angrily. "Who do you think you are? The fucking Samaritans? I'm not going *anywhere*."

"All right, all right," Dafydd said and sighed. "But my locum finishes on the seventh of December. Are you going to be ready to go back to work? I should tell you that there's talk of hiring a new partner, on a permanent basis."

"Great," Ian said gruffly. "I'm thinking of taking early retirement."

"But what are you going to live on?" Dafydd protested. "Your pension won't be up to much and I don't suppose Sheila has spared you any savings."

Thorn didn't like the tone of the conversation and started to whine. The dog came up and leaned against Dafydd's thigh, pressing insistently. Ian sat slumped in the kitchen chair, looking awful.

"Why don't *you* take the job?" he said. "You seem to be liking it just fine."

"Don't be stupid. I've got to get back to Wales or I'll lose *my* job. I've got a marriage to try to save, although I think I've lost it already. I mean, I can't just stay here forever, now, can I?" Dafydd pushed the debris on the table to one side. "Look here. Don't use me as a reason not to go back to work. You can beat this, you know. You need some treatment. Hell, you're only forty-five years—"

"Forty-four."

"I'll help you. I'll arrange something, Vancouver or Toronto, anywhere discreet. I'll lend you the money. I could try to stay on for a while . . . Hell, it's only a phone call. But I'd only do it to see you beat this. That way you can get on your feet and come back triumphant. Slash Sheila's earnings and tell her to go fuck herself. Fix up this place. Have a holiday—"

Dafydd stopped abruptly when he saw that Ian's shoulders were shaking. Thorn was jumping up, trying to lick his master's face. Ian was crying silently, but his body heaved and shook as he tried to hold in emotions that seemed to threaten to make him howl. Dafydd looked at him, startled by his anguish. He searched for something to say, but Ian wasn't the sort of person who would take comfort in trite words and he seemed to shun physical contact. Nevertheless, Dafydd reached over and placed his hand on his shoulder, and gradually the shaking subsided. Ian grabbed a used paper napkin and blew his nose, his head still bent into his concave chest.

"You know what I found this morning?" he said in an unsteady voice, laughing quietly. "Your old boots and the skis. I took them out of the shed so you could have a go."

"That's nice, thank you. But, Ian, did you take on board what I was saying just now?" Dafydd insisted, exasperated. "You can't bury your head in the sand. Something's got to give. And I can't let Sheila place the drugs on me any longer. You two seem happy to risk it, but I can't. That would just be one disaster too many for me."

Ian shook his head as if to clear away the unpleasant onslaught. He got up and poured them both a drink. Dafydd wanted to shout *no* and pour the glasses down the filthy rust bucket that passed for a sink. But he didn't. He felt spent, tired, hopeless. Ian's emotional outburst had brought to the fore his own seemingly unsolvable situation. Who was he to give advice? They sat quietly for some time, Dafydd listlessly scanning the *Moose Creek News,* Ian's eyes far off, somewhere between shots of Demerol, topped up with whiskey and sustained by cigarette after cigarette.

"I had a wife once," Ian said suddenly.

"You were married?" Dafydd put the paper down and stared at Ian. "You never said."

"Her name was Lizzie. I loved her. I loved her to death, *literally.*"

"Oh, God, no, Ian. How do you mean?"

"She choked to death on a piece of turkey, a Christmas turkey which I'd cooked myself." Ian laughed grimly. "And she'd decided to become a vegetarian on January the first, and she really meant it."

"God, Ian. That's terrible beyond words." Dafydd reached over and touched Ian's knee. "Were you . . . there when it happened?"

"Yes, me, a fresh young doctor. But for all my medical training, I couldn't save her. I tried the Heimlich maneuver, but now that's a no-no, so I suppose it aggravated the situation. I tried to get at the fucker with a finger and then in desperation a pair of tweezers. It was almost impossible to hold her down. Finally I did a tracheotomy with a Swiss army knife, the sharpest thing I had. She was blue already, almost dead, and I must have panicked. I made a hell of a mess of it. There was blood everywhere. I'll never get that picture out of my mind." Ian laughed again, an eerie howl, somewhere between mirth and anguish. "The police had me locked up for murder until the autopsy was done. You couldn't blame them. I felt like a murderer myself. I kept getting confused and thinking I'd stabbed her to death. Even when the cause of death was established, everyone looked at me sideways. They were most reluctant to let me go."

Dafydd was rigid with horror. *So this was Ian.* It explained everything. "How long ago was this?"

"Oh, some eight months before I came here."

God, how had they never shared this? And they were supposed to have been friends! Compared with Ian's tragedy, how relatively cushy his own catastrophe had been. Where Derek was concerned, it had been a slap on the wrist and then only his own guilt and angst to deal with. But this! How could a man

ever get over such a cataclysmic event? The answer was obvious. No man could.

"But you did all you could," Dafydd said, feeling totally in-
adequate. He reached over and shook Ian sharply by the arm.
"You couldn't possibly have expected more from yourself.
You're only a man."

"A man?" Ian looked at him with disdain. "I'm supposed to
be a doctor."

Dafydd slumped in his chair. "Yes, I know what you
mean."

Ian tossed back the contents of his glass. "Dafydd, old buddy. I know all about it. Sheila told me what happened to you.
Shit, man, a child . . ."

They lapsed into another long silence.

"Have you any family anywhere, Ian?"

"Not anymore. Not that I know of."

"How do you mean?"

"My parents died in a house fire, I think I told you once. I
was adopted. After medical school I lost contact with my adop-
tive parents. We . . . fell out."

"Have you never thought of trying to get in touch?"

"Christ, no. I . . . I was always a disappointment, never
quite up to scratch. Hell, I got my degree and finished my training . . ." He stubbed out the cigarette with force, grinding the
butt hard around the ashtray. "They were quite old, anyway.
Dead by now, I'm sure."

They sat without speaking, each with his own thoughts.
Dafydd was gripped by his own sense of unreality. Ian's story seemed to have catapulted Dafydd further away from his
own cozy life, which now seemed irrevocably shattered. But
it wasn't! He had to keep reminding himself that he must go
back to pick up the threads. Which threads? His home might
have been sold, just like that. He would soon be in court facing
charges for drunk driving. His marriage might be over. Was all
this really true? Could this really have happened?

"I met Mark in the pool this morning," Dafydd said finally,

bringing them back to the here and now. "He's one strange kid. He insisted that I'm not his father."

"He doesn't look like anybody," Ian said, lighting another cigarette and inhaling deeply.

"You didn't tell me that it was you who took the blood tests for the DNA," Dafydd said quietly.

Ian looked away, smoking insistently. "I had no idea what the blood was for. She refused to say." He tipped his glass up and swallowed noisily, then poured a little more into both glasses.

Dafydd was shivering with cold watching Miranda and eight other girls, all of them quite a bit smaller than her, practice their figure skating on the ice rink behind the rec center under the glare of vicious strobe lights. This formed a large part of his relationship with the kids; taking them to their various activities in the evening, standing by waiting for them to finish and taking them home, thus liberating Sheila from the tiresome task. She seemed to have come to terms with the fact that people were talking and speculating, and Miranda took no heed of her warnings to keep her mouth shut. And people *were* talking. He noticed looks, winks, and nods from people he didn't know, but who now knew him, either from the hospital or from his being pointed out by others. The errant father come back to do the right thing.

"Look at this, Dad," Miranda called to him. She pirouetted clumsily in her orange snowsuit, incongruously garnished with a white tutu around her plump waist. Dafydd tried not to grin and applauded silently with his sheepskin mittens. She was a nice kid. There was nothing very difficult about her in any way, although her obstinacy and self-assurance were somewhat reminiscent of her mother.

They had fun going for junk-food bonanzas when Mark wasn't with them, and they did so today after the figure-skating practice, giggling over the monstrous pile of corn chips with sour cream and melted cheese that she loved.

"You should watch out for those evil saturated fats," he tried to tell her. "You don't want to become a real roly-poly."

"Give me saturated fats galore." Miranda chortled. "You wouldn't believe the fights we have at home about food. Mum's just as bad. Everybody wants different things. It's a nightmare. Can I have a chocolate milkshake?"

"You watch it or you won't fit into *this*"—he lifted up the limp, discarded tutu—"even without the snowsuit underneath."

"Dad, you know those sneakers I was telling you about . . . ?"

"How much?"

"Twenty-eight."

"All right. What the heck?"

"Thanks, Dad . . . Dad?"

"What else?"

"Couldn't you and my mum . . . sort of . . . go out?"

"Oh, Miranda. You're really smart. You can see for yourself that your mum doesn't like me much. Anyway, I'm married. Have you forgotten?"

"But if she did like you and your wife left you, you would, wouldn't you?"

"My dear girl. I'll be straight with you. My wife may well leave me, not because of you, don't worry, entirely because of me. You might think I'm Mr. Nice Guy, but I'm capable of being very stupid and making all sorts of mistakes. You'll find that out soon enough. But going out with your mother is a mistake that neither she nor I is likely to make. And don't be disappointed. It's absolutely for the best. Trust me."

"Me and Mark . . . I bet we're mistakes, too, right?"

Dafydd looked at her pretty face, her eyes narrowed in suspicion.

"No, Miranda," he said. "You two are very special. I look at the two of you and I'm amazed I had anything to do with it. I never thought I had it in me. It's a bloody miracle."

CHAPTER *18*

Dafydd. Got your message. Well, guess what? I've accepted the offer. Mr. and Mrs. Jenkins came to look at the house and they just want it. They don't need a mortgage and are keen to get in asap. The searches are being done as I write, and the contract has been sent off to you for your signature. Send it back right away. I'm renting a self-storage in Barry, and if you're not back by completion I'll just have your stuff (what's left of it) moved in there.

Now I'm going to have to spring something else on you, I'm afraid. I would like to have my share of the proceeds in order to buy in with Paul, as a partner. I don't want to be his employee and it's an investment I cannot pass up. He's doing extremely well. We're starting on the job in Dubai in just a few weeks' time. We're flying out there next week to meet the owners and the architects. Best, Isabel. PS Very good news: your Russian icon has been restored completely. It wasn't cheap but it's on me.

Dafydd printed out the e-mail and deleted it, then disappeared up the stairs before Tillie could detain him. She was so sensitive to his moods, he didn't want her to see his face.

It was increasingly difficult to reject her genuine concern, tell her to butt out and not ask questions.

He slammed the door to his room a bit too hard and threw himself on the bed. He read the e-mail one more time. *Sold!* He felt as if his life had been sold. No, he shouldn't have allowed it. Where would he live? Where would he take the children if they ever wanted to come to visit? Then again, there were always other houses . . . or an apartment. She hadn't said anything about where *she* was going to live, as in a permanent residence, *or with whom.* Bloody woman, stupid bloody adulterous hussy. Stupid, beautiful, clever, remarkable Isabel . . . his beloved wife. His nonwife, his lost wife, his ex-wife, Paul Deveraux's woman . . . He punched the pillow and tried very hard to remind himself that so far he had no proof. He *could* be imagining it. She'd not admitted to anything, bar the fact that she'd lost all respect for him. How could there be love without respect? She couldn't write an e-mail like this and still love him. Affair or no affair, she just didn't love him anymore.

He crunched the paper in his hand, gritting his teeth and gathering the purple velvet counterpane against his face so that Tillie wouldn't hear the muffled sobs that escaped from his throat.

It felt like sailing, sailing on snow. There was no other way to describe the feeling. He'd waxed the skis, but in every way they were as good as when he'd used them all those years ago. The conditions were perfect, and it felt as if he didn't need any effort to propel himself forward on the hard-packed tracks. Swimming was paying off; he felt fit and robust. Thorn had lumbered behind him for a few minutes, but had then given up and returned home. The sun was merely skimming the horizon, yet the midday was clear and crisp and the heavens blue. It was only minus twenty-two, not so cold as to freeze the wax or the tips of his fingers and toes. He felt exhilarated by the momentum, which extended to all his senses, his mind sharp, his vision and hearing acute. The weak sun glittered on the snow crystals, and the blinding white seemed to fill him. He'd forgotten the beauty and the starkness of the white.

Some time later he looked up from the tips of his rushing skis and noticed that dusk was setting in. How quickly it happened. He dug around his sleeves to look at his watch. It was a quarter to two. Damn, it was later than he'd thought. At once he turned around and set off in the direction in which he'd come, faster now. He felt himself go damp under his warm clothing. Still, it felt good, adrenaline adding the burst of energy he needed for the distance to Ian's cabin.

He seemed to have come farther than he realized. Darkness fell quickly, but he could still discern the tracks. The main tracks would get him straight back to the road, but there had been one or two minor tracks diverging among the trees. He thought of the consequences of taking a wrong turn and getting lost. Getting lost in the dark, deep in the woods, at temperatures that would freeze an apple solid within seconds. An element of panic now added to his speed. It was quickly getting much colder as the sun took its fragile warmth away with it. As he darted along the trail, he stared into the middle distance onto the bluish ground, scanning for the ridges left by a trapper's snowmobile, ridges and lines that his life now seemed to depend on. The trees towered black and menacing. Fear of losing his way drove him on now, and he could feel himself sweating.

Finally, coming around a bend in the tracks, he saw the road and, beyond, the lights of Ian's cabin. The relief slowed him almost to a stop. He was exhausted. His eyebrows and lashes were thick with frost; even the moisture in his eyes threatened to freeze. He set off again, feeling weak, as the charge had drained every last bit of energy from him. The muffled sound of Thorn barking inside the cabin was the sweetest intonation he'd ever hoped to hear. The old dog still had a hearing and a *knowing* as keen as in the days he came to meet Dafydd on the tracks. Even Ian looked agitated as Dafydd fell in through the door.

"Are you out of your mind . . . you bloody idiot?" he roared. "You didn't even take the flashlight."

"I lost track of time . . . I almost lost the track, too." Dafydd flopped into a chair and tried to unlace his boots and free his cramped feet.

"Tip this down." Ian handed him a glass of whiskey and bent to help him with the stiffened laces.

"It's not really the best thing for hypothermia . . . or stupidity," Dafydd said, "but if you insist." He swallowed the acrid liquid and drew his chair up to the woodstove, removing the layers of clothes one by one. The panic ebbing away had left him feeling like a wrung-out rag. He'd forgotten the precautions and the care a human had to observe in the depths of the arctic winter. How very easy it would be to cease to exist, by doing nothing, just being out there, getting lost, freezing.

"It's called death by omission," Ian said, as if he'd read his mind. Thorn looked agitated and wandered back and forth across the room on his arthritic legs. He whined softly as if distressed, his eyes droopy and melancholy.

"Yeah, which makes me wonder," Dafydd said sharply. "Have you fed this mutt?"

Ian didn't answer but went into the cupboard and poured dry dog food into a plastic bowl. He put the bowl on the floor, but Thorn didn't even look at it. Ian went to stir a stew on the stove. The aroma was pungent with wild game. He tasted it on a teaspoon, then shoved two mugs right into the pot, scooping up the lumpy mixture. He handed a dripping mug to Dafydd.

"Put some of that on Thorn's food," Dafydd said. "You can't expect the poor thing to just eat that sawdust all the time."

"You're full of good counsel today," Ian said irritably.

They drank the stew without the benefit of a spoon. Dafydd felt he had to bring up the subject of Ian's return to work, but Ian seemed closed to any discussion about his future. Now that Dafydd was doing his job, there was no need to pull himself together. It appeared that he was just hoping it would all resolve itself with no action taken on his part. His was a life by omission. Dafydd's suggestions about checking himself into a clinic had been dismissed or forgotten. In fact, his alcohol requirements had increased sharply again. A move from the cabin into town was out of the question.

The stillness and the quiet felt oppressive to Dafydd. The cabin had been like a refuge at times, but now that Ian had let go of the last vestige of discipline and routine and was just drinking continuously, the atmosphere of the place had an ominous feel to it. It was frightening to watch a man, a friend, in the process of self-destruction. Dafydd couldn't help but wonder if he was partly responsible for bringing it about. He'd certainly facilitated Ian's current state by bringing him booze and drugs and by doing his job for him.

"I'm seeing the kids at seven," Dafydd said to break the silence. "I'm taking them to the movies."

"So Sheila doesn't mind you going public?"

"Nah, I think she's given up. Even people in the hospital seem to know," Dafydd said, feeling sleepy. His eyelids began to quiver.

"I think I should tell you about those blood samples," Ian said suddenly.

Dafydd opened his eyes. "The ones for the DNA test, you mean?"

"I didn't actually take them myself. I mean, I didn't draw the blood myself."

"No? Who did?"

"I don't know. I think she did. Anyway, she just had me sign that they were theirs." Ian paused and looked down into his mug. "I don't suppose it's relevant, but I thought I'd tell you anyway."

Dafydd leaned back into the chair and held his feet up toward the heat of the stove. "It makes no difference. Nothing could have been faked. Nothing could imitate my own blood. The actual tests were done in England by a certified prognostics company, with blood that I provided. Whatever sneaky scheme that woman may come up with, this is not one that she could have faked . . . unfortunately."

Ian nodded, patting Thorn's head absentmindedly. "Is that how you feel . . . still . . . that it's unfortunate?"

"I don't know. I feel really confused. It seems that my marriage is over. I think my wife has fallen for someone else. And now she's sold our home. At the same time I'm starting to accept that Mark and Miranda are mine. It's a strange paradox, this loss and gain. Hell, I seem to have no choice in all this stuff that's happening to me. But *if I am* Mark's and Miranda's father, it's my job to make sure they're okay. Anyway, I want to."

"The only way you can really do that is by staying here. Can you really leave those unfortunate kids with *her*? It's like leaving lambs in the care of a werewolf."

Dafydd shook his head, his eyes closed. "They're tough kids. I think they'll be okay. Sheila loves them in her own fucked-up way, I'm sure."

Ian shook his head. "Be that as it may, she's a woman with no conscience. You should be here."

Dafydd hovered on the brink of sleep, his limbs aching with weariness.

"I know," he said at last.

"Miranda didn't want to see you," Sheila told him, smiling triumphantly. "That leaves you and Mark."

"Where is she?"

"She's sleeping over at Cass's house."

Sheila was wearing tight black suede trousers and a red polo neck. The bright red and her orange hair clashed unpleasantly. Dafydd was surprised: she was always so immaculate and well put-together. The black circles under her eyes were pronounced, and she was wearing too much makeup. Her face was whiter than usual. Stress was showing in the tautness of her brow and the rigidity of her jaw. She must have known she was less than beautiful because she looked pained when she caught him studying her face.

"I'm going out," she said curtly, "so send him home whenever you want. He's got a key."

Dafydd said nothing and stood fast by the front door. Entering into any discussion with Sheila almost always ended in sharp angry exchanges. He'd handed over his first paycheck to her, with *Make payable to Sheila Hailey* on the back. The two tellers at the Royal Bank would have a field day. Most likely the bank wouldn't accept it anyway, although Sheila was willing to take the chance since she was quite friendly with the manager. Any type of transfer using the bank would have been noted all the same. It seemed confidentiality was not an employee requirement this far north. Dafydd smiled at the thought. "Moose Creek whispers": the creative ramifications that were possible with such a piece of information. He only hoped they didn't reach the children, although they themselves didn't seem to give a damn about things like that. The complexity of adult relationships and adult morals was something they had seen aplenty, and not just at home.

Mark sauntered down the stairs, dressed in a pair of overlarge jeans hanging way down his hips and trailing the floor around his clumpy trainers. His hair had been shorn.

"What!" Dafydd exclaimed. "What happened to your ponytail?" Mark glared at his mother and started to put on his parka. Not another word was said. They left and wandered toward town.

"So do you want to see *Riding Home*?"

"About that little moron who becomes a champion rider? Sure, why not?" Mark shrugged his shoulders.

"Or do you want to go to Beanie's?"

"Why don't you have a house so we could just hang out and watch TV?"

"Well, we could order a pizza and watch TV in my room."

"Whatever."

An hour later they were installed on the purple bed, propped on a rolled-up quilt, surrounded by cheese-free artichoke and onion pizzas, popcorn, olives, cherry tomatoes, grapes, and a big bag of mixed nuts, plus a two-liter bottle of Coke. The television had been pulled up to the foot of the bed, with *The Last Wave* at full blast, an old film starring Richard Chamberlain.

"I'm pretty sure he's a faggot," Mark commented.

"I've never heard that," Dafydd said, his mouth full.

After a few minutes Mark turned to him and frowned. "Are you gonna hang around here forever?"

"I don't know what the hell I'm doing, to be honest."

"You could get a house, you know. Or a trailer. Maybe you could get a computer and a microwave and stuff . . ."

"Yeah, well, that's one option I've considered. How would you feel if I did?"

"It's up to you, isn't it?" Mark shrugged his shoulders, feigning indifference. "You could get a car, or a pickup, and a snowmobile . . ."

"Do you mind if I ask you something? You don't seem to have any relatives, apart from me, of course. Doesn't your mother have family?"

"My mom said I shouldn't tell you."

"Why not?"

"Because it's none of your fucking business."

"Are those your words or hers?"

Mark considered this for a moment, enjoying the idea of it. Then he looked over, his colorless eyes actually focusing on Dafydd's. "We have a grandma. My mom's mom. She lives in Florida." He turned back to the action on the TV and placed two tomatoes in his mouth, one in each cheek. "They hate each other, my mom and her. I lived with her for a year." He pressed his cheeks with his hands and a spray of pips shot from his mouth.

"I didn't know that." Dafydd handed him a wad of napkins. "Did Miranda go, too?"

"Nope. The old lady hates girls."

"And . . . what was it like?"

"Crap. She hates me, too. Mom figgered Grandma dug boys cos she digs men, but she didn't." He glanced at Dafydd and sniggered, "Grandma sent me back. Mom thought she'd seen the last of me. She was pissed off as hell."

Richard Chamberlain was having a hallucination inside his car, debris and dead people floating all around the car, which appeared to be underwater.

"I don't know if this film is suitable for—"

"Shhh . . . this is the best part."

They engrossed themselves in Richard Chamberlain's trials and tribulations as an honorary aboriginal in Australia predicting the arrival of a tidal wave. When it had finished they switched to a game of ice hockey.

"What about your grandfather? Is he dead?" Dafydd asked during a commercial break.

"Dunno," Mark said, while concentrating on tearing off a hangnail. "I think he was English like you. He left when Mom was ten. He was real disappointed because she was a redhead, so he would have hated me, too." Mark shrugged, as if being hated on account of his coloring were perfectly natural and justifiable. Dafydd looked at the boy beside him with a sudden overwhelming feeling of compassion.

"And did they never hear from him again?"

"Sure, he sent checks so that Mom could stay in boarding schools, cos Granny didn't want her around to cramp her style. But I guess her dad didn't want her, either." Mark laughed suddenly, a high-pitched unnatural guffaw. "You don't like her, either, right? It's okay cos most of the time I don't, either. Poor Mom. Some guys like her, though. She is kinda pretty despite her red hair." He looked pleadingly at Dafydd. "Don't you think?"

Dafydd flinched, hearing the pain in the boy's voice. "Yes. Your mum is very pretty. And she's smart, too. So are you." He punched Mark lightly on the arm. They fell into silence as the hockey game started up again. Dafydd had a flash recollection of an interaction he'd had with Sheila a very long time ago. She said that Dafydd reminded her of someone, a pompous, self-righteous so-and-so. Someone she could never please enough . . .

"I figger Miranda is yours, but I'm not," Mark declared abruptly.

"Yeah, you said." Dafydd looked at the boy. "But that's not possible."

Mark chuckled mockingly. "Look it up in one of your medical books. It *can* happen, if the woman—"

"Yes, I know," Dafydd interrupted. It annoyed him how the lad had a way of belittling him, just like his mother. "But the statistics show it's probably one chance in a million, maybe ten million." He felt stupid as he said it, and Mark looked at him with resigned tolerance. He sighed loudly and shrugged his shoulders. "If it means a lot to you . . . *Dad,*" he said and turned back to the TV.

"Anyway, it was your blood, not Miranda's, that proved you were my kid."

Mark said nothing but repeated the trick with the tomatoes, then handed two to Dafydd to try. "Mom hates you, you know."

"My God, Mark. The way you tell it, the whole place is just a cauldron of hatred. Do you know anyone who doesn't hate or dislike everyone else?"

Mark glanced at him but ignored his question. "No, not like that. Press them with the inside of your cheeks as well. Press hard until they explode."

"Would you come to visit me in England if I go back?"

Mark stopped chewing and looked down at his hands. "I kinda thought you'd stay here . . . You got a job and all."

"My real job is back in Wales. I don't know if I can stay here forever."

Mark was quite for a moment. "Well, fuck off, then," he said and turned away. His narrow chest hunched into itself and his head, now pathetically bare, sank low between his shoulders. He was unreachable for the rest of the hockey game. When it finished he'd fallen fast asleep. Dafydd felt an urge to stroke the knobbly shoulder of this sad young person, to impart a little bit of human warmth. Mark was the most dour and dispirited child that Dafydd had ever met. The little affection he ever seemed to get was Miranda's horseplay. He never minded her punches and hair ruffles and lubberly hugs. It was unthinkable to send him away, to separate them. He needed his sister, and she needed him.

Tillie was knocking on the door and calling his name. Slowly he floated up from a deep, murky dream, surfacing to the insistent noise. His brain was slow to identify the circumstances. After a second or two he realized that, while he was a man in a foreign place, and a doctor by profession, he was *not on duty*. It was something else. He came to with a jolt and jumped out of the bed.

"*Coming*," he shouted and hunted for his bathrobe.

"It's the hospital," Tillie said when he opened the door. "They have an emergency and need your help. They asked me to tell you to come up straightaway."

Dafydd threw on his jeans and shoes without socks, pulled on a sweatshirt and his parka and darted down the stairs. Tillie had her car out at the front all warmed and ready.

"Thanks, sweetheart," he panted. "I bet you regret my tenancy. I'm nothing but trouble."

"No, you're not . . . you can stay forever." Tillie looked over at him as she drove up the hill toward the hospital. He heard the unmistakable ring of infatuation and avoided meeting her eye. Tillie's short-lived marriage had come to an end when her older husband had passed away ten years ago, basically of old age, and she was a woman reborn, a chrysalis emerged from a cocoon of fat into a pretty butterfly. She'd probably known very little of passion between a man and a woman. Dafydd glanced at her dainty profile, the small delicate face and the tiny hands holding the steering wheel. There must be scores of lonely men in this town who would be delighted to fall in love with her and her thriving little B&B. But he must, *at all cost,* disabuse her of the notion that *he* was *it.* One more complication in his life and he'd have a nervous breakdown.

She dropped him by the emergency door and he ran toward the main theater, where he was met by Janie.

"A trapper has been mauled by a grizzly, not far from here. He's stable, but he's practically torn to shreds. No apparent internal injuries. Just a few broken ribs and a dislocated shoulder. Thank God he was wearing a lot of clothes. And a friend was with him. This guy's gotta have a guardian angel."

She helped him pull his gloves on after he'd scrubbed up. She moved closer to him and whispered, "Lezzard is on call but he'd been at a party. His wife couldn't even rouse him. Nadja was second on call, but I called Hogg to explain the situation and he thought I should call you. She's so . . . inexperienced." She stood back and looked at him. "You don't mind, do you?"

"Of course not," he said. "So I take it Atilan is anesthetizing?"

Janie nodded, then said quietly, "Sheila's not here, in case you wondered."

"Thank God."

She looked at him but said nothing.

During the long hours of piecing together the ragged flaps of skin where the deathly claws of the grizzly had torn the flesh of the man, Dafydd asked Janie how it was possible that a grizzly was on the prowl at this time of deepest winter.

"It's possible that the kid disturbed him. Grizzlies do wake occasionally, probably in the foulest possible mood."

Dr. Atilan, a quiet woman of Hungarian background, suddenly spoke up from behind her mask. With her heavy accent, she told in gory detail of a Spanish cyclist who'd been mauled by a black bear in the summer of 1998. He'd been determined to be the first person to cycle the whole length of the new highway, all the way from Wolf Trail to Tuktoyaktuk. A local man had driven along, some eighty miles south of Moose Creek, and seen a bicycle lying at the side of the road, one wheel still spinning.

He'd stopped and heard cries from among the trees, where the unfortunate man had been dragged by the bear. The bear was scared away by the motorist's shouts and screams and the fool-hardy Spaniard was rescued. He'd topped the record with over four hundred stitches. He still sent flowers to the hospital every sixth of July from Bilbao, where he was now a schoolteacher.

"What about the kid from Coppermine?" Janie asked. "He was in pretty bad shape." She turned to Dafydd. "This Inuit boy was attacked by a polar bear. It was all very dramatic because there was a blizzard—and this was March, April this year—a blizzard like you've never seen. They were going to fly him to Yellowknife, but the weather was so bad they flew him here, since we were about the nearest."

"Polar bear!" Dafydd exclaimed. "I thought a polar bear encounter was pretty well lethal."

"The story goes that a dog saved him."

"How did he fare?"

"He was here for a few days. It was touch and go, then we transferred him to Edmonton. He needed a lot of surgery and he lost a leg. Incredibly brave. He never once cried."

"How old was this kid?" Dafydd asked, leaning over the delicate task of closing up a gash in the man's groin.

"Twelve or thirteen," said Atilan, looking up from a medical journal she was reading. "Big for his age. What a beautiful child. We all fussed over him, he was so special."

"Kids are often much better patients than adults," Dafydd said. He straightened up and arched his back to relieve the strain of bending forward over the hapless trapper. "When it comes down to it, kids are a lot more stoical." A faint picture of Derek Rose flashed through his thoughts, a child whose glassy, sunken eyes had asked questions that his mind was too young to formulate.

After four hours of operating, the team emerged from the theater, exhausted but heartened. Dafydd had counted two hundred and eighty-seven stitches in total, but, still, he felt good about the job he'd done. The man, a young Métis, married with a small child, would be terribly scarred but would not be unduly handicapped. At least he'd had as good care as he would in any major hospital, and he was alive.

Janie's daughter, Patricia, had trespassed into the cafeteria and started cooking breakfast and making coffee. Soon the staff from the night shift was drawn to the darkened dining room by the smell of frying bacon. An atmosphere of comradeship and team spirit prevailed. Perhaps because Sheila Hailey wasn't there, Dafydd thought. It had not escaped him that she wasn't very popular, yet she had her allies.

Although he didn't eat meat very often, he tucked into a big plate of bacon and eggs with hash browns. Someone else took the liberty of making pancakes, and he had several of those, too.

Between mouthfuls he said to Dr. Atilan, who was sitting beside him, "You know, years and years ago I was up that area, near Coppermine, where that kid came from, the one you were telling us about. It must be the starkest place in the world, but incredibly beautiful at the same time. Do you remember what the community was called? There were very few, as I recall."

Atilan shook her head. "A small hamlet, I think. Some Inuit name, probably."

"Black River," Janie called from down the table.

Black River. Dafydd saw it written in his own hand on countless envelopes—*Black River*. What a coincidence. Such a small place. Maybe he'd even met the injured boy's parents, although there were precious few younger people there. His thoughts turned to the woman he'd been lucky enough to love. He remembered her long hair trailing across his naked skin, her stone carvings that he'd cradled in his hands, the northern lights coloring the sky above her humble house. Was she still there? He turned the thought away. Wasn't his life in enough of a chaos?

CHAPTER *19*

Dafydd.
Don't know what to say. Good for you to have made
such progress with the children. How nice. And your
locum, congratulations. So you won't be home for
Christmas. I'd not expected you, so you needn't be
concerned. House sale proceeding.
Completion early January. Dubai was great, thanks
for asking. So, no worries.

Cheers, Isabel

Isabel was drifting away, like a ship receding on a wide sea, becoming smaller and smaller, merging with the horizon. He thought about her objectively, her charisma, her quick temper, her beautiful, sharp profile, her unusual charm, even her jealousy and obstinacy, and he could see that he had been lucky. He was thankful to have been her husband.

The strange thing was that he no longer minded. Was this proof of his shallow feelings, some kind of barrenness of spirit? This woman he thought he had loved so passionately was slipping from him, apparently on to better things, and now, without even having noticed the shift in his feelings, he found in himself no real grief or distress. The last pang of regret had been detonated in a sudden final torrent of tears and after that he'd felt light . . . almost cleansed. He searched inside himself, his feelings, his reason, and he couldn't understand this lack of pain and remorse. Perhaps it was anger. He felt she'd abandoned him to deal with something that turned out to be as bewildering as he'd ever experienced, bar Derek Rose and the aftermath. She'd not supported him, not trusted him. She never grasped that he believed himself innocent of the charge, truly innocent, until his mistake was written starkly in that damned report, confirming his paternity. It appeared that she had shelved the whole project of her marriage to him, and transferred her hopes and ambitions to a new goal, to be indispensable in the world of grand design. To be rich and powerful, possibly even famous.

Dafydd's ambitions, on the other hand, had shrunk. If Isabel had ever feared that his newfound children would draw him away from her, she would have been right to fear it. The sense of paternal responsibility had been awakened in him and he could not turn his back on it, no matter what the future held. His destiny was linked to this sense within him, peculiar as it was.

Dafydd drove up to Ian's cabin, and his headlights splashed on the broad arse of Hogg's four-wheel drive, which was blocking the yard. A stab of apprehension hit him. He'd not confronted Ian again regarding the transport of Demerol, but a few cursory searches of the car trunk had yielded no incriminating packages. Still, a few times he'd been horrified at his own nonchalant attitude. It wasn't something he could persist in ignoring. Handling stolen goods, drugs at that, was a criminal offense, which put him right alongside Sheila. He would have to make sure it never happened again.

He wondered what Hogg was doing there, and in what state he'd found Ian. It was just before seven, around the time that Ian had his evening fix. Dafydd felt he had no choice but to join them, since the sound of his car must have alerted them to his presence.

"Oh, jolly good, jolly good," Hogg said as he came in. "Just the man we want to talk to."

Ian was sitting at his kitchen table, looking as awful as Dafydd had ever seen him. Thorn was lying on an old moose hide in the corner, whining softly.

"I was just trying to convince Ian here that we really do expect him back on Monday, since you've completed your locum with us," Hogg said wearily. "Haven't you?" he added, looking imploringly at Dafydd. He looked tired, the thick mop of dark hair strangely incongruous on top of his white, puffy face, like a cheap and ill-fitting wig.

The three men looked at each other, each waiting for someone else to take charge of the matter. Ian's passive indifference and Hogg's weary irritation left the business to Dafydd. As they both looked in his direction, he knew what they were waiting for, but he knew his compliance would be disastrous for Ian. The man needed to get back to some semblance of normality. He needed the discipline of work, although at the same time Dafydd knew that, let loose on patients, Ian could be dangerous in his present state of intoxication. It would be irresponsible to put him in that situation, now more than ever.

Dafydd was trying to formulate some acceptable statement to this effect when Hogg abruptly broke the silence. He turned to Dafydd, his face tense with exasperation and annoyance. "Now, why beat around the bush? I don't think Ian is in any shape to work at this present moment."

He took a step toward Ian and put his hands on his plump hips. "Look here, my man. We've worked together for a good many years, and for that reason I think I owe you . . . some concessions. As a doctor I can't fault you, but this last year or two . . . well, I don't think we can go on much longer like this, do *you*?"

"Oh, don't bother," Ian said, looking up at him. "You know as well as I do that you can't get rid of me unless I've fucked up. You can't put a single thing on me. I'm entitled to sick leave and that's where I'm at. I'm in no state to start working on Monday."

"I can see that," Hogg said, his voice dripping with sarcasm.

"Give me until the new year. I'm sure Dafydd won't mind staying on till then. Do you, Dafydd?" There was a new tone to Ian's voice. His defiance was mixed with a cry for help, a pitiable plea for time. It touched Dafydd deeply, and he felt like rushing to his friend's side and begging him to stop this appalling destruction, to pull himself together, but he could do no such thing in front of Hogg. Both Hogg and Ian were looking at him now, awaiting an answer.

"All right," he said, "to the first of January . . . *but no longer.*" He looked directly at Ian, but Ian's gaze was fixed on the floor.

"Jolly good." Hogg made a move toward the door, then hesitated. He turned back to Ian. "I'm afraid you're going to have something in writing from me. You know this is truly a last resort. I don't like doing it." He shrugged in a gesture of helplessness but got no response from Ian. He glanced at Dafydd and there was in his eyes a genuine look of remorse. Dafydd wondered how much this man really knew of the situation. How could he be oblivious to all that had been going on under his very nose for so many years? Perhaps his passion for Sheila had made him look the other way.

Hogg buttoned up his overcoat and left. Dafydd closed the door on the icy darkness and heard the engine of the four-wheel drive roar as Hogg made his way around Ian's car and down the drive. Then he emptied the Co-op bags on the kitchen counter and opened a tin of dog food.

"You can see that I can't cover for you anymore," he began. "I have to return your car so that you can start taking charge of your life. I feel I've done you a disfavor. It's been very foolish of me."

"We said January the first. Why not leave it like that? It's the right sort of date for a fresh start."

"*No!*" Dafydd exclaimed. "Can't you see it's no good? You'll be in a worse state than you are now. Why not use this time to dry out? If you don't want to go anywhere, you can do it right here. I'll help you."

"I'll cut down on drinking, but there's no point in stopping the Demerol. It doesn't affect my work performance. I function just fine on it."

"*Ian,*" Dafydd practically shouted at him, "you know you shouldn't be working under the influence of drugs. You're endangering patients' lives."

"I've not killed a single patient," Ian shouted back, getting up from his chair. "I've never killed anyone except my wife."

Dafydd went around to where Ian was standing and grabbed him by the shoulders, making him sit down. "Ian, listen. Stealing drugs is a criminal offense. Your luck is running out."

Ian slumped back into his chair. "Oh, fuck that. That's harming no one. Anyway, it's Sheila who's doing the stealing."

"In that case you're going to need your car and get your supplies yourself."

Ian got up and went into the bathroom. Thorn sniffed at the food in his bowl and returned to his moose hide. Dafydd looked around the cabin. The place was falling apart. There were patches of ice on the walls where the logs had shrunk and the insulation fallen away. The ceiling looked waterlogged and bulged as if it were about to burst open at any moment. The carpet on the floor was unrecognizable of color and material, just a blackened oily surface, scuffed and torn.

Ian came out, his eyes at half-mast.

"I'm surprised you have any veins left," Dafydd said bitterly.

"Just leave it, will you?"

"Look, I'm phoning for a taxi." Dafydd placed the car keys on the table. "I'm bringing you no more food, booze or drugs. Whatever you need you have to get it yourself. I'll only help you if you decide to help yourself. I'll do anything . . . but the decision is yours."

"I'll think about it."

There was nothing more to say. Ian dozed torpidly in his chair while Dafydd waited for his taxi. Twenty minutes later, when the car pulled up in front of the cabin, Dafydd got up. He leaned to look into Ian's dull face and said, "I want you to do one thing for me. Let me borrow your password for the computer system. As a locum I have no access. There's something I want to check."

Ian opened his eyes, then got up and, finding a pen, he scribbled a series of numbers on a scrap of paper. Wordlessly he handed it to Dafydd. They looked at each other for a moment.

"Quit it, Ian . . . Just do it," Dafydd said emphatically, putting a hand on his friend's shoulder. "It'll hurt, but you can do it. I'll come and look after you. You know where to find me."

The office was dark but for a table light. Dafydd had closed the door behind him, but it was unlikely that anyone would have any business in this part of the hospital at this time of the night. He turned on the computer and waited. When it asked for his password he inserted the numbers on the scrap of paper and scanned the various programs that rolled up on the screen. He clicked on *Intensive Care Unit* and came up with a list of options. *Reason for admission* seemed as good as any. He typed in *bear attack* and a list of names appeared. His heart beat hard against his chest as he quickly scanned the names. There were twenty-two in all, covering several years. Halfway down the list he saw it: *Charlie Ashoona, Black River, Kugluktuk (Coppermine) region, Nunavut. Next of kin: Uyarasuq Ashoona, mother.*

Dafydd sat back and stared at the name. The glare of the computer screen in the dark room made the letters jump out at him. A bizarre possibility occurred to him. Could this have been the boy that Joseph had referred to, Sleeping Bear's son? Was this really possible? He looked at the date of birth, December 5, 1993. He couldn't concentrate enough to calculate months and years; it all blurred hopelessly into a jumble of numbers. He grabbed a pen and wrote months and years as little lines on a pad of papers. He finally saw that the date of the boy's conception coincided roughly with his and Bear's visit to Black River.

Had Uyarasuq and Bear . . . ? No, he couldn't conceive of

it. But Bear had willed half of his life savings to a boy in Black River. Joseph said that he had fathered . . . What a terrible thought. He recalled the strong affection that Bear and Uyarasuq had for each other. What did he know of the relationship they had? What did he understand of their way of thinking? His cultural prejudices about age and sex and morality probably had no application up there, in the arctic wilderness. Oh, God! Dafydd felt his limbs go weak as the odds spun around his skull, like on a demented and unstoppable roulette wheel.

"What the hell do you think you're doing?"

The sudden clang of the sharp voice in the dark and empty room made him jump. He turned and saw Sheila coming toward him in quick strides. Reacting instantly, he reached forward and pulled the plug out of the socket. The computer pinged and the screen went blank.

"You have no right to meddle with hospital records. How did you get in?"

"I work here. If I need to look at patients' records, I will."

"You have every right to look at the written records. For your purposes, that's all you need. I know for a fact that you have no password to the computer records. They're not for the likes of you. I'm reporting you to Hogg."

"You do that," Dafydd said coldly. "Why don't the three of us have a long chat? I'll arrange it. There are a number of things I think need reporting."

"Really?" Sheila's face altered slightly, although her aggressive stance didn't change. "Like what?"

Dafydd said nothing, but didn't get out of the chair. She moved closer to him and shoved her forefinger toward his face. "If you think Hogg is going to listen to anything you'd care to say about me, you are sorely wrong." Her eyes blazed angrily but there was apprehension in her face.

Dafydd thought of Ian, and he had a sudden flash of rage. He was getting to the point where he no longer cared if he compromised Ian. It was time that someone did something to stop the wretched destruction that she was helping him perpetrate on himself. He looked at her finger, which was still jabbing toward his face.

"Stop sticking your finger in my face," he growled, shoving her hand away with some force. "Is there no end to your depravity? And to think you're in charge of two defenseless children."

"You watch it," Sheila hissed. "If you want anything to do with your kids, you watch how you tread. There's nothing depraved about me taking you to the cleaners. It's what you deserve. That's what men like you deserve. You think you can run around sticking your stinking little member here, there, and everywhere and get away with—"

"That's not what I'm referring to," Dafydd snarled, cutting her off. "I'm talking about what you're doing to Ian."

Sheila stared at him, speechless, but she quickly recovered. "I don't give a shit what or who you're referring to. Whatever it is, it has nothing to do with you. You keep out of my life or you'll never lay eyes on your kids again. I'll blow the whole saga wide open. I can prove what you did to me. I'll tell the kids . . . in gory detail."

"You would? You would actually do that to your own children?"

"Yes, and I've got proof. Trust me, you won't like it." She smiled now, thinking she'd regained the upper hand. She folded her arms under her breasts and stared down at him. She always searched for a weakness, and now she thought she could use the kids as her weapon, but it wasn't going to be so easy for her, not this time. He'd see to it.

"I don't believe you. You're full of shit." Dafydd pushed his chair away from under him, knocking it over. "But okay. You do what you have to do, and I'll do the same."

Before she could answer, he turned from her brusquely and left the room.

At 8:55 a.m. he stood ready and waiting outside Rent-a-Ride, a small office on a side street at the edge of town. It was clear that a car was indispensable, and in Moose Creek his driving ban was overruled by need. He smiled as he remembered a conversation of long ago. Who was it who told him that he'd never walk the streets of this town, since it was either too hot and dusty, or too cold and slippery, or he'd be too drunk? Someone very cheeky. His face fell in astonishment when none other than the proclaimer of this truth marched up the street with a large bunch of keys in her hand. Martha Kusugaq looked no different despite the passage of years. Her eyes lit up when she saw him.

"The sexy young doctor," she squealed. "I do declare."

"The doctor, maybe. Sexy and young are questionable," Dafydd said, laughing.

"This time you're here to stay, aren't you, young man? The Lord only knows how badly we need someone of yer ilk," she said, shaking his hand vigorously. "I sincerely hope you take over from old Hogg. He'd never admit it, but he really oughta put his feet up."

"Whoa . . . easy, Martha. I'm just here for a visit. How are you?"

"Let me open this door and I'll tell it like it is."

She fiddled at length with the bunch of keys, trying several before she hit on the right one.

"Judging by those keys, you've got lots of interests," Dafydd said.

"You got that right!" Martha said. "The old man left me for a floozy and I got meself married to a younger man, one with real ambition." She hopped behind the counter and took a gold pen in her hand. "Now, before noth'n else, let me get you some wheels. They're all perfectly reliable, I do declare . . ."

He couldn't concentrate on what the kids were saying. Mark was dragging him by the arm. Miranda was behind them, pushing at the sled and shouting at them to pull harder. The two of them were talking, shouting, and laughing uncontrollably while trudging up a steep pit, up to their thighs in snow.

"What's the matter with you, Dafydd?" Mark cried. "Are you in a bad mood or something?"

Dafydd was astonished at Mark's unexpected high spirits. He grabbed the lad by the waist and tackled him to the ground, but Mark was stronger than he looked and managed to trip him up. They rolled a fair way down before they managed to stop.

"Look at you," Miranda yelled. "It'll take ages before you can get back up. I'm going by myself." She threw herself headlong on the sled and started hurtling down at some speed.

"Watch it," Dafydd shouted, alarmed at the sight of his daughter accelerating past him like a bullet. It was a broken leg or a neck injury waiting to happen. Suddenly Mark hurled himself at him and they fell again, rolling and sliding farther down the hill, the soft snow filling up the insides of their collars and sleeves. Miranda was at the bottom in a heap, laughing like a maniac.

"That's it," Dafydd shouted, sitting up in the snow. "Get a grip. Your mother will have a fit when she hears about this."

"It's none of her fucking business," Mark said smartly. "Anyway, do you really think she gives a damn?"

"Of course she does."

"You're a bit naive, aren't you," Mark said, looking at him condescendingly, "for a grown man?"

The little shit's got *that* right, Dafydd thought as he brushed the snow out of his hair and put his toque back on his head. "She will give a damn when I bring you back in an ambulance with broken bones and hypothermia."

They both looked down at Miranda, who was suddenly motionless in the snow. Mark pitched himself after her, slid down through the soft snow and attempted to lift her up. She weighed a good ten kilos more than he, and it proved difficult. She made herself into a dead weight and started wailing. Dafydd looked on and realized how deep was the difference in their maturity. He'd heard that it was usually the other way around, but Mark was like a cantankerous old man, dour and introspective, whereas Miranda could revert to an infantile state in an instant.

There she was, hysterical with both laughter and feigned agony, kicking her legs like a two-year-old. She would get cold lying there, but Dafydd didn't have the energy to interfere. He remained sitting on the slope for a moment. He'd not slept even a full hour during the long night, thinking and turning over what he'd discovered. The idea that Sleeping Bear could have impregnated that lovely young woman during their visit seemed totally ludicrous. Much as he reproached himself for his prejudices, he could not conjure up an image of the two of them embracing. Bear was old enough to be her grandfather, even great-grandfather. There could, of course, have been some other man, although she'd said she hadn't been with anyone for a long time. But was it naive of him to believe this? Why should a young woman not have had lovers? The other possibility, the one that was making his head spin, was that Dafydd himself had fathered the boy. *Oh, Lord, was this really a possibility?* The dates said it was.

Like so many times over the years, the minutiae of his love-making with Uyarasuq, every detail, frozen on the network of his senses, came back to him. She had said she was "safe" in terms of her cycle, but he knew how totally unreliable that was, so he'd used a condom. The soft peals of her laughter, and his own mirth, at the inevitable inelegance of covering a stiff penis with a rubber garment, he remembered it clearly. But condoms do fail, they do break or tear. Not often, but they do. Especially if they're out of date . . . her tightness, his size . . . she'd taken it off him in the dark . . .

Dafydd leaned forward, hiding his face in the crook of his arms, trying to suspend his agitation. He didn't want to think about this now, not here with the children. He looked down at them where they now were hurling snow at each other, Miranda yelling and laughing, Mark quiet, laboring in concentration.

Why wouldn't she have told him? And why didn't Sleeping Bear tell him? Maybe he tried to. It was imperative to get hold of Joseph and ask him more questions about Bear's urge to write him a letter. Maybe this was what Bear had wanted to convey. But he was old and tired; he couldn't write; Joseph didn't care, so Bear decided to leave some of his money to the boy. Because he felt responsible for what happened, or because of his strong ties to the family. Or because fundamentally he disliked his own grandson. Oh, God, where would he go with this? He needed to know absolutely. He had to know.

There was a hand on his shoulder.

"Why are you just sitting there like that?" Miranda was peering at him. "You're a drag sometimes, you know. I was only kidding. Letting off steam, like. You didn't take it seriously, did you?" She rubbed his cheeks mercilessly with her icy mitts, and he grabbed her wrist and tried to shove some snow down the collar of her snowsuit.

"Daaaaad," she screamed. She never missed an opportunity to call him *Dad*. It seemed to mean such a lot to her that she finally had a father, although he was under no illusion that it was *him* she loved, for himself. Sure, they'd become friends, and she could see that he was solid, dependable, generous, and in time perhaps she would come to feel he was the real father she yearned for. Thankfully she was a well-adjusted young girl, normal, in spite of her mother. Mark was a person unto himself, virtually impenetrable. How would they feel when they discovered that perhaps they had a brother . . . "Oh, Christ." Dafydd groaned out loud.

"Christ . . . *what*?" Miranda tried to wrench herself free from his grasp on her sleeve.

"We're . . . late."

"Late for what? You don't even have your watch on, stupid."

"Who did you call stupid?" Dafydd shoved another handful of snow against her collar and then shouted for Mark to hurry.

They ran up the hill to warm up and got into the large, gas-guzzling Buick that Martha had rented him at a "mighty discount," and he drove them back to Tillie's.

Tillie hadn't been shocked when he'd told her that Mark and Miranda were his. She had her sources—he'd never discovered who or what they were—and she'd known for weeks already, before he'd even introduced the children to her.

"You're not the first man to fall for that woman," she'd said primly. "Someone should have told you to take care." She nodded meaningfully, referring no doubt to some sensible precaution, but in her eyes there was hope. "Will you be staying, then?"

Although Dafydd knew in his heart that he was using her disgracefully, Tillie was delighting in the gratification of vicarious motherhood. She'd not had any children of her own and now she took great pleasure in cooking for Dafydd and the twins and joining in with them at the table in the breakfast room. Miranda had taken to her straightaway and loved to hang out in the kitchen and help her bake cookies and buns, something her mother had never done. Tillie's living room, with the bigscreen TV, was also a free-for-all. Even Mark seemed to take to her; he sometimes took the trouble to make her laugh with his piercing comments about the human condition, delivered in his deadpan way. Dafydd thought of the various ways in which he could compensate this lovely woman for her kindness, any way except by making love to her and making promises he couldn't keep.

"Dafydd, you look exhausted," she said to him as he slumped on her sofa watching some inane game show that the children seemed to like. "Let me get you a gin and tonic."

"Tillie, you're an angel. Make it big, please. And make damned sure you put that on my bill. Write . . . *one bottle of gin* on my account—in big letters."

Tillie laughed, delighted. "That bad, huh?"

"If you get drunk," Miranda warned him, "I'm outta here. I hate drunk people."

Mark spoke in his monotone without turning his face from the rantings of the game show host: "Your precious dad is just as gross as anybody else when he's drunk."

"How do *you* know?" Tillie exclaimed, outraged. "Your father doesn't get drunk."

"You've seen now," Dafydd told her apathetically. "Mark's right. I'm just as bad as anyone."

Half an hour later he sat up with a start. The clock on Tillie's wall said four-thirty.

"Come on, kids," Dafydd called out, suddenly remembering that he was on call as of five o'clock. "Get a move on. I'll walk you home."

"No, drive us," Miranda whined. "My legs are hurting from you making us run up the hill. *And* it's snowing."

"You're unfit," Dafydd chided her, suddenly tired of their company, tired of having to talk, of having to be sociable when his head was in a different place altogether. "We're not taking that monstrous vehicle four hundred yards down the road. Get real!"

Tillie bundled them all in like a mother hen and they set off down the road to Sheila's house. It was dark, but the streetlights shining their yellow glow on the freshly falling snow made the town look jolly, fresh, Christmas-like. Two shiny new snowplows, with fierce searchlights, scraped their way along the main road in both directions, the giant blades curling back the quickly freezing snow like huge strips of butter and leaving them neatly in fold upon fold along the middle of the road.

Sheila's house lay in darkness. Mark fished out his key, and they let themselves into the house.

"Will you be okay?" Dafydd asked them.

Mark looked at him with a face that said, *Where do you think we've been for the last five thousand years?*

"'Bye, then." Dafydd bent forward to offer a frost-ridden kiss on Miranda's cheek, but she was already off, and the door shut firmly in his face. He stood there a moment watching the lights come on all around the house. In many ways they were thirteen going on twenty-three. They had plenty of practice at looking after themselves. He had to concede it was lucky he came to them so late. Years and years of worrying about little children would have been harrowing, knowing and not knowing what their mother was doing to them and the impotence of being so far away.

He turned back toward "downtown," kicking at the snow as he went, hands deep inside his big parka pockets. Tillie would be waiting, and he couldn't really dismiss her and disappear up to his room, not after the cozy afternoon in her living room. It was no good. He'd have to rent a house or something. Someplace where the kids could run riot and he could have the privacy he yearned for, but how long could he draw this out, and to what end? His last phone call to his directorate manager in Cardiff had not been altogether pleasant.

"What's going on, Woodruff? Have you no intention of returning to your position? Your locum wants to move on. He's a good man, in fact. We wouldn't mind him staying on."

Was there an implied encouragement to resign behind those words, or was he being paranoid? "I can't come back for another few weeks, for personal reasons. I really must ask you to extend my sabbatical. This has to do with discovering children that I didn't know existed."

"Children? Good heavens, Woodruff. You should have said. Look, we do value you tremendously, but you can't stay away forever. You're setting an example here." Dafydd chuckled to himself as he turned a street corner and stepped over a pile of dog shit. If the guy only knew the sheer number of children it may amount to.

On an impulse he stopped at the Northern Holiday Hotel. A squat man was chipping and shoveling furiously to clear the ice that would have their big-spending customers slipping at the entrance. Dafydd greeted him with a nod and went in.

At the back of his mind was Ian. He'd not seen or heard from him for three days, and he was starting to worry. The lavish reception had several private phone booths, and he shut himself into one of the teak-lined cubbyholes. He took out a pen and a scrap of paper, and his credit card, and he dialed Ian's number, which he knew by heart. Then he looked at the pen and the paper and wondered why he'd taken them out. His knees went weak. He put his finger on the telephone cradle, canceling the call. He knew now why he was there, why he'd gone there in the first place. Yes, he *was* concerned about Ian, but Ian wasn't the reason he was inside this booth.

Three phone calls later, he had a number on the piece of paper. He recognized the number. It had flashed across his retina when he searched and found what he was looking for in the patients' records.

His finger trembled as he pressed the numbers, slowly, one by one. His mouth was dry. It rang twice.

"Charlie here!" The breaking, croaking voice of an adolescent boy.

"Hello, Charlie. My name is Dafydd Woodruff." He swallowed hard before he could continue. "Is your mother there?"

"Sure thing . . . Mom." His voice was distant and hoarse as he called to his mother. "A David Walruss on the phone."

"Hello?" Her sweet voice, her lovely accent. How well he remembered it.

"Uyarasuq. It's me, Dafydd . . . Dafydd, from long ago. Fourteen years ago."

"Dafydd." He could hardly hear her, she spoke his name so softly. A pause lengthened, then she said, "Where are you, Dafydd? Where are you calling from?"

"I'm in Moose Creek. I'd like to see you. Soon. I'd like to come up and see you. I need to speak to you." He spoke quickly, out of breath, trying to stop himself, knowing he should ask how she was, make small talk, be polite, restrained.

"It's . . . I'm . . . Why are you there?"

"Listen, Uyarasuq. Sorry, but I've got to ask you. I know I'm probably totally out to lunch here, but I must know. Your son, Charlie, he isn't *my* son, is he? Tell me the truth, please."

She was quiet, and he cringed at his blundering tactlessness. He hadn't meant to be so clumsy, but he'd already lost his equanimity and there was no point in pretending otherwise. He implored her once again, "Please, Uyarasuq, tell me."

"Yes, Dafydd . . . Charlie . . . is your son."

"Oh, Christ, woman." Dafydd felt a flush around his neck and sweat broke out all over his body. "Why didn't you tell me?"

"I felt it wasn't right to put that on you. Perhaps you don't remember, but you went to some lengths to prevent him happening."

"Of course I did." He tried to calm his voice and not seem so agitated. "That was for your safety, just as much as for myself."

"Well, I guess I should apologize," she said coolly. "But despite your precaution, I got pregnant. I'm *not* sorry. Charlie is the best thing that ever happened to me."

"Oh, please . . . wait." What was he wanting to say? He'd not planned it. At once he was terrified that she would cut him off before he'd even been able to express his concern, his genuine interest, his need to know about his son. How different it felt from the news of Sheila's children, this son whom he had fathered in some semblance of love.

"Listen, none of that matters now. I won't ask a thing of you. I found out that Charlie had a terrible . . . accident a few months ago. And that he lost his leg. I'd like to—"

"How did you find all this out?" she asked sharply.

"From the hospital." Dafydd shifted legs. He felt weak in the knees. The booth was airless and the heat of the light was making him feel faint. Much as he wanted to go on talking, asking questions, he felt he needed to end this conversation soon or he'd pass out. "Someone in the hospital told me about Charlie. How he was airlifted to Moose Creek. How brave he was—"

"Oh, yes, the nurse. Nurse Hailey," Uyarasuq said slowly, quietly. She paused. "I want you to know, she is the only person I've ever told about you being Charlie's father, apart from my father and Sleeping Bear. I felt bad telling her because I knew you'd worked in Moose Creek, but she didn't seem to remember you. I guess she must have informed you after all. She shouldn't have. I asked her not to tell anyone."

"No, in fact it wasn't Miss Hailey who told me," Dafydd said, bemused. "I heard about Charlie because of his dreadful trauma and injuries. The staff are still talking about him. I mean, it's only a few months ago. They all remember him with a lot of affection. I got curious because I was told he came from Black River, so I looked him up on the hospital records and that's how I found out he was *your* son. When I saw his age and date of birth I realized that . . . in spite of precautions, he could be mine, too. I can't deny it was a bit of a shock."

Uyarasuq said nothing for a few moments and he gave her time to take it in.

"But . . . so this isn't why you've come to Canada, because of Charlie? You were already here when you found out about him?" Justifiably she was puzzled.

"No. Yes. But listen. That's another story. All I care about at this moment is to see you and meet Charlie. How is he? How is he recovering?"

"He's doing well. We've just come back from seeing a specialist in Toronto and he's been fitted with a state-of-the-art leg. It's quite a gadget, and he loves gadgets, so they're making hopping friends with each other." She laughed her distinctive bell-like laugh and Dafydd laughed, too. Thank God, she could laugh—after what they'd been through.

"If it's okay with you, I'm going to book a flight up or hire a plane or whatever it takes . . ." At once he stopped himself, mortified by his audacity. "Ah . . . are you . . . with anyone? Will anyone be upset by my coming?"

"No, don't worry." He could hear her smiling. "There was, for a while, but he couldn't cope with Charlie's misadventure, the time that I spent . . ."

"I'm sorry."

"I'm not."

"I'll phone you as soon as I've found a way to get up there."

"There is the mail . . . a plane that comes once a week . . ."

CHAPTER 20

Dafydd hung up the phone. His hand was still trembling. The truth of Charlie was overwhelming. A son. No, *another* son. He put his hands to his head and shut his eyes tight. A deep breath. He fumbled with the door, a folding concertina job, but it had jammed shut in some way. He struggled to open it and felt panic setting in, not a panic based on fear, but a deep inner effort, something trying to burst forth from the very pit of his being. Everything seemed off beam, mixed up, crazy. He stopped struggling and shaking the door and looked through one of the little windows at the large chandelier in the foyer. The many lights were dazzling. He stared at them as his mind worked furiously. His breath was slowing . . . it was important to stop. Something was coming to him, like a word on the tip of the tongue, hovering painfully in his subconscious, in front of his eyes, if only he could see . . .

Sheila. She knew. What did it mean? She was the only one . . . It couldn't be? Oh, no. It couldn't? He drew a sharp breath as an outlandish possibility finally dawned on him. As the pieces fell into place, he saw it was the only explanation. He reeled in shock, bracing himself with his outstretched arms against the walls.

There was time, still some air left. He was not about to suffocate. Quickly he fumbled for his wallet and got out his credit card, stuck it in the slot and unfolded the scrap of paper. A drop of sweat ran down his forehead into his left eye. He swore and dialed.

"Ashoona."

"I'm sorry. It's me again. Uyarasuq, I just need to ask you one more thing. I know it's a weird question, but just tell me. Did Sheila Hailey take blood samples from Charlie when you came to the hospital?"

Uyarasuq was quiet for a moment. "There were many blood samples. Charlie needed transfusions and—"

"Yes. I'm sorry, of course, but what I need to know is: Did Sheila Hailey *personally* take blood samples from Charlie? And did she take them from you?"

"Oh, yes. When we came there, she dealt with just about everything. She was incredibly quick and efficient. I was very grateful for everything she did for us. In fact, she seemed more in control of the situation than the doctor. Why do you ask?"

"Look. I know I sound like a jibbering maniac, but your answer to this question has clarified something for me. It's got nothing to do with me and you and Charlie. I'll explain it all when I see you."

"All right, Dafydd."

"I'll see you very soon. Take care."

He hung up and then his knees really insisted on giving way; why stand when he could sit? With his back against the wall, he sank slowly to the floor and just sat there, grateful for the privacy, the enclosure, like a safe and hot womb. Sheila must have stolen their blood. The implications were almost too much to take on board.

There was a knock on the door and an anxious face peered down at him from the window. The door rattled, but his feet were wedged against it.

"Sir," the woman called out. He recognized her as the haughty receptionist with the blood-red lipstick and piled-up hair. "Sir . . . are you all right? Shall I call for a doctor?"

"I *am* a doctor," Dafydd called back to her and waved. "Come to think of it, I'm the doctor on duty."

Refreshed by a glass of water and chastised by the implacable demeanor of the receptionist, he was back in the telephone booth.

"Please, sir, don't close that door," she called after him in her clipped voice, looking at him over the rim of her spectacles.

Dafydd called the hospital and spoke to Janie.

"Listen, don't ask any questions," he told her firmly, "but I can't be on duty tonight. I wouldn't do this if I didn't have to, but can you call Hogg or Lezzard or whoever? Someone's got to take over."

"All right . . ." A sensible woman, she knew not to query his reasons. "Don't worry. Atilan is here anyway. I'll ask her."

Next he called Ian's number. While it rang he took several deep breaths to bring himself down to a normal, friendly, chatty form.

"Brannagan."

"It's me, Dafydd."

"How are things?"

"With me, great. How about you?"

"All right."

"What's happening out there, then?"

"Not much."

"Are you feeding that dog of yours?"

Ian was quiet for a moment. "Yeah."

"Why don't you come into town? I'm at the Northern. In the bar. Come and join me. It's nice and quiet. We could have a . . . Coke or something."

Ian laughed loudly, like his old self. "Ah, what the heck. Why not? It's like a tomb out here now that you're not coming 'round. I'll be right there."

Half an hour later Ian appeared in the bar looking as though he'd actually groomed himself a bit. He was wearing a pair of tight-fitting black jeans with the old silver belt buckle of many years ago. He had a white shirt on, and he'd pulled a comb through his hair, which had grown quite long down his back. Dafydd suddenly saw the man as he remembered him. In the dim light of the doorway, he still looked dashing, as skinny and gangly as a teenager, with the hardness of his face adding that dilapidated careworn look. Three women at a nearby table nudged each other and looked him over appraisingly.

Closer to, his illness showed appallingly, his eyes sunken, his skin sallow and puckered. The distended liver. A habitual cigarette hung loosely from his mouth, and he puffed effortlessly without the need for hands. He was certainly not on the wagon. Immediately he signaled for a beer and when it arrived he asked for a double Jack Daniel's to go with it. Dafydd put his Coke aside and asked for the same. This called for something strong.

The bar was dark and fairly quiet and Ian seemed relaxed, almost happy. They sat in a red velvet booth and spoke of old times, Dafydd doing his best to hold off, not to think, to wait awhile. Gradually they were lulled into the false idea that all was well and they were just good old friends getting drunk together. Nevertheless, Dafydd felt a tightening in his throat when he saw Ian laugh his huge bawdy laugh, and he laughed as loudly himself to cover up the sadness of it all.

"Ian, I want to ask you about something," he said after a lull in their reminiscences. "It's on my mind and I can't lay it to rest. I've just discovered that a woman I . . . made love to, up in Black River, has a son." Ian stared at him, his face suddenly somber. "This kid," Dafydd continued, "was mauled by a polar bear and was brought to the hospital here." Dafydd snapped his fingers in front of Ian's frozen face.

"*Hello* . . . are you in there? Brannagan, are you taking this on board? I thought you'd be delighted . . . have a field day. Imagine that, I must have got laid more than once in my life. Excepting my dear wife, or *ex-wife* as she's bound to be when she hears about *this:* every time I go anywhere near a woman she gets pregnant."

Ian didn't laugh. "What do you want to know?"

"What do you know about this boy? He was brought here in late March this year. Did you see him? You must know about it."

"Yes, I remember him well."

"Go on, then . . . ?" Dafydd laughed drunkenly, covering up his crystal-clear sobriety, nudging Ian with his fist. "Tell me all about it. Tell me everything you know about him."

The sparkle had gone out of Ian's eyes and he hung his head, avoiding Dafydd's insistent gaze. "I knew I would have to tell you eventually," Ian said quietly, "but I was starting to hope it would be later rather than sooner."

"What the hell are you talking about?" Dafydd prodded him again.

"You're not going to like what I'm going to tell you, Dafydd." He stopped and put his cigarette out at length. "That boy is your son, all right. Where do you think Sheila got the blood for the DNA test?"

Dafydd grabbed his arm hard. "So you *did* know about it?"

Ian looked up into his face, speechless. "How did you find out?" he said after a moment.

"Never mind that," Dafydd growled. "What I want to know is how much *you* know about it. I was really hoping that you weren't a party to this conspiracy."

"I wasn't." Ian had sunk farther into his chest, out of shame or drunkenness, or both. He looked down toward the floor. "Not to begin with."

"How did Sheila do this?" Dafydd grabbed him by the arm again and shook him sharply. *"Tell me how, damn it."*

"Oh, come on, Dafydd, it was easy. In her capacity as the nurse on casualty, she simply took blood samples from both the boy and his mother. Nothing unusual about that . . . Don't we always? But all of it didn't go to the lab. Somewhere along the line she obviously had this incredible brain wave, so she helped herself to some, took it home and put it in her fridge . . . or freezer . . . can't remember which."

"But, *why* did she do it?" Dafydd shook his head in confusion. "She couldn't possibly have known that the boy was my son."

"She found that out straightaway. Within minutes of them arriving. She asked the mother for their next of kin, but the woman had no relations. So, quite correctly, Sheila demanded to know the identity of the father . . . and you know how insistent she can be. The mother was frightfully distressed and she spilled the beans. And why shouldn't she tell? She thought her son was dying, she didn't care about anything else."

"*So Sheila found out that I was the boy's father.*" Dafydd's face was inches from Ian's, his voice cold with barely controlled rage. "*And she decided to steal my son's blood, and his mother's blood, and pass them off as Mark's . . . and her own.*"

"Yes."

"But for fuck's sake, *why* do it? Why did she want to nail *me*, thousands of miles away?"

"Because she had the means. Settling old scores. A long-held grudge. Money. I don't know . . . Ask her. Perhaps she just wanted to see if she could get away with it."

They were quiet for a moment. Ian lit a cigarette and inhaled deeply. His hands were shaking, and he tossed back his Jack Daniel's. "Sheila is remarkable like that," he said, almost in admiration. "Whatever else one may say about this scheme, it was incredibly ingenious. I've always thought she was a textbook psychopath, but, boy, she sure is shrewd with it."

"Yes, I'm full of positive regard," Dafydd snarled sarcastically. "And you've known about this since when?"

"Not when I signed the papers to say I had taken the blood, but later. Sheila got apprehensive when you came here and she wanted to buy my cooperation. She told me how she was finally going to nail you. I wanted to tell you, but then I saw that you got on with the kids . . . and I liked having you around. I kept putting it off. Sheila was threatening me. You know Sheila and I've been . . . sort of in cahoots . . . for a long time. Through no choice of my own."

"Bullshit!" Dafydd exclaimed. "There's always choice. How could you sink so low?"

"Well, there it is. I'm not proud of it."

"What about Mark and Miranda?" Dafydd felt a stifling sensation crawl up his throat, admitting what he knew already. "Those poor kids are no relations of mine whatsoever. This is what all this means." Again he shook Ian by the arm. Ian's head wobbled loosely on his neck.

"No, it doesn't look that way, does it? . . . I'm sorry."

"Oh, God." Dafydd tried to control his conflicting emotions, taking deep, slow breaths. He'd grown to really care about those two luckless children. He'd actually almost come to believe they were his.

"But . . . for God's sake, whose are they, then? They're *yours,* aren't they?"

Ian laughed listlessly. "Nah . . . I doubt it. Can't you see? She's getting all my money already. She wouldn't have to be my dealer if she could just ask for child support. That doesn't make sense, does it?"

Dafydd didn't want to admit it to himself, but beyond the fury that he felt about this swindle, this ruthless exploitation of his gullibility, there was also a small sense of relief. For this reason his outrage was even greater on behalf of Miranda and Mark. A cruel trick wantonly perpetrated on them by their own mother, for the sake of a few dollars, or to get back at him for some real or imagined transgression, or just a game, the result of her resourcefulness and ingenuity. He slammed his fist on the table, rattling the glasses. People turned and looked with good-natured curiosity. The bar had filled up and was becoming noisy and jolly. His outburst was nothing out of the ordinary.

"You can't be all that surprised," Ian said, looking up at Dafydd. "You never actually *did* fuck her, did you?"

A couple of seconds passed in which Dafydd came as near as he'd ever come to smashing his fist into another man's face. He could even anticipate the crunching of nasal material and the jaggedness of broken teeth lacerating the skin of his knuckles. "You *bastard*," he snarled, his jaws locked tight by the effort to control his aggression. "You knew all along I couldn't argue with the DNA results. How the fuck could you keep it up and look me in the face, day after day?"

There was a commotion by the bar. A small balding man in a crumpled suit was trying to pick a fight with a couple of Indians. People were taking sides, laughing uproariously. Both men looked in the direction of the fracas, and the tension was momentarily diverted.

"Look," Ian said, sounding more composed, "I knew this would come out eventually. I would have told you, believe me. I've even written it all down and signed it. I've got two letters in the cabin, each in triplicate. In the cupboard by my bed. Just in case . . . you know?"

"In case you drink and drug yourself to death one of these days. So you can clear your conscience posthumously?" Dafydd said coldly and turned his face away.

"Yeah. Something like that." Ian rose from his seat. "I've gotta go home now, or I won't be able to drive. I'm going now, Dafydd. I'm very sorry, believe me, I am."

Dafydd didn't look up when Ian left. He couldn't look that man in the face. The waitress brought another round and he took a beer from her. He sat there for a long time, one hour, two hours, he had no sense of time passing. He sat paralyzed, staring into the smoky haze that hung in the cavity of the mock-barn-style ceiling. Mainly he thought of nothing, as if this bombshell had blasted from him the last of his emotional reserves. What stood before him was the total uncertainty of his future and behind him the falseness of his past. He didn't know how to go forward and he could never go back. What he had was lost, irrevocably ruined. He thought of Isabel. How much this information would have meant to him a few months ago. To tell her it was all a mistake. That she'd been wrong about him. That he hadn't lied. He hadn't impregnated that despicable woman . . . Now it meant nothing. He doubted he would even bother to tell her. She probably wouldn't believe him anyway and her opinion of him didn't interest him anymore. What really concerned him was how he was going to tell Mark and Miranda . . . and how they would cope with this news.

Then he became aware of something niggling him, an insistent sharp knocking in his chest. He tried to let it go, to let everything go, but it wouldn't allow him. The knocking, like the unrelenting ticking of a clock, grew louder and sharper. He wondered if it was his heart, but feeling the pulse in his wrist told him it wasn't. He closed his eyes to try to discover its meaning. Immediately an image came to him of a small fox dashing through a forest in the darkness. Its feet sank deep into the snow, but it ran on and on and on, struggling toward its destination, panting with exertion . . . *If you learn to be quiet, the little fox will come to you. He will tell you things no one else will.*

Dafydd's eyes popped open and he looked around him, bewildered. Then it hit him, and he ran, knocking drinks off tables and causing people to shout out at him. As he ran, he searched for his keys in his pockets, the ice-cold air in the street waking him to reality. He drove as fast as the road, and the car, would allow him, hunching forward, trying to peer into the darkness beyond the headlights. He was no longer affected by the booze he'd drunk, but the fear in the pit of his stomach made his bowels churn. He needed a shit and he wanted to throw up that last beer, all the beers he'd drunk. But there was no time to waste. Finally he reached Ian's drive and swerved crazily on the ice, skidding sideways, and got stuck in a snowdrift. He got out and ran toward the cabin. The distant sound of Thorn barking loudly and insistently—a bark different from any he'd heard—made him shiver with fear. The lights were on and the door was ajar; he dashed in, dreading what he would find. When he'd ascertained that Ian was not in the cabin he hurled himself into the toilet, emptying himself, as if his insides were expelling everything that had passed.

Thorn was demented. He attempted to soothe the dog but there was no point and it wasted precious time. He searched everywhere for the flashlight, and ended up finding it where it was always kept. He tried to calm himself; panic was not going to help. He dressed himself in everything of Ian's that he could find, and flashlight in hand he set off. Thorn was whining now, a grating scraping whine, and then he went quiet. He trotted purposefully into the dark woods and Dafydd had to run to keep up with him.

About fifty meters into the darkness, Dafydd called out to Thorn. He ran back and rummaged wildly around the cabin for matches, newspapers, and bits of kindling. He threw things about, and when he'd finally located everything he needed he flung it into a dusty rucksack hanging on a nail by the door. Thorn was sitting motionless in the snow waiting, and again they set off. There were no footprints, but he relied on the dog. After a moment he saw the sharp, fresh tracks of skis. Ian had taken the skis. It would be almost impossible to catch up with him. He had no idea how long he'd been sitting in the bar after Ian left: two hours, maybe more. The darkness was dense under the trees, but he could see stars in the sky offering the palest light in the clearings. The flashlight shone weakly. Thorn's skinny flanks were moving laboriously some yards ahead of him. No doubt Thorn had attempted to follow Ian but had been ordered back, or had not been able to keep up.

Suddenly he remembered these woods on a hot autumn day. Thorn was a boisterous puppy and he'd hunted down a wild hare. The fleas on the hare, once loyal to the master that fed them, abandoned their dead host and jumped wildly onto the nearest warm furry body. In the animal world there is no loyalty to the dead. Oh, God . . . no. He was driven by guilt and by horror. If he'd just paid attention to what he saw, what Ian had confided in him, he would have known this was coming. Now it was perfectly clear. In fact, he *had* known it; he just hadn't acknowledged it. He'd been too bloody obsessed with his own problems. None of them was remotely as ghastly as Ian's. None of them was life-threatening . . . Ian had been asking him for more time, always just a little more time, before the inevitable.

Thorn was slowing down to a walking pace. The dog couldn't hold out much longer. Dafydd ran past him and didn't look back. He couldn't care for the dog as well.

"*Ian,*" he screamed at the top of his lungs. The subsequent sharp intake of breath caused him to retch. The air had just about frozen his lungs. It wouldn't do to scream. He would just have to make sure he didn't lose the trail. He began to fear for his own safety. Even if he might be able to make a fire—and that could prove difficult—he still had to find his way back. He stopped for a moment and looked behind him. His footprints had made faint impressions in the hard-packed snow. If Ian had decided to get off the track, he would never be able to follow, not on foot. He cursed himself for not grabbing the snowshoes that were hanging on the cabin wall. Hysteria made for poor planning. He was grateful that this was the very trail where he'd skied a couple of weeks ago. He kept looking around, shining the flashlight into the darkness between the trees to try to locate how far he'd come. There were few landmarks apart from some clearings and minor undulations of the ground. He crossed the cut line he remembered, a long, open ribbon of cleared ground. Beyond it was sheer wilderness, the path of a trapline making a circle of thirty, forty miles. He wondered how far he'd go. Soon he would be risking his own life. He was dressed for the worst, but no amount of clothes allowed for exhaustion and a stop for rest or sleep. It would be a long sleep. The cold was already seeping into his hands and his feet.

In the far distance he could hear the howling of wolves. He ran on but found he was running in the direction of the ghostly sound. This was his nightmare come true. He'd had this dream many times, more as of late. The leg-hold trap, the red blood in the white snow . . . and the howling wolves. Had he perhaps predicted this, or was it his own son he'd seen . . . on death's door, trapped by a polar bear in the high Arctic.

He was slowing down, fatigue setting in. Suddenly the decision to act alone seemed foolhardy. He should have raised the alarm and organized a search party. But Ian would never have survived such a delay.

"*Ian,*" he shouted desperately, covering his mouth with his glove at the intake of breath. It made him giddy, and for a moment he seemed to be running and falling at the same time. He could go on no longer. The tracks of the skis still vanished into the distance. He fell to his knees. "Ian, please . . . answer."

The wolves started up again. They were nearer. He mustn't shout in case it attracted them. He thought he'd read that they didn't attack people, not unless they were starving, or rabid, and the person was near death anyway. They killed and ate dogs, even large huskies. Wolves worked in packs, and they were highly intelligent. Oh, my God . . . he got up and ran on. The idea that Ian could be attacked and ripped apart, eaten alive . . .

Suddenly, a few steps ahead of him, in the wildly dancing beam of the flashlight, he could see the tracks of the skis curving sharply to the right, straight into the trees. He felt new hope. Ian couldn't ski very far in the deep snow; it was simply impossible. As soon as Dafydd ran off the track he sank in to his hips. In places the snow was hard enough to carry his weight, and he climbed up and down the snowdrifts on all fours for some ten or twenty meters.

There, against a tree, sat Ian. He had a half-smoked cigarette in his mouth. He sat straight up, his eyes closed, his bare hands folded in his lap. He had his parka opened at the neck but the hood pulled low over his forehead. The skis and poles lay neatly by his side.

"Ian, thank God . . . Ian." Dafydd fell before him and hugged his awkward body to him, cradling him. "Talk to me, come on, Brannagan, just say something." He sat back and patted Ian's face. "Wake up . . . *Wake up.*" He shook Ian's shoulders hard, but there was no response. He felt desperate. Ian could well be at the point of death and there was little that Dafydd could do for him. His hands were numb with cold, and he feared taking his gloves off to make a fire, but he had no choice. He ripped them off and frantically yanked the paper and the kindling from the rucksack. It seemed pathetic to even attempt to light a fire in the snow with a few papers and a couple of sticks of kindling, but a fire was the one thing that saved lives in extreme cold. So he tried, sweeping the flashlight around him for twigs or branches that could serve to get the fire going. Everything was covered with the white, beautiful snow that he so loved. He cursed and fought his tears; crying was another hazard he could not afford. His fingers were becoming more numb by the second. As he fumbled with the matches, most of them fell out of the box into the snow. He cursed. As he tried again he dropped the box itself. He plunged his hand into the snow to retrieve it and it was as if his hand had been thrust into a raging fire. He bit his teeth together and snarled in anger and frustration. He tried once more with the other hand. As he grappled in the snow, the pain made his vision blacken and small icy pinpricks danced on his eyeballs. He could feel nothing with his hand and could grasp nothing. The matches were lost and the flashlight was dimming. Quickly he put his gloves back on, knowing that for some of his fingers it was probably already too late. Ian didn't move. Dafydd pulled the hood of his parka back off his head and shone the light in his face. His expression was peaceful—in fact he looked almost happy—but his exposed hands were as white as the snow itself. If he lived he would have to make do without hands; his circulation had long ceased. It would not be easy, but people did; it wasn't unusual in the Arctic.

He noticed with dread that underneath the parka Ian was wearing a T-shirt. He'd had no intention of trying to stay warm. Dafydd took the half-smoked cigarette from his frozen lips and started rubbing his face and shouting at him, then slapping his face with his gloves. One hard slap made Ian fall sideways. The reality of Ian's condition finally became entirely clear. He was dead, practically frozen solid. Dafydd had suspected it all along but could not deny it any longer, not without denying that he, too, was gambling with death.

He sat back in the snow and looked at his friend. Ian was dead. All that was left lying awkwardly prone in the deep snow was a shell, a shrunken, hollow, dried-out shell. How easily his sparse flesh had frozen. In the distance he heard the wolves, farther away now, howling their tormented song.

There was only one thing to do, and that was to get himself to safety. For a moment he contemplated trying to remove the ski boots from Ian's feet and fit them on himself so that he could ski back, but he knew his fingers and toes would be beyond redemption with such a maneuver, so he got up and straightened Ian against the tree, just as he'd found him. He grabbed the flashlight between the palms of his gloves.

"Goodbye, friend. You've finally found peace," he said and stood for a second in front of the rigid body, then he turned and started the trek back.

He ran, he stumbled, he swung his arms around wildly to restore the circulation to his freezing hands. He clenched his teeth to stop the tears from coming.

The aftereffects of the alcohol made his mouth dry, leaving a stale residue of beer and whiskey; his body was dehydrated. He'd not eaten anything for many hours. The thought of the afternoon tea with Tillie and the children seemed light-years away. Everything was different now; nothing would ever be the same.

He stopped on the cut line and hung the rucksack from a branch, so that the way to Ian's body could easily be found in the morning. The flashlight was giving off the last of its energy and after flickering for several minutes it died. It was pitch-black among the trees. Dafydd peered into the distance, trying to perceive the light from some clearing. Still running clumsily, hindered by the thickness of his clothes, he picked his way as best he could along the tracks. Finally he could see the distant lights of the cabin. There was no joy in it. A part of him would have welcomed the icy sleep that Ian had chosen. It was not a bad way to go.

Inside the cabin was the devastation that he'd left as he'd thrown Ian's belongings around. He closed the door and went to the woodstove. There was not a speck of an ember with which to start it up. He took his gloves off and saw that his fingers were red and swollen. Big watery blisters were forming around them. The pain was excruciating, but he felt relieved. Dead tissue had no sensation.

Again he had to hunt for matches and when he found some he managed to light a wad of toilet paper. He threw a cornflakes packet with its contents on top and then set about looking for other burnables. There were plenty of logs, but the kindling and the newspapers had been stuffed into the rucksack. Into the stove went unopened and unpaid bills, paper plates and napkins and a broken wicker wastepaper basket. Soon the fire was going and he put in the smallest log. Fire seemed to mean something. It was precious and had to be looked after. Without it, God knows how he'd go on. He felt delirious. He looked in the cupboards for tea and food. He put the kettle on the stove and ate a moldy cheese out of its packet, standing in the light of the fridge door. He laughed at the fridge. A fridge in this climate? There was a bottle of white wine, half drunk, in the fridge door. Holding it between his palms he poured it down his gullet. The cold liquid ran down his cheeks and beyond his collar and down his chest. The kettle started boiling, and he took it off the stove. He shoved in several logs. He went into the tiny bedroom. To his surprise it was quite tidy. Ian had made his bed. Dafydd pulled the covers back, an act of intimacy that he felt he had earned. Fully dressed, he laid himself down, pulled the quilt over himself and fell deeply asleep.

It was still pitch-black outside when he woke. At first he wasn't sure how he came to be there, but then it all came back to him at once. The events of the night physically knocked him backward, and he remained flat, flattened, staring at the ceiling. He couldn't move even if he'd wanted to, but he had no desire to do anything but just be motionless, totally still. His mind was dull, and his hands throbbed viciously. Finally he turned his head. There was a small digital alarm clock on the bedside table. It said 5:37 a.m. A moment later a tiny sound reached him, a mere breath. He threw the covers off and jumped up, causing waves of giddiness. Holding his head, he ran, crouching, into the main room.

Thorn . . . where was Thorn? The poor old dog. How could he not have remembered him? As it was, Thorn had been in the cabin all along, lying soundlessly in a corner, catatonic with grief or pain. Dafydd fell to his knees by the dog and hugged his limp head. Thorn didn't respond, but the dog's wise old eyes were open and looking into nothing. They had seen all they wanted to see. Thorn's breathing was as light as the sweep of a feather. Dafydd rubbed his back legs and Thorn whimpered softly. He knew that Ian had pills for the dog's arthritis, and he went into the bathroom to search for them. The pills were nowhere to be found, but in a box on top of the mirrored cabinet he found the vials. Ian's vials. Dafydd stared at them. There were twenty or so of the fragile glass tubes, filled with the noxious substance. Overwhelmed with emotion, he grabbed the box with his wrists and went to smash it onto the floor. He raised the box over his head and drew breath for the effort, but there he froze. Gently he put the box down on the lid of the toilet. With his hugely swollen fingers he picked up a handful of vials. He looked for a syringe. There were no clean ones, and he went searching for one in the garbage. None there. Finally he located Ian's briefcase and there, among prescription pads and samples of drugs, he found a large syringe and some hypodermic needles. He tried hard not to weep, but tears were streaming down his face, and with fingers the size of golf balls he drew one vial after another until the syringe was entirely full.

With Thorn's heavy head cradled in his lap he injected every last drop into the dog's quivering flank. As he went out, Thorn looked up at Dafydd and gave an imperceptible movement of his tail. A few moments later he let out a mighty sigh and expired. Finally, Dafydd could let go and he sobbed until his chest could take no more.

Of the three RCMP officers, he knew Mike Dawson, the senior officer in town. Dafydd had treated him recently for a persistent leg ulcer. He was due to retire, and Dafydd had suggested that his affliction was serious enough to be considered a just cause to come off early. Not a chance. Dawson was a man with scruples.

They had brought two snowmobiles and a large-person-sized sled. A black tarpaulin was neatly folded under six nylon straps. Dafydd couldn't bring himself to tell them that Ian's body would not easily acquire the appropriate shape for the narrow sled, and he avoided even thinking of how they were going to fit him on it. He offered to lead the way, but Dawson pointed to his hands and said he should be in the hospital, not in the woods. But Dafydd refused to leave. His hands could wait. He agreed to stay in the cabin and gave the officers the best directions he could. The cut line was easy to find and from there, the rucksack indicated the way.

After rolling Thorn's body into Ian's quilt, Dafydd went into the bedroom and opened the little cabinet that acted as a bedside table. Among other papers and documents were six envelopes, bundled into two lots held together by rubber bands. One bundle also contained a small package. Both bundles had one envelope with *Dafydd* written on it in a large and steady hand. With difficulty he managed to open one of them. He read the letter it contained slowly and carefully.

> *I, Ian Brannagan, hereby acknowledge that I aided*
> *and abetted Sheila Hailey, head nurse at Moose*
> *Creek Hospital, in perpetrating a fraudulent act, in*
> *order to dispatch blood allegedly belonging to Sheila*

*Hailey and her son Mark Hailey for a DNA test,
to falsely prove that Dr. Dafydd Woodruff was the
father of Mark and his sister Miranda.*

*This blood was obtained from Ms. U. Ashoona,
of Black River (Nunavut), and her son Charlie,
without their knowledge of its intended usage. Dr.
Dafydd Woodruff is the father of Charlie Ashoona,
a fact Ms. Hailey established when the boy was a
patient in the Moose Creek Hospital, and which allowed her to perpetrate the elaborate deception. My
own part in this consisted of putting Mark's and Ms.
Hailey's names to said blood samples without having
taken them myself and thus authenticating them for
the use in said DNA test.*

*Subsequently Ms. Hailey confessed her deception
to me. A new DNA test involving all parties will easily establish the veracity of my claim.*

Ian Brannagan

A PS added a note meant only for him:

*Dear Dafydd, I sincerely hope that when you read
this letter I will already have summoned the courage
to tell you in person. If I haven't, I hope you will
forgive me. I'm weak in more ways than you know.
Ian.*

The other two envelopes, presumably containing the same letter, were addressed *To whom it may concern.*

He opened a letter with his name on it from the other bundle. It read:

*I, Ian Brannagan, hereby acknowledge that for the
past thirteen years I have been personally involved
in the theft of Demerol and other psychotropic
drugs from the Moose Creek Hospital. I've suffered*

*addiction in various degrees of severity over this
period and often been in need of large amounts of
drugs. I have been aided and abetted in this theft by
Sheila Hailey, head nurse of said hospital. Ms. Hailey has been the only person in charge of dispensing and accounting for the usage of these drugs, at
said hospital, and she has procured them for me in
exchange for money. I leave behind me as evidence
a cache of several thousand empty vials, mainly
having contained Demerol. They can be found in
two wooden trunks at the back of my shed. Further
evidence is a cassette tape containing two recorded
conversations (done by me without Ms. Hailey's
knowledge) between me and Ms. Hailey. They
speak for themselves. My bank statements and Ms.
Hailey's may also show consistencies in withdrawals
and deposits, representing transfers of money made
by me to Ms. Hailey as payment for her complicity
in the thefts.*

*My reason for writing this letter is that I feel Ms.
Hailey has abused her position, has used extortion
and intimidation for her own considerable financial gain. I pledge this to be the whole and absolute
truth.*

Dr. Ian Brannagan

Dafydd remained sitting on the bed for quite some time. The
immense responsibility contained in being in possession of
these two letters slowly dawned on him. The letter denouncing Sheila as a compulsive thief and ruthless drug pusher
would almost certainly result in a long prison sentence and
that would leave her children parentless—subject to what awful system?

The letter telling of her theft of blood and the remarkable
swindle she'd conjured up would result in Dafydd no longer being able to help those children in any way. Once it was discov-

ered that he was not their father he would have no more rights to Mark and Miranda than a perfect stranger. That, in the end, summed it up.

He looked out of the window and wondered how long the Mounties had been gone. He would have to make up his mind very quickly. He now understood why Ian had written two letters instead of one. He was leaving the choice to Dafydd. In a matter of minutes he would have to decide which letter to hand over to Dawson, one or the other, or both, or neither. Perhaps Ian foresaw the whole situation and the predicament that he was putting Dafydd and Mark and Miranda in.

Again he wondered if the children could have been Ian's. Could Ian really take that knowledge with him to his grave? Perhaps that's why he had fostered Dafydd's loyalty toward them. He knew his time was up, and he could see what a potentially good parent Dafydd was, at least in terms of consistency and kindness.

Dafydd heard the faint purr of engines. It was now or never. A voice inside him said: Let the full force of the law descend on Sheila for *all* her crimes. Another: Exonerate Sheila, and the twins will be cared for, perhaps not in the way they should be, but they would still have a mother, and you are free of her. A third: Let Sheila pay the price for being a crook and a drug dealer, and let everyone go on believing that you are the children's father, a role that you yourself must then continue to play for however long . . .

Dafydd looked at the two letters, one in each hand, as the purring got nearer.

CHAPTER 21

" I think you'd better take a look at this," Dafydd said to Dawson while they were watching the two junior officers load the ill-proportioned sled into the van. They were standing in the snow outside Ian's cabin, which now looked as dejected and ramshackle as if it had been abandoned for decades. Dafydd, his hands wrapped in makeshift bandages, handed Dawson the envelope.

"Brannagan left this letter in triplicate in his bedroom," he said to the officer. "One was addressed to me. It's easy to see what caused this tragedy."

Dawson took off his gloves to open the envelope, then fumbled around at length inside his coat for a pair of spectacles; having located them, he scrunched them onto his face. His features tightened as he read, a stern folding and pleating of his brow denoting the seriousness of the matter. His mind was conspicuously mulling over the contents as he was trying to get around the enormity of Sheila's criminal dealings.

"Holy Jesus," he exclaimed, having finally understood the full meaning of Ian's letter. "If this is true, it would be absolutely astonishing that she's got away with it."

"I knew something was up with Brannagan," Dafydd lied effortlessly. "I blame myself for not realizing he was on large doses of drugs. Goes to show, I've been out of general practice for too long."

Dawson was grimly shaking his head. "That woman . . . There have been a few things over the years. I shouldn't mention them, of course, but I've had my suspicions."

"Oh? Like what?"

Dawson hesitated. "Can we stick to Dr. Brannagan for the moment?" he said. "I've heard you've been seeing quite a bit of him as of late. In your opinion, Dr. Woodruff, you don't think this was an accident? I mean, do you think such an addiction is strong enough a reason for a man to take his own life?"

Dafydd looked at Dawson, whose face looked open and trusting. He seemed to know an awful lot about everybody, but in a small place like this and the many years he'd spent there it wasn't surprising. Anyway, it was a perfectly fair question.

"Perhaps not in itself, but Dr. Brannagan was suffering from a long-standing depression, which is why I've been looking in on him. Sadly, he refused to acknowledge it; he refused all help. Perhaps it was the fear of discovery, too."

"Wasn't he going a bit heavy on the booze as well?" Dawson lifted his hand to make bottle-tipping motions. "My sources tell me he was getting through a couple of bottles a day."

"Well," Dafydd said smartly, "your sources may be exaggerating some, but yes."

"Still, one wonders," Dawson mused, "what makes a man want to freeze to death."

Dafydd flinched at the thought of the other bundle of letters, which had stayed firmly in his pocket. He himself was now guilty of another colossal cover-up. He had no idea yet where this would lead, yet he knew it would send Sheila to jail, and if he didn't follow through with his impulsive decision it would leave the children at the mercy of the social services.

As if sensing his unease, Dawson said, "We'll have a thorough look around. Perhaps we'll come up with something."

"Why don't you start where Brannagan suggested?" Dafydd motioned with a nod toward the shed, and Dawson called on his colleagues to follow. The shed contained many relics from Ian's life in the cabin, and the bulk of them were in two trunks. Dawson opened the clasp of one and pushed back the lid. There was the bounty of little glass containers, years and years' worth of misery, and possibly some pleasure, forming the explanation and conclusion of Ian Brannagan's decline. The men opened the other trunk, and all three wrote in their little notebooks while keeping their fine pigskin gloves on to keep out the cold.

"We'll take these with us," Dawson said, and the younger two carried the trunks to the van. Dawson was about to start on the cabin, but Dafydd detained him.

"I'm not up on Canadian law, but I have to say I'm concerned about the children. What sort of punishment is Miss Hailey likely to get for something like this? Of course, the children have me, their father, but this is going to be hard on them."

Dawson shook his head. "Oh. It'll be a bad one. Years. She better get her hands on one hell of a good lawyer."

Dafydd smiled in spite of himself. "She's got her hands on one already, as it happens. A real shark."

"Well," Dawson said, thumping Dafydd on the shoulder in sympathy, "now that you've mentioned it yourself, if you don't mind me saying, I knew the reason you came up here. These things have a way of reaching me. When I heard, I did feel for you. It appears you knew nothing about these kids of yours, huh?"

"That's correct," Dafydd said, feeling uncomfortable and casting around for a change of subject. "Another thing. I'm afraid I gave some medication to Brannagan's dog this morning, for compassionate reasons. He was on his last legs, literally. He was very old and completely devoted to Brannagan. I think he'd have willed himself dead had I not helped him along. Is there any chance you could take him? If possible to keep them together . . ."

The men were ordered to have a quick look around the cabin and take the sad bundle to the van. Dawson tried to insist that Dafydd come along to the hospital for treatment of his frostbite, but he declined. After the Mounties had left, he returned to the cabin one last time, wondering if there was anything of Ian's he would like as a memento of his friend. In the end he took the skis and poles that the Mounties had brought back from the scene of Ian's death, a poignant reminder of Ian's last journey, and shoved them in the back of the Buick. He closed the door to Ian's home and hoped to God he'd never have to bear the misery of seeing it again.

The Buick was positively stuck. He cursed himself; why hadn't he asked Dawson's men to help him? Resorting to placing his parka under the wheels and anything he could find outside, he finally dislodged the damned automobile and steering with his wrists he drove it away, never once looking back.

As he drove toward the hospital, he marveled at the theory of mind over matter. He'd carried on all morning, his frozen hands his only implements, having been able to largely ignore the pain, but now the agony asserted itself ferociously and he felt drained and nauseous.

"Who's here today?" he asked Veronica, a new nurse from Winnipeg, who came toward him in the corridor. Her face was quite white and she looked distressed.

"Hogg, Lezzard, Kristoff," she said, staring at the filthy rags around his hands. "Atilan just left." She took a step closer to him and whispered, "They've all just come up from the morgue. I guess you don't know . . . Ian Brannagan froze to death last night."

Dafydd patted her lightly on the shoulder. "I know."

"I didn't really know him," the girl half sobbed, "but it's horrible."

"You'll get used to these sorts of things. They happen frequently here. I knew Ian quite well and, believe me, he's at peace."

The girl nodded, wiped her eyes with a tissue and continued down the corridor.

Hogg looked up with a start when Dafydd came into his consulting room, pale, disheveled, wild-looking, his hands before him.

"Yes, I found Ian," Dafydd said preemptively. "I'll tell you about it in a minute if you could just see to my hands first."

Their eyes met briefly, then Hogg swiftly removed the lengths of cloth.

"Dear, dear, dear, dear, dear," he crooned, "not pretty, not pretty." They both studied Dafydd's hands as if they were a couple of raw slabs of liver in a butcher's shop. Hogg prodded the dark, watery blisters and shook his head.

"What about that one?" Dafydd said, alarmed, wiggling his left ring finger to attract Hogg's attention to its blackening tip.

"Yes, I'm looking at it, old chap. Very bad, very bad. Very bad indeed," Hogg said, rubbing his chin. "Dry gangrene. I'm afraid the thing had better come off."

Dafydd flinched. "Not the whole finger, surely?"

"Just a little bit, just a little bit." Hogg patted his arm reassuringly. "Just the tip, to the joint. We can do it now. The sooner the better. It won't take a moment."

He called for a nurse to assist him; Veronica appeared and was sent off again for the necessary implements.

Hogg injected local anesthetic and Dafydd watched impassively as the tip of his finger was swiftly cut around with a scalpel and the bone snapped off summarily with a pair of surgical pliers, then the flaps of skin neatly sewn over it. Hogg was a master; he'd done quite a few in his day. Dafydd looked at the gangrenous bit of flesh that had just belonged to his finger lying pathetically in a steel bowl, a scrap that a hungry dog wouldn't even look at. Quietly he said goodbye to it. He should be devastated, knowing what it meant, but his guitar had been stolen and was part of a past that no longer seemed real. Operating would not be a major problem since he was right-handed.

"I hope the rest will be okay," he said.

"The others are fine, old chap. Don't you worry, don't you worry. You look like you really need to rest. I want to ask you about Ian, but we can talk about it later." He applied antibiotic ointment to his fingers and bandaged both hands, then gave him a dose of intravenous antibiotics. "Veronica, could you take my car and give Dr. Woodruff a ride home?"

"In a moment," Dafydd said to her. "Can I call for you in a little while?"

Once alone, the two men looked at each other. Dafydd felt impossibly weary, but this was his last task before he could retire to his purple grotto, pull his covers over his head and not speak to anyone for twenty-four hours.

"Andrew, could you please retrieve the envelope that's in my left coat pocket and read it?" Dafydd instructed. "I'm doing you a favor here." Hogg should know about the drug theft so he could be prepared.

Hogg looked mystified, guarded, but did as he was told. He got the letter, opened it, read it and blanched. "Oh, no, Sheila's never . . . It was Ian," was all he could say before he buried his face in his hands.

"Come on, Andrew, I think you know better. Sheila has been supplying Ian for years and years. Don't try to tell me you didn't suspect it."

Hogg didn't move or speak, his face hidden.

Dafydd raised his voice. "Look at me, Hogg. Don't try to deny it. Ian is dead, partly because of her."

Hogg looked up suddenly. "Has anyone else seen this letter? It was sealed."

"I'm afraid so. The letter exists in triplicate, all three signed by Ian. I've given one copy to Mike Dawson, along with the tape recording. For Sheila, the game is up, I'm afraid."

"How could you?" Hogg burst out. "How could you do that to the children, *your* children? You do realize they're going to be motherless, don't you? Sheila will be finished, she'll go to jail . . ."

Dafydd stared at him, astonished. Even after all this, Hogg would have wanted him to get rid of the evidence and absolve Sheila. "How can you go on covering for that woman?" he said scornfully. "After all that she's done to everyone, to Ian, to you even. *You* might be held accountable for this, don't you realize?"

"I know." Hogg sank in his chair and again covered his face with his hands. A muffled cry escaped, and another. He appeared to be crying. "I know she is . . . can be . . . troublesome. You've got to understand, she's a very complex person, so damaged . . . I'm very fond of her . . ." Hogg moaned. He took out his man-sized handkerchief and blew his nose. His heartbroken expression sickened Dafydd. At the same time he felt sorry for the man. He'd never realized how totally he worshiped Sheila, although it had always been plain that he was in love with her. No wonder Anita had left him. For Hogg there was only one woman.

Dafydd made an abrupt decision. Why not? Hogg might as well know. "I'll show you what else she's done. If you look in my inside pocket there's another letter in triplicate. This one I kept from Mike Dawson. I'm only showing it to you so that you know I do very much care about what happens to the children. I'm doing this so that they won't fall into the hands of some dreadful fostering system or, worse still, an institution."

Hogg stared at him blankly. He looked as if he couldn't take any more, but he got up slowly and rummaged inside Dafydd's parka for the other bunch of letters. He slit one of the envelopes with the letter opener on his desk.

Dafydd looked at him as he read. Soon there was a noticeable change on his face. He sighed deeply, his brow softened and he looked up at Dafydd with genuine warmth.

"Thank you," he said simply.

"Thank you?" Dafydd barked at him, exasperated. "I'll look after them for a time, but I can't go on lying to them forever. I can't go on letting them think I'm their father. The whole thing is madness—can't you see?—and it's all Sheila's doing. It's destroyed my marriage, everything."

Hogg seemed undeterred in his gratitude. "You misunderstand me, Dafydd. I'm not thanking you for wanting to look after them. I'm thanking you for . . . You would not believe how much this means to me, Dafydd." He leaned forward, putting his elbows on the desk for support. His eyes were red and swollen. "You see, Mark and Miranda are *my* children," he said slowly.

Dafydd stared at Hogg for a long moment, then burst out laughing. "I don't *believe* this. Don't tell me *you're* involved in this farce? Why on earth didn't you tell me in the café, that day, when I said *I* was their father?"

Hogg looked affronted. "It's no laughing matter. I was distraught. When you dropped that bombshell on me I thought Sheila had lied to me all these years and just milked me for child support." He sat back wearily, big stains of sweat having appeared in each of his armpits. "I guess I should tell you . . . Sheila was involved with another man at the time of their conception. I think she hoped that he was the one who had fathered the twins, but she soon found out that this was not the case." Hogg let escape a mirthless laugh and shook his head. "If only she'd have asked me, I could have told her straightaway. I was the one who'd referred the man for a vasectomy.

"By the time she found out it was too late to do anything about the pregnancy. Thank God. She would have aborted my children. I was desperate to have them, I would have done anything. I offered to bring them up, on my own if I had to. In the end we compromised. I promised Sheila I'd always support them financially, be there if they needed me . . . love them . . . even if she insisted that it be from a distance. Then you came along . . . How could I argue when you told me you'd had DNA tests?" Hogg shrugged his shoulders repeatedly as if to throw off the memory of their meeting in the café. "It wasn't a very pleasant discovery."

Dafydd was so thrown by this new revelation that he could barely comprehend it. He'd been convinced that Ian was the father of the twins, but he'd been wrong. "And the children . . . don't know anything?"

"Of course not. Sheila wanted it this way. First because of my wife. I could understand that. Finally, when . . . Anita left me, I thought we could be a family at last, but Sheila didn't want that. With her dreadful background she's frightened of commitment. I fully accepted that. Nevertheless, I hoped she would change her mind one of these days. We've always been . . . quite close."

Dafydd shook his head in amazement. "Do you realize she's been fleecing *everyone:* you for child support, Ian for drug money, and I was to be her next victim? No wonder she's stayed around this place. I couldn't understand why a woman like her would waste her life in Moose Creek, but this explains it perfectly. She's been building up one hell of a nest egg. You've got to hand it to her. She's a big-time hustler, a con woman . . . in fact, a real professional crook."

Dafydd watched with some gratification as Hogg squirmed in his chair.

"Please, Dafydd, let me keep this letter."

"What are you going to do with it?" Dafydd demanded. The poor man must be in turmoil. The letter was further evidence of Sheila's criminal character and would put her away for the fraudulent paternity claim as well. On the other hand, by handing it to the police Hogg could go on to prove his own paternity—and claim what was rightfully his.

"Sure, have the damned thing, keep it, but I have copies," Dafydd said.

"I need time," Hogg whimpered. "We need to think this over very carefully."

"You know what, Hogg?" Dafydd said. "They are *your* children, not mine. They should be your first priority, before you even think of Sheila. Let me give the letter to Dawson." Hogg moaned quietly, but Dafydd could see that a change was taking place. His words had hit home. "Those children need you, Andrew. You've known them all their lives, you've cared about them. Go on . . . go and see Dawson yourself. Tell him the truth."

Dafydd's energy abruptly came to a full stop. He felt woozy and worn out. He got up and went to the door. Outside was

Veronica, sitting primly on a chair, waiting for him. "I'll have that lift now," he said to her and smiled. She smiled back.

Hogg called after him. "Dafydd, wait." His tone was humble, apprehensive. "When that injection wears off, you'll be quite uncomfortable. Let me at least give you a shot of Demerol."

Dafydd stopped. "All right," he said, suppressing a smile. "If there's any to be had."

Tillie's eyes were large when he staggered past her up the stairs. "Dafydd," she called after him. "What's happened to your hands? Where have you been?" He found in himself no answer to her question, so he just continued toward his room, fumbling for his keys but not being able to get his hands into his pockets.

"Help," he called feebly, and Tillie came darting after him.

"Oh, my God," she cried. "What's happened to you?"

"Keys in my pocket," he said and raised his arms to give her access to his body. She searched him for the keys and extracted them from his trouser pockets. Opening the door, she supported him as he staggered toward the purple. He fell on the bed and groaned. Tillie started unlacing his boots and as she did he fell into a twilight zone of sky blue, and he soared upward as if his outstretched arms were wings. He could feel her unbuttoning his trousers and he didn't resist as she pulled them down and away from him. The sweater was another matter. He had to wake up a bit so that she could carefully peel it over his bandaged hands.

"Oh, my God," she moaned. "Darling Dafydd, what have you done?"

"Where is your source?" Dafydd murmured. "He's slipping."

"Why, what's happened?" Tillie demanded as she unbuttoned his shirt.

"My friend is dead," he said without opening his eyes. "My marriage is over. My children are not my children and I'll never play my guitar again and it's been stolen anyway and my home has been sold to some horrible people and I'm high on Demerol. Very good stuff. I've missed out all these years . . . Dang."

"Oh, Dafydd." Tillie took his face between her little hands and kissed him on the forehead repeatedly. It was very pleasant to be kissed, and he smiled. Next she was kissing him on the lips, tiny quick kisses, covering his mouth from one corner to the other. He put his arms around her and she hugged him back fiercely. Then he nuzzled his face against her soft hair and drowned in her embrace, losing himself there.

The next thing he knew they were both under the purple velvet, and she was still kissing him, and he was starting to kiss her back. It felt so nice, so warm, so wet. He realized vaguely that he was almost naked, perhaps he *was* naked. Never mind, at least she had clothes on. He could feel her hands stroking the skin on his back, his buttocks, his hips. It was so enjoyable he didn't want to stop her. Something stirred in his groin, a pulsating, throbbing, and he drew her nearer and squeezed her to him with his forearms. She rolled onto him and his erection became lodged somewhere between her knees. Her body was so short, so small. It felt weird, depraved, like embracing a child. This incongruity, her childlike form and her womanly desire, abruptly brought him toward the surface of cognition, and he saw that he was seconds away from tearing her clothes off with his teeth and having her. He so wanted to be engulfed and swallowed up, transported, carried away to some other place, but it was madness. Tomorrow he would wake up . . . with Tillie. It wouldn't feel right; he knew he would regret it.

"Tillie, no," he said weakly. "We mustn't."

"Why not?" she argued and continued placing her hot little lips all over his.

"You're taking advantage of me. It's not right. I'm drugged up to the eyeballs."

Tillie chuckled. "That's good."

"No, really." He was quite awake now and he pushed her gently away from him with his forearms. "My hands are hurting terribly," he lied. "I've had a finger *amputated*. Please, Til-lie. I can't do this. I'm really sorry."

She looked down at him, frowning. "Amputated? Oh, Dafydd, that's awful." He could tell that she knew what he was really saying. He just didn't want to do it because he couldn't follow it up. Her disappointment was palpable. She rolled away from him and readjusted her clothes.

"I'll get you a cup of tea," she said quietly and left the room. Seconds later he was far, far away.

Dafydd made his way slowly through town. If it weren't for the endless churning of his mind around all that had passed in the last forty-eight hours, and the rendezvous that he was going to, he would have really enjoyed the bustle of Frontier Days, a yearly festival consisting of dog-team races and other, more as-tonishing contests. From all over town came the yapping, whin-ing and intermittent wild barking of the dog teams as they were tied to posts or vehicles on various pieces of cleared ground waiting anxiously to compete. The dog-mushers and their fami-lies, from all corners of the Northwest Territories, as well as the Yukon, Alaska, and Alberta, were welcomed guests, and the atmosphere of gaiety, sport, and general abandoned cheer was further enlivened by the tawdry Christmas decorations that seemed to have gone up overnight all around the town.

Dafydd steeled himself for the encounter. There was Mike Dawson, sitting in his car outside Sheila's house when Dafydd arrived at precisely eleven o'clock, the appointed time. He nod-ded at the RCMP officer, who looked grave and motioned for him to get into the passenger seat.

"I had no choice here," he said, slightly apologetically. "I've got to bring her in. This is no trifling matter, it's big-time crime. She'll be prosecuted for theft of hospital property, sale of con-trolled drugs and fraud. To top it off, Andrew Hogg came in this morning with some new evidence. I take it you know al-ready?"

"Yes, that's why I want to speak to the children. I can tell you it was a hell of a shock," Dafydd said earnestly. "I was just getting used to the idea of being a father."

"I'm sorry for you, Dr. Woodruff. All this must have caused havoc in your life. The scheme she cooked up was astonishing, really." Dawson seemed almost impressed. "I think you need to get yourself a lawyer, too. It's just a formality; she's confessed to it all. You'll need the letters or e-mails she sent you, and the DNA certificate, and any other evidence, but your lawyer will brief you on all that. I'm just telling you so you can put things in motion."

Dafydd sighed heavily and opened the car door.

"One hour," Dawson said, "no more. Tell the kids. Perhaps you could mention to her to pack some personals, if you don't mind . . . that sort of thing. I'll be here and Hopwood will be at the back. Just so there won't be any question . . ."

Dafydd rang the doorbell and Sheila let him in. Mark and Miranda stood anxiously behind her, obviously knowing that something serious had happened. As soon as he was inside the door, Sheila ordered the kids upstairs, much to their bewilderment and annoyance. She was in no mood to offer him any refreshment. She just waved a hand in the direction of the living room. They sat down on opposite sofas.

"What have you told them?" Dafydd asked quietly.

Sheila wasn't her good-looking self. Her eyelids were swollen and she was pale and gaunt. She wore no makeup, and her outfit, normally so immaculate and figure-flattering, consisted of a shapeless jogging suit in knobbly pale blue cotton.

"Oh, they know you're not their father. I told them this morning. Anyway, do you really think something like this can be kept under wraps in Moose Creek for as much as a day? Don't be an idiot."

He swallowed the bile he felt rising, the anger that could so easily unleash itself. He remembered suddenly having hit her in a flash of anger, all those years ago. How very easy it would be, how satisfying, but he had to restrain his antagonism just for this one more confrontation with Sheila. At the same time he was astonished, almost admiring, at her complete lack of contrition. There seemed to be not a trace of shame or mortification at being so summarily exposed for all that she'd done.

"I know Hogg's their father," Dafydd said. "You don't deny it, do you?"

"That's no concern of yours," she countered tartly. "Why are you here anyway? Why don't you fuck off home? You have no business here anymore." She threw him a derisive glance. "You're dismissed."

"No, I'm not going anywhere just yet," he said reasonably. "I want to make sure Mark and Miranda are cared for . . . properly. I'm pretty sure that Hogg will be happy to have them, if they want that. I could easily apply to foster them myself since they know me well. I made some inquiries, and at their age they'll have some choice over who they live with."

"You've got to be kidding," Sheila said with sneering incredulity. "You're just as pathetically tenderhearted as I'd counted on. Now you're proposing to take on my kids, knowing that they're not yours."

"Yes, why not? I could move in here for the time being. That way we wouldn't upset them more than is necessary."

Sheila stared at him. "Go to hell," she said. "Do you really think I'm going to let you move into my home and take over my children?"

"Okay. So scrap that one. What are the alternatives? Live with Hogg, their natural father, who really cares about them, here in Moose Creek, or perhaps elsewhere, or go to stay in Florida with your mother?"

Sheila managed a sarcastic laugh. "My mother? How did you know I had a mother? It'll be a cold day in hell when she's going to want children around her. She hates children with a vengeance. I can vouch for it."

He said nothing. He looked out through the window at Hopwood, Dawson's young colleague, where he was in the yard, watching the house from behind, freezing his butt in too short a parka. Dafydd tried not to smile as the young man, unaware of being watched, was slapping his arse and running briskly on the spot.

"Well, okay," Sheila said after a moment. "Hogg is the obvious choice, being their father. I've not talked to him, but I'm sure he's more than willing." She smiled to herself.

"Do the kids know . . . ?"

"That he's their father? Not yet. Someone else can tell them. I've had enough lip from them for one morning. I don't need any more."

"For once, Sheila, just for once," Dafydd blurted angrily, "can you put your damned narcissism aside? This is not about you and your needs. We are trying to think about what's best for the children here, *your children*."

Sheila smiled wryly. "You didn't think about them when you exposed me, did you? I think it's *me* I've got to worry about now, seeing that you've landed me in it."

Dafydd stared at her. Her selfishness was almost unbelievable. "You're despicable," he growled. "What you did to Ian is utterly contemptible. You're the worst kind of criminal. And to think I almost considered destroying the evidence against you with my own hands." He looked at his bandaged hands with bitterness.

Sheila looked up. "That's enough. Get the fuck out of my house."

Dafydd didn't move. He smiled at her. "Already, as we speak, the *Moose Creek News* is writing up something very savory about you . . . and me, of course. I tried to talk to Mr. Jacobs this morning, to stop it, for the sake of the kids, but he refused." Dafydd shrugged his shoulders in mock helplessness. "News is news."

The officer in the garden was looking uncomfortably cold and was glancing constantly at his watch. Furtively, he lit a cigarette and puffed intently at it as if the cigarette itself were the primeval source of heat.

"We're running out of time," Dafydd said, looking out at the freezing lad. "I want to speak to the children."

"They don't want to speak to you," Sheila said.

"I do," Mark said and came forth from the hall. He looked at his mother contemptuously. "We've been sitting on the stairs. We've been listening to every fucking word you guys said." He turned to Dafydd and barked, "I told you, didn't I? I knew you weren't my father. Why the fuck didn't you believe me?"

"I really thought I was," Dafydd said, reaching over and trying to touch Mark's hand. "But Mark, listen, my feelings for you haven't changed."

Mark stepped back. He was trembling. He stared at Dafydd, his face contorted, barely containing his angry tears. "I don't want *any* fucking father," he shouted. "Now we're supposed to go through the same shit with Hogg."

Miranda had come to the doorway and looked on with large, frightened eyes. Dafydd jumped up and went to her. "I'm so sorry, sweetheart." He put his arms around her.

She started crying and limply returned the embrace, pleading, "Can we live with you, Dad?" Suddenly she pushed him away and ran up to Sheila. With her fist clenched she leaned over her mother and screamed, "*I hate you . . . I hate your guts. I hope you go away forever and I get to be adopted. You're a shit mother. I hope you have to stay in jail until you die and never come back. You're horrible and ugly and hateful . . .*"

While further streams of abuse and vicious recriminations were hurled by Miranda at her stunned mother, Dafydd quickly went to the phone out in the hall.

"Tillie, there's a crisis," he whispered as soon as she'd answered. "Can you hear it? Is it possible to accommodate two more guests for a few days? Two very delicate and vulnerable guests . . . Great. Thanks, Tillie. We'll be over in about half an hour."

CHAPTER 22

Dafydd stood by the road and watched the dog-mushers prepare for the fifteen-mile race. This was serious business and many months of planning went into the affair. The dogs were handsome, rugged creatures, but the noise they made was deafening. From time to time he wandered up and down the crowds of people, searching for a face he'd only seen once. A native of British Columbia by the name of Baptiste Sharkie, owner and pilot of a four-seater Cherokee, would take a passenger for a reasonable fee more or less anywhere accessible. Dafydd had seen him once briefly in the surgery, to renew a prescription. He was a tall, broad-shouldered man of about Dafydd's own age, forty-five or so, with roughly etched Indian features and a broad-set mouth with a look of rarely having smiled.

People were thoroughly bundled up against the low temperature, and as the time edged past midday the sky seemed to darken quickly. With a terrific amount of noise, both canine and human, plus the shooting of a loud weapon of some sort, the first team was off, followed shortly by another and another, all accompanied by the same amount of discord. Dafydd passed the onlookers and attempted to see their faces through the buttoned-up hoods of their parkas. When he'd failed to locate his man, he moved on to the sports ground by the rec center. A flour-packing contest was under way, a quirky sport with massively built contestants carrying bags of flour on their backs, starting at five hundred pounds. Momentarily he forgot his mission as he watched in astonishment a man staggering forth with eight hundred pounds of flour in bags stacked high on his back.

"But hello, there, my young doctor," Martha Kusugaq shouted above the din of the cheering crowd. "I'll back ya on the next one. You're a fine specimen of a man, good and fit-looking. I'll put a few bucks on ya." She eyed him up and down. It appeared that she'd had a few.

"Not manning the office today, Martha?" Dafydd reproached her. "And I thought you were such a workhorse."

"Nah," Martha sneered. "S'Chrismas. Hubby's doin' it. That man o' mine is too soft. He's getting lazy on the back of my virtue. Can't seem to get it right." She hiccuped loudly.

"Martha, you've not seen that fellow Baptiste Sharkie, from Fort St. John, the tall guy with the Cherokee?"

"Course I seen him, sunshine. Whatcha . . . looking for a ride?"

"Well, yes."

"So use the Buick I gave ya. There's noth'n wrong with it."

"There are no roads leading to the place I'm going."

"Well, hell, why don' you juss say so?" she quipped. "Last I seen, that pilot guy was in the Bear's Lair. He'd had quite a bit already, mind."

Dafydd took his leave and Martha shouted after him, "Hey, wanna do the log-sawing contest with me? I'm mighty powerful." He smiled back at her small, stout figure, standing there, feet planted firmly apart, not doubting her power for one minute. "Mind, those hands aren't gonna be up to much, 'cept keep yer outta mischief." She cackled rudely, pointing out his bandaged hands to the people around her.

He found the man he was looking for in the Bear's Lair, sitting glumly at a table watching two women, performers or customers, dressed in flouncy dresses and fishnet stockings, doing a cancan on a table. At closer inspection they were probably customers. Although the performance in itself wasn't too bad—spectacular, one could say—the girls were definitely a bit long in the tooth for the job, extravagantly broad across the arse and with thunderous thighs, plus they were drunk. Nevertheless, dozens of men were crowding in, leering and applauding.

"Excuse me, Mr. Sharkie. Can I speak to you for a minute?"

Baptiste Sharkie turned his head slowly toward Dafydd. His eyes tried a close-up focus on Dafydd's face, but they were clearly not up to it, so he shut them.

"What about?"

"Can you fly me to Black River tomorrow?"

"Shit! Assa long way," Baptiste said, sighing stoically. "What time?"

"The earlier the better," Dafydd said with rising optimism. "As long as you've recovered by the morning."

The twins had been installed in a room next to his and in the morning he watched them playing Scrabble with Tillie at her kitchen table among the remnants of a multi-course breakfast. None of them seemed bothered by his imminent departure, and they barely looked up from their tense game.

"Look, Mark," he said, tugging the boy by the sleeve of his sweater. "Can I just remind you that Hogg is coming here this evening? He just wants to see you and talk to you. Explain a few things. You know you've not got to make any decision about anything. As I told you, you can stay here as long as you like."

"Well, *I'm* not ready," Miranda said irritably. "I want to stay here with Tillie. Get over it, like . . ."

"Mark?" Dafydd held the boy by the shoulder and shook him lightly. "Are you okay with that?"

Mark turned and looked Dafydd in the eye. "Am I okay? You've got to be kidding. Because we're kids, we're just being pushed around by adults all over the place. At least my fucking mother is out of the way. One down"—he glanced around him—"and, like, ten thousand to go."

"Let them be . . . for a while," Tillie said firmly, avoiding Dafydd's eyes.

Mark turned to her and said quietly, "Tillie, I didn't mean you. Okay?"

A look of complicity passed between the two, and it heartened Dafydd to see that Mark was capable of genuine warmth toward someone other than his sister. If Ian's diagnosis of Sheila as a psychopath was correct, perhaps her removal would be the making of her children, although there was no telling what damage she could have already caused them. There was clearly something in it for Tillie, too, a welcome break from her loneliness. The three of them seemed to cling to each other in defiance. He looked at them with sudden tenderness; they were the most unfortunate of rejects, cast out and disconnected from any semblance of normal family life. But there was a toughness about these children, and only hours after the ghastly scene with their mother they had been chatting quite normally and tucking into a large dinner that Tillie had gone all out to prepare. They already knew everything about Ian's suicide, their mother's criminal offenses, and Hogg's resignation. They knew Hogg was their real father and that he'd asked to be their guardian.

And Tillie . . . whose existence had been built around her enterprise and a need to protect herself from the vagaries of predatory men. She was a true woman of the north, strong, resilient and married to hard work, but still a woman. He recalled with remorse the way he had rebuffed her attempts to seduce him. He'd never wanted to treat her that way, but he had not known how to do it sensitively.

"Thank you, Tillie." On an impulse he went to her and pressed his lips hard to her forehead. Their eyes met for a brief moment. He went to Miranda, who offered her cheek up for a kiss without taking her eyes off her letters. A quick enfolding of Mark's awkward shoulders, and he was off on the assignment that had dominated his sleepless night.

Baptiste was waiting for him at the Northern as he'd promised. His eyes were very hooded and alcohol seeped through his pores, creating an aura of toxic vapors around his body, despite an obvious attempt to clean himself up. He was freshly shaven and his long black hair was wet and slicked back from a broad, brooding forehead.

"All set, then?" Baptiste asked in a weary monotone. They went out to his pickup for the five-mile drive to the airfield. "It'll be seven hundred dollars, if that sits all right with you," he said, "each way."

"Fine," Dafydd said, not having a clue what to expect. "But I might be a day or two."

"I can wait, so long as there's accommodation," said the tall man. "Is the place dry?"

"I believe so," Dafydd said, glad at the idea of at least one sober flight. "It was last time I was up there. Mind, that was years and years ago."

The flight was squeezed into the couple of hours of daylight. It was fairly safe in terms of the pilot's fitness for the job—he was an old hand—except he took great delight in telling Dafydd that he was famous in the whole of the western Arctic for the feat of having written off three planes . . . and still lived to brag about it.

Dafydd all but forgot his dread of flying as they swept so close to the ground that he could clearly follow solitary bears, moose, and herds of caribou as they bounded across the land, startled by the noise of the plane. The forest grew ever more sparse, the trees getting shorter and thinner along the shores of frozen rivers, and finally they were flying over the desolate tundra, which rolled on for seemingly hundreds of miles, as flat and unadorned as no other thing on earth. The only living things that passed on it were a pack of some ten musk oxen, which fled under the rumble of the Cherokee's engine. They pressed close into one another as they ran, their shaggy guard hairs floating about them in graceful slow motion. Farther still, as they were approaching the edge of the Arctic Ocean, an isolated polar bear lumbered along the vast expanse of blinding snow.

Black River looked different from what he remembered. Some of the old bunkers were still there, but many new houses had been built, joined by a strange network of passages or funnels, an apparent conduit for services. The spire of the white clapboard church was still the only thing reaching up into the sky, and attached to it now was an ugly mast for some kind of transmission or other. Baptiste circled the settlement, shaking his head in disappointment.

"Now, this is one place I never seen," he admitted, after having told Dafydd he knew every town, village, and settlement from Dawson City to Churchill. As Baptiste expertly lowered the plane through the air toward a rather inconspicuous runway, Dafydd was at once overcome by apprehension, a sinking in his abdomen. This extended journey of his, from the now-distant morning of having received Miranda's letter, was taking him to hinterlands in both mind and body, situations that he wouldn't have been able even to imagine just a few months earlier. Here, on the edge of a frozen sea, surrounded by icebergs of glass blue, where the daylight hardly came in the winter, he had a child, a son who'd seen more danger and felt more pain than he had in an entire lifetime, a young man of the wilderness, a native Inuit hunter.

Uyarasuq and Charlie were waiting for him. They were expecting him, had seen or heard the plane at a distance and come quickly to the airfield. He hopped out of the plane and ran up to them but then found that he was lost for words, and the three stood looking at each other, studying each other's every feature; there seemed to be no hurry for greetings or explanations. Finally he approached Uyarasuq and gave her a quick hug, then shook the boy's gloved hand with his own bandaged one. Charlie was a well-developed young man and tall for his age. At once Dafydd saw something of himself in the startlingly handsome face, an undefinable resemblance of character. His eyes were his mother's, black and slightly oriental, likewise his high cheekbones, but his mouth and his forehead were Dafydd's. His hair was as dark as the night, but curled at the temples in a way that only Dafydd knew how. When he broke into a sudden grin, Dafydd smiled back in instant recognition. Any doubts were completely dispelled. This was his son.

After giving Baptiste some directions to a house with a room, they walked slowly toward their home. Charlie had the sturdy body of his mother's people, but with Dafydd's relative height. He looked impressive, unbeatable even, in his determination to minimize his dreadful handicap, although he limped and walked with the aid of a stick. Poised in himself, he focused all his concentration on his steps. Intermittently he glanced up at Dafydd and nodded, as if to reassure him that things were going okay. Dafydd nodded in agreement and tried not to stare in return, but he couldn't help his fascination and covertly studied each of them in turn as they walked along.

Uyarasuq's winter pallor reflected the ice and the snow of her land. On each of her cheeks was a round coin-sized red dot, the legacy of freezing the tips of her prominent cheekbones once too often. Up close he saw the tangle of tiny broken veins, but from a distance they looked like rouge applied by a child's hand. In Dafydd's world those could be removed swiftly with a laser, but Uyarasuq was probably not aware of such treatment, or else not bothered by the evidence of her hardships. Her hair was very long now, still thick and coarse like a horse's tail, cascading like a shiny black river from her knitted woolen cap, far down below her waist. In every other sense her appearance was unchanged, seemingly timeless. Her face was as smooth as a teenager's, her teeth as blinding white as the snow. Only her clothes were different. Smart woolen trousers and an intricately embroidered white woolen parka, trimmed with some soft white fur, a work of art in itself. Expensive-looking gloves and boots, matching and no doubt handmade.

They saw not a person on their way, although there was definitely some curtain-twitching along a row of identical houses. Dafydd was anticipating with some dread the idea of them living in the one-room box that had been the location of his most passionate encounter, the place where his son had been conceived. Surely not? She must have inherited her father's house.

It was neither. On the edge of the village was a building set on steel stilts apparently driven deep into the ground. It had large windows on two sides, and smoke rose straight up from a large cylindrical metal chimney. Dafydd climbed the curved staircase leading up to the front door, intrigued by the unusual design. Uyarasuq smiled at him.

"Don't tell me you've forgotten what my house looks like?" she teased him.

"You've spruced it up some," he said, wondering what sort of fortune Bear had passed on to his friend's only grandchild, the sole son of his hapless doctor. Not much, if Joseph's word was anything to go by. Half of practically nothing.

While Uyarasuq helped her son divest himself of his coat and boots, Dafydd wandered around the open-plan living room, trying not to look nosy. Evidently the two of them wanted for nothing. The furnishings in the house were sparse and plain, but there seemed to be all the latest in gadgetry. All around there were stone carvings, bigger and more powerful than the ones he'd seen all those years ago. They were also darker, some almost frightening.

"This house is not my father's legacy, just in case you wondered," Uyarasuq told him proudly, noticing his scrutiny. "Nor the money that Charlie inherited from Bear. I've put that away for his education."

He took off his parka and sat down on a carved wooden chair, looking at her. She stood in front of him and crossed her arms. He wanted to smile, such was the childlike defiance of her posture, but he managed not to.

"It's the money of the *kablunait*," she said, smiling herself now.

"For heaven's sake," he said, laughing. "Sit down. It's none of my business, but tell me all about it anyway."

They had a pot of tea and a plate of sandwiches, and, settled on the sofa, she answered his questions about her growing success. *White man* was buying ever more of Uyarasuq's work. Two galleries in Vancouver and Toronto were vying for her carvings. During the winter months she worked in her father's house, which was now converted into a studio. In the summer, larger carvings were made on a concrete platform in the open air, with Charlie's and two other young men's assistance. She'd been offered a solo exhibition in a small but up-and-coming gallery in New York, but Charlie was still too needy for her to contemplate leaving him in the care of friends.

Charlie, who had plonked himself on a beanbag and so far just listened, protested. "Aw, Mom, that's not fair. I'm not *needy*. I told you a trillion times, New York was more important than my stupid leg." He rapped his knuckles on his bionic leg to show its hardiness and lack of needs.

Dafydd looked at Charlie. "If the exhibition is that important, I could stay here with you. Or we could all go." He turned to Uyarasuq, realizing how presumptuous he must sound. "If that's any help to you."

The boy rolled his eyes in exasperation. "She's blown that one already, by saying no."

"Now, come on," Uyarasuq said. "There'll be others. What's the rush? Anyway, I can hardly keep up. Carving takes time; there's only ever an edition of one."

Charlie's frustration was evident. He looked at Dafydd as if appealing for support. "My mom here is a technophobe. There are amazing machines you can buy—air hammers, high-speed sanders, drills, electric carvers—but Mom insists on doing it the old-fashioned way. When I've finished learning the hard way, I'm gonna do it differently, get the right equipment to keep pace with my ideas."

"Right," Dafydd conceded, careful not to take sides.

"I've got lots of ideas, you know."

"I'd like to hear about them."

Dafydd looked at the young man who was his son, trying to meter out his eagerness, his fascination with the child that he thought he'd never have. Here he was in the flesh, Dafydd's imprint on him as clear and as sure as anything he'd known in a very long time. Charlie was looking at him expectantly, willing him to affirm the need for technological devices and contraptions. Dafydd could see how much a boy needed that balance between the masculine and the feminine. He'd lacked this himself, growing up with a widowed mother and a sister. Mark's haunted countenance came to him. Another fatherless boy, yet what a difference between this brave and dynamic young man, bursting with a will to survive, to grow and succeed, and the "whatever" attitude of Sheila's luckless son.

He felt suddenly guilty about his newfound sense of wonder. The commitment, affection, and empathy he still felt toward Mark and Miranda brought with them the rage he felt about Sheila. It flared inside him for a moment and his fists tightened involuntarily, but his anger drained as quickly, realizing he had her wicked inspiration to thank for this astonishing discovery.

Charlie cocked his head and looked at Dafydd with narrowed eyes, studying his face and clearly wondering at the flashes of emotion that just passed over his features. Then he smiled, having reached some conclusion of his own.

"I guess I'll leave you guys to catch up, huh? Anyway, there's stuff I've got to do."

"No. Don't leave," Dafydd said, cursing himself for his errant concentration. "I want to ask you . . . I want to know all about you."

"No worries, man," Charlie said. "Once you get me yakking you'll wish you hadn't." He lowered his voice in mock threat. *"I'll be back."*

He flung his leg gracefully in an arc and let the momentum of its weight bring him to a standing position. Then he laughed. "At least it's good for counterbalance, and as a doorstop, and for scribbling notes on."

When he'd closed the door behind him, the room seemed to empty of a whirling energy. Suddenly it seemed much larger, hollowed out. Dafydd looked at Uyarasuq and laughed, and she laughed, too, guessing what he felt.

"How can someone as remarkable as him grow out of a soil as bleak as this one?" Dafydd said, shaking his head.

"There's a lot you don't understand about this soil."

"You're right," he said, chastened. "There's certainly nothing bleak about those who live on it."

He got up and went to sit beside her on the sofa. They looked at each other quietly for a while. Momentarily he was flooded with the memory of feelings he'd once experienced. He fought an urge to embrace her and hold her close, to impart some of the strength that Charlie's near-fatal ordeal must have taken from her. Impulsively he wanted to promise her everything, pledge all he had, all he owned, all of his care and his time, but he knew he should restrain himself and not overwhelm her with gushing sentimentalities. Nevertheless, something had to be said to express how he felt.

"I think it's you. It's nothing to do with the land. You've created an extraordinary specimen of a child. I don't know how to express how very deeply I feel about that. Grateful, moved, profoundly impressed . . ."

Uyarasuq looked away, flustered by his declaration. "Hey," she said with a chuckle, "you don't know him yet. And even if you're right, I think *you* may have had something to do with it."

"Not a lot." He took a few deep breaths. His hands were shaking and there was a tightness in his chest. Afraid of dissolving into some uncalled-for emotional mess, he leaned back and thought of some change of subject. "Tell me about this," he said, gesturing at the room.

"Ah, the house," she said with obvious pride. "A young architect I met in Vancouver designed it for me in exchange for one of my carvings. We met at the opening of an exhibition and he somehow took to my work. I thought it was more than a fair trade, especially as he got some funding for me to have it built. It's a prototype for houses built on permafrost in many places now."

Dafydd looked at her and wondered how many men there had been in her life since Charlie was born. The young architect must have been quite taken with her, and he felt a sharp pang of something akin to jealousy for the years that he'd not known anything about her and their beautiful son. He realized now that in some ways she had changed considerably. She was distinctly more sophisticated and assertive; she'd been to many places and met many people. And money meant power, independence, and choices. Yet here she still was. Her essence seemed unaltered; she still blushed easily, laughed the quick, merry laugh of her father and had that innate feminine reserve that had so attracted him was still there.

She had no fear of silence like so many women in the fast world. As dusk deepened, they sat for a while with their own thoughts. The fire that she'd lit in the cast-iron grate mesmerized him. He was exhausted by the events of the last few days and perhaps he dozed for a moment or two. When he opened his eyes she had a piece of hide across her knees and was sharpening a carving tool on a smooth oval stone. From some other part of the house came the inexpert strum of a guitar and Charlie singing an old Dylan song. Dafydd sat immobile, straining to hear it. He had played and sung that tune himself, not so very long before he lost the tip of his finger, lost his guitar and vowed never to play again. The boy's voice was in the full flush of change, and the shuddering bass alternating with a squeaking falsetto made Dafydd want to giggle hysterically, yet with an alarming feeling of tenderness.

"Did I ever tell you I play the guitar?" he asked.

She looked up from her work. "You didn't," she said and shook her head.

"A bit of a coincidence, wouldn't you say?"

With an amused look on her face she returned to her task, and both of them listened, sometimes smiling, sometimes cringing. A sudden exclamation of disgust, and with a final resounding twang the guitar went quiet. Ah, the frustration . . . how well he knew the feeling.

The silence restored, he went back to contemplating the chisel gliding over the oval stone in a smooth curling motion. Uyarasuq's fingers guided it with long-gained practice and infinite patience, as if she had no idea of time and didn't mind how long it took to sharpen. Dafydd was yearning to go and talk to his son, see his room, play his guitar, listen to his part-child, part-man's voice, but there were more questions and he needed answers. In breaking the silence he sounded sharper than he meant to, and it startled her.

"Why didn't you tell me? I wrote you several letters. You never even acknowledged them."

Without answering she put the tool down and rolled up the stone in the hide. She got up and stood for a while looking out of the window. Billions of stars punctured the blackening dome of the sky.

"I felt it wasn't right. You didn't mean for it to happen," she said finally and turned to him. "Remember, you came prepared." She blushed and tried to hide a smile at some recollection of his preparedness.

"I would really have wanted to know," he insisted. "You should have given me the benefit of the doubt. I would have helped you, done anything, arranged—"

"That's just it," she broke in, frowning. "I didn't *want* anything 'arranged.' Once I realized I was pregnant, my life changed. I wanted that baby. There was another purpose for me here, while keeping my father's last years. He lived to see his grandson walk and talk and it made his last year full of joy. That in itself made it all worthwhile."

"I didn't mean it like that," Dafydd said somberly. "I meant I would have helped you in any way you'd have wanted. I, too, would have loved to have seen that remarkable son of mine grow up." He felt the clump of tension in his chest return and swallowed repeatedly. The emotional impact of this meeting was near-impossible to hide from her. He wondered if he would have left everything behind and come back to the woman who bore his son. Probably not: it would have been such an outlandish venture into completely foreign territory. But there was no way of knowing how he would have felt. He'd been in love with her, after all. He'd missed her deeply.

Seeing his distress, she came back and sat down beside him. Touching his cheek lightly, she said, "I'm so sorry, Dafydd. I thought it would be terribly unfair to put that sort of pressure on you. I felt it was something I had to take responsibility for."

"I'm sure you could have used my support."

"My father was old, but he was there for me. He supported me. He helps us still, from beyond."

She glanced at Dafydd, checking for signs of skepticism, and then said quietly but vehemently, "My father saved Charlie, you know. He knew how to enter the body of animals, in life as well as in death. His spirit took possession of the dog that fought off the bear. He and the dog became one. I expect Charlie himself will tell you one day. When my father thought he might not save Charlie he tried to help him pass through, but Charlie changed his mind. He chose to live. Perhaps he knew you were coming."

Dafydd stared at her.

"It may even have gone further back than that," she went on. "The night of your phone call my father came to me in a dream. He told me that Charlie went out on the ice purposely to meet the bear. It was his spirit's way of calling for you. He called to his father across the oceans, and you came all this way to find him. Only his near-death was strong enough to reach you and bring you here."

Dafydd was shaken. It was an extraordinary concept. Perhaps Sheila was just a pawn in a greater game. His head shook against his will.

Uyarasuq misunderstood this and she looked at him defiantly. "My father lives in the spirit world and he knows these things. He was a true *angatkuq*. You of all people should believe it. You gained some of his knowledge yourself."

"Could you not have tried to find me?" Dafydd cried. "You

could have tried. If you believe in that dream, in your father's words, it means that Charlie's suffering was futile, the loss of his leg—"

He stopped abruptly as Uyarasuq burst into tears.

"How was I to know this? I am not an *angatkuq*," she sobbed. "I had been waiting a long time for Charlie to ask me who his father was. I was dreading the question, having to tell him you were long gone, far, far away, with another life, and knowing nothing of him. But it wasn't that he didn't want to know. He's so sensitive . . . He was waiting for *me,* giving me the choice to tell him. Oh, God, how I've regretted my silence. First for Charlie . . . and now for you, too." She blew her nose on a handkerchief that Dafydd handed her from his pocket. "That is something my father could have told me. But he always said that each of us takes the path that we are meant to take. Some choose the most painful and difficult. Mine must be one of sheer stupidity."

Dafydd wanted to be angry—he had every right to be—but what did he understand of this, her dilemma? He gazed into the fire in the hearth, the crackling logs. Abruptly it brought back a picture of the old man, Angutitaq, and he remembered the subtle transformation that the shaman's power had bestowed on him. Angutitaq had tamed the child spirit that had haunted him, and made the fox his ally. He'd tried to teach him to become one with the fox, but Dafydd had not been ready. Yet, the little fox spirit was always there, hovering on the edge of his inner vision, willing him to be quiet. Perhaps if he'd been quiet, and listened, he would have known that someone was waiting for him, calling to him from across the oceans.

Maybe it was not too late to learn. His lingering resentment had no place in this endeavor. Dafydd surrendered his bitterness. He looked into the fire and watched it burn away, felt it dissolve into ashes.

"Yes, your father was a true *angatkuq*," he said at last. "I did gain some of his knowledge, although I think I was too young to understand it . . . or perhaps just unqualified."

"But do you honor that knowledge? Do you believe in it?" she asked him, quite sternly despite her tears.

"I do," he said. "I want to find it within myself. Being here helps. At least it reminds me of what is beyond me and what isn't."

Her face went soft and she laughed. "I, too, need reminding."

"Indeed." He took her right hand in his and examined it at length, stroking the carver's cuts and calluses with the tips of his damaged fingers. "Just look at this hand. It's battered. It's fared even worse than mine."

"Don't hold my silence against me, Dafydd. I've paid a terrible price as it is." Dafydd looked at her, and etched beyond her innocent face he saw the terrible fear and the anguish. His frustration over the lost years already belonged to the past, and his sorrow for Charlie's pain . . . he was here now.

"All right," he said and smiled. "Just don't ever do it again."

The man and the boy stood at the window. It was midmorning on one of the darkest days of the year. They watched in silence as the light extended slowly out of the eastern sky. The sun moved, invisible, below the horizon to the south. At almost fifty below zero everything was silent and utterly still.

"I hope you'll be here when the sun returns to our land," Charlie said.

"When is that?" Dafydd asked.

"Towards the end of January."

"I think you'll find it difficult to get rid of me."

Charlie was about to say something, but he caught Dafydd's look of uncertainty and he stopped. Although the future seemed large, endless, full of hope, it was too soon to speak of it, and Dafydd just hoped that Charlie trusted him. Charlie nodded sagely, smiled Dafydd's own smile and they turned their faces back to the arctic morning.

"It happened out there somewhere?" Dafydd said, looking out at the bleakness of the frozen sea.

"I'd like to show it to you," Charlie said. His eyes didn't waver from the panorama but his voice shook slightly, telling of his apprehension. "It's only approximate. Uyarasuq and I put a carving there to mark the place, but when the ice broke up it sank into the sea. I named it *Ice Trap*. It was her best carving ever, but it was scary too. I memorized it so that one day I can carve it myself."

"I would have loved to have seen it. Better still, owned it," Dafydd said.

Charlie turned to look at him. His dark eyes were grave. Dafydd saw in them the depth and the strength that were far beyond his years. Coming back from the brink of death had aged him, made him a man.

"I'll make it soon and I'll give it to you as a gift," he said. "For finding me."

"I'll treasure it," Dafydd said, putting his hand on the boy's shoulder.

"I've measured the distances roughly. Anyway, I remember the place pretty well."

"If you want to show it to me," Dafydd said solemnly, "we must go there."

"Today?" the boy said. "Let's do it now."

"Are you sure?" Dafydd asked, responding to the slight tremble of the boy's chin, the sudden unnatural brilliance of his eyes.

"Yeah." He smiled a grim smile. "Now that you've arrived, I'd better tackle it again, huh?"

"Would you like your mother to come with us?"

"No, let's not wake her," he said. "I heard her chipping and rasping at the *Old Hunter Wielding Axe* all night. Sometimes I wonder if she ever sleeps. I've told her the kitchen is out of bounds, but it always looks like a damned quarry in the mornings. We have stone dust for breakfast, for Christ's sake."

Dafydd chuckled. "We'd better go, then, before twilight does. Let's leave your mum a note."

"Call her Uyarasuq. I'm old enough."

The bleak midday light left no shadows, and they clambered with difficulty over the jagged ice blocks that clogged the shore. Sharp pinnacles of transparent ice shot up into the sky at crazy angles. Charlie struggled with his bionic leg, uttering unintelligible foreign curses under his breath. On all but one occasion he refused Dafydd's hand, needing to negotiate his way by himself. His arms were strong and helped compensate for the frailty of his lower body. More often than not he hauled himself around, placing his hands on the jutting ice slabs and swinging his legs forward. Dafydd carried his stick and a rifle under his arm. Even for the able-bodied, the shoreline was hell to cross, in some places outright dangerous, with snow-covered crevices and sheets of ice as slippery as if oiled. At the same time the vigorous exercise kept them from getting too cold.

Once they came out on the clear frozen waters, it was easier to make headway. They walked slowly in silence, Charlie leading the way, his limping more pronounced as he got tired. Half a mile out on the sea ice, he stopped to get his bearings, then turned some forty degrees westward, and they continued for some three hundred yards.

"This is it," Charlie said suddenly. "This is where they found me."

Dafydd looked around at the bleak panorama. He felt quite vulnerable just being there on that vast arctic sea. Every few moments it rumbled like thunder, the ice falling or rising on the tide, rearranging itself. A crack like a gunshot startled him, as did the hissing of a fissure racing across the ice. Charlie paid no heed to the sounds, and Dafydd tried hard to follow his example, but the openness, the lack of barriers, the want for anywhere to hide, to run to, deepened his feeling of vulnerability.

Farther out, a large ice-covered island loomed high, and distant icebergs, immobilized by the solid density of the frozen seawater, looked menacing despite their luminous beauty. Behind them could be any number of polar bears, ravenous from the long, dark winter. Abruptly the terror of Charlie's deadly predicament descended on him, and he had an overwhelming urge to pick the boy up in his arms and race across the ice.

"Would you like to tell me about it?" he asked, trying to hide his panic, determined to let Charlie be in charge. It was Charlie, after all, who'd been hunted down and his body torn by the jaws of the giant white bear. He needed to hear it. Nevertheless, he was afraid to have his son's account of his fight with death.

"I want to tell you," Charlie said, "but not today. Today we just look at the place, all right?"

"All right, Charlie. Good idea. Whenever you're ready, I want to hear about it, about everything that happened, every detail."

"I'm not scared," Charlie hastened to inform him. "It won't bother me to talk about it, and I'm not scared of going hunting by myself again. I'm going as soon as I can trust my new leg."

"Really?" Dafydd looked at him uneasily. "How will you protect yourself, in case . . . it happens again?"

"Dogs," Charlie said. "I'm gonna get myself a good old team of Siberian huskies, the toughest dogs in the world."

"Good thinking," Dafydd conceded. After all, one lone injured dog had fought off a large male polar bear and saved Charlie from being eaten alive. The dog may or may not have been imbued with the spirit of Angutitaq, but she had held off her own death until the bear had given in. The dog had sacrificed her life for her master. The bear was probably still out there, no doubt remembering the husky bitch that tore open the tendons in its hind legs.

"But no dog will replace the one that saved me," said Charlie. "I'd give my other leg to have her back."

Dafydd nodded. He thought of Thorn, trying to show him the way to his dying master. Man's best friend, indispensable in this barren and dangerous land.

"I'll never hunt a bear," Charlie said now. "Actually I don't think I really want to kill anything. Not unless I'm starving. Like that bear. When you gotta eat, you gotta eat." He laughed. "Believe it or not, I don't hold it against him."

A wind started up, and small grains of snow whirled around their ankles. They stood there for another moment, Dafydd's arm around the shoulders of his son. But with the wind, the cold was quickly seeping through their clothing, numbing the flesh.

As best they could they hurried shoreward. This time Charlie allowed Dafydd to hoist him up over the worst of the ice blocks. They scrambled over them in silence, Charlie's face poised in concentration, their bulkily gloved hands grasping each other with difficulty. Darkness was falling quickly and the wind had increased, whipping fine, dry snow in hard gusts across the land. Freezing and blinded by the icy particles, they stumbled in the direction of Uyarasuq's studio. The distant echo of a mallet pounding rhythmically against a chisel let them know they'd come home, safe and sound.

ACKNOWLEDGMENTS

With thanks to Simon & Schuster, my publishers, and Sheila Crowley, my agent, and to the many writers, friends and family who supported me in writing *Ice Trap*.

I'm indebted to Helen Thayer, the first woman to walk solo to the magnetic North Pole. Her extraordinary book *Polar Dream* provided me with invaluable facts about polar bears, arctic dogs, and sheer survival. Her story inspired me to search deeper for my own courage and to undertake a journey of my own, albeit a very different one.

Cell-Mate Diagnostics patiently answered all my questions about the marvels and mysteries of DNA, and thank you to those who enthusiastically gave information about old British motorbikes, Demerol addiction, Italian liqueurs, the behavior of fleas, and taxi driving in northern Canada.

My greatest thanks to John Sewell, who has supported me stoically, morally, and financially in my quest to be a writer.

ABOUT THE AUTHOR

Kitty Sewell was born in Sweden and has lived in Spain, Canada, England, and Wales. After running an estate agency in the frozen north of Canada, she trained as a psychotherapist and then as a sculptor. She now divides her time between Wales and Spain, where she owns and runs a fruit plantation.

Ice Trap, her first novel, was short-listed for both the Crime Writers' Association's New Blood Award and the Wales Book of the Year 2006, and won the BBC Wales Readers' Prize.